The
Road of the Strong

The
Road of the Strong
A Romance of Colonial Cambodia

George GROSLIER

Foreword by
Henri COPIN

Edited by
Kent DAVIS

Translated by
Pedro RODRÍGUEZ

Featuring
Colonial Battambang Today
Revisiting George Groslier's Setting for *The Road of the Strong*
by Tom KRAMER

Including the complete French text of the original 1925 edition:
La Route du plus fort

DatAsia Press
MMXVII

About the cover:

Using a 1931 illustration of Angkor as her background, designer Rebecca Klein gives us a vision of the author's protagonist, Hélène Gassin. Next to her is one of her husband's epynomous automobiles; the Roland-Gassin belonging to her host, Pierre Ternier, *résident de France* in northwestern Cambodia. See the Publisher's Notes for more details.

Acknowledgements

With gratitude to **Nicole Groslier Rea** for her guidance and inspiration
in reissuing her father's works.

With the editor's special thanks to the Groslier family, and to Sophaphan Davis,
Jon Dobbs, Meng Dy, Tom Kramer and Duffy Rutledge for their special contributions.

A **Translation Fellowship** from the **National Endowment for the Arts** (NEA) awarded to Pedro Rodríguez helped this effort. Established in 1965 by the United States Congress, the NEA is an independent government agency that has awarded more than $4 billion to support artistic excellence, creativity, and innovation for the benefit of individuals and communities worldwide.

To join the discussion on how art works visit the NEA at **www.arts.gov**

Production Credits

Editor: **Kent Davis**

Associate Editor: **Lia Genovese**

Translation: **Pedro Rodríguez**

Cover design: **Rebecca Klein**

Text design: **Daria Lacy**

French proofreader: **Sandra Bourgi**

Archival assistance: **Darryl Collins**, **François Doré** and **Joel Montague**

DatASIA Press — www.DatASIA.us

© Copyright 2017. DatASIA, Inc. Holmes Beach, Florida

First Edition

ISBN 978-1-934431-16-0

Library of Congress Pre-Assigned Control Number: 2015942984

Printed simultaneously in the United States of America and Great Britain.

Table of Contents

THE ROAD OF THE STRONG

APPENDICES

LE ROUTE DU PLUS FORT (1925)

George & Nicole Groslier

At the front gate of their home in 1923. The Groslier home still stands behind the National Museum of Cambodia at the corner of Preah Ang Makhak Vann (St 178) and Preah Ang Yukanthor (St 19). Hopefully this landmark of Cambodian history will be preserved.

Dedicated to

Nicole Groslier Rea

June 15, 1918 – February 12, 2015

Loving daughter of George Groslier
who inspired and witnessed
the publication of her father's literary works
twice in her lifetime.

George Groslier

At home in Phnom Penh circa 1924.
With Gilbert (born Sep. 8, 1922) and Nicole (born June 15, 1918)

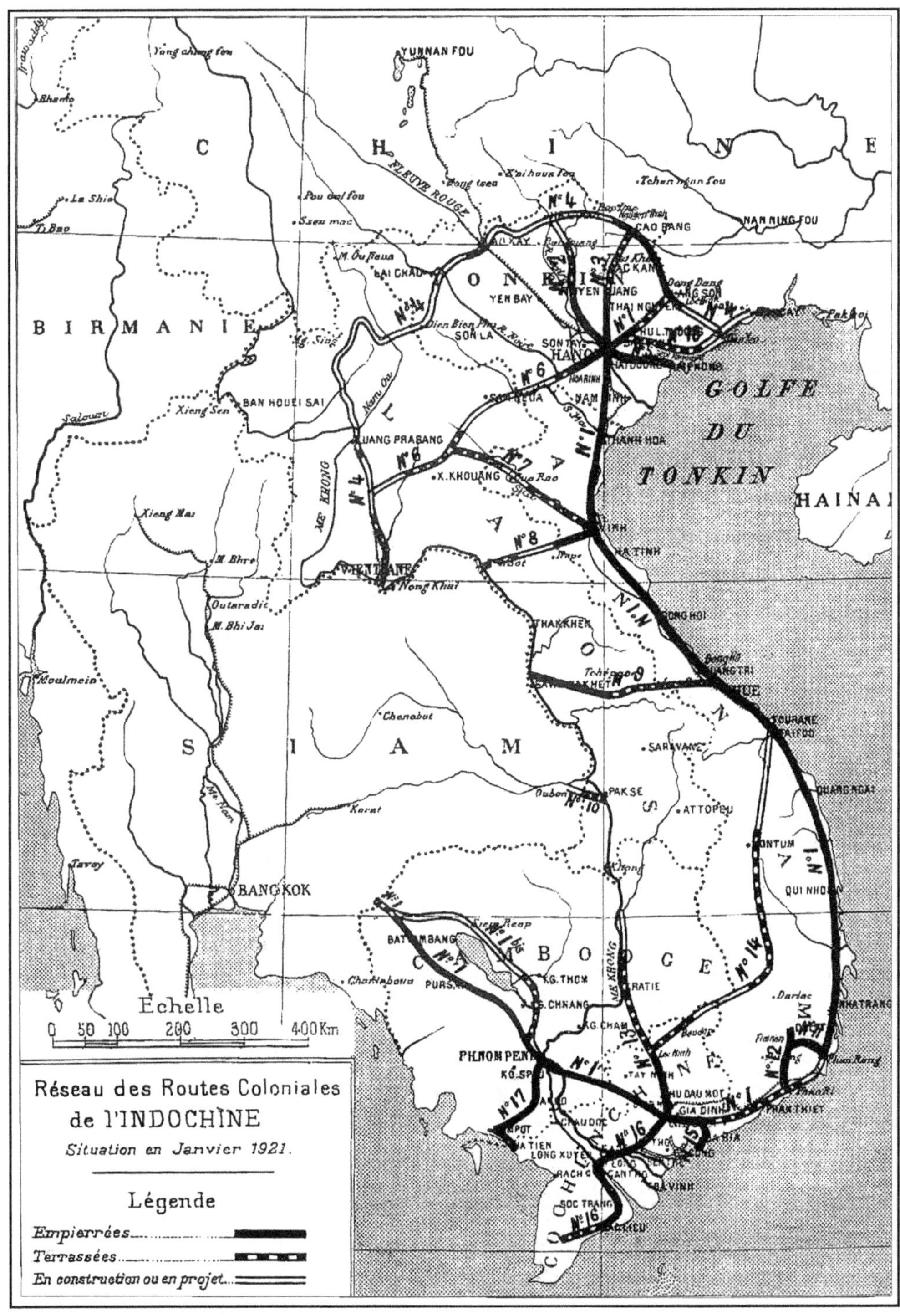

The colonial road system in French Indochina. January 1921.

Foreword

The Strong, and the Beautiful Girl with the "Crab Fat" Colored Sash

"We are all symbols…"

Published in 1926, *The Road of the Strong* is Cambodian author George Groslier's first novel. *Cambodian* author? Yes, Cambodian! While it is true that Groslier was not Cambodian in a legal sense, he was indeed born in the land of the Khmer and was undoubtedly among the first Frenchmen to be. More importantly, he was Cambodian in spirit, in his passion for the country of his birth. It was an *informed* passion, if the reader will forgive an apparent oxymoron, for it resulted from painstaking study, and from a fascination with the history and culture of a country that, ten centuries earlier, when Angkor loomed large, had established one of the largest empires in Asia.

Today, nine decades after the appearance of *The Road of the Strong*, the author, the era of the book's writing, the colonial context, and the very setting of Cambodia itself seem far, far away—in space and especially in time. Most of us can only claim vague familiarity about any of it. We should thus take a moment to review the history, that we might fully appreciate this singular book and the rich contradictions of a man and his time.

A French Cambodian

First the author. Born in 1887, George Groslier was nearly forty when he wrote his first novel, although he already had seven non-fiction books and dozens of academic publications to his credit. Cambodia had seen his birth and would see his death as well, in 1945, at the close of the Second World War when Indochina was under Japanese occupation. Groslier died a terrible death, under the clubs of the Japanese military police. The *Kempeitai*, as it was known, had arrested him because he was an amateur radio operator, and therefore under suspicion of passing information to the resistance. His tomb reads *"Mort pour la France"* ("died serving France"). *"And Cambodia"*, we might add, so entwined was his fate with his second homeland.

Groslier was the son of a French civil servant who had arrived in Cambodia in 1886 to serve a Protectorate established in 1863. The king of this small, embattled, declining country—all but dismembered by rapacious neighbors Siam (present-day Thailand) and Annam (present-day Vietnam)—had just signed a treaty to ensure its survival. France was a recent arrival to Cochinchina (present-day South Vietnam), so the alliance was of mutual benefit: Cambodia gained not just an ally but, indeed, a protector to keep under check the ambitions of its more powerful neighbors, whereas France tightened its grip on Cochinchina by gaining access to the backcountry around the great port of Saigon. There flowed the Mekong, considered at the time a possible gateway to the vast Chinese market. In reality, however, the Cambodian protectorate quickly gave way to a Cambodian colony, governed by France. The year 1887, when Groslier was born, saw the official founding of the Union of Indochina, a federation that included Cambodia and the three provinces of Vietnam, with Laos joining in October 1893 in the wake of the 'Paknam incident'[1] a few months earlier. *Indo-China* lost currency to a new term, *Indochina*, which underscored the area's geographical identity: a vital crossroads east of India and south of China.

---

1   In July 1893, three French ships were sailing off Paknam, at the mouth of Siam's Chao Phraya River, when a Siamese fort fired upon them. France won the battle and in the following months proceeded to blockade Bangkok ultimately ending the Franco-Siamese war.

Groslier spent the first two years of his life in Cambodia, before his mother decided that conditions there were intolerable and returned to France, taking young George with her. Her husband stayed behind to continue pursuing his government career. She would never return to Cambodia but, twenty-one years later in 1910, George would. In France, he undertook his studies in Marseille and then in Paris, where he attended the École des Beaux-Arts to become a painter. There, he trained in his craft and competed for the Grand Prix de Rome.[2] His failure to win turned him toward a career in colonial service, but his strivings nonetheless made him a lifelong devotee of art. Thenceforth he enjoyed the spectacle of life as he might a good painter's palette, and his writing reflects this artistic vision.

"The Revival of the Khmer Arts"

Returning to the land of his birth—rediscovering it—was a shock for Groslier: one might even say a rebirth. In getting to know the small country of Cambodia, he found grandiose traces of the vanished empire of Angkor, with its refined civilization, imposing temples, its ruins, mythological and religious references, and its enigmas as well. He sojourned in Angkor, studied ancient Khmer art, and soon knew his subject well enough to deliver a series lectures in France and Belgium. Gaining political access through his wife's family, he was appointed to conduct reforms when the General Government of Cambodia decided to overhaul the country's arts curriculum. He was in any case eminently qualified, with his Beaux-Arts education, his knowledge earned in the field, and his own artistic ideas. In fact, Groslier wrote a number of texts on Khmer art. His first book, *Cambodian Dancers: Ancient and Modern*, appeared in 1913, followed in 1916 by *In the Shadow of Angkor*. In 1918, in the pages of the *Revue indochinoise*, he published *La Convalescence des arts cambodgiens* and *L'Agonie des arts*

---

2   A prestigious French scholarship competition for artists of all types. Winning the award essentially ensured a successful career, however Groslier narrowly missed the mark.

cambodgiens in quick succession. In 1925 he published *La Reprise des arts khmers*.

The scope of the reforms far exceeded any simple teaching of Cambodian arts. The idea was to serve Cambodia, help it rebuild an identity, and burnish French prestige as well—and at the same time to generate revenue through an expansion of tourism and promote Indochina through the cultural treasures of the Khmer. What Groslier undertook in 1917, in the service of both countries, was a rich and complex task. He was to found an institution intended to prompt a true renovation of the Khmer arts, in keeping with the reforms begun after King Sisowath's trip to France, in 1906. This renovation, jointly undertaken by the Court and the authorities of the Protectorate, needed rekindling, and Groslier was stationed at the bellows. He was to found a new and independent École des Arts, basing it on his own view of a people resigned to smiling obscurity, while preserving the memory of a glorious past cut off, as it were, from its cultural identity.

For Groslier, Khmer artistic practice was above all utilitarian and functional, not aesthetic. He wrote as much in *Étude de la psychologie de l'artisan cambodgien*, an article published in 1921, as well as in *Études sur l'art khmer*, published in 1923. The first principle in Groslier's curriculum was to put exclusive control of Cambodian art in Cambodian hands.

> Despite training as a painter, Groslier would never teach at the school. "I am not Khmer", he declared, and the "fundamental principle" of the School was "only to make Cambodian art and only to have it be made by Cambodians".[3]

Foreign influence was to be avoided entirely. In hindsight, we might complain that such a doctrine produces artists devoid of originality. As he wrote elsewhere, however, "my job is to defend,

---

3   Muan, Ingrid. 2001. *Citing Angkor: The "Cambodian Arts" in the Age of Restoration.* Doctoral Thesis, Columbia University, New York, pp. 77-78.

by all means within my power, the Cambodian tradition."[4] We should note, by way of contrast, that the guiding principle behind Hanoi's École Supérieure des Beaux-Arts d'Indochine, founded in 1925 under Victor Tardieu and Nguyen Nam Son, was to renovate the traditional arts while at the same time opening the way to Western influences, and that school was a remarkable success. For Cambodia's arts, though, everything depended on George Groslier's particular conception of Khmer ways. His was the capital influence on the École des Arts, which he directed; on the Musée Albert Sarraut, which he later designed, oversaw in construction and curated; and finally, on the Direction des Arts (1920–1944), which oversaw the other institutions.

Such were Groslier's circumstances in 1926, when he published *The Road of the Strong*, his first novel. He was an artist, a scholar, a central figure in the protection and rejuvenation of Cambodia's artistic patrimony and in the inspection of historical and archeological antiquities. In this last capacity he was instrumental in the arrest and trial of André Malraux, a man destined to become a major writer and a minister under French president Charles de Gaulle. At the time, however, Malraux was a young adventurer, and a thief of bas-reliefs from the small temple of Banteay Srei, in the Angkor group. If we look beyond this high-profile affair, however, what shines through in Groslier's actions is a profound commitment to the restoration of Cambodia's cultural identity around its Angkorian past. Groslier served France and its colonial prestige, but served his vision of Cambodia as well. By that year of 1926, he had published some thirty-five articles on archaeology and a further dozen on "indigenous" arts, all in academic journals of repute. And so the question arises: what could have driven an established scholar and man of action to write a work of fiction— namely, *The Road of the Strong*?

---

4   Quoted by Gabrielle Abbe in "Le Développement des Arts au Cambodge à l'époque coloniale, George Groslier et l'École des Arts cambodgiens (1917–1945)", UDAYA, *Journal of Khmer Studies*, 12, 2014 (published in 2015). This preface owes a considerable debt to the article and its wealth of information.

A Colonial Myth

The answer—or answers, for this is no simple matter—is of course to be found in a careful reading of the book. Let us come right out and state our hypothesis: unlike expository or scholarly writing, fiction permits a juxtaposition of different, even contradictory, points of view, and can thus reflect the ambiguities of real life. In *The Road of the Strong*, Groslier glorifies the colonizing power of France, while also celebrating a Khmer art of living. The same tension is drawn tauter in his second novel, *Return to Clay*, which is an apology for "de-civilization", a celebration of the Khmer art of living as a return to man's natural state, and a condemnation of Western "pseudo-civilization", itself presented as a sort of "de-civilization." It is a veritable reversal of the values of the colonial doctrine, founded on France's "civilizing mission."[5] "The white man's burden" Kipling called it! The two novels elucidate each other, for *The Road of the Strong* contains the germ of the revolution in *Return to Clay*. Let us explore a little further, without spoiling anything for the reader.

The first thing to note is that *The Road of the Strong* belongs to the then-nascent genre of "colonial literature", one definition of which concerns its relation to colonial ideology. Certain works glorify it, with clarions and regalia. Others are subtle in their support. Groslier's title contains an apology for "the strong": that is, for the colonizer faced with the passiven,f China.a.t be here? born in Cambodia people of Cambodia. It is the strength of the West, with its technical mastery, dealing with the fatalism attributed to Asian man; it is the road as symbol of technical superiority. But it is not merely an expression of domination, for the road is "blazed by the strong for the weak", given by France to Cambodia. The protagonist, Résident Ternier, a top civil servant in the Protectorate of Cambodia, lives his life in devotion to his mission, to the roads

---

5   In French, *mission civilisatrice*. A code characterizing the responsibility of France to introduce civilization, technology, education and rule of law into their colonies in Africa and Indochina.

that link beings, bring villages into the world, open up economies, and guarantee security and peace.

"We had come, and in a few years had built a new city between gardens overhung with century-old mango trees. [...] Places once isolated by days and days of travel we have now linked to the rest of the country by roads", he says. The road theme runs the length of the novel, structures the story, and sets out the characters. It opens in the French countryside where Ternier, on holiday, meets automobile manufacturer Roland Gassin and his wife Hélène. Later, the Gassins travel to Indochina where the focus shifts to urban automobiles on colonial roads—roads that Ternier is responsible for building and maintaining. The message is clear: mother country and colony are complementary. There is, in the pragmatic view of colonial ideology, mutual benefit.

Moreover, the representation is very much of its time. The period between the world wars saw the development of maritime, air, and land transport, and with it the birth of tourism, though of a kind still limited to the élite. As distances shrank, people built mansions in the colonies, around the Mediterranean, in Indochina, at Angkor. Already in 1908 the Duke of Montpensier was shuttling between Saigon and Angkor by car, without losing so much as a bolt on the way! Though towed by buffalo out of many an impasse, his "Lorraine Diétrich 24/30 HP with reinforced American chassis" scaled the stairs at Angkor Wat to tool around the monumental grounds! The Croisière Noire and later the Croisière Jaune demonstrated the automobile's power to dissolve geographical, cultural and political frontiers in the world.[6] Eiffel's metallic architecture made it possible to build bridges, like the Long Biên Bridge in Hanoi, or to lay down a railroad, with countless works of engineering, all the way to southern China. In

---

6   The Croisière Noire (Black Cruise), was a 20,000 kilometer auto expedition in Africa organized by André Citroën to promote his brand of cars. The trip lasted from 28 October 1924 to 26 June 1925, just a year before Groslier published *The Road of the Strong*. Six years later, Citroën organized the Croisière Jaune (Yellow Cruise) in Asia, which ran from 4 April 1931 to 12 February 1932.

its extensive photo spreads, the newspaper *L'Illustration* offered up a vision of colonial development, associating it with efficacy and modernity. Throughout Indochina, 1920 was a year of economic growth (and of heavy taxation for peasants). By 1930, a Cambodia far removed from that of 1863 could boast some 9,000 km of roads, laid down largely by *corvée* (roadwork performed in exchange for tax relief) and would soon have a railroad to Siam. In 1931, the Paris International Colonial Exhibition would promote the colonial system at its apogee (with its decline close at hand), around a reproduction of the temple of Angkor Wat right in the middle of France's capital city.

Thus, Groslier built his fiction on his experience of reality and his vision of the colonial endeavor. Other writers—like Roland Dorgelès, with his reportage *Sur la route mandarine*, or novelist Henry Daguerches, with his *Le Kilomètre 83*, which imagines an episode in the construction of the Cambodian railroad—sketch these representations as well, in their own way. In sum, there was at the time a consensus: to colonize is to work toward progress, and the road is indisputably a symbol of colonization.

This affords us a first reading of the novel as the reflection of a certain reality. Résident Ternier, now back to his post supervising road construction in northeastern Cambodia, learns that Roland and Hélène Gassin are headed to Indochina to investigate automobile manufacturing opportunities. He extends an invitation to the couple to discover his Cambodia, with its landscapes, its cities, its wilderness, its forests, its pagodas, its inhabitants, and its French expatriates. Hélène arrives first while Roland concludes his business deals in Vietnam. The colonial builder thus begins showing the newly arrived urbanite the significance of his undertaking, and its usefulness both to France and to Cambodia. Chapter after chapter he details the daily tasks and the value of a mission that is larger than the individuals involved, and transfigures them: "It had entailed…the simultaneous enrichment of two civilizations. Their labor on a road benefitted not just their own country or clan but also that of another people."[7]

This colonial chronicle culminates with an official reception, at which a narrow, tuxedo-clad French society—with silverware, fine wines, French cuisine, decorum and protocol, old, picturesque colonial anecdotes, and a useless, decorative Cambodian governor—gathers around Résident Ternier. Groslier describes, with acerbic wit, the microcosm that makes the light of civilization glow out in the bush, in the middle of the night, around the veritable beacon that is the Résident: "From this man radiated roads […] white with moonshine, spanning his province like the symbol of the great pacifying hand he had laid upon it. Within this star […] more than three hundred thousand souls lay asleep. Every guest who raised his crystal glass into the prosperous air had done his duty, as well."

The novel abounds with references to the endeavor, to its protagonists, to its beneficiaries. They are at times needlessly insistent, and go so far as to suggest that Résident Ternier, and thus France, has in fact taken the torch from the great ancients, the creators of Angkor and its royal roads. "You will make your road, commands the one to the other. For ten centuries you have been dreaming and degenerating. The time for dreaming is over. Today we forge." This is the purpose of creation in fiction: to fashion myths that take reality as their basis and elucidate it.

Under the Gaze of Women

And yet, if in his ideal world the character of Résident Ternier seems at times as monolithic as a statue, and all but impervious to doubt, Groslier's story provides a glimpse of another world, a parallel and different world. Beside the Cambodia that the Résident

---

7   Indeed, Ternier goes on to say: "All colonization, says one claim, operates on a principle that is false, or at least debatable, and at times even inopportune, but for this the colonists are not responsible." The apology for the road leads to meditation on the legitimacy of the use of force that forms the basis of any colonization. The idea would be taken up later by Albert Sarraut in his *Grandeur et servitude coloniales* (1931).

shows (and demonstrates), we attain another, more complex reading through the eyes of the two women, Hélène and Vetonea.

It is Hélène, the urbanite with the fresh view, who, in making her discoveries, first reveals the charm of the villages, the bucolic scenes of daily life, the slow carts, the paunchy junks, the markets, the children at play, the men traveling on foot, the sounds, the scents, the odors. It is she who, after the official reception, sings the praises of the simple village *sala*,[8] which welcomes the traveler without fuss but not without courtesies. It is she who lends an ear to the carts, "these carts [...] forever criss-crossing the country. Today they were going to sing for her. They are elegant vehicles, put together like living bodies. Their axles hiss and grind, changing their inflection with every change in the turn of the wheels. On and on they cry, for as long as the road lasts. They are loudest in the forest, grumble in the morning, and shriek in broad sunlight." It is through her eyes that Groslier depicts the perfect ballet of naked bodies walking in the forest: "His changeable architecture is prestigious through and through. The shield-like convexity of the thorax and back, the twin weaponry of the arms, the legs propelling the marvelous machine. [...] What sincerity, what loyalty can be more earnest and forthright than frank nudity? [...] And something else as well, liberty, radiates from the whole, which the very air sustains and smiles upon."

This hymn to the state of nature, to the original beauty of bodies and beings, to the liberty that they exude, is the core subject of Groslier's second novel, *Return to Clay*, but its germ is present here, in counterpoint to the hymn to *civilization*. *Naked man* is not quite the same symbol as *the road*. Groslier reveals more of himself as he goes along. While his characters engage in peaceful meditation with the fall of night, the author speaks up, to address...whom exactly? We do not properly know. Himself, perhaps: "You have escaped your routine. You have slipped your yoke. You have set

---

8   A village house kept specifically for travelers to stay the night in.

aside convention to see something else. [...] Free! You have sought to be free! [...] Nature lies dead between your cities; here it reigns supreme. In your world man remains forever remote beneath the many masks he borrows; here man is naked, and in the richness of his nudity stands in opposition to you...."

And this strange chink in Ternier's scabrous armor, this avowed weakness for full-bloom liberty in the natural setting of Cambodia, expands as the story advances, until we reach a troubling confession: "I am the civilization necessary to man, you say, the civilization dictated and desired by man. [...] [T]his entails something else: that you...are the strong. However gently you set your broad hand upon the world, whatever the saving certainties you set loose upon it, you will kill."

Behold civilized man become pervious to doubt.

That Subtle, Proud Girl with the "Crab Fat" Sash

It is, then, through the eyes of a woman, Hélène, that this other reality, different from that of an ideological discourse, is established. But there is yet another woman who plays a key role in the novel: Vetonea, Termier's little native wife, the *prâpôn*, a "subtle, proud girl... [with] a light ocher complexion." In the mass of Cambodians who populate the book, none of whom are treated as true individuals, Vetonea alone is sketched with specificity, in a singular portrait high in contrast. Is she a secondary character? Yes, absolutely, for she is the little wife forbidden to show herself, "that disconcerting creature: the native consort of a European man," "an emanation of the land and the sum of its charms." But she makes her entrance at a pivotal point in the book, and redirects the story. What if she were the novel's true protagonist? But I will say no more, dear reader! Make your own discoveries, and carefully observe young Vetonea, "fresh and dry, and as agreeable as ivory," a little idol whom Ternier thinks he can "tame", for all kinds of good reasons that appeal to the strong.

She is to me the true cause of the oh-so-powerful Résident's unavowable weakness, and the true symbol of the Cambodia with which Groslier was so madly smitten, in every sense, and that he depicts in so many marvelous watercolors throughout the story, evoking the settings as they arise, their forms and colors bursting luxuriously forth: "knots of ginger, water-lily flowers, Chinese chestnuts, the shredded flesh of dried fish, bean sprouts like larvae in agglomeration, skeins of transparent noodles, stacked small jars of fermented sauces, jars of red chalk resembling a paste of corals, black tobacco, regular ranks of spade-shaped betel leaves, peanuts, brown saffron." Groslier the painter could not resist colors and shapes, and went so far as to paint "rubbish heaps: as lovely, almost, as the stalls themselves" and matter "disintegrating in brilliant coquetry before it could rot."

I reread this book many years after discovering it and am struck by the marvelous opportunities it provides to arrange symbols, or even create myths, that coexist with their differences, and their contradictions, and their contrary meanings. Road versus path. Civilization versus nature. Progress versus liberty. One can take the position that man's will should dominate, that man should take action and transform reality, and still betray a violent attraction for all that must vanish as a result of one's action. An attraction, or perhaps a preference? To these opposing tensions everyone will attribute the meaning they see fit.

As for Groslier, he brings his book to a close with an instance of magnificent ambiguity: "Your road crosses a region, and, like an arrow, pierces to the heart. Onto the road the automobile manufacturer will dispatch his machines. But the crossed region will strike at his heart as well."

Henri Copin

October 31, 2017 — Nantes, France

Henri COPIN

Henri Copin is internationally recognized as a leading specialist in French colonial literature for his lectures, critiques, works and analyses that help these historical masterpieces live again.

Copin first traveled to French Indochina in his mother's arms after his birth in Paris in 1945. There, he spent his first 16 years in Vietnam and Cambodia witnessing the Indochina War, the waning of French presence in the Indochinese Peninsula, and the early years of Cambodian, Laotian and Vietnamese independence.

A century of shared history between France and Indochina drew him to devote his professional life to the culturally rich literature of the region. In 1994 he received his degree at the Sorbonne, with Harmattan publishing his thesis in 1996: *L'Indochine dans la littérature française des années vingt à 1954, Exotisme et altérité* [*Indochina in French Literature from 1920-1954, Exoticism and Otherness*]. He was appointed Professor of Humanities at Saint Louis, Senegal and taught at the Center for Applied Linguistics in Dakar before returning to France where he is now a permanent professor and lecturer at the University of Nantes.

The
Road of the Strong

George Groslier

*"It is at times a grave misfortune
that human nature is so complex and so simple,
that man's perspicacity, subtle as it is,
should walk right past profound and beautiful things
without even a hint of recognition."*

I
Spice-laden Air

Out on the road through lovely Auvergne, somewhere between Royat and Fontanat.[1] To one side, gently sloping meadows; to the other, springs bubbling lively and cool from the rocks. A medley of slanting sunbeams and trickling water, and a tiny rainbow hovering over the moss.

Driverless, hood propped open, a motorcar stood idle. Inside, a couple resigned to their circumstance. The man a strapping lad above thirty years of age, the woman slim and blond, with the long, slender hands one has often seen on Italian ladies since the Quattrocento masters.[2] The car was a Roland-Gassin, equipped for the road and, like the road, dusty.

Out on the same road to take in the lovely June evening was a second car, it too a Roland-Gassin, and of the same model. The Annamite[3] at the wheel was driving at a crawl, and behind him

1 Now called Fontanas, this scenic village, 5 km west of Royat at the top of Puy de Dôme, has been popular with painters since the 19th century. Royat itself is renowned for hot water baths, the perfect cure for the aching bodies of colonials visiting home. [www.tourisme-royat-chamalieres.com]

2 An abbreviation of *millequattrocento* (1400), *quattrocento* is a shorthand for the Italian fifteenth century. The masters in this case are the great Italian painters of the time, like Sandro Botticelli and Leonardo da Vinci. (Groslier was himself a skilled painter, trained at the École des Beaux Arts, in Paris.)

3 'Annamite' was used as a general term for 'Vietnamese', including people from Tonkin and Cochinchina, even though 'Annam' corresponds only to Vietnam's central area.

lounged a man lost in the landscape and delighting in the hour,
a short pipe clenched beneath his bushy, drooping moustache.
Glimpsing the car in distress, the man sat up, called for a halt, and
addressed the couple.

"Have you run into some trouble?"

"Magneto's gone dead, Monsieur."

The man alighted and introduced himself.

"Pierre Ternier, *résident de France*[4] in Indochina."

"Roland Gassin, carmaker. My wife."

Bowing, Ternier turned with a smile toward the open hood.

"A poor advertisement, Monsieur, but I am familiar with the
make."

A new gurgle from the cool springs—the giggle, in fact, of
Madame Gassin. The cars had made each other's acquaintance, and
the ice was broken.

"Our driver has gone to Royat to fetch a new car. We're
expecting him."

"I am myself stopping at Royat. Pray, do not wait here. Allow me
to drive you."

Aboard they climbed, and the functioning car got back under
way.

Words flow easily between people of the same stratum, out in
the countryside, under such conditions. The Gassins had planned
to reach Clermont by evening and push on to Saint-Étienne
on the morrow. Ternier, meanwhile, was planning to stay on in
Royat, for the waters, and especially to wander about at the foot of
the Dômes,[5] before rounding out his holiday in Paris. Colonists,
even the eminent among them, are little known in France, but
the couple were quick to grasp that they were in the company of

---

4 This title reflects a political appointment to administrate a sub-region in one of the five
provinces of French Indochina: Tonkin, Annam, Cochinchina, Cambodia and Laos. The
résident would in turn report to the *Résident-Supérieur* in his region.

5 The Dômes are the dormant volcanoes of the Chaîne des Puys, a mountain range within
France's Massif Central.

a distinguished man. What's more, a customer had run into his manufacturer—the man responsible for a renowned automotive brand, then enjoying quite the vogue—on the road in Auvergne.

The evening continued at the Hôtel du Parc, where Ternier had taken his lodgings, while his car went back along the road to look for the Gassins' driver. The repairs were going to take hours. There was a nip in the air. A small table was set up in a hall that overlooked the park and gave a glimpse of the mountains. To decorate, heather of amethyst yellow was arranged in a great crystal bowl. The friendship that would bind the Gassins and Ternier was forged then and there. They looked at one another frankly, spoke in agreeable tones, and harbored no guile in their peaceful hearts; an easy sympathy was quickly established.

In short measure they met again in Paris.

Roland Gassin was not one to stand still. Having inherited a factory in Levallois-Perret from his father, he had surrounded himself with select personnel. Self-assured as he was in matters of business, he had rapidly put the innovations of his engineers to use and achieved enduring success. He held to the often highfalutin notions of those who triumph by following a well-blazed trail and readily conclude that anyone who fails in life must be some sort of oaf. The steady effort such people make gradually obscures the role that luck has played in their lives. They know neither misery nor betrayal. Like one of his engines, Roland Gassin was himself a complex, highly elaborate mechanism, with every component precisely aligned and controlled.

His wife, whom he had met in his industrial milieu some ten years earlier, was of a different, less easily defined character. We shall try to understand her by observing her in life. Madame Gassin's urbane virtues and simple ways defied analysis. She seemed eminently supple and feminine—feminine women are so rare these days. Nothing about this woman was apparent to the eye. Not that she was a dissembling sort; quite the contrary. She was uniformly enameled in a lovely, pure color, with no fissure to be seen. But was it the enamel that was colored, or was the stuff underneath showing through a transparent top coat? One could not say. Win her confidence, and she would get chummy, and seem to place herself under your wing. Her charm lay perhaps in a strong will that she never exerted, as if it were superfluous, for, after all, she was a woman and judged you to be a gallant man. Madame Gassin said she would do this or that, and then went ahead and did it. "Off I go," and she would rise and depart. "Tomorrow at ten o'clock," and the following day she would appear at ten. "I'll write," and she would write. In everyday life these little resolutions have but a feeble hold on us; we seize on the slightest pretext to shrug them off. And yet it is by shouldering these slight burdens—far more than by engaging in vain, herculean labors—that we reveal our strength of will. This is, no doubt, the truly feminine dimension of will. It subtly follows its course, never drawing the man's attention, until one day the man yields. By then it is too late for him to take up the iron rod and vanquish the woman.

Madame Gassin loved her husband, and he had a tender affection for his companion of rare quality. The happy trust he showed in her, their community of tastes, the delicate and timely attentions they exchanged prove at least that Gassin was mindful of the object of our inquiry.

Did Madame Gassin hope, through some painstaking sense of modesty, to conceal at all costs the qualities of her heart, so as to reserve them for her own use? Did she believe that too diaphanous a veil would sully her sentimentality, as it would the secret contours of her body? Was it pride or scruple that kept her from revealing anything she considered a weakness? Did she suppose, out of stubborn principle, that any passion shown her husband would no longer belong to her, and that this gave her all the more reason to withhold it entirely? Had she made her love into a secret ritual? Did she believe that by merely speaking of love she would divulge her own? Did she, in fact, love at all? All these questions we could have answered in a moment's time with a yes or a no by seeing whether Madame Gassin replied with candor to our privately made allusions or, instead, stanched the flow of our words by staring off into the distance.

She was, mind you, neither a snoot nor sanctimonious. She had no fear of words, and a witty allusion could get a laugh out of her. It spooked her sensibility, however, when an inquiry approached the heights or depths of feeling, the regions where she truly dwelled. She was like one of those birds that live only in the far corners of a forest or at great heights. Moreover, she had great affection for her sister, an elder sister, named Annie Belgrand. Few were on an intimate footing with Annie, for she had lived a retired life ever since a terrible train crash had mangled in an instant both her husband and her ten-year-old boy.

A final stroke, which the account to follow will not make, will sufficiently refine our portrait of Madame Gassin. She was one of those women who know how to listen, and whose intelligence lies plainly on their face like a luminous mask. Her bearing and her curiosity toward you were like a question hanging latent in the air as she sat erect in her armchair, ankles crossed, eyes wide open and fixed upon your own. Sifting your words for every valid morsel, she would stir your need to speak. Such attentive women keep their allusions discreet and their questions insidious. In revealing yourself to them you discover who you are. From the imbecile who does not flee at their approach they can draw forth sensible words. They have a deep and brilliant inner life, for in reflection they must know how to listen to themselves as well. Their ability to "attend" all manner of men endows them with a wide, florid, polished learning by virtue of the talent or conscientiousness of these same men, who transmit this learning to them, and whom they wisely select for the purpose. And men hasten to recognize the depth and superiority of such women, for an attentive ear flatters their vanity and satisfies them that their words are not devoid of interest.

Ternier was not immune to this charm, especially since Madame Gassin showed more than her usual curiosity toward this idle, haughty, courteous passer-by. In the brilliant circle of the Gassins' regular society—engineers, businessmen, industrialists, and other upstanding citizens—certain members, especially women, were susceptible to the *esprit nouveau*.[6] Or, rather, the conversations turned on matters to which Madame Gassin had grown accustomed. Certain men of letters would stop by, as would artists. Dinners were refined, and winged words would glide through the wafting aromas. Yet there was no clash between the new guest and the guest of yesterday evening. His turn of mind, his erudition, his moral qualities caused no mishap. They blended right in with those of the Gassins' select, uniform milieu.

The colonist made his mark with the prestige of the distant, unknown lands he came from. His conviction, the occasional coarseness of his conversation, his freedom with paradox were so much new music on novel themes. Whether Ternier described the colonial administration or depicted indigenous life, whether he held forth on civilizational programs, planned or carried out, or limited his conversation to anecdotes and memories, Madame Gassin felt as if she had new, spice-laden air to breathe. She was his best listener, abandoned herself more completely to this atmosphere than anyone else, though Ternier was careful to banish from her mind any fanciful notions or sense of adventure. In particular he gave the lie to that tenacious, absurd *colonial legend* in which so many misinformed people delight. Indeed his words carried great weight with her, for the "colonial" or "exotic" novels she had read had left her with dubious impressions and artificial tableaux. The *résident's* revelations and sobriety, disconcerting though she still found them, served as an invitation to advance by dint of logic through

6 New way of thinking—literally, new spirit or new state of mind. The passage might be referring to the *esprit nouveau* in French letters, a movement spearheaded by poets like Guillaume Apollinaire, John Perse, and Max Jacob, who sought to give free rein to their imagination, break free from traditional forms and rhyme, and explore modernity and the quotidian: in short, to explore what was happening on the street. (The central image of this novel is, of course, a road.)

this unfamiliar territory, on well-laid roads lit by his tranquil good sense, and allow herself to be led along by the trailblazer's deep conviction.

Thus the Gassin house, at 27 Avenue d'Eylau,[7] had a distinctly colonial season late in the year, until Ternier returned to his post, in the Sangkae province of northern Cambodia.

---

7 A prestigious address, on the heights behind the Trocadero.

II
A Most Agreeable Couple

"My dear Doctor, you can repeat yourself every hour if you like. We must still make do with what we have."

"We can scarcely make our vaccination rounds."

"I am only too well aware! Every chance I get—in reports, in private letters, in official letters, orally—I ask the Résidence Supérieure and the local medical chief for an extra doctor. There isn't one. They need doctors all over the place."

"You realize, Monsieur le Résident, that we are meeting the guidelines."

"I know, Maillard. I know."

"But it isn't enough to do our duty here. We could be of great help all over the province, yet here we are pinned down in Sangkae and the outskirts."

"As the engineer from Public Works and the school's headmaster and the ranger all tell me at every audience. They're shorthanded everywhere. We've just got to bear our share of the burden."

Doctor Maillard had the joviality of small, well-fed men, lively eyes behind the pince-nez, a clean-shaven face, and salt-and-pepper hair in a regulation cut. He had watched the center expand under Ternier's leadership, and the two men had a close understanding, both being bachelors, smitten with their respective professions and the country around them, and engaged in the same enterprise. For more than five years without a holiday the doctor had dwelled in Sangkae. His father and mother had died early and all his ties to France been severed. Such is the fate of a great many colonists, who gradually stop looking to the West. The gruff voice could not obscure his friendly manner and kindliness. These had accomplished more among the natives than the prestige of a science that has so far failed to win their confidence; it rather intimidates them, subjects them to conditions whose import they fail to comprehend. The incredible modesty of the women accounts for much of this repugnance. The formalities of medical consultations, with their palpations and auscultations, remain for them insurmountable.

An orderly brought in a telegram.

"Ah!" exclaimed Ternier, scanning it. "What have we here?"

"Are they giving you a medal?" asked the doctor.

"I have often spoken to you of the Gassins, that pleasant couple I met in Paris during my last holiday."

"The automobile manufacturer?"

Ternier handed the telegram to the doctor:

IN SAIGON TO SET UP SUBSIDIARY. THINKING OF PAYING YOU VISIT SOON. LETTER TO FOLLOW. KIND REGARDS AND FOND MEMORIES FROM THE GASSINS.

"Did they never hint at this trip?"

"Not once. And I'll be damned if I'd given them any thought. We've exchanged a few commonplace letters since my return here. Should work out well, this visit. You're going to meet a most agreeable couple."

"Especially the woman, you've said, no?"

"Especially her. Intelligent woman. He's the engineer-businessman, the hard worker, perhaps less open to the outside world. Excellent for the colony too that he's thought to come establish his firm in Cochin China. Every customer gained will be wrested from the American makes."

"A Frenchman from France coming here, daring to come here himself, to try his hand at business. Why, we should have him stuffed and mounted."

The promised letter arrived the following evening. Madame Gassin had written it, apologizing on her husband's behalf. Between negotiating with the banks, finding suitable premises or a site for construction, and studying labor and the local means of production, he had more to do than he'd bargained for. In short, it seemed he would be stuck in Saigon for something more than a fortnight. As for Madame Gassin, she had formed a dreadful impression of the city. She felt stifled there and didn't know what to do with herself. A pit of boredom. Thus she was thinking she might leave her husband behind as he set up his company, venture on ahead, and wait for him at Sangkae, in that Cambodia whose charms Ternier had so eloquently extolled. Could he wire his assurance that she would not be too much trouble and might find a hotel room? Ternier wired his assurance.

Thereupon a car equipped at Saigon crossed Cochin China, switched to Cambodian roads, stopped for a night at Phnom Penh, set out once more at dawn, and five hours later, hot and dusty, pulled up beneath the porch of the Résidence of Sangkae. Madame Gassin stepped out, a happy flame dancing in her eye, a wind-whipped flush on her cheek. But it seemed to Ternier that she had slimmed down somewhat and that her features lacked their former calm and spiritual detachment. Unskilled and unpracticed in the art of reading the female visage, he pushed his examination no further.

Besides, who can rightfully claim to read the face of a woman?

That very evening Madame Gassin settled into in a big, corner room at the bungalow, with large verandas looking east to the river and south to the trees of a neighboring property. The *résident* had had the furnishings rounded out with a heavy table of ruddy wood grained like marble, a rocking chair, flowers, some silks to relieve the nakedness of the walls, and some fine linen on the dressing table. He stopped by to review the arrangements himself and once again recommend the traveler to the bungalow's manager,[8] an obliging Chinaman[9] who carried on his watch chain, as a charm, a little golden pig inlaid with fragments of diamond.[10]

---

8 Groslier calls him a *gérant adjudicataire,* a manager who has won some sort of public contract with the bungalow, presumably after a call for tenders.

9 The editor recognizes that modern dictionaries identify this as a derogatory term. Here, the translator has included the archaic demonym *Chinaman* to maintain the informal character of Groslier's narration and usage consistent with the era (1931). Like current uses of such terms as *Englishman* and *Frenchman,* Groslier's use is not derogatory.

10 Most likely a symbol of the man's birth year from the 12-year Chinese zodiac cycle, which is also used in Cambodia. The years are: Rat, Ox, Tiger, Rabbit, Dragon, Snake, Horse, Goat, Monkey, Rooster, Dog and Pig.

III
Tableau and Method

Ternier would doubtless have preferred to receive Madame Gassin at the Résidence. He did not propose it because of the proprieties on which Madame Gassin, being out on her own, might well have insisted.

"It doesn't worry me in the least to see you lodged here," he had said to Hélène. "Your room has an excellent orientation and a fine view. The manager is devoted to me and has every reason to take good care of you. I'll be keeping an eye out."

As tidy as a décor, the view unfolded before Madame Gassin's eyes in warm opulence. The riverbank was bathed in shadow; the far bank blazed in sunlight. Between them flowed the river, its median waters already swift, draining the mahogany sands. One could see it coming from a long way off before it drew even with the bungalow, spread to a breadth of more than two hundred meters, and then, up north, veered off. Hélène leaned on the sill.

Below were craft of every displacement, from the narrow pirogue to the tall Chinese junk, its prow sunk between two painted eyes. There was a whole bobbing city breaking apart and coming back together amid the peaceable activity of a population that mixed all races.

The naked feet of women fetching water had rubbed lustrous paths into the golden bank. Amid the huts the scintillating pediments of two pagodas rose above the scene. To the north and south, crowning men, land, and water, a curtain of deep verdure girded the horizon.

The eye lost its bearings in the variety of species. The tufted, broad, ragged leaves of banana trees; the scattershot of lemon trees, sprinkled with the pearly orbs of champa flowers; the feeble, insubstantial, jagged tamarinds; here and there a jackfruit with the dark luster of its rounded leaves. Squeezed into these tall, dense, unbroken copses was a gray-stiped colonnade of areca trees. And wherever the eye settled the coconut palms burst forth to every height; isolated, clustered, or flattened against a swath of the horizon, they brandished their metallic fronds. Mixed into this were the panaches of bamboos. And Hélène could make out still other trees she did not yet know, among them opaque giants of a black green that gleamed like a lacquer in the sunlight; organized and solid they stood, like formations of rock: mangoes.

In spots between junks and up against the bank the river went slack, losing the sky's reflection and the current's shimmer. Here the curtain of trees flipped upside down and set pirogues to bathe in foliage. The traveler felt herself gradually yielding to this intimacy between things and living beings. It was as if her own flesh were being absorbed, diluted in the light. Hélène was going down to the river, entering a sort of dispassion, multiplying. In her as in the flowing water the sky and the works of the land were becoming double.

Ternier paused a moment, not to interrupt her contemplation, and then said:

"It is all yours, Madame. It is a particularly lovely time of day, and I do believe that the land of Sangkae has turned itself out for you. The new town, the one we are building, is on this side of the river. I will give you a proper tour tomorrow. If you would like to observe native life, cross the river and make your way beneath those trees on the far side, the ones the sun is shining on right now. You can ask the manager for a sampan, if you'd like to avoid going around by the bridges. Better yet, telephone me, and I will send you a car. I would gladly spend the evening with you, but, unfortunately, I am chairman of a committee that is meeting in a few minutes. At any rate, we dine together, at eight o'clock. Nothing fancy. I will introduce you to Dr. Maillard."

"Very well. Hurry along, then. And thank you. You have set me up like a princess."

Ternier was on his way out.

"Oh, by the way! The car—send it to me right away."

❖ ❖ ❖

It was the Roland-Gassin in which, a year and a half earlier, Hélène and her husband had returned from the cascades of Fontanat. The door clattered shut, and the car made its way over a bridge of reinforced concrete across from the Résidence. It then took a left onto the bank-side road and settled into a walking pace.

Madame Gassin was now penetrating into the heart of that green horizon whose extent she had just surveyed. She was leaving a mark in the red earth beneath vaults obliquely lit by horizontal sunbeams. Each house was ringed with a festive garden to support the architecture of large trees. Hibiscus with flowers ablaze, a few yellow and red tufts of canna lily in front of a hut, the white clump of an amaryllis, oleanders. Lining the properties along the path was a rank of cacti speckled with little flowers like shuttlecocks set upon rackets, or a jasmine bush. Near a door, under a small roof, was an earthen jar of water for thirsty passers-by: here, then, is where men dwell, while the rest of us languish.

Hélène sought out these men. Too many revelations confounding the eye; too many things she had never seen and did not understand. She would have liked to isolate these creatures, the

expressions on their faces, the details of their clothes, and focus
her mind on them. Impossible. Her eyes could not shake the
dazzling splendor of a tree in which she had glimpsed the rhythm
of a human motion, the bulge of a chest draped in celestial blue.
She descried a wrist encircled with a bracelet of braided flowers,
another with a ring of gold. The blood-red ground seemed the
source of the ruddy hibiscus, as if the red of the flowers were in
fact the red of the ground drawn out, and ignited as it was pumped
to the blossoms. Along with these visions she took in the fruit-
tinged fragrance of the air and the somewhat heavy limpness of the
perpetual shade. In short, Hélène could not separate living being
from thing. Her gaze slid with equal delight from a fold of fabric
to the colors of the fold and on to the gesture that animated them.
And in her mind, just like that, a palm tree took up the human
gesture and continued it above the street, in this village shaded like
a wood.

Asking the driver to stop, nestling in her corner of leather, she
opened her intellect to the surrounding fertility.

"I'm just a tiny little thing…," she murmured.

Oxen passed. She saw and recognized open watermelons in a
basket. There was a steady thump from a paddy mortar, operated
by a woman standing atop its pestle. Farther off young men sat idle
in daydreams, staring off toward the river before them. Two bare-
necked cocks, standing tall on their madder-colored legs, made
a sudden, mad scramble for some fish guts and came to blows.
Small children had gathered around the car. Then a decrepit old
carriage, with the stuffing coming out and rattan patchwork and
two rope-harnessed horses to draw it, came rattling along the road,
transporting Chinese women with baskets in their laps. Bonzes
advancing in Indian file and draped like Romans crossed its path.
Flowers with a pale-yellow core were coating the ground at the
roadside, the last of them dropping from a barren tree, its trunk
and branches gray, twisted, and scaly.

"Move on, Driver," said Madame Gassin.

She passed a dilapidated Chinese pagoda, with a decorative, openwork circle on either side of its door, and some other huts, where the women were preparing meals by clay ovens. And then, suddenly, she saw an old, abandoned brick house with three semicircular arches set upon leaf-embellished capitals. Two lateral staircases, forming a horseshoe, led to the upper floor. The roof, with its heavy flashing, had been darkened by sunshine and rain. There were earthen balusters of emerald green and the ruins of stucco ornaments, all of it outmoded and melancholic and cracked and marbled with lichen. The house had been built more than a century back. Its candid architecture mixed the keen grace of Chinese décor with bastardized Louis XIV lines; it was the architecture that the Jesuits had brought to China in the sixteenth century, and that had then spread all the way to Manila and Singapore. Stumbling upon this house, a dumbstruck Westerner sees flashes of grandmothers in puce-colored gowns. He scans the little courtyard, where the grass pushes up between the bricks, for the unhitched sedan. He searches beneath the areca trees, between the Cambodian huts, and at the riverside with the bobbing pirogues.

"Stop!" Hélène commanded in a gentle voice, and leaned as if out a window.

There were two naked little children, red with the earth they had been playing in. They had bulbous bellies with big navels. Their features behind their stern expressions were already well defined. One was sitting by a hedge and looking at the other, who was speaking, or, rather, busy meeting some absorbing need and occasionally uttering a word to indicate what he was doing. Tableau and method might have dated to the dawn of man. The seated child had his back to the road and had not heard the quiet car come to a halt. The other was too busy to see anything.

The busy child had etched a rectangle into the dirt and laid a leaf at each corner.

"*Phtéa*," he said.

"*Phtéa*," repeated the other.

"What are they saying?" whispered Hélène to the driver.

"House."

Hélène saw the house at the edge of the grass.

"*Stoung*," the first child said.

"*Stoung*," approved the second, opening his mouth and raising an arm, with his little fingers spread.

"River," whispered the driver.

On this river the game master set a shard from a blue bowl, saying: "*Touk*."

"*Hoeu*!" replied the spectator, dropping his arm now that his doubts had been satisfactorily addressed. "Boat," the driver had translated. Things were getting serious, as the traveler, astonishingly, could see. All around her she could see the landscape the child was recreating. Ripe mandarins gleamed in the sun. A blackbird eviscerated a papaya and hovered there to keep level with it. The blackness of the bird, turning violet in the shadows, stood out against the yellow of the exposed pulp.

All of Cambodia was nodding off there, all of it contained and symbolized in a corner of its territory. The river crosses it end to end. The huts are all the same and clump together. They are enriched and protected by these same trees; they are unified in traditions that reach back centuries. Everywhere the same sensuousness, simple and still; the penetrating hold of things on minds that never suffer the torments of thought. But what about those children just now?

Yes, those children were already men. House, river, and sampan, and even their game, limit the span of their lives. By the age of two they know their destiny, and run out the clock without paying much heed to the passing stranger, or to the races mixing around them. No complication and nothing new will arise. Later they will simply cover their nudity with fabric, to rouse the pangs of love.

The car crossed the river once more. Speeding up through the French town, it reached the bungalow just as the electricity was advancing like a shot down the avenue, stringing luminous points along its path. A large, dusty mail truck that had set out that morning from Phnom Penh hurtled by like a whirlwind, hauling a trailer and crammed with natives. Madame Gassin had scarcely climbed up to her room and set down her hat before dusk began seeping in. The river sank between its banks. And when she set her elbows on the sill once more to reflect on the day's many impressions it was night that came to meet her.

IV
"We, the French"

Turning the morning cool to advantage, Ternier collected Madame Gassin at dawn for a walking tour of the French town.

The verdant riverbank is studded with huts, and upon it dwells a somnolent population, idle for the past ten centuries, subjugated, grown too old. The earth is split, the gullies stagnant with filth. Mosquitos flourish. From time to time the cholera, endemic, cuts a man down. Death claims one child in three. Man and beast drink from the river. Pagodas gleam in the sun, and chants rise into the night. Trees sag with fruit alongside waters brimming with fish. Rice fields scintillate as far as man has cared to push his plowshare. The population pays its tax to a Siamese mandarin.

And then, though any change to this state of affairs seemed impossible, there came a sudden intrusion. The thick, deep tuff lay scattered with the ashes of a hundred generations. The landscape had endured in stasis. A native girl would wed on the same spot, and by the same rites, as her great-great-great-grandmother, and the words uttered within the pagodas had gone unchanged for more than three hundred years. It was to this place that we, the French, had come.

"We, the French," Ternier had said, and it seemed to her that he stood up straighter as he made his meaning clear. He had not said "Westerners," for none but the French could have come if events were to take the course they had in fact taken. None but the French if the bonzes were to keep meditating in the pagodas, the chants keep rising into the night, the girls keep marrying in the manner of their great-great-great-grandmothers, inside makeshift pavilions decorated with white fabrics and sculpted banana trunks. We had come, and in a few years had built a new city between gardens overhung with century-old mango trees.

"Yesterday, Madame, on the far bank, you saw native life, with its calm and its liberty. Places once isolated by days and days of travel we have now linked to the rest of the country by roads. Here in this square, behind those trees and between the blue walls, stands the post office, with its telegraph and telephone lines. It serves also as a depot for the buses, which depart in all directions. Dying children? We will presently be passing in front of the hospital, with a maternity ward for natives and pavilions scattered in a park. Farther on is the bank. Our schools were no sooner opened than they were filled to capacity. We expanded them. In Sangkae live more than a thousand Chinese, source of the region's activity and commerce. For them we laid out broad roads lined with solid, bright, salubrious houses. In the gardens along this avenue you will see the houses and offices of the French, founders of this young city. One day electricity flashed on, and there was ice on every table. With all the marshes drained, we can now dispense with mosquito nets on most nights. Tomorrow the train station will rise. You will have seen the airfield and hangars to the right on the road in from Phnom Penh.

"We have built our city three kilometers long, and charmingly laid it out along the bends in the river. It is a city with no garrison. The few soldiers we had called in at the beginning have left, as they were not needed. We have set up our city and our authority without firing a shot. These houses and boulevards were built with

Chinese and Annamite labor, and with the ten-piastre[11] tax paid annually by every male Cambodian. We have also built the safe, hygienic market where the Cambodian buys and sells; the guarded roads where he need no longer fear highwaymen; the hospital that heals him free of charge; the school his children freely attend; the offices where he need no longer be under the mandarin's thumb; the bridges he can cross with his carts, without unmooring a sampan that the current can carry off; the factory that provides his pure water and his light. We have staked out his properties, so the weak can hold land without fear of the strong. We have called in veterinarians to care for his livestock. And all along the riverbanks the steam launches have increased his commerce tenfold.

"Had he no need for this? Why, then, has he not left? He is at liberty. Why has the population quintupled in five years? Why are our mail bags filled with his letters? Why are our launches and our charabancs[12] filled with passengers? Why have all the city's vacant lots been purchased? Why do children from the traditional pagoda school go on to attend our primary schools? And why are our clinics full every morning for our open consultations? The wilds and liberty lie a mere five kilometers from here. Could it be because, within the strict limits of this urban center, the pagodas continue with their prayers and the same old traditions live on in every hut?"

⚜ ⚜ ⚜

Ternier and Hélène took a street that ran beneath a vault of trees. It led between sidewalks and *compartiments*[13] to a square with a

---

11 To stabilize currency in the region, the French introduced a silver *piastre de commerce* in 1885. In 1930 its value was pegged at 1 piastre to 10 French francs.

12 There has been considerable crosspollination between French and English in the terms they use to designate buses. The English word *charabanc* derives from the French term *char-à-banc* (carriage with benches). Groslier uses a different term, *auto*, short for *autocar* (motor-coach, or omnibus), which is in fact derived from the English term *automobile*. The charabanc was an early motorized bus, popular in France in the 1920s, and is in all likelihood what Groslier has in mind. In Britain it was used, for instance, to convey factory workers to the seaside for holidays.

13 A French word for a type of shop-house made of wood or masonry built in towns and villages during the colonial period. Generally a business, shop or restaurant located on the

grand theater, where every evening Siamese and Cambodian actors played *The Ramayana.*

The street was inhabited almost entirely by Annamites. Upon the shops and the open houses to either side Hélène saw carmine spots lengthen and come into focus. Gradually the strange, shifting designs coalesced into script: family plaques. The black wood of these plaques seemed to evanesce, leaving the glimmering letters of gold or mother-of-pearl miraculously suspended. The panel would change from house to house, as would the ancestral altar piously maintained in each house's recess.

At every door was a creature in rags, a filthy woman inserting a long fingernail into her hair for a careful scratch, and behind her, in the heart of the darkness, catching venturesome glints of daylight, were the two scintillating chandeliers, the perfume burner, the vase for ash—a Shrovetide[14] mummer with the full-on bronze mystique of a chapel for a backdrop. Gummy-eyed humanity in the foreground, and beyond it a tidy, glittering ritual: a dragon in mid-leap at the corner of a plinth, or a sculpted bat in decorative flight.

"It is," said Ternier, "a curious phenomenon too often overlooked, this mixing of Asiatic races in Cambodian towns. Side by side they live, and yet they liberally retain their respective customs, beliefs, and tatters. The Chinese and Annamite streets are all alike in this little city. The Hindu in his white loincloth passes after the Malay with his velvet cap. Whereas foreigners will take a house of masonry in the city center, the Cambodian will stay on the outskirts. He has no taste for business and prefers his gardens and his airy huts."

There were sundries—wads of cotton, sacks of rice, piles of dried fish, heaps of skins—on display, spilling onto the sidewalks.

---

ground floor with family living areas above.

14 In various Christian calendars, the celebratory days (e.g., Shrove Tuesday, also known as Mardi Gras) that precede Ash Wednesday (i.e., the first day of Lent, the six weeks of contrition and abstinence that precede Easter).

There were bare-chested Celestials[15] at table in the shops, sharing a soup as they waited for another launch or dray to unload. The thin morning air was filled with the dry clack of abacuses and the clicks of porcelains being unpacked, but two hundred meters farther on it all came abruptly to an end.

There the hectic street became a deserted road between banana trees and rows of areca. Left and right all was arbors and little groves, in which Madame Gassin recognized the tableaux of the previous day. There was no comparison to be made between what lived on the city street and what lived here. They crossed a square, with its plots for construction. The tall grass transformed it into a savannah, with round dunes of white sand. The road came to an end there, beneath an enormous flamboyant. As regular as a spray of flowers in a vase, the tree upheld its flowery dome on multiple trunks, and the ground was red with its fallen petals. In its shade slept a Cambodian stretched out on his cart, the draft shaft upturned like a swan's neck. To the east a cinema was going up. Farther off stood the wall of a school; the voices of children carried over it as they droned through the alphabet to the tune of a canticle. There were occasional passers-by: a trio of blue-pated bonzes, a Chinaman, a swift soup merchant slipping beneath the weighty yoke from which his portable kitchen swung. Atop one of the sand heaps turkeys dozed, their breasts slit open and their guts held in their beaks.

The *résident* led Hélène through the market, which spilled out from a metallic hall onto broad sidewalks. To enter the chaos of opulent color that is Far Eastern food is to travel through a wonderland. The stalls are so many mosaics painted and varnished in the flames of the sun. So felicitous is the haphazard array of merchandise, so opportune the gleam of the peppers upon stacked gourds, it is as if the merchant had wittingly set the scene by the principles of some subtle pictorial art.

---

15 A 19th century term for Chinese emigrants, derived from Celestial Empire (Tianxia), a traditional name for China.

Hélène moved between odors as crisply separate as sunlight and shade. Jasmines proclaimed their presence for twenty meters around, bathing in a flowery fragrance the pyramid of enormous gourds beneath them. The pineapples were piled in baskets, and the light, hitting their scaly facets, cooled their golden bronze with a sky-blue glaze. And then came the baskets of gleaming violet eggplants, and the banana flowers, with their violet-tipped, madder-colored spindles, and everywhere the dented peppers, with their deep varnish, incisively green or violently carmine, appearing to the eye as their pulp tastes to the tongue.

Ternier next led Hélène between small, makeshift shops, the partitions between them buried under banana bunches. The shops jutted out from walls spiked with a thousand, versicolored horns, through which the sun shone ragged like cotton through a card. The stalls—more gray, more complicated—were crammed together here. There were knots of ginger, water-lily flowers, Chinese chestnuts, the shredded flesh of dried fish, bean sprouts like larvae in agglomeration, skeins of transparent noodles, stacked small jars of fermented sauces, jars of red chalk resembling a paste of corals, black tobacco, regular ranks of spade-shaped betel leaves, peanuts, brown saffron. There were kitchens with great hunks of lard and quartered chickens and lacquered ducks.

It was a labyrinth, a chemistry to set the senses reeling, a seething sea of protean-seeming things taken up by proffering or selecting hands, and through it all there flowed a prattling crowd. Fair-chested Chinamen, Annamites sheathed in black, Cambodians of every quality. There were hearty peasants shouldering watermelons; yet more Chinamen, bloodstained and unloading pork quarters; native policemen; a few Tonkinese women in black turbans and cachou-colored dresses; children of all ages, naked, straddling a hip, one playing with a crab.

The patrons hastened to beat the coming heat. They shouted, squeezed between piles of fruit, and glided into steamy kitchens.

They bore an increasingly heavy circular basket on a jutting hip or dangled a fish from the tip of a cane.

On the ground, at the edge of the sidewalks, finally, were the rubbish heaps: as lovely, almost, as the stalls themselves. An already blazing sun was sucking life from this death of matter, from this matter that it had birthed, that was disintegrating in brilliant coquetry before it could rot. Coconut halves looking, with their alabaster insides and russet fur, like the broken craniums of dolls; mango stones to which thousands of green flies clung like an emerald pulp; the conical opercula of bamboo shoots; the amber viscera of fish; pineapple skins like the molt of reptiles skinned alive, the almond-green spinning-tops of water lilies—all manner of polychromatic things, jumbled together, shunted aside with a broom like confetti and streamers at a theater door after New Year's Eve.

V

"In spite of it all."

Ternier sent for the driver and asked Madame Gassin:

"You are not pressed for time, I trust?"

"Free as a bird."

"Well, then. It's four o'clock. Let's venture another thirty kilometers from here and take a look at a well-situated pagoda: Wat Romduol.[16] The road through the rice fields is not too bad. How about it?"

"Need you ask? Let's go."

Hélène seemed tired, but her eyes shone beneath her gray buckskin hat, which was decorated with steely pearls and secured, in soldier-like fashion, by a chinstrap. Her simple, straight-hanging dress emphasized the slender body beneath. The whiteness of her hands, the mauve rings around her eyes, and the hint of languor in her bearing were belied by incisive gestures, the energy in her voice, and especially the bloom in her gaze.

---

16 The actual distance from the Battambang Governor's Residence to Wat Romduol is only 3.6 km. Groslier's original French text cites the distance of 30 km above. Either they went for a long joyride, the distance was mistaken, or there is another Wat Romduol, but no other wat by that name is now known.

"Overflowing rivers and the first rains have flooded part of the countryside. This is the time of year when they prick out the paddy, and when the sunsets are at their loveliest. Not too fast, Driver."

As soon as they emerged from the foliage of the center a vast, sunny plain opened up around them. The straight, white road and the telegraph lines converged at a distant point. The Roland-Gassin, steering wheel immobile, glided along toward that same point, through the lukewarm sou'wester of the monsoon.

"A solid road!"

"It has just been resurfaced. It goes all the way to Sisophon, eighty kilometers from here, and past that a path has been cleared for more than a hundred kilometers. In three years there will be cars at the foot of the Dângrêk Mountains. The northernmost reaches of Cambodia and, through the passes, the nether regions of Laos will be opened up. On our side, we will also have opened up the northeast provinces of Siam."

"And this path, is it practicable by car?"

"Not yet. The first storms have riddled it with furrows, and the bridges are not yet finished. I am to review the work next week."

"Would you take me along?"

"It's not exactly a stroll in the park! The only way to get around is by horse or cart. It is a sandy region, and water is scarce at this time of year. It will be a five- or six-day journey."

"Do not stoke my enthusiasm."

"You will come along with your husband."

"He won't be here in time."

"He has abandoned you, this man!"

"I've nothing to complain about. It's rather *I* who has abandoned *him*! Saigon is a stifling city. Two days and a traveler has exhausted its charms, and afterwards there's nothing but boredom."

Cambodians up to their calves in rice-field water were pricking out paddy. The still water was a mirror between the young stems, and in the sky's reflection the rice seemed to be growing in the clouds. Women in muddy clothes were tying the nutritious grass into streaming bundles. Some children were fishing with a basket. In this season, as in the fable, the fish had quit the flooding rivers to stray into the countryside.[17] Men were standing atop sticky, mud-spurting harrows to guide paired oxen around in circles, with mandarin blackbirds providing an escort.

Hélène absently set a hand on the car door. The leather flap of a compartment in the coachwork bore, in high relief and doubly ringed, the initials of the car's make: RG. The touch of it troubled her, and with a flutter of her eyelids she hastily withdrew her hand. To mask her gesture and turmoil, she hastened to repeat her question:

"Would you take me along?"

"Do you realize the responsibility I would be taking on?"

"Are you afraid?"

"I fear it will be a rude expedition. It is no place for a woman. We must expect storms and hardships."

"You prefer not to trouble yourself?"

"I have no wish to see you deprived of every comfort."

"Did you not often tell me in Paris—yes, I seem to recall—that a tour was quite practical, that one could have a tablecloth smack in the middle of the forest, and that in two hours the natives could raise an impeccable shelter? I will exempt you from the tablecloth."

"So much is true for a man, but not for a Parisian lady straight out of Avenue d'Eylau."

"All right."

---

17 Note needed. No idea what fable this refers to.

Madame Gassin thought for a moment. On the telegraph wires pairs of kingfishers flashed sapphire wings and swelled their flame-licked crops.

"Well, then, I will go alone," she concluded with a smile.

"I categorically forbid it!"

"The powers of your office do not extend quite so far. And, besides, no one forbids me anything."

"Would you have me ascribe your insistence to female obstinacy?"

"Would you counter it with male bias? Listen for a moment, and you'll soon understand my wish. You've told me so much about this wilderness! Here I am with the only chance I'm likely to get to venture into it. I have the best of guides at my disposal and needn't cause him too much trouble. And you expect me not to jump at the chance?"

"What you are saying, then, is that I myself have encouraged you to undertake this trek?"

"You yourself. Would you like evidence from my memory, proof that one must never speak in front of the children? We are on Avenue d'Eylau. Present are Madame Gassin, her husband, two or three minor characters, and a *résident* on holiday. This *résident* is telling lovely stories, and the Parisian natives are following him in their minds through the forest. He says something like 'For hours without cease columns of black ants slither along, brilliant and sinuous like a rivulet of spilled lacquer. Holding out a hand beneath certain trees, one can feel a steady shower of little grains, like a little hailstorm, and it lasts the morning. The path one cuts and tears and stamps to clear vanishes in a matter of days. The stem left for dead will have returned to life, shoots will already have sprouted from machete-opened wounds, the wasp nest will have been rebuilt, the beast one killed will have been dismembered....' Was that about it?"

"There is not much there to fire the imagination."

"Shall I continue?"

"Not at all—or, if you do, select a new author."

"Not much to fire the imagination, you say. No. But is one master of one's imagination? Ought one to curb it when life seems a bit too monotonous? Even without maligning this life—do not misunderstand me, please—even while finding fulfillment in it, one can yet have a burning, legitimate curiosity stirred up by the right occasion. Such is my case. And happenstance has brought me here, where just the past few days have far outstripped your words and the pictures I had formed listening to them. Don't leave me stranded halfway, my friend. Have you any idea of the wonderful memories I hope to carry home, how precious they could be to me when I am once again living in France? Your surroundings here no longer strike you as anything special. The country has subsumed you into itself. But I'm just passing through. I am but a traveler, living in a state of enchantment. Just thinking about the preparations for the trip, and the chests for the carts, and the waiting horse—I'm like a little girl in toy land!"

"Where's Crusoe when you need him?"

"Yes, call in Crusoe! He saw a human footprint in the sand—and his solitude was at an end."[18]

"The winds effaces such prints, and then nothing remains."

"I'd like to see them first."

"Then you shall see them."

Horn tooting, they crossed a village. Madame Gassin glimpsed sugar-palm tufts, Chinese shops built of thatch, a cactus hedge,

---

18 I.e., Robinson Crusoe, marooned protagonist and narrator of Daniel Defoe's novel (published in 1719) The Life and Strange Surprizing Adventures of Robinson Crusoe, Of York, Mariner: Who lived Eight and Twenty Years, all alone in an un-inhabited Island on the Coast of America, near the Mouth of the Great River of Oroonoque; Having been cast on Shore by Shipwreck, wherein all the Men perished but himself. With An Account how he was at last as strangely deliver'd by Pyrates—better known as Robinson Crusoe. The footprint in the sand is that of an escaped captive of the island's cannibals. Crusoe famously names him Friday.

scattered huts in a tight colonnade of palms. Other, great trees reared up, surrounding a shaded square and a pond strewn with pink lotus. It was the pagoda, roofed with golden antefixes[19] like yellow bonze togas. And once again the sun blazed on rice fields as far as the eye could see.

Hélène turned slightly toward Ternier.

"You'll see. I'll be a very good girl. You won't have to trouble about me at all. On horseback when necessary and for as long as necessary. You cannot imagine what this chance means to me, what it means just to make the trip... I'll be so proud to travel down your road, to see it for myself and understand how it pushes on toward the regions it will awaken... Surely my esteem for your work cannot be a bother to you."

Setting aside his usual curtness, Ternier softened his tone:

"In my isolation, Madame, your esteem is precious indeed. But consider the demands that courtesy and affection have placed on me. Charge of this province falls to me, not because I am Pierre Ternier but because it is my duty. I must safeguard even the most miserable bit of straw, I must watch over the rice, and if birds steal the grains then I am a bad watchman. You pass through, and so I watch over you as well. You become my guest. I must keep you in health and help bring about your wishes, and I gladly accept the duty. But my conscience intrudes with a grave warning: 'Keep special watch over this one,' it says, 'for she is alone and counting on you.' And I am all the more concerned with your peace of mind because, as you yourself have just reminded me, you are here above all because of promises I made. These promises, Madame, must be kept. Should some accident befall you, I will have lied. Should some calumny sully your good name in the slightest, I will have lied. Should the shadow of a doubt cross your husband's mind, I will have lied. You do not understand. You look at me in wide-eyed

---

19 Ornaments placed on the eaves of classical buildings to conceal the ends of joint roof tiles.

astonishment, because as a woman you are accustomed to being carried along. But the man who does the carrying looks at things from a different perspective. If he accepts a burden, however light, he owes it to his fellow man, or to himself, to carry that burden, intact, from point A to point B, or else he lies. Yes, he lies. I am well aware of the tendency in this day and age to mince words. If our man refuses a burden, we will say he is fearful, or feels himself unequal to the task."

"There is no dishonor in that…"

"No, but let him cede his claim, then, for he has usurped it."

With a screech of the brakes the car came to a sudden halt. Blocking the road was an enormous statue of ill-cast bronze, scaly and sticky with mud, with an upturned muzzle and a fiery eye. Was she keen to pounce on the travelers? No. She turned ponderously about and set off, taking to a pond. She was a buffalo. Some pond herons fluttered away.

"Since we are making plans, here is another. In three days I will be hosting a big dinner to celebrate the rosette that the Legion of Honor has just bestowed on the governor of the province, an old servant of the Protectorate. At this dinner you will see just about the entire center in attendance: some forty guests."

"Why, it's a godsend! I'll have a double bill: colonial society *and* the splendor of an official reception."

"Put it on your agenda. Do not, however, expect to find a Negro behind every guest and almehs[20] lounging at the back of the hall. The people you are going to see are civil servants to a man. They are tranquil and bourgeois and have nothing whatever to do with the overly colorful portraits that certain chronicles have seen fit to draw. You have my word that the men will not swap wives during

---

20 Egyptian courtesans. In other words, says Ternier, don't expect the Western dream of the Orient

the meal and that none of the beds at the Résidence are 'deep as tombs.'[21] Things will not be quite so picturesque."

"I'll try to take heart."

"You just might walk away convinced that milieus of a kind are quite similar wherever you find them, be it in France or in the colonies or, indeed, anywhere else in the world. Our expatriate society, they say, is dissolute and wasteful and eager for advancement, but that is because it is never matched against comparable elements elsewhere. It is as if in Europe the world of high functionaries or of high commerce—in short, the upper crust—were nothing but purity and integrity, order and harmony, elegance and erudition; as if everyone were in his proper place, and it were impossible to find a hint of intrigue, a single adulterous desire, the slightest sign of ambition! But why should an individual transported here and placed under the same social conditions see all of his vices amplified and not one of his virtues? Why should a man who steps aboard a ship in Marseille be instantly deprived of his moral, intellectual, and professional faculties?"

"I gladly concede the point. Yet in the long run the climate, and certain opportunities that the colonies open up, and the advantageous salaries, and even…"

"Stop right there, so that I can reply to each item in turn! You will find no European labor here. The most modest expatriate is already a foreman or a shop manager. Nor will you find an aristocratic class, or people living off landholdings, or politicians. You will search in vain for a liberal milieu, by which I mean

---

21 From Charles Baudelaire's poem "Death of the Lovers" ("*La Mort des Amants*"):

We shall have beds rife with faint odors, Divans deeps as tombs, And, on shelves, strange flowers, Abloom for us beneath more beauteous skies.

Vying to consume their final ardors, Two blazing torches our hearts shall be, Reflecting their double light In the twin mirrors of our spirits.

On an evening of pink and mystic blue We shall trade a single fulmination, Like a drawn-out sob, laden with farewells;

And later an Angel, true and joyous, Cracking open the doors, Shall come revive The dulled mirrors, the snuffed-out flames.

writers, artists, intellectuals, independent scholars, theater people. Except in Saigon and Hanoi, then, the population into whose midst you have wandered corresponds exactly to our French bourgeoisie, to the very people who have been entrusted with our affairs of state and our commerce. Here independence is illusory, for there is no merchant or lawyer who has not at some point been obliged to hitch his wagon to the government's train. As you can thus easily understand, there reigns here from top to bottom a certain discipline, whether it is acknowledged or not, whether it is quietly combatted or clumsily accepted or more or less discreetly imposed. The result is a powerful, indissoluble atmosphere, which no one dreams of leaving, and which exerts an influence. That said, in judging the colonial milieu we ought to separate this influence from that of the colonized country itself. We should endeavor to determine whether the miasmas one breathes from Cochin China to Yunnan rise from the ground or have simply been imported by us, and are therefore to be found, if sought out, also in the department[22] of Indre-et-Loire or Allier."

"It nevertheless seems to me that the heat and the humidity must alter the temperament of certain people."

"That is so. Over the two or three months of summer the heat drains energy and diminishes effort. No one will deny it. But here we set off in another direction, towards, as you say, the subject of temperament. Temperament is not mentality. At any rate, note that we are devising more and more ways to deal with the heat and would manage to suppress its effects if only our sacred routines did not get in the way, if only we adopted some rational measures in our architecture, city planning, office hours, and diet. In fact, we are putting up a poor struggle against the climate. It affects us, and we are to blame. From the human—or, better yet, the social—point of view, the key thing is to determine whether the healthy amount of work, the amount necessary for our colonial responsibilities,

---

22 The territory of France is divided up into *départements*, which correspond roughly to counties.

matches up with our total capacity. If in France I can do ten units of work and actually do ten, then I have achieved balance. If here I can do eight and actually do eight, then the balance has not been lost. And yet I feel that I can do as much here as I could in France. As you can see, my Résidence operates like a prefecture and the doctor treats the ill as needed. As a result, I am close to thinking that many colonists are more productive at their colonial posts than they would be back home at similar posts, because they are called upon to make greater efforts while surmounting more obstacles."

"So you wear yourselves out faster. There are many drawn faces here."

"Are there no hale faces? Why the difference? We have taken to blaming the climate for a great many ills that the colonist carries within him, and which he would suffer from in Dijon as well. In principle, no one is permitted to leave metropolitan France[23] who is not sound in body.

"But the reality is different. Also, let us not permit the past to cloud our judgments. Over the past fifty years many of our countrymen have perished to prepare for the already wholesome present we now enjoy. Let us mind their sacrifice and not vilify the results of their abnegation. Disease is receding with the marshes. Compare a thousand people in France with the thousand Frenchmen now inhabiting Cambodia. The level of health is higher here than it is there."

"That is not to be believed."

"Yet it is quite natural for it to be so. If you doubt it, I can provide the most exact statistics to back it up. The drawn faces you see—do not linger on them too long. Most such faces vanish after a month of colonial life. Especially when it comes to women, seek the cause not in the rigors of the climate but in idleness, a bad diet,

---

23 I.e., European France, nearby islands (e.g., Corsica) included, as opposed to the colonies (e.g., Cochin China) and protectorates (e.g., Cambodia). At present the term is used in opposition to French overseas territories (e.g., Martinique).

and fear of exertion—and, indeed, fear of the very fresh air and sunshine that they avoid at all costs. Out of a hundred women in France how many have pale, drawn faces beneath the make-up and the powder?"

"Pale people for Pink Pills!"[24]

"Precisely. Are you yourself not a bit pale today? And you haven't yet been here a fortnight."

"Already I'm a victim of the climate! None of this is common knowledge in France. With every passing minute it grows more apparent that the picture we've formed of our countrymen's lives in the colonies is false and absurd."

"Ah, but not every colony is like our Indochina."

"Is it not already negligent not to know that Indochina stands apart? Now that I've seen it for myself—seen a bit of it, that is!—I'm sure I'd feel no compunction if my son settled down here, had I a son."

"You would react like any other mother. The separation…"

"Perhaps, but it'd just be a matter of the separation. It's true…"

"That counts for a lot. Anyway, as I was saying a moment ago, you will see the whole of the post's society at this dinner."

"A sample."

"A mixed sample, for I invite everyone and just about everyone shows up."

"The seating arrangements must demand real strategy."

"It is indeed a complex matter. I would place you to my right, but you would grow bored and I would not be able to tend to you as I would like. So I will sit you between M. Barrois, the

---

24 Pink Pills for Pale People— originally produced by Dr. William Jackson, of Schenectady, New York—was a patent medicine claiming to cure such ailments as St. Vitus's Dance. The rights to it were sold for a pittance in 1890 to Canadian businessman and politician George Taylor Fulford, who made a fortune selling the pills. They were distributed as far afield as France, South Africa, Australia, and China.

treasurer-paymaster, and our national and renowned forest keeper general, Tubinque.

"Tubinque is probably one of the last remaining true characters from the heroic days of the colony. The old colonists have committed to memory a great store of amusing or rowdy stories, a hundred tomfooleries whose protagonists are still remembered. They would fill a most curious volume. You might enjoy catching a few echoes."

"And you have but one representative of those days long past?"

"You will see that he suffices. The new generations are more complex, calmer, and often more insidious. The broad joke had its value. I see no other stand-outs to recommend to you among our guests."

"And the women?"

"You will see for yourself. A few sweet ones—homebodies, unfortunately. Too many peignoirs languishing beneath fans. Not a trooper among them. Our tennis courts are practically deserted. In general, French women take no interest whatsoever in the natives. They ought to play a charming, salutary role amid the women of Cambodia. They would be warmly welcomed, met with a child-like, discreet curiosity. But French women too often reserve a sort of disdain for these yellow Cambodians, these little hags—these *congaies*, as they delight in calling them.[25] From this disdain they exempt only diamond-studded princesses, who happen to be the least interesting native women in the land."

"Will we have any of these princesses to dinner?"

"No, no princesses. They are to be found only in Phnom Penh, in and around the Royal Palace. We will have the eldest daughter of the governor, who burned his wife last year."

"Good God!"

---

25 In Vietnamese, *con gái* means "young girl" but in French colonial context it was used for any woman kept as a temporary wife.

"I mean to say that he is a widower. You see, they burn their dead in Cambodia."

"Ah! That's better, especially for a decorated man."

❖ ❖ ❖

They reached the riverside pagoda of Romduol. Below them junks were gathering. The sunset was a riot of color in the west, its festoons reflected amid the hyacinth-mauve flowers afloat in the river. An Annamite woman, thighs agleam, was rinsing herself with water. Other women, fresh from a bath, bore flat vases on their hips. Every sampan carried a lit hearth from which smoke, like a mast, rose straight and narrow. A glaze of luminous shadow lay on the thatch of the deckhouses, and here and there the vanishing sunbeams put down a glint of amaranth. The treetops, meanwhile, blazed on in the furnace above. It was the serenity of evenings perennially new, banishing all thought of citizenship and fatherhood and marriage, abolishing the duties of man, casting aside his freshest memories and most pressing plans. At this hour man is utterly forsaken, stripped of all but his gaze as he contemplates this mesmeric bonanza, this transmutation of lead into gold.

They went through the massive gate of the pagoda, which scintillated on the far side of some banyan trees. There were young men at play, passing a rattan ball[26] back and forth, their chests bare and loincloths gathered between their legs. One of them would get set to return the ball only to see it intercepted by another; clenched muscles would instantly release, an effort no sooner prepared than gone to waste. From there the eye was drawn to the left, along a line of huts perched on piles, in which bonzes were meditating. Amid bell-shaped stupas green with moss, the temple held aloft the curves of its roof as if crowning itself.

---

26 Records of the game of *sepak takraw* (*sepak* = kick in Malay, *takraw* = woven ball in Thai) date back to the 15th century in Malaysia and the 18th century in Thailand. As northwestern Cambodia was under Thai control until the early 20th century it is logical to find the game there, and it is still popular today.

Like that of every other pagoda in the land, this roof had all the grace and cadence of an ode to the heavens. Its two faces, very wide and steeply pitched, curved as they rose, providing a gentle path for the sunlight to glide on. The varnished tiles shone with yellow and green, light's twin daughters among the colors. Held aloft by the pitched sides, the ridge of this golden, emerald-trimmed roof wormed its way into the air, where it gleamed like a sabre. Up it went until there appeared a second, smaller roof, like a saddle upon a stallion. Thus the ode's first stanza. The second was the spire, the arrow. In profile the double roof was a drawn bow letting fly. Pyramids in telescoping stages, like cups of cut crystal. Golden elegance, as slender as a stipe.

Such aerial structures symbolize the artistic genius of this people. Their decorative motifs and music have the same supple precision. They live in a doze, but their art, sole display of their existence, smolders on. Thus the serpent indolent in the sun becomes the lash of a whip when it sloughs off its skin. The curve, which for us evokes a sag between two supports, has a different sense here. Only one end maintains contact with earthly material; the rest dashes off to the horizon, takes flight, but with astonishing activity, with a jolt and a spring. Upright curves, with the spark of life in them. The draft shaft of a cart, the crescent of a junk, the *épaulières* of a dancer, the handle of a tool, the neck of a guitar—all of these curves the Cambodian has traced, taking inspiration from the thrust of the reptile or the palm tree. It is upon these exaggerated curves—curves transposed up an octave, as it were—that the pagoda roof is set. Each is to the eye what the cicada's cry is to the ear. The gaze, wherever it first alights, is led upward. Like a happy woman receiving her lover with open arms, the pagoda spreads its roofs to the sky.

Said Madame Gassin:

"The men who conceive this architecture love the sky. That much is plain. I have already seen them at dusk, squatting and staring blissfully at the setting sun."

"Yes, indeed. A child here has hardly started to walk before he is launching a kite into the sky and offering up his nakedness. Every quarter of the moon is celebrated. In short, man and heavens are carrying on an unbroken colloquy. Observe the way a Cambodian goes about his day. The least of his acts, though its meaning escape you, will have some motive related to the sun's presence. Pagodas and houses are oriented to the east. And within a house the bed is aligned north to south, lest the sun be sullied by the soles of the feet of the man it puts to sleep and awakens. One must wait for a propitious day before setting off on a journey, or getting married, or burying a loved one. The rest of us, we have no such love for the heavens; we do not partake in this steady commerce with the celestial lights."

"Our masters are lower," added Madame Gassin.

They were moving away from the pagoda. She turned back toward it. With the dying day the gilding of the pediment was being snuffed out. As if to continue giving something of itself, something more ethereal than the curves of its structure, the pagoda tinkled the airy bells hanging from its gutter. The last of the daylight spread a pearly ash around the visitors as they set off for Sangkae.

"What an odd contrast!" said Hélène. "A whole other way of life, from a whole other age—there it is, framed in the windshield, between the headlamps. The peaceful huts streaming past, each the same as the next, and all of them unchanged for centuries, as you've said. In a short while our electric light will literally illuminate life as it was I don't how many years ago. And just an hour ago I was in my room, the epitome of our civilization, and the endpoint of a telephone line. All we must do is spin the wheels of this car a few times, and we're transported to a world different in every way from our own, where everything is foreign to me and I recognize nothing, where I am lost and yet find myself in the clutches of some irresistible poetry, some vast calm. Yes, it is very odd."

"No doubt the deep voice of the land, heard by all."

"Perhaps, and speaking with its primitive simplicity. And I feel as if I did in fact understand it."

"Though not a single tree in the flora is familiar to you; though the new beings and things take astonishing forms."

"In spite of it all."

⚜ ⚜ ⚜

Who could describe the beauties of dusk in this place, on the banks of the Sangkae River, along all the rivers of the land? A certain cool rises from the waters, a cool so refreshing after the blaze of the day that it adds a note of sweetness unknown in the twilights of the West. This is the hour to step out of the black houses. The quiescence begins at the elusive moment when the sun prepares to redden and still grips the earth by the treetops and the hillsides.

Over the course of the day the sun has stirred the land to powerful action. Light and shadow have violently spread, and there was ardent work to be seen even in a motionless leaf. Then, after the enthusiastic finale, the orchestra falls silent and a poignant silence settles over the hall. The earth moistens underfoot, and the world, like a receding landscape, shades into a smudge. Sensations take on the tenderness that a ripe fruit must feel in the wraps of its generative blossom.

Children settle down, and the hair of the men remains moist from ablutions. Livestock return on their own initiative to their shelters, near the huts. Distant peacocks call from their perches. Minute by minute bits of sky slip and collapse, cut free by arrows of light. A breeze—intermittent, like the exhalations of some vast belly—gathers, lifts, and sets down banana leaves so vast that they tear. One watches as the breeze makes its way through the tree clumps, rising, parting the coconut palms, and penetrating at last the black mass of the mango trees, where all trace of it is lost.

The headlamps were switched on, for night had spread rapidly. The eyes of oxen gleamed like twin flames of phosphorus, as did the eyes of the birds in the road, bedazzled and taking flight at the last second. Wisps of smoke from the huts wound themselves into the air; the natives were burning aromatic grasses to drive off the mosquitoes. Here and there a headlamp would reveal a family gathered within a dwelling. Some fluid, rhythmic thing—a flute song—would wrap itself around the car, then uncoil and fade away.

Had he looked at her, Ternier would have seen that Madame Gassin had thrown back her head to face the sky with her eyes shut. She looked dead.

VI
Vetonea of the Crab-fat Sash

"Hello. Are you alone?"

Madame Gassin was standing at the door to Ternier's office.

"Come in! Come in!"

"I was passing by. So this is the *résident* at work."

"This is the *résident* at work."

"You intimidate me, and I'm a bother."

"I intimidate you, and you are a bother. Fine. Take a seat anyway."

"I'll pop in and head right out."

"Ah. Goodbye, then!"

The room was more than eight meters to a side, and larger still with the verandas. A double door at the far end gave on to the secretariat. A ceiling fan was spinning, its bouquet of lamps in oscillation. Tall cabinets lined the walls. In the center stood Ternier's solid-wood table, its Henry II style rectified by Chinese cabinetmakers, whom Indochina will not be rid of even by Judgment Day. Wires for the telephone and a porcelain reflector lamp hung from the ceiling to the desk in multicolor coils. Administrative files lay strewn about with the arrogance of parvenus receiving nonentities at home.[27] Between two doors hung a sculpted monster head, with two great elephant tusks jutting from it like crescents. Stray chairs stood adrift on a floor of gleaming, polychromatic tile. And an opulent leather armchair, for visitors, yawned before Ternier's desk.

"I trust you'll fish me out later," said Hélène as she tumbled in.

An orderly came in and went out, gliding along on his bare feet, carrying papers that Ternier gave a once-over and signed.

"It is most kind of you to drop by amid my paperwork."

"I hadn't yet seen you at the ministry."

"Ministry? Ministry? But there is actual work being done here!"

"I've no doubt, and retract the word *ministry*."

Ternier paused to consider a file of yellow telegrams.

"Would you mind?"

"I'm not even here."

"Tri!" he called.

A secretary materialized. His gray hair was gathered into a chignon beneath a pongee turban. His chest was sheathed in a black tunic fastened with little gold buttons under one arm. Below the loose, silk pantaloons the tips of his yellow shoes stuck out like duckbills. Raising his glasses to his forehead, he approached with compunction, hands clasped.

"Is all of the traffic information there?"

"Yes, M'sieur R'sdent."

"Take a letter."

---

27 A parvenu is a person from a lower social class who has gained wealth, fame or influence, but not sophistication or manners so their behavior remains vulgar. In Groslier's scene above, Ternier's disorganized files reflect the rude and detached state that many nouveau riche affect.

The Annamite let his glasses drop back onto his nose and skipped away on tiptoe to fetch a pad.

"*'Telegram to Résuper.*[28] *Traffic report. Most of Colonial Route 1B damaged by rains yesterday and strong storm last night. According to Siem Reap delegate: (1) From Kampong Kdei to Damdek almost all recent embankments built to close breaches carried off, but detours remain solid...'*

"Have that?"

"Yes, M'sieur R'sdent."

"*'(2) Road clear from Damdek to Siem Reap except sector 200 meters from kilometer 278, where recent embankments thoroughly...'* No. Put '*moderately.*'"

"*'Moderately.*'"

"*'...water logged. All breaches blocked off, with detour arrows placed 150 meters ahead.'* That's all. Read it back to me."

The interpreter's singsong, now throaty, now nasal, lay somewhere between a litany and a vocalise. When he finished he peered over his glasses at the *résident*.

"Good. Send it off."

With a slight bow he took his leave.

"How well kept your roads are!" said Hélène, who had listened attentively.

"Yes. Quite fickle they are."

"Is it like this every day?"

"Yes. The rains are starting up, and all the work done in the dry season is going to be put to the test. The embankments will be tamped down, and the waters will pool unevenly on either side and seek out a channel."

---

28 I.e., to the *résident supérieur*, Ternier's superior.

"Won't they find one?"

"Yes, but not always through our scuppers, bridges, and culverts. So they end up cutting through the road, or submerging it."

"And you get word of this?"

"Day by day. The native authorities keep watch over every ribbon that cuts across my district, from one end to the other. At the first sign of trouble their emissaries converge on the nearest telegraph. Within a few hours a detour has been set up to join the severed ends. During the big storms we might get fifty to sixty breaches— eight or ten of them serious—for every hundred kilometers of road."

"What an undertaking!"

"Not an undertaking. Care. We treat the inevitable wounds that any living, breathing, functioning body incurs for its efforts. These shifting roads inspire love. In the time I've been here I have come to know my network in its entirety, kilometer by kilometer, whether it was laid down by me or by my predecessors. I know all its ills. The engineers who serve at my side might change, but I remain. I am the memory of my roads. I know where this or that road was taken ill last year and where it stood fast. They seem fixed, monotonous, and bare as you travel along, but I have seen them struggle, change form, oscillate with the tiny adjustments we must occasionally make to their original routes. I have seen them gain their bridges. In this we rescued them from a desperate situation. There used to be fifty cars and drays passing through here daily. Now the roads bring me two hundred. The quicker I repair the breaches and venture out to palpate the rough backbones myself, the more I scrutinize them during the dry season, the more vehicles they carry to me. Ah, they are not an ungrateful lot! Weary and potholed and puddled and rutted they may be, but onward they slog, the courageous things. The vehicles might pass slowly, but pass they do. And that, you see, is the main thing. If two hundred cars and a thousand carts and three thousand pedestrians and fifteen thousand oxen and a hundred fifty horsemen use every kilometer of my roads in a day, then I know my province is doing well. I know its pulse is normal and every hut has everything it needs."

"Yes, that is the main thing. To pass through," said Hélène dreamily.

"It is the main thing. You made the trip from Phnom Penh in five hours."

"Upon a magnificent road."

"Ten years ago you would have been five days crossing the savannah, on a horse or in a cart. It is worthwhile for a *résident* to watch over the roads. He sees to their every need."

"I had no idea when I first arrived that you had done so much to prepare my trip."

"I have been preparing, the *résident* has been preparing, a hundred trips—all trips. Where you pass now sixty men were working yesterday. This evening my telegram will warn all the cars, the passenger-stuffed charabancs, and the drays weighed down with their merchandise to proceed with caution at such-and-such spot. If there is a flood, or an irreparable breach, I must inform the business enterprises within hours. They are always dispatching some share of their capital out onto the road, and have thus placed their trust in me. When all is said and done, all human lives and all human fortunes converge on that road. On its health depends the health of the country."

"And it's a lot of work."

"In these parts it is three-quarters of a *résident's* work."

"Three-quarters of his responsibility."

"That depends on the *résident*," said Ternier, smiling, "for he does not act alone. He commands; he oversees; he makes suggestions under the authority of his *résident supérieur.* The Department of Public Works operates under the authority of its department chiefs."

"I see. One can pass the buck."

"Precisely."

"In the short time I have been in Indochina I have come to understand that the Department of Public Works is a convenient scapegoat."

"The *résidents* as well. Would you like to know a secret?"

"If it wouldn't be indiscreet."

"Here just as in France the administrative and technical services are either dreadful or excellent."

"Not much of a secret."

"But true. The trick is to know how the men on staff conceive of their social role."

"There are no duties."

"Moreover, what we've established here is a community that is meticulously organized to dispense with the individual yet is perpetually subject to the individual's whim."

"And with that, I'm off. By the way, can you still see me?"

"What do you mean can I still see you?"

"In this armchair. I seem to be sinking deeper and deeper. Oof! Here I am. When will you be showing me your great road?"

"I will be organizing that. Hey! So short a visit?"

"I'm already cross with myself for having taken up *this* much of your time."

❖ ❖ ❖

Emerging from the Résidence to walk across the park, Madame Gassin spied a native woman heading in the opposite direction, the sun- and shade-speckled path trailing behind her like a peacock's tail. At every step the advancing bare foot shunted the folds of the loincloth onto its companion. Like a writhing reptile the silk fringe of red and green spooled and unspooled on the ground. The long, solid-color national tunic floated a bit around her hips. It was tighter near the top, snug on the chest and arms, and a delicate neck emerged from a long, triangular opening. In the sunlight the silk sheath shone with the luster of copper gone green and purple. The fabric stretched over the twin domes of her breasts, which jiggled as she walked, and once again over the tips, with a hint of brutal, juvenile insolence. The shifting shadow on the earth glimmered with ochre and violet.

When she crossed paths with the woman Madame Gassin took note of the tiny folds in the tunic under the arms, the bronze tinge on the saffron-powdered neck, and the heavily bejeweled hands. The woman had massed her white sash atop her head but held one end of it in her hand, the intervening translucent stretch casting a mauve glaze on her face. From beneath the edge of this veil two gorgeous, somnolent eyes glared at Hélène, who turned away. Pressing on, the woman rounded the porch and entered the Résidence by a side door. An orderly on his way out saluted her, brusquely righting himself and doffing his helmet. Since he also saluted Hélène when they crossed paths she asked:

"Who is that lovely Cambodian woman?"

"Madame Résident," replied the orderly.

⚜ ⚜ ⚜

It was indeed Vetonea, Ternier's native wife, the *prâpôn*, which is to say "spouse."[29] She was a subtle, proud girl. From her mother she had inherited a light ochre complexion and a tall frame; from her Siamese father, finesse in the joints. This father, a mandarin under the Siamese government, had returned to his country after the retrocession of the provinces,[30] leaving behind his Khmer wife,

---

29 The official laws of Cambodia define three classes of *prâpôn* and their rights (*Les Codes Cambodgiens*, p. 62. 1881).

30 After the final sack of Angkor by Siamese troops in 1431 the northwestern provinces of Cambodia came under Thai control (including Battambang and Siem Reap). In 1863, King Norodom of Cambodia entered into an agreement with France to become a protectorate

who was pregnant at the time with Vetonea. The two women had lived somewhat miserably, the mother now working in retail, now pricking out paddy, now running errands; the girl "placed" to pay the mother's debts until Ternier took notice and "placed her on his throne as well as into his bed."

When she first made her entrance into the chambers of the Résidence—decked out in a sampot as stiff as waxed canvas, wrapped in a sash the color of saffron, wearing over her ear a flower scented with bleeding-hearts, and under escort from her mother, a little boy, and two old women—Ternier had taken Vetonea aside and delivered, in the florid Cambodian he spoke so well, the following epithalamium:[31]

"Beautiful Vetonea of the crab-fat sash, I take you henceforth to be my wife. I shall give you forty-five piasters monthly. Behold here two rooms, and another, yonder, for washing. Behold to the west a stair. It leads to a door through which you may enter and leave as you wish. This shall be your domain. Here you may sleep, smoke, sew, braid flowers, bathe ten times a day, and do it all again. Of course, you will not spit on the floor or chew betel. You may chew betel outside, as long as it escapes my notice and your teeth remain white. Do you understand? Excellent. There is nothing to tax the understanding. Now, it is absolutely forbidden for you to stray anywhere else, even when the house is empty. It is forbidden to take the great staircase, to cross the other rooms, to show yourself in the parlors or at the windows of the façade. Disobey once, I will repeat these proscriptions. Disobey twice, I will punish you. Disobey a third time, we will divorce. You understand this as well, do you not? It is no more complicated than the rest.

"Your mother is an honorable woman. I am very fond of her. Here are two hundred piastres for you to give her. You are to

---

of that nation. In 1906 French negotiations forced Thailand (then Siam) to cede these territories back to Cambodia.

31 A paean, in the form of a song or poem, to a bride. In ancient Greek the word literally means "from the nuptial chamber."

ask her to leave Sangkae for, say, Kralanh. I shall instruct the governor to cede her a small plot of land and have a straw hut built for her, at my expense."

Vetonea had joined her hands and brought them to her forehead. Ternier had continued:

"Do not thank me. He who honors his parents honors himself. So, your mother is off to Kralanh. She will be comfortable there. Most importantly, she will be eighty kilometers away, for our marriage carries with it a new and final condition: I do not wish to see any visitors here. As I have said, you may come and go as you please, but I do not want the entire province parading through the Résidence—every day a new set of old women who will always be your aunts, and boys of all sizes who will always be your little brothers. This, by the way, is for your own good, and will spare you much trouble.

"Voilà. Keep to your interests by living peaceably, and you shall be happy. Look around. It is lovely here, and big. Better to smoke a cigarette in this bed than to fish for eel in the mud, under the sun. If you are a good girl, I shall buy you sampots, a lace parasol, perfumes, and a handbag—anything you like. Vetonea, dear girl, you are lovely to my eye. I like you very much already. Now that I have spoken and you know everything, would you like to stay with me?"

Ternier had remained seated as he spoke, with Vetonea standing between his legs. Head down, she had been twisting the end of her sash, assenting to all of the terms, which to her, little wretch that she was, seemed splendid indeed. One point, however, had begged for clarification. Swallowing her saliva, Vetonea had asked:

"Eating. How do I eat?"

Ternier had burst into laughter.

"As you like."

After a further silence:

"Is the price of food included in the forty-five piastres?"

"All right, then. I pay a supplement for food. How much?"

"Five piastres. I know a woman who can prepare the food and bring it to me here."

⚜ ⚜ ⚜

In just a few months the lovely girl with the yellow sash had become that disconcerting creature: the native consort of a European man. There she is, forever in her many-hued silks, an emanation of the land and the sum of its charms. You speak; she replies. You reflect; she is still and silent. In what is her life spent? In watching. She observes. Missing nothing, she adopts your habits, and even your tics. She lurks about you, her tranquil, velvety eye smoldering with the black flame of indubitable intelligence. Why? Raise your eyes; she smiles an infantine, confident smile. Lie down; she takes up the fan and comes near. You prepare to depart; she hands you your helmet and has slipped into your pocket both handkerchief and restocked cigarette case. You come home; she has been waiting. Where have you been? She does not inquire, and already knows. If she knows not, she will know shortly. She has sprinkled flowers into your toilette water, for a fragrant touch, and set the bedroom in order.

How very fine life is every evening in the lithe arms of one's land of exile. There is an ineffable odor of firm flesh and peppery skin, of slender hands and tiny feet, of a glabrous body meticulously shaved under the arms, fresh and dry of sweat. Her calm suffers your embrace with modesty and good will. The *prâpôn* is your object in the absolute sense, so supple and passive that she returns your image like an imprint. She grasps everything you say. Though ignorant and unlettered, and unable to read her own language, she knows your papers, for she has observed which ones you take up in what circumstance and the manner in which you handle them. Take a cigarette from the box; the woman offers a match. The shower water stops flowing, and here she is with a towel, for she has been squatting behind the door, listening to the water. Let me be! She lays out on the mat like a fallen flower. And the egotistical, sated man thrives. Let him take heed.

All is indeed well if he can withstand her unyielding grip, which is all the more sure and ineluctable for her inability to betray her own nature, her apparent passivity and submission. She satisfies a man's base instincts if he is vulgar, cradles his imagination and artistic sense if he is superior and discerning. All is well if his hand remains firm and his mind lucid; if he is never the dupe; if he too keeps a keen eye open; if he is not timid; if he maintains his life in balance and tells himself daily that the woman could leave tomorrow, that another just like her would take her place; if in stepping out of the house where she awaits him he does not imagine that he is leaving behind a mistress; and, finally, if he does not mind that she slip out during his absence to meet a militiaman or an interpreter—the lover who collects her pay—and enjoy the harmonious embrace of her own kind.

Such a man sees the trap. He understands that he alone can lose at this game. It takes more than a few months for a people to rise to the level of another people, though their arms interlace, and if the higher does not sink to seek out the lower. And how tempting it is to sink! A man needn't spend himself to ruin. All is available at his command. Every craving of his egotistical heart that he must suppress among his own kind he can here satisfy without encountering the least resistance. He triumphs effortlessly. He needn't be well built or intelligent or enterprising. His plebian hands can still seize the idol. Whoever he might be, he attains love without a struggle. He can have at home a woman who obeys him. Little by little his exaltation builds, for he believes that he is raising up his spouse, and that he is ennobled with every conquest.

Why, indeed, should she be inferior just because she is of another race? She has a heart and a soul. Are they in fact the same as ours? Does she make the same use of them as we? The assiduity, the obedience, the discretion, the close attentions, rather than qualities she compels herself to display, are qualities atavistically administered. To your eye they gradually assume shades of love, and day by day they sap your good sense. You make comparisons, to find comfort. No Frenchwoman would be like this! Certainly not. And the Frenchwoman now seems heavy, thick, vulgar, and loud, for you have that slender, supple, passive body forever before your eyes. Western ablutions begin to seem complicated, ridiculous, for you now get along splendidly with a perpetually fresh loincloth and a sash. The Frenchwoman suffers from the climate and sweats, and fusses with her repellent fleeces, whereas this native woman remains fresh and dry, and as agreeable as ivory. It is so.

Then you take a further step toward what you see as a liberation, the salutary individualization of your masculine nature. It now irritates you that the Frenchwoman you've met at the friend's house you still frequent pipes up with a rejoinder—the imbecile! She does not stoop to collect the cane that has slipped from your grasp—the uppity hussy! Back home you are royalty, but here you are forever fighting for your life. How very tiresome! Back home you are at least a peacock, and sit upon your bed in "royal ease,"[32] whereas here you must likely settle for being a jay. Come, little idol! Come here, with your innocent soul and primitive virtues! Place your hands over my eyes, and let us away from vulgarity and convention. The fine, dry hands alight upon your eyes. All things considered, it wouldn't be so bad.

But things are not like that, not at all. From this moment on everything changes. The supple slave wears a hard gaze that you cannot fathom. At times she gets irritated. You yield, for how could you gamble away such happiness when you have just now awoken to it? One day you find the *prâpôn*, the sweet little child, in a sulk. As you yourself have said, why shouldn't she too have the right to be a woman? She has that right, and exercises it. And the very thing

---

32 In the posture of royal ease, or *rajalilasana,* the right leg is drawn up to support the right arm, usually at the elbow, and the left leg either hangs or lies horizontally in a half-tailor fashion.

that made you recoil from women of your own kind, the very thing
that drove you to the native, now reappears before you in a fresh
guise. And the fetters snap into place. You are Samson shorn.[33]

You still play the tough-minded man, for you do not yet believe
in your shackles. Wait a little. If these do not suffice, others will
be found for you. Dexterous hands will serve your vices, or one day
the *prâpôn* will be with child. By sex or habit or languor, by all of
your failings, by your pride or timidity, by your very sense of duty—
for it was you who planted the seed in that belly—you will be
definitively ensnared. A fallen man, you say? Oh come, come, now!
It was *you* who wanted this, was it not? For crying out loud. After
months of cohabitation, embraces, conquests, and poetry, with a
half-blood you yourself have engendered, you now have the gall to
claim yourself free of entanglements? Incidentally, the timid native,
invigorated with the strength you have fed her, is now dominating
you, and the intelligence that you acknowledged in her, that quite
real intelligence, has pinned you hopelessly down. Oh yes. Go
ahead and sport that jaunty expression, but mind the clock, and do
not tarry at the club or your friends' house, for if it displease your
passive servant she will refuse this evening to unknot her sampot.

She now knows what you earn, and you have given her the keys
to your armoire as well as management of the *boys*. Is it not she who
selects them in the first place? Thus at all times and in all corners
of Indochina men of all ages and stations, from customs agents
to *résidents supérieurs*, captains of industry to scholars, soldiers to

---

33 The birth of the biblical hero Samson (Judges 13–16) is foretold by an angel to the barren
wife of Manoah. The angel warns that Samson is to be a Nazarite: a Jew who is not to drink
wine or have his hair cut. Samson marries into the Philistine clan and performs a number
of feats of strength: he slays a lion, kills thirty Philistines, kills a thousand more (this time
with the jawbone of an ass), and carries off on his back the gates of Gaza. Samson later falls
for a second Philistine maiden, named Delilah. At the behest of her countrymen, Delilah
nags Samson into telling her the source of his strength. After three lies, each followed by a
failed attempt on his life, he finally tells her that he mustn't cut his hair. She cuts off seven
locks while he sleeps. Now no stronger than an ordinary man, Samson is captured and
bound to the pillars of a house. There, with the Philistines celebrating upstairs, Samson
prays God that he be granted his strength one last time. His prayer is answered, and he
pulls down the pillars, collapsing the house and killing all within, himself included.

bankers, find themselves mired in the same romp, hollowed out and emasculated by a Cambodian *prâpôn* or an Annamite *congai* who is now withered by motherhood, bereft of the fleeting charms of her race. Ready for anything, capable of anything, she smiles with her betel-blackened mouth. Like a praying mantis, this subtle, patient female, this poor little insignificant native girl, with hands joined, and all the requisite niceties and bows, makes a meal of her mate.

Ternier, who was not on his first one, knew that Vetonea would be like the others. Thus he had taken precautions. He was, of course, obliged to foil some early gambits. First the meals delivered from town became pretexts. One day the child hired for the purpose was replaced by a woman who lingered while Vetonea took her meal. The following day she lingered for Vetonea's digestion as well. Ternier imposed new measures. Later Vetonea made the case that she needed a servant. "All right," Ternier had said. "I will select one, and she will become my second wife." Vetonea insisted no further. Then he found the lovely *métisse* strolling through the grand parlor of the Résidence, which was off limits. Vetonea was informed that in two days' time, on the thirtieth of the month, she would be paid forty piastres instead of the usual forty-five. She thought hard on this. Her condition being, at any rate, honorific, not to mention lucrative, she insisted no further.

❖ ❖ ❖

"Madame Résident," the orderly had replied.

Hélène twirled her parasol and continued on her way. She went through the great gate, where stood two large, eighteenth-century cannons mounted on naval carriages.

A native was leaning there, gaping like a simpleton. Once the European lady had advanced some hundred meters he set out in pursuit.

❖

VII
The Lustrous Trace of Man

Phnom Banon is one of the many mounds scattered throughout Cambodia. Generally a hundred to a hundred fifty meters high, these mounds loom over a landscape of otherwise uniform flatness, and thus even their modest elevation affords the traveler a vast panorama. From the top his gaze can sweep across the earth into the far, bluish distance, where, rather than come to a tidy end, the land evanesces into the vapor-ridden air.

Some of these summits—like Phnom Banon, accessible by a monumental flight of a hundred steps—harbor the ruins of a temple. The monks of the ancient monasteries were wearing down these slabs some ten centuries before the monks of the present day and, like their modern analogues, would at propitious times gather here, in the liberty of an open sky, to meditate upon the metamorphoses of the gods.

The temple of Banon was built on a platform. So confined is the chosen setting that the outer wall's main gate opens right onto the landing of the staircase, which dips down almost sheer before tempering its grade on the lower skirts of the slope and alighting, limply oblique, on the plain. Farther on the eye glides across the green mottle of a lake. All of this unfolds before the rising sun. The rest is but plain and forest.

A further element in this landscape was the monsoon. Madame Gassin, Ternier, and Dr. Maillard did not feel it during their ascent, but it hit them, pasting the clothes to their bodies, as soon as they reached the rust-colored slabs up top. They could see it climb, as it were, through the myriad leaves of the trees, the smudgy stillness of the distant landscape throwing its sun-drenched motion into relief. The same contrast made everything in this airy spot more vivid in hue and tone. The shadows in the stones were so many lakes. In the sunshine the doctor's proffered hand had a vermilion contour. And the trees whose tops reached the platform were so brilliant and green that one might have been looking at them through the yellow lens of a sun glass.

Below lay the ashen checkerboard of dry rice fields. The floods had not as yet reached these parts, and the parched earth had soaked up the first rains. The little ridges left over from the previous year had the country carved up into squares the size of a hand. Fainter, more tortuous lines snaked their way through the matte, regular network. These were the thousand paths taken by the natives, laid down and polished by their bare feet. Strips of earth caressed by the flesh of man; a labyrinth bestowed upon the land by the creature it conveys from house to work, from work to love, from birth to death.

It is a land to obsess the mind. Survey it from atop some piddling mound, and instantly it reveals man, the creature concealed in its bosom. Nary a bruise in these parts, and not a road traced out in iron. No harvest or belfry or smoke. Nothing below but desolate, copse-ridden terrain, matted and wooly like the fleece of a kid. It all proves unexplored, unexploited, threatening. And yet there it lies, taut and gleaming: the complex canvas of fine filaments, woven hour by hour by men living out peaceable lives, passing precisely where their predecessors passed, stepping in the very prints of those other bare feet.

"From here, Madame," said the doctor, "you can once again see what has so forcibly struck you already: human life wedded harmoniously to the land, with no intellect to speculate in the name of progress or introduce its instruments or impose its will. Reptiles leave a lustrous trace in the sand; behold now the lustrous trace of man, all that you discover of human life."

"You're headed for a scolding from Monsieur Ternier."

"Oh, he agrees deep down, and when he's not off on his roads."

"Especially since the doctor is talking such sleep-inducing poppycock and has you looking down, where there is nothing to see," interrupted Ternier. "Take a look instead at this quite visible temple, with its five crowning towers—the art and intelligence of those same, allegedly nature-bound men. As for my roads, keep in mind that ten centuries ago, when they built this temple and six hundred others just like it, those same men laid down a great many roads, on levees. We find traces of them everywhere. Their length, were we to add it up, would equal that of the roads that we Frenchmen are laying down now. What would you have us believe, Maillard? That the near-vanishing of all this is a good thing? I am of your same opinion. That what we have before us are a people and a country that can make do without? I concur. Do you intend to linger atop your mountain and observe? I won't begrudge you your contemplation. But I, dear friend, prefer to rebuild what has been destroyed, to make better roads than those that have failed to last. I would rebuild temples if I could. There are ten of us who think this way, whereas you are alone in your philosophizing."

"You are the strong."

"By God, yes! There is matter for debate, but it is a fact. Better to stick to the facts. We are the strong, and we must put our strength to *some* use, no? "

"Your cynicism is repugnant."

"No, Maillard. You bind your patient to amputate a gangrenous limb, and he screams in pain. At that moment you are the strong. Let the man scream; you saw away. Why not instead fall into contemplation before that rotting leg, that collaborative work of nature and man?"

"A doctor is justified by the disease and by the happy result of his intervention," said Hélène, with an air of candor.

Ternier looked upon her at length, then:

"Madame, a moment ago the doctor accused me of cynicism. Permit me not to share your opinion. When he cuts off a limb the doctor does not know that his operation will succeed. No."

"But I hope it will. I take that last chance…"

"When I lay down a road I do not know whether it will succeed. I take the last chance left me to restore a region to life—and not to precarious life, not to a life I deem precarious just as you deem your patient's life to be threatened. I bring that region back to the active, prosperous life that our times demand. That is the thing. Now, if I am mistaken it's too bad, and too bad for the patient if the doctor is in error. Acting as the strong, we have done what we thought best. Perhaps there exists some other justice, some other equilibrium, than ours. Let it intervene, then! Also, Doctor, permit me to remind you that we are your guests today. You have promised us an excellent lunch atop this hill, a lunch complete with ice, no less. Stay here and contemplate your rivers as they run dry if you like, but at least tell us where the picnic chest is."

It was a feast day, and pilgrims by the hundred were visiting the temple to salute the lofty Buddhas. On their way up the three Europeans had already spotted groups of such pilgrims, scattered about on the rocks for a rest, weary from the weight of the edible offerings they had been hefting. Mothers were taking advantage of the pause to suckle babies. Having laid their sweaty sashes out to dry, men sat with legs spread, each foot resting on a different rock.

Through the temple grounds flowed a crowd renewed regularly by the hour. East of the temple the faithful were offering up their hair to the divinities. Broad, round-bladed razors were carving tracks of violet and blue into black heads, and a mat of hair was gradually forming on the ground, mingling with the dead leaves. Propitiatory candles burned within the sanctuaries, before every plinth ancient or modern.

The crowd glided along through the galleries or spread out on the esplanade beneath the open sky. Bedecked with big jewels, hardy girls from the thiamkars[34] went about hand in hand among the groups. Also present were old women one would have thought incapable of walking, so wrinkled was their skin, so juttingly did the clothes hang on their bones. Flocks of children, women with little ones astride a hip, and vigorous men with workman muscle and charred, leathery skin draped in vain, shimmering sashes.

The monastery chief came to greet the *résident* and insisted on accompanying him to the *sala*.[35] He was a grand old man. As he spoke the wind sculpted his ample toga and flattened white hairs on arms of cinnamon red. From the *sala* came a deep murmur carrying a xylophone tune. Though no more than a roof set on columns, the shelter was engulfed in darkness, the effect of a dense crowd. One's cheek grew warm with the animal warmth of the place. The odor of so many bodies, thickened with sandalwood cosmetics and unable to find an egress, mingled with the insipid vapors of hot rice and melting candles, the fragrance of cut flowers, and the bitter note of the soups. The musical instruments, ranged at the far end of the shelter, could scarcely penetrate the atmosphere with their sound. By the golden trail in the river of bodies flowing past, however, one could still make out—wholesome spectacle—a long file of eating bonzes and, at times, the bright speck of a plate of rice. A child howled, holding flowers against his little belly. White-clad women, old, sanctimonious, and seeking redemption, carried vessels of water to the saintly men. These without a glance took the vases in their food-smeared hands and chomped away on pumpkin purees.

---

34 A Khmer term for a rural village.
35 An open pavilion common in Southeast Asia and used for shelter from sun and rain.

❖ ❖ ❖

The doctor and his guests went up to the temple courtyard to take their own lunch, settling beneath a tree of gleaming leaves. The picnic chest was set down and opened near a gutter stone in the shape of a monster, through whose elephant trunk, a thousand years earlier, water had flowed for the ablutions of the idols. The arrival of the three Europeans disrupted the banquet in the *sala*, and part of the crowd drained off in curious pursuit. The Europeans suddenly had twenty-odd servants making themselves useful just to get a closer look at the dishes and the forks. The rest of the audience took a seat on the steps or in the gaps of the surrounding galleries. Children in file and women by the bunch had gathered round, and soon bonzes added their sunflower splashes to the tableau.

The people had made an exceptional journey of several leagues, on foot or by cart, to take part in a sacred pilgrimage, but the two Frenchmen and this white woman, with her blond hair and her gray dress, offered an unparalleled spectacle, all the more so as the man with the moustache obscuring his lips was the *résident* himself. There he was, eating out in the open, before their very eyes, with no mystery or fuss about him. These poor country folk were seeing the thing that they often spoke of among themselves, the thing that those returning from the city—civil servants, furloughed militiamen—told of with such an air of importance. Ah! The round, golden buns that substitute for rice—and no rice on the table! Most curious. So it is true that the French take drink with their food!

The whispering came to a sudden hush. The circle of children closed in. Men craned their necks. From sawdust the doctor was extracting ice, frozen water, *tök kâk*.[36] Marvel of marvels! Solid

---

36 Scotsman William Cullen is credited with inventing artificial refrigeration in 1748, but it was nearly a century before ice-making machine patents were filed around the world and the industry took off. This Western technology clearly made a strong impression on the peoples of Southeast Asia, most of whom had never seen ice, snow or even frost. Groslier's Khmer language example above, *tök kâk* (alternate transliteration *dteuk kak*), means "water hardening or stiffening", with *kak* also used for cement, tar or paint. The

water that burns at the touch, a rocky crystal that vanishes within the hour. Could it be so? Could men without learning, the sun's beloved children, credit their senses?

Ternier passed a block around in a copper cup. All took it in hand with the same caution. Some smiled; others examined it closely, every which way. A black, hoary man set a finger on it and, incredulous, impenetrable, stared off into the void. Another, of subtler cast of mind, noticed that his finger left a trace in the vapor that covered the cup. And the block shimmered in stupefied hands, and struck a brilliant contrast with the severe, gray camaieu[37] of the walls.

In this incredible setting the ice became to Hélène's eye a miraculous gem borrowed from the gods and passed around a crowd on whom its simple contact conferred sought-after virtues. Was this not the same as when simple people sought for happiness or fertility by rubbing the breasts of certain statues, polished by the caress of such countless hands?

A young voice rang out in the most utter stupefaction, a charming voice that hung suspended in the silence. Ternier translated:

"A young woman has just discovered that the chunk is shrinking."

A murmur ran through the crowd. Some then took a sip from the melting ice, and from every suntanned volunteer without exception the cold water drew forth a wince, no matter that the gullet it slipped down was already thoroughly corroded by betel and peppers and curries.

Laos call ice *nam kon* (water chunk), the Thais, *nam kang* (water hard) and the Vietnamese *nước đá* (water stone).

37 Term derived from *cameo,* the name for a type of relief sculpture in which the raised (positive) image is executed in some shade of white against a dark (and negative) background. A camaïeu is a painting in which subject and background are depicted in different shades of the same color, usually a color other than the subject's natural one. This makes the painting resemble a relief. Gray camaïeu is called grisaille. Yellow camaïeu is called cirage, a term whose literal meaning is "executed in wax."

After a pensive silence Ternier said:

"Doctor, I am reminded of what we were debating just a moment ago. From atop a hill the mind more easily takes flight. A symbol-loving poet, if he were with us now, might echo your thoughts and say: so many brilliant or astonishing things melt away in immutable settings, slip through our human fingers, and no one can say for certain whether their melting is not a good thing, whether their true use is not different from the one we assign, and whether the hands in which they vanish are enriched or impoverished."

Like the Vishnu brandishing a disk in a neighboring sanctuary, the doctor raised the amber slice of juicy pineapple speared on the end of his fork and replied:

"If the Résident himself is dreaming, we are all—I beg your pardon, Madame—screwed."

VIII
"Why speak? Everyone know."

Never one to nap, Ternier was reading at midday. The sun was dazzling, but only bits of the light were filtering in through the shut louvers of the veranda. In the gleam of the floor tile the white bed matched the raised white mosquito net. The fan flashed its shiny disk, and the only sound from outside to break the room's shadowy calm was the clank of a distant ox bell, and that from time to time.

Seated on a mat, chest bare but for the sash around her breasts, Vetonea was rolling cigarettes with a little cardboard device and a stick. Rather than glue them, she was cinching the cigarettes with a delicate paper ribbon, knotting it and festooning the tiny loose ends with a scissor. She worked diligently, supple upon her hips, legs crossed before her. Without raising her head she looked up at Ternier and observed him. Lowering at length her gaze, with a cigarette turning in her fingertips, her face blank and her tone detached, she said as if to herself:

"French lady come again this morning."

Ternier was still engrossed in his book. The native looked up, took in the length of him, observed, and then dropped her gaze once more. She finished the cigarette and started in on another. In the diffuse light, beneath the black blot of her short hair,

Vetonea's slender shoulders took on a greenish hue. Hints of bistre underscored her chin and the crease of her arms. She tried again:

"Nhê… She is very pretty."

Now, trimming her knot, she seemed to fall into thought. She set down the cigarette, adding:

"She has big feet."

"Ah," said Ternier, who though still not listening was now aware that Vetonea was speaking to him.

She took a pinch of tobacco, stretched it between her extended fingers, raised her eyes, lowered them.

"She come here often, French lady."

Inert, Ternier looked at Vetonea. He had understood. She knotted her paper band, cut it with the scissor, and bent forward to blow the fallen triangular snippets from her lap. She crossed her arms behind her and stretched. She adjusted her sash, baring for the space of a second two impeccable breasts, with tips like violets. She once more took up the tobacco, spread it on her paper, and said, evasively:

"That woman very bad. I know."

Laconic, Ternier commanded, "Be quiet."

An ice cube had just melted away in his coffee. He took a swallow and returned to his book. Vetonea rose and approached. Then, set in her course, she nudged aside the book and squeezed, sinuous and bewitching, under Ternier's arm.

"I know things," she said.

And in twenty punctilious details the *résident* learned that Madame Gassin had spent one of the past few nights at Captain Thévenet's house.

"Are you mad, Nea?"

"I not mad. I know."

"Who says so?"

"Everyone know. The *boys* of hotel, the cook of Doctor Maillard, and Chinaman Li, who saw Madame go into rickshaw."

"I forbid you to say such things, Nea. They are lies."

"I tell my husband."

"Be quiet. I forbid you to speak of this again—to anybody. Understand?"

Stony faced, Vetonea wriggled free and returned to her mat.

"If I hear that you are continuing to spew such rubbish you will be leaving this place."

"Why speak? Everyone know. Everyone speak."

"But *you*—you hold your tongue."

She fell silent. With a delicate breath she separated two sheets of rolling paper. Ternier returned to his reading, or at least took up his book.

⚜ ⚜ ⚜

At dusk two days earlier, after a stroll, Hélène, the doctor, and Ternier had been sitting out under the pergola, their iced glasses sheathed in a mist evocative of peach blossoms. There had been fireflies flashing in the trees. Footfalls had broken the silence, and a voice had said:

"I hope I'm not interrupting."

It had belonged to a visitor, Captain Thévenet, recently given command of the infantry brigade.

"Not at all," Ternier had replied, rising to meet the officer, who, young and slim, with dark hair and a warrior's cast, had stepped into the light. As he thought back on it now it seemed to Ternier that something unusual had occurred when he introduced the man, something that at the time had not held his attention. Upon said introduction Captain Thévenet had stepped toward Madame Gassin, and she, in proffering her hand, had assumed so haughty an air and blinked so imperiously that the visitor suffered a moment's hesitation before making his bow, wordlessly. Ternier had hardly taken note of these subtleties before the return of Madame Gassin's smile restored balance, and thereafter the conversation had flowed.

The visitor had come to set a time for departure the following day; he and Ternier were to inspect the dilapidated target butts.[38] They had agreed to go at dawn, and a half-hour later the officer had retired. Since the doctor and Hélène were dining at the Résidence, the cozy evening had continued until eleven o'clock. Then Maillard had accompanied Madame Gassin to the hotel. It must therefore have been afterwards that she had gone out again.

How much stock to put into this calumny? None as yet. The calumny had merely been formulated. Ternier denied it and shoved it aside, but it wormed its way into the lines of his book, and his sips of cold coffee now left a metallic aftertaste. He would rather have heard nothing, but his mind kept circling back to that little incident two nights past. He had thought nothing of it at the time, but the more he pondered it now the more troubling it became. He shrank from the inquiry, but on it went. If she'd lied Vetonea wouldn't have a leg to stand on!

Could this not be some intrigue fabricated by Vetonea to protect herself from a European lady who had assumed a sudden importance in the *résident*'s private life? Powerless as she felt to influence the most trivial of Ternier's decisions, wouldn't the *indigène* be all the more vigilant in safeguarding her fortune? What exactly was Hélène? She had no idea, knew nothing about her—except that she was a woman, a lone woman. Vetonea was piecing things together as best she could. Suppose the all-powerful *résident* wanted to take Madame Gassin for his wife? What then?

---

38 A mound into which projectiles are fired from guns for target practice.

Vetonea would have no choice but to pack up and leave. Thus she was resorting to the sole weapon at hand: insinuation. Now, Vetonea was certainly not without guile. Why, then, would she be so careless as to cook up such a story? She must have figured that Ternier would check it. A *résident* knows all within his bailiwick— when, that is, he wants to know. Impossible, then. Vetonea had invented nothing, nothing at all. On the contrary, she would have been very sure of herself before uttering a word.

I will look into it, Ternier said to himself. I don't give a damn if someone makes up a story about Madame Gassin's being Captain Thévenet's mistress, or even if someone proves it to be true. What matters is that things be settled in my mind. I must find out whether my brotherly trust and attentions are misplaced—or, indeed, whether I should grant them even greater importance, so as to defend an unfairly sullied victim. Any doubt will henceforth be intolerable to me. Her intelligent curiosity, her enthusiasm, that desire of hers to delve into our local business, her spontaneity, her strivings to improve her mind: could these be just a blind, a way for her to meet with a lover and carry on an affair? It is possible, and it is her right. And I suppose it is mine to take some precautions.

Two days later the *résident* was set in his course. With morning coming to an end the orderly, as usual, announced Hélène. Ternier found her swaying to and fro in a rocking chair. In manly manner, she had set her hat on the coat rack on her way in. Her hair capped her in copper. A dash of red livened her lips, and a necklace of Auvergne amethysts offset her pale blue eyes.

"Madame," said a sullen-browed Ternier, "our conversation will not be taking its usual course this morning."

"Indeed, you're looking rather stern. Should I be concerned?"

"We will get to that. You and I are at once old and new friends. We met by chance. You received me in Paris with a charm and graciousness that I will not forget."

"You have done better than that for me here since my arrival."

"I am doing what I ought and what I can, everything I can. And I do it without reservations, with all the joy and unalloyed satisfaction it gives me to have you here. Pray, could you assure me it is the same with you?"

He eyed her intently. Hélène bestirred her lips, as if the words were rising up only to die upon that threshold. Nervously she began fingering the amethysts. At last she banished her confusion by admitting it.

"What you say troubles me. What do you mean?"

"I am asking, in other words, whether the reasons for your presence in Sangkae are indeed—that is to say, are entirely those that you have given me. And, I would add, if there are others, do you have sufficient trust in me to confide them?"

Hélène lowered her gaze and thought for a moment, then replied:

"I trust you enough not to lie, my friend. No, I have not given you all my reasons for being here. Although I trust you enough not to lie, however, I do not, or do not yet," she painfully added, "feel the sort of trust I need to confide those reasons."

"I thank you for speaking frankly, though I am sorry to hear that your reassurance in my company goes only so far."

"Oh, I felt quite reassured up until five minutes ago. You yourself have set a limit on things with your questions, because what I have let you see so far apparently no longer suffices."

"There is no reason to bring your pride into this. A father sees his daughter sink into melancholy or believes her to be suffering under some sort of threat. If he frets over her well-being is his duty towards her, or his trust in her, in any way diminished?"

"You speak of fathers. I am not your daughter. In everything you know of me, in the thoughts I have been able or wanted to share, I warrant the delightful courtesy you have always shown. Or at least so I believe, for I have never thought you an ostentatious man, pulling out all the stops at every occasion. You are my dearest friend, and I say this not without some measure of pride. Just by being around you—even if we are, as you say, new friends—I have already learned… How shall I put it? I have learned to take the measure of an act. Have you led me astray? Have I started down the wrong path? To answer you that I would need to owe you a confession, and I owe you no confessions…"

Hélène sat back and thought hard.

"No, I don't believe I do."

After a second pause she began again:

"My admiration for you, my affection—they do not compromise my independence."

"Let us speak calmly. God forbid I infringe on your independence. You have retained your frankness as well?"

"Every bit of it, as I have just shown you."

"Yes, you have been frank, which is precisely why I have found you rather ambiguous since your arrival. Like a cloudy spring. Pray, do not interrupt me. I do not intend to start a discussion. I simply wish to lay out my thoughts for you, as a man, even if you cannot do the same for me. Yes, by God, you belong to your husband. It is an independent thing to venture forth. But sometimes one loses one's way, and then one is no longer independent. One can venture forth arm in arm with one's husband, as long as the rhythm of married life brings one back every evening to hearth and home. Then, I imagine, it feels good to be independent. But here, for the past week, you have been alone, six hundred kilometers from Saigon. True, Monsieur Gassin should soon be arriving, but he is not here yet. The hours go by and slip one's notice.

"You are, then, alone. I understand the merits of the surroundings in which you are living out this solitude, but grant that I do not know you well enough to understand *your* merits. Do not furrow your brow. What would you have: bland compliments or the plain words of a man who speaks as a friend? When I say I do not know you well enough to judge your merits I mean that I intend not to fret needlessly over what you might do, but also not to fall into some ill-considered oblivion and neglect the duties incumbent upon me by the simple fact of your arrival in my little kingdom— duties to which I have strictly committed myself. It is no doubt ridiculous for a man to watch over a woman. That responsibility lies with the husband who has let you go. He undoubtedly knows you better than I. Be that as it may, you are at present between the two of us, as it were, and when we look at you we do not at all see the same woman. Your husband sees you through the filter of his confidence, of your past together, of all the tender and solemn words that have passed between you, of the compact in which he has placed his trust. He sees you as he has made you, or as you have evolved over your ten years of life together. I, Madame, see you without these intervening conditions. I see not a particular woman but a woman, a person, a human being. What one knows in the cold light of day—that is to say, objectively—does not permit one to foresee what will become of so eminently versatile a creature, a creature so fragile that its self-assurance is worse than a chink in the armor; it is, all too often, a cause for blindness and inexperience. Your husband believes you armed for the task, just as you believe yourself to be. I see you as vulnerable. He has clad you in his love, and you have reached into your own love to draw forth the peace of mind with which you set out on the road. Beware lest the lovely dress and brilliant sword... What's on your mind? You seem not to be listening."

"Yes, yes, I am listening! I am all ears! You asked me not to interrupt."

"In short, you are not safe here."

"I am grateful to you for telling me."

"This is no time for levity. It is not advice I wish to give you. You are clever enough to supply that for yourself, if it is not too late, and too much of a woman to ignore it just because it comes from me. You needn't fear a sermon either."

Ternier rose, clasped his hands behind his back, and planted himself before Madame Gassin. Leaning back in her chair, she looked at him from below.

"Listen carefully. Captain Thévenet is here. He has only recently come to take up his post at Sangkae. I introduced him to you. I say introduced, but it's only a manner of speaking, for I had a strong impression that you already knew each other. A gesture on his part, a blink on yours, and then a feigned coldness. That is what I saw. I am not conducting an interrogation, mind you. Anything you see fit to keep from me is none of my business. That said, there is another matter to consider.

"As you can well imagine, the arrival at a post like this of a pretty woman, traveling alone, preceding a husband who has been held up with business elsewhere, does not go unnoticed, however logical the chain of events. Here we are in the thick of native life, and the natives, with their myriad bare feet and their idleness and their readily malicious curiosity, observe all that is European. At the hotel there are *boys* up and about at all hours, day and night. They have keen ears and keen eyes. Every house, whether it belongs to the brigadier of the gendarmerie or to me, has but walls of glass. Anything we say at table quickly makes its way around. Anything we do is generally known in time. Do you see what I am getting at?"

"You seem bent on telling me."

"Well, then, Thursday night, as everyone from the Chinese manager of the opium den to the postmaster's cook knows, you withdrew from my house and went to the hotel at about eleven o'clock. You then went right out again by the door facing the river. You walked some hundred meters along the bank before hiring a rickshaw and stopping at Captain Thévenet's house. He is a bachelor…and without a *congai*. It is known, moreover, that although there were no lights on at his house he must have been expecting you, because once you had gone inside he closed the door behind you himself, after checking to see that no one was about on the street."

Hélène closed her eyes and pressed her fingers into them, leaving her mouth half-open in an expression of unspeakable suffering. Ternier had turned around and was pacing back and forth. Her hands still tense, she brought him to a halt with calm words:

"And have you been told when I departed?"

"My dear friend, the volunteer observer, or observers, having seen you go into that house, in the middle of the night, and in that manner, had, I imagine, seen enough. The story has nothing to say about when you got back to your hotel. It simply and crudely says that you are the captain's mistress, and that you have come to meet him under the good auspices of the *résident*—for the intimacy between you and me, which we have no reason to hide, is also common knowledge. Forgive the harsh words; detail often has a brutal edge.

"I've given you the European gossip of the town, first so that you'll be prepared, second to assure you that I am not one to buy into gossip. I stick to the facts; everything ends wherever they end. I speculate no further and have no desire to suppose anything else. Again, I speak as a friend. To make things perfectly clear, let me add also that I am prepared to help you, if necessary."

"Thank you, my friend. Are you not surprised that I have contested none of what you say?"

"I am not surprised. You would have disappointed me had you raised your hackles. It's no use putting on a show when the facts are blatant. And I have been careful to say that I ask for no explanation."

"Certain explanations are not to be given."

"I am of the same opinion, and did you not tell me so a moment ago?"

"But there are also explanations that *may* be given."

"Make good use of them."

"These I do owe you. I am not the captain's mistress, no. I am no one's mistress. I went to his house, as you know. It was the first time. I came out ten minutes later and have not been back since."

"I appreciate your clearing up the point, and I am quite satisfied with what you say. Experience often shows up the falsity of certain appearances. A lone woman who goes to a lone man's house at night can, of course, spend the night, but she might equally well do nothing of the sort."

"It all depends on the woman."

"If you like. I prefer: 'It all depends on the circumstances.'"

Hélène smiled painfully. Then, after a long silence, during which Ternier continued his stroll:

"And what if I *were* the mistress of Captain Thévenet?"

"You have no fear of words, at least. If you were I wouldn't like it as much. You are a married woman."

"Is this you speaking?"

"I am doing my best to reply. Only, do not misunderstand me. I appeal to no general laws, or even to the broadest convention, for I see no commonplace couple in your marriage and do not hold you to be any ordinary woman. If your husband is being fooled, that is of no importance and leaves me indifferent. He had only to look after his interests, make himself indispensable, make sure he took precedence in your thoughts and in your tastes. I recognize your right to take a lover, but I cannot condone a decadence in which you belong to two men at once. You have, I imagine, pride enough to make a choice—to leave your husband, if he no longer pleases you, and take the lover, if he has managed to conquer your affections. You want for nothing, have no children, and are seductive enough to inspire deep passion, the sort of passion you yourself can muster. That is why it would hardly please me that you were the mistress of any creature, even a member of the elite, if you were also still the wife of Roland Gassin. That would be neither elegant nor clear. For the rest, that whole legal and religious apparatus out to quash the adulterer for the sake of egotism, I care not a whit. You would disappoint me only because you would have to lie and scheme, and thus reduce yourself to duplicity and all the usual dirty tricks of the game. Clear, hearty living—there is nothing so beautiful as that, especially for a woman, because it is harder for her than it is for a man. Here is my lover! Hats off to the woman who proclaims it in broad daylight, with a boldness that only *seems* insolent, in light of our stringent conventions. But she must not proclaim it between her husband and her lover. I will stop here, for it is not my purpose to stand in judgment over adultery. This is about you, whom I like to think of as inhabiting a higher plane, without any misgivings or disapproval or complicity. I see you proud and shiny and unalloyed like a well-struck medal."

Hélène shuddered. Ternier, still at his pacing, did not see. She was following him with her eyes, nostrils narrowed, and terrible indecision writ upon her face.

"It would be too easy, as well! You would have gotten free with a lie, under the pretext that Saigon was boring you and you wanted to venture out into the country and see the friend who was welcoming you out there. Suppose that your departure was planned, or that you seized an chance opportunity, or even that the opportunity was forced on you—your lover would be at your beck and call, and your husband held in reserve. How utterly commonplace in a land where bachelors abound and lie in wait, where morals are loose and sensuality is advised. One need only stoop to it, and stoop to it one does. Yes indeed, it would disappoint me to see you lower yourself in that way. This is not timorous rectitude on my part. I simply balk at common acts. Low-hanging fruit are sullied by the dust of the road, whereas the fruit up top remains unblemished; but one must climb to get at it, and one generally finds it unripe.

Dreamily, Hélène said:

"The fruit up top, is it better than the fruit below?"

"One needn't wipe it clean. What virtue is there in easy conquest? What is my obedient *congai* worth next to a woman I could have gotten to know, merited, won, wrested from herself and from others, if I had been able, if perhaps I had known how, and if my life abroad had not always kept me away from the sort of societies where fair maidens cannot be bought with money, like courtesans, but give themselves to one man: the strongest, or the ablest? Is the path not always open to do as others do and pick the low-hanging fruit? Taking thy neighbor's wife—a bargain. You operate without being seen. I would understand if you went to that neighbor, said, 'I like your wife. Watch out! I'm going to do everything I can to take her for myself,' and then took her, through sheer effort, by every available means. Now, there's an adultery of a different color! A man on the hunt. Look around for philanderers of that stripe. You can count them on your fingers."

"No doubt, but what if the woman takes the initiative? What if she decides on the conquest and…under the conditions you've just set?"

"She is at liberty. As for me, it would no longer be the lowest-hanging fruit; it would be fallen fruit. I have no pride in the matter; I esteem myself no better than a moderate catch, and mine is not the physique of a conqueror. What good to me is a woman at loose ends who throws herself at the feet of the first man to walk by? This one's no good; all his qualities and virtues on display, like a frigate under full sail with the whole crew turned out topside. How could I be sure under such circumstances that I rather than another… And what if the woman later realizes that she's made a mistake, gotten carried away? Since you ask about this specific point, I think true love is obscure, animal, violent in origin. Without a struggle, without the man's attack and especially the woman's defense, if the law of the strong in every sense of the word is not operative, if the male expends no effort in a proper search, if he feels no sense of conquest, if he enters into love without pride, without imperious need in all his faculties, let the man be forewarned that his love will be bland. Having too easily attained it, he will feel no ardor in preserving a property whose value he fails to appraise. But let us return to the business at hand. My only concern is you. In about ten days your husband should arrive. Do you still plan to meet him?"

"Why do you ask me that?"

"After what I have just said and recent events I think it necessary."

"Nothing has happened for which I owe my husband an explanation."

"Do you not think that to silence the talk about town…?"

Madame Gassin let out a nervous laugh.

"I don't care a fig about gossip!"

"That is all I needed to hear. Are you at peace?"

"I have never felt better."

"Then let us forget we even spoke."

"No. You have told me some precious things… Woman, in sum, is an unfortunate animal, forever hunted. Of all that is directed at her, what is *not* an attack? I nonetheless feel able to mount a defense…"

Her voice took on some bitterness.

"…but not an attack. I must admit that I am far from indifferent to the security you so carefully ensure, and dare to guarantee by every available means. It in no way injures my pride to accept it."

"Madame, you are a wife out on her own, an exquisite woman come for a visit."

"I am, you said, a well-struck medal…"

"And medals are worn in full view, on the chest."

"A lovely spot."

"The heart lies beneath."

"The heart, wellspring of pride…," added Hélène, rising to her feet.

"As you say: the pride of beating beneath a medal."

"You will lose it, lose the medal, when I depart."

"I will preserve the memory of wearing it."

"It won't have been too much trouble?" asked Hélène as she proffered her hand.

"There are perhaps burdens that grow heavier in remembrance."

"It's time for me to go; you're going in for gallantry."

"I go about it clumsily. You need nothing at the hotel?"

"Nothing. I'm being treated like a queen. I've run out of room for your flowers."

"Until this evening, then."

"Until this evening."

⚜ ⚜ ⚜

They were under the porch. To all appearances becalmed, Madame Gassin took her leave and advanced a few steps before suddenly wheeling about and hastening back, turning an anguished face on Ternier. She leaned on him, tottering.

"But what's the matter? You're going to fall! Come inside and rest…"

"No! No! Never mind that! Listen. I'm a miserable wretch. You've just raked me over the coals, and I've done everything I can to hide it from you, to hide it from myself. Believe me, I am unnerved, mad! Have pity on a helpless woman. Would you have me get down on my knees? Look! Here I am. This is not an act! I wish I were dead! I wish it were all over with! It's as if everything were slipping away. But don't you forsake me. Must I beg for your esteem? For the love of God, no more questions. Forget everything you've told me. What I'm asking makes no sense, but you are generous. A woman is not always her own mistress. I would love to explain everything! Oh, I would love to! But that is the one thing that's forbidden to me. Would you take me by force, like a brute, if you wanted me and I fought you off? No. Impossible. You cannot know more about me than what I've told you, but let me retain your trust. Let me continue to be the Hélène Gassin whose portrait you have painted. It's true to life. Just say it, and I know it will be so. If you could look inside me, see the bloody tatters. You want confidences. You want them now. Tell me! Do you?"

She was regaining her strength. Her eyes were riveted on Ternier, and their bewilderment began to subside. She was dabbing her lips with the handkerchief clenched in her fingers.

"No, Madame, no. And I assure you that everything that has just been said by you and by me is erased."

In a brusque gesture too swift for him to counter, Hélène grabbed Ternier's hand and brought it to her lips; then, frightened by her own gesture, cast it away.

"Thank you. And now let me depart, as usual."

"Until this evening?" said Ternier once more.

"Until this evening."

From the height of the porch, which was wreathed in the dazzling, sad violet of a streaming bougainvillea, he watched Madame Gassin move away, stepping lightly on the red earth of the path. Her figure dimmed and lit up alternately as it passed through the mottle of shade and sunlight beneath the trees. Out the gate she went. Now, opening her parasol, she was nothing but a long, slender blot of mauve hanging from a disk, and soon she had dissolved altogether in the light.

…A woman, she had said, is not always her own mistress.

IX
A Perfect Dinner

Ternier had called for the portico, the veranda, and the central
parlor to be decorated with white and pink lotus. The petals had
been turned out by hand, to enlarge the already enormous flowers.
They engulfed the base of the pillars and were arrayed elsewhere
in stages, obstructing the view of the archways at the far end. They
smelled faintly of lemon and in the glow of the flaming chandeliers
overhead had the mother-of-pearl luster of shells. A few of them
were fluttering beneath the four ceiling fans. Petals loosed by the
whirlwinds floated on the reflective tile as on a pond.

The dining room adjoined the hall. The dining table, white and
pink with the same floral abundance, almost ran the length of both
rooms. Three great, open windows at the far end shed a little light
on a blooming papaya and the trunk of a giant rubber tree. The
night was superb. The air was hot but not stuffy, for the fans kept it
circulating. Car horns were honking outside.

Madame Gassin and the doctor arrived early. She was dressed
in a backless, almond-green dress with ornaments in raised gold.
A simple strand of pearls adorned her neck. She looked at once
dazzling and discreet, so deft in her bold elegance that poise veiled
her nudity, softening its glint. At one point the doctor noted a
vague disquiet in her eyes and inquired after her health. She replied

with a smile. Perhaps he had been mistaken, or perhaps she began watching her conduct; whatever the case, she thereafter stymied his curiosity.

The Cambodian governor entered with his daughter, each dressed in the national dress, a sampot, bound about the middle. His, of white brocade and gold, was of a sort that is no longer to be found in the country. Hers was of iridescent silk, pink and silver, with fine folds. The sole pin on the governor's tuxedo jacket was a cross from the Legion of Honor. His daughter, in Siamese style, was wearing a sort of chemisette, short and frilly with lace. A dozen salters of finely meshed gold thread or mail lay heaped on her left shoulder and ran to her right hip, which itself shined with hollow hoops inlaid with diamonds. Her fingers were heavy with rings, a small embroidered handkerchief hung at her waist, and she teetered about on Louis XV heels, from France.

Her face lacked beauty but not finesse. Her hair was cut short, like a man's. It was curled in front into a deep-black roll and glistened with fragrant oil. A little powder had given her skin a gray hue of bistre.

Timid through and through, she sat like a good little girl, her feet dangling from a European chair made for bigger people. Her greetings came with a smile of great charm and a slight, automatic nod. She proffered an unclasping hand, tiny and dry. She was enigmatic and puerile, becoming and awkward, and but faintly ridiculous in the Asian and European blend of her finery. Hélène, won over by this timidity and native grace, took a seat next to her, and the two women exchanged smiles, for the daughter knew not a word of French.

The parlor was filling up, each new automotive rumble heralding some new couple's arrival. The doctor had declared to Madame Gassin his intention to serve both as her ordinance officer and her adjunct *résident de France* at Sangkae, so as to elucidate matters both military and civilian. He began naming the new arrivals and took charge of introductions.

Drawn together by their affinities, some ten ladies converged into a small committee, their apparent independence ill concealing a keen attention to hierarchy. Though news was slow to travel from the mother country to this hinterland of northern Cambodia, French fashion was cleverly and quite closely followed. Mindful of the approximately two months she had spent covering sixteen or eighteen thousand kilometers—almost half the circumference of the earth—Hélène found the brilliant fabrics and evening gowns surprising amid the pink lotus flowers and the plentiful light.

The men, dressed in black slacks and white tuxedo jackets, kept to themselves. In groups they consulted the table-seating chart in the veranda. With the aid of a secretary, the adjunct *résident* was handing each man a card with the name of the lady entrusted to his care. A few guests, lacking transport of their own, had yet to arrive and were waiting to be collected by the Résidence car or the doctor's, both serving as shuttles. A brouhaha of good cheer had already settled in, and two *boys*, arms spread and laden with broad platters, were serving cocktails.

Many a scrutinizing gaze settled on Hélène, because she was foreign, and many another absently scanned the room for Captain Thévenet. One has little control over such alternative impulses, which are at any rate less unkindly than complicit. The captain, who, like the other men, had given Hélène the most natural of greetings, was set upon by the director of the waterworks and electric plant and by the militia inspector, a small man with a head so round and obstinate that he looked like a ball-and-spike toy.[39]

The wives of the banker and the coach-office manager were soon monopolizing Madame Gassin. The former, skinny and aloof, told

---

39 A ball linked with a string to a stick that ends in either a cup or a spike. The player, manipulating only the stick, tosses the ball into the air and tries to catch it in the cup or on the spike. Variants include cup-and-ball (English-speaking world), *kendama* (Japan), *boliche* (Spanish- and Portuguese-speaking world), and *bilboquet* (France).

of the scant pleasures that a woman could expect from outpost life, far from Hanoi and Saigon. In those cities one at least had amenities, a theater season, and ranking administrators to mix with. For a traveler arriving from France, like Madame, the interior of the country was no doubt fascinating, but after eight years in the colony one no longer knew what to do with oneself and would "lose one's taste for anything." The coach-office lady demurred, for she was always busy at home and never had time for everything. And *she* had no children! Indeed, the bank lady had a boy and a girl, aged five and eight, Madame. She could not put them in school with the little natives, and it was most distressing for their future. Moreover, she always had them in her charge. The instructor was giving them private lessons, but they were getting little out of it.

Ternier came by, diligent in his duties as master of the house, striving for wit with every guest and not always attaining it. Cocktails arrived to lend a hand.

"Have you had a cocktail, Madame? Was it chilled? Another? *Boy*, come here."

Thus he managed a complete circuit of the parlor. That much, at least, was done. From time to time Hélène cast her eyes around the room, seeking him out among all the unfamiliar faces, all those men with stiff folds in their hefty white jackets, and when she spotted his graying hair and bushy mustache, his tall stature and the high cut of his spencer, she felt less alone and took up the conversation with renewed interest. The doctor touched her arm just as a lady in a pearl-gray crepe splashed with big, madder-colored flowers was asking for her first impressions. There was a man with him.

"Monsieur Tubinque, who will have the pleasure of escorting you to table."

She saw a man of medium height with a pointy, Mephistolic goatee. He declared in cavernous tones that he was most honored. The company began heading for the dinner table, as the *boy*,

Ternier's right-hand man, a big Sino-Cambodian *métis* serving here as maître d'hôtel, had with perfunctory ceremony taken up a position in the center of the room to announce:

"Monsieur le Résident is served."

"Egad! The man's a regular undertaker! Downright lugubrious!" said Tubinque as he escorted Hélène. "You know, Madame, that's the extent of his vocabulary. Speaks not a word of French. Is this your seat, Madame? No. I'm mistaken. Farther on? You jest!"

Starting, stopping, craning over every card to read the name, Tubinque had Hélène a bit off balance. At last he pulled out a chair. Taking a seat himself, he muttered to Hélène, cupping a hand over his mouth as if to confide a secret:

"I've got to be careful. At a dinner like this at the Résidence of Kampong Chhnang,[40] back when I'd just arrived in Cambodia, I escorted this lady to table—the teacher's wife—remarried since, to a Corsican; lives in Tonkin now. So my mind wanders and I pull the chair out too far. Blam! The lady ends up sitting on the tile! Didn't know what to do with myself. How's that for a pickle? She just wanted to die, that lady!"

Ice cubes gleamed in the glasses. The Bristol board read PROTECTORATE OF CAMBODIA, in gold ink, below the monogram of the Republic. Farther down:

CURRIED PURÉE OF FOWL

WRASSE BRAISED IN CHAMBERTIN

DUCKLING FILETS IN SALMIS

TRADITIONAL ROAST HAUNCH OF VENISON

ARECA SALAD

ASPARAGUS IN CHANTILLY SAUCE

SOURSOP ICE CREAM IN MERINGUE

---

40 Capital of the province of the same name, just north of Phnom Penh.

Fruits and cakes

The wines listed were Gris de Lorraine 1888, Sauternes 1889, and Pommard 1893.[41] The inevitable silence at the start of any meal quelled all conversations, but they had soon found new life, punctuated by the clatter of cutlery.

"Is this your first time in the colony, Madame?" asked Tubinque.

Hélène had heard this question once every minute for the past half-hour.

"My first, Monsieur," she replied.

"Ah, well, I've been in Indochina for twenty-three years now, and I've just about had my fill of the place. I met Résident Ternier back in 1904. He was just starting out. In fact, he'd quake in his boots on account of the big lakes. There were fish out there that'd spit in his face! He didn't want to go on living. He'd pull at my coat and call for his mother. Want proof? The customs man of Kampong Luong[42] was cooking shrimp at the front of the boat and almost burnt up the whole show coming to his aid. It's no joke, those fish. They'll follow you around! They'll stick their heads out and spit water in your face!"

In support of his tale Tubinque would lean in toward Hélène with the confidential hand cupped over his mouth or give her a poke with his elbow.

"All kinds of funny animals hereabouts. One time it was monkeys on the cape road. I was with the Public Works overseer. Poor old rascal—died from water-cress poisoning. No joke. Ate too much and took a bath right afterwards. He'd take his baths in a barrel and stay in there for hours at a time, with his wife hollering like a polecat on account of him spilling water all over the place. Well, that day there was no getting him out of the barrel, he was

---

41 Despite the remote upcountry location French wines were *de riguer*. This selection includes a white Gris (Grey), also called "pelure d'oignon" or "onion skin" for its pale range-pink hue; a sweet white Sauternes from Bordeaux; and a red Pinot noir from Burgundy.

42 A floating village on the southern shores of the Tonlé Sap Lake.

so fat. The *boy* heaved at him like an ass at a cart. How's that for a pickle? This was at Pursat. Me, I was leaving the next day and had my bags to pack. It was rough, I tell you. Took us a sight more than an hour to get him out of that barrel. An hour—can you believe it? Like that time with Duston, a newspaperman. I'd invited him to lunch. He was lodging with me. We were downstairs waiting for him and taking our Pernod—you could still get Pernod[43] back then—and all of a sudden there's water leaking from the ceiling and dripping down on our heads. The deputy's wife called for an umbrella. Just wanted to die, that woman, because she was wearing one of those dresses made of whatchamacallit. You know—stuff that stains easy. So I go see what's what, right? And I find the man squatting in the bathroom fast asleep and still tugging on the shower chain! Talk about a deluge! I was out thirty piastres in repairs. No joke. He'd fallen asleep! Must've tippled something fierce that morning. Out like a light, and the imbecile'd sat on the drain! No way out for the water!"

"But what about the monkeys on the cape road?" asked the lady to Tubinque's left.

"Ah, yes! The monkeys! They were plucking a marten."

Eyes went wide.

"No joke. Nasty creatures, those monkeys. They'd captured the marten out on the road and were plucking it like a hen. Fur everywhere. Plucking it, I tell you. That marten just wanted to die. It was hollering like a polecat, and the monkeys pulling every which way. Pluck you bald, tear you limb from limb! It was a ghastly thing to see up in those trees. I told this story to What's-his-face there, the ambassador. You know—Froleau. He was on an official visit to Angkor. I'd had a landing stage put up to receive him on, right? So then the waters go and recede. He arrives eight

---

43 In 1797, Henri-Louis Pernod began distilling absinthe in Switzerland, later founding Maison Pernod Fils in 1805. The powerful (45–74% alcohol) anise-flavored spirit became infamous for causing hallucinations, insanity, crime and addiction. It was banned in Switzerland in 1908, followed by the United States (1910) and France (1912).

days earlier than announced, so now the landing stage is three hundred meters inland. We had to wade through mud when he disembarked. Nearly caused a diplomatic incident. Fortunately, I wasn't there! Neither was the government's delegate. Only Noël was there to receive him."

"Noël?"

"He was the Negro—the bungalow Malabar, head of transport, darker than life. The ordinance officer was raising a hell of a hullaballoo. 'There's no one here to receive the ambassador! There's no one here to receive the ambassador!' Over and over again. So in dulcet tones the Negro says, 'I am here, Lieutenant! I am here!' But the lieutenant couldn't see him. It was the middle of the night! Noël just wanted to die. Turned yellow, he got so sick. No joke. This wrasse isn't bad."

Hélène thought at first that Tubinque was launched on another story, but then she remembered the menu and saw he was talking about the fish. As Tubinque made his usual splash at the corner of the table the gentleman to Madame Gassin's right was eating with a diligence that smacked of fervor and logarithmic calculation. He had given a slight nod on releasing his escorted lady's arm and on taking his seat turned to Hélène to give another. Since then he had seemed so busy that the two women hadn't even thought to disturb him. He dared not laugh at Tubinque's stories, lest he seem to be listening, but at times his lips would twist or the veins in his temple flare as he chewed.

Ternier surveyed his table. The tiny young Cambodian woman, struggling to slice duckling filets, was casting around a timid glance after every bite. She was seated next to the inspector of the native guard, who knew a little Khmer. Smiling prettily, she listened attentively as he spoke, the diamonds of her jewelry emitting the occasional glitter. There were happy faces all around. The men seemed hale. The wine glasses glowed with lovely notes of pale yellow or reddish black, and the sweating ice-water glasses left damp rings on the tablecloth. Above the row of heads visible before her, beyond the lotus table-runner and the fruit cups, Hélène could see the *boys*, slim and spry in their starched white jackets, dashing about with their eyes half closed, deftly tilting a bottle between guests or dropping into a glass, from unclenching tongs, a scintillating cube of ice.

Tubinque continued to hold forth, enlivening with his bonhomie and regaling with his anecdotes, but Madame Gassin was now catching only snippets of his conversation, for a warm glow of well-being had pervaded her. From afar the doctor would send a complicit signal. Sometimes her gaze would cross with Ternier's, and he would smile. Course followed course in clockwork succession.

❖ ❖ ❖

It seemed in that hall as if no thought that might arise among the forty guests could meet with a threat or a regret to chase it away. Past the park the river was lit by the fires of its junks. Prayers rose up from neighboring pagodas. Five kilometers from this impeccably laid table, from this opulent French world, from this handful of white-clad men and cheery women lay the broad expanse of the wilderness, with its savannas and forests.

Tonight in this place teeming with flowers, bestrewn with the sacred lotus of the ponds, a man, tenth of his race to arrive, with peace in his soul and a vigorous throb in his heart, smiled amid twenty other men, his collaborators. He drank the wine and broke the bread of his country. The telegraph and telephone were silent. From this man radiated roads—past the ponds, toward distant towns, and on to the foot of the border mountains they radiated, white with moonshine, spanning his province like the symbol of the great pacifying hand he had laid upon it. Within this star of twenty-eight thousand square kilometers more than three hundred thousand souls lay asleep. Every guest who raised his crystal glass into the prosperous air had done his duty, as well.

The bored banker's wife; that vulgar woman there, obscure female who between courses wiped the concavities of her teeth with her tongue; the young sweet one yonder; and the others, all the others, were living blind, yearning foolishly for their homeland or indiscriminately exaggerating the depth of their exile. Still, they were present and accounted for.

In the past or at present, wittingly or not, unbidden or compelled by an order, all these people—every half-family short a father, mother, or child; every exile, doubtless a volunteer; every errant soul, though he err to earn a living—had played an eminent role. True, it might not have entailed turning a wheel, occupying an ordinary station, or conducting by their particular means the daily business of a community. It had entailed, rather, the simultaneous enrichment of two civilizations. Their labor on a road benefitted not just their own country or clan but also that of another people. Their egotism did not profit them alone. All colonization, says one claim, operates on a principle that is false, or at least debatable, and at times even inopportune, but for this the colonists are not responsible. See above. In the colonies there are but laborers— indeed, to judge by the scope of their task, good laborers.

Names like theirs are etched into the stones of Sangkae cemetery. The bearers of those names would doubtless be satisfied to see straight roads, a school, a dispensary, and a hygienic market in the town where only sixteen years earlier they were leveling the land and breathing in its pestilence. At dinner this evening perhaps not all the heirs to the precursors' legacy are of superior mind or nature or even terribly generous in spirit, but all are at least dutiful. When they look upon the *résident*, their common, direct chief, their eyes quicken with a slight glimmer. However complex their feelings, whatever their loyalty, their attention manifestly settles on him. In his professional rigor, in the firm devotion to duty he demands, in his conviction—in all this he evokes more than the notion of authority. His rank is of no concern. He is not merely the man who records individual assessments in files. He is above all the man who has built the house to which each guest will later repair in the cool of the night. He is the captain mindful of everyone's safety. And everyone, feeling infinitely fragile on this far side of the world, turns in the end to him, to thank him for being there.

❖ ❖ ❖

Before Monsieur Barrois, discreetly fading into the background, Madame Rougemont explained to Hélène that the soursop ice cream was made with the pulp of a large green fruit. It felt to Hélène like chewing a paste of fragrant flowers. The *boys* having passed around the aquamaniles—the cut and folded citronella leaves suggesting insects—Ternier rose and led the way through the hall to the verandas. On the way Tubinque confessed to Hélène that he had eaten too much and was bound to suffer an ache in his lower back on the morrow. But that was nothing to the old police commissary! Boy! Why, after a meal like that he'd still be famished. Back home he'd gulp down a potato salad and eight hardboiled eggs, with the shells, and drink three cans of beer, one after another—and never burst at the seams!

People quickly came back together in knots. The men snipped the bands off Manila cigars tied off at the end. The scent of the women's Three Castles tobacco wafted about, and was dispersed by what the doctor termed the "little maelstroms" of the fans.

"Not too bored, I hope," said Ternier to Hélène, bringing her some coffee.

"Bored? I'm delighted. A perfect dinner, an all-around success."

"There will be dancing a little later."

"Dancing too?"

"Dancing too. All the pleasures. Do you play? Perhaps a game of bridge?"

"No. I'd rather mingle."

Two bridge tables had already been set up. In a corner of the parlor three ladies and an officer were preparing a game of mahjong, a Chinese import of two or three years' standing in Cambodia. It was already all the rage elsewhere in Indochina and in the English colonies. The players performed the initial mixture, and the clatter of the hundred forty-four dominoes colliding and rubbing on wood pierced the din of the room. Hélène tried to follow a few games.

One of the ladies explained her "wall," the "seasons" finely engraved and colored in the bone, the ace of the bamboo suit sporting a bird with spread wings, the many images of varied significance. As more tiles were laid out the pattern grew more variegated and finical, like a puzzle composed of decorative, delicate pieces. The original rules called for the use of a special language. When placing a tile at a particular spot one would declare "Making the hill bloom," or "Fishing the moon from the bottom of a well."

"A rather difficult game that takes a while to learn," her tutor was saying, "but simple once one has understood. The combinations are infinite."

⚜ ⚜ ⚜

Hélène moved on, and was joined by Madame Rougemont. A group, consisting of two gentlemen and Captain Thévenet, broke ranks to make room. The officer's gaze crossed Madame Gassin's. After the slightest of hesitations she came to a dead stop.

"Well, Captain, have you repaired that target butt?"

"Yes indeed, Madame. The job is done."

"And was it your skirmishers one heard yesterday morning, at dawn?"

"The wind was carrying. There was indeed target practice yesterday."

"I thought we were under attack!"

Madame Rougement fanned herself, her expression a little too indifferent. A slight blush rose to Hélène's cheek.

"Do you dance, Captain?"

"By God, Madame, not very well."

"We shall find out a little later."

The officer, befuddled, twirled his moustache. Hélène left no time for his silence and embarrassment to transpire. Smiling, she said:

"I suppose you will ask me?"

"I thank you for the honor…"

"And you, Madame, do you dance?" she asked her companion, leading her along by the arm.

"It is quite hot, Madame. Besides, I am not up on the latest steps. Nowadays everyone is doing the foxtrot or the shimmy, whereas I am still doing the Boston."[44]

Soon thereafter a skinny woman with a pained expression took to the piano. The *boys* cleared the hall, and a dozen couples glided along to the blunt, jerky rhythms of the day's dances.

"Let us open the ball together," said Ternier to Hélène, leading her out.

The next invitation came from a young bank cashier, and when the piano struck up a foxtrot the Captain bowed before Madame Gassin. She stood erect and composed in his arms, her eyes downcast. Most of the guests followed their progress,

---

44 The foxtrot, generally danced to swing tunes (in four), is two slow steps (forward or backward) followed by two quick steps to the side. The shimmy is a shoulder jiggle performed with the arms held out to the sides. The Boston is a two-step danced to a brisk tune in two or four with a triplet subdivision (e.g., a polka). The one-step, mentioned further below, is related to the Boston and amounts to walking in time with a partner. All of these dances were popular in the early twentieth century, but the foxtrot really caught on, naturally enough, in the swing era, after the 1920s. As Madame Rougemont suggests, it would have been the new thing at the time of the novel. The foxtrot lives on today as a "standard" dance in ballroom-dance competitions.

peering through other couples. Broad streaks like the blazing bands on certain Chinese vases gleamed on Hélène's lamé dress. Conversation ceased among the ladies. For a moment Hélène and the Captain found themselves at a certain remove from the others. Keeping her partner in place and her eyes downcast, with her lips almost motionless against his shoulder, she uttered the following:

"Ternier knows I went to your house."

"The whole town…"

"What do you plan to do?"

"Rest assured, I will never say anything."

She gave his hand an anxious squeeze, and in a long glide they made their way back among the other dancers. Hélène was smiling. There were a few beads of sweat on her forehead. She released the officer's hand momentarily to grab a rogue lock and smooth it into place, a reddish down coming into view beneath her upraised arm.

Her only other dance was a one-step, after which she felt a bit weary. She wasn't accustomed to such heat, and it caught her by surprise. The rest of her time she spent chatting with the ladies, picking up town gossip and some contradictory claims about life in the colonies. The lovely night went by at the windows. Ternier was playing bridge. And once more the *boys* went around with soda-water glasses, cups, and a *marquise frappée*[45] in a great, frosted crystal pitcher. Bottles of whisky, lemon, and sherry clinked on a platter. The fans blew around the wrappers of straws. When the piano fell silent the talk and rustle of mahjong took precedence. Conversations fell to a whisper. And amid their spray, in vases at the foot of the pillars, the lotus wilted.

---

45 A cocktail of iced Champagne with seltzer water and lemon juice.

X

The Burning Secret

They set off for Sisophon in the afternoon two days later. Riding in the Roland-Gassin were Hélène, the doctor, and Ternier, and riding in the Résidence car a secretary, the cook, and a *boy*. The baggage had been dispatched that morning on one of the service trucks that shuttle between Sangkae and Sisophon. At that final outpost, where the gravel road came to an end, they would have to switch to horses and make their way north along a path cleared through the glades, a first stage of seventy kilometers. Beyond that the future road pushed on as a mere swath, veering northwest for some twenty-five kilometers more to the edge of the great Chong Kal forest.[46] With Hélène along, Ternier had limited the daily trek to twenty-five kilometers. This put them three days from their destination.

Ternier would make such a sweep every three or four months, to check up on the road work and prod the native authorities. Every time he set foot in these regions he would penetrate deeper into the living flesh of the land, and thus some share of the population would for the first time behold a European, the Louk Thom[47]: the big gentleman, chieftain of the province, whose name all from the

---

46 In Oddar Meancheay province to the east of Banteay Chhmar and directly south of O'Smach, location of an important pass through the Dângrêk Mountain Range.

47 In Khmer *louk* is a term of respectful address, like "Mr," while *thom* means "big." So, literally "Mr. Big."

lowliest caretaker of an administrative pavilion to the governor himself would utter twenty times daily to threaten or pledge, prompt or counsel.

⚜ ⚜ ⚜

Baking in the sun since morning, the road wavered ahead in the heated air. It lay on a crest between grassy, sloping shoulders, a gutter cutting properly across every hundred meters. An infinity of dragonflies, abdomens erect, had settled on the telegraph wires running to the right. The telegraph posts, made of rot-proof wood and blackened at the base with coal-tar, diverged from the road wherever it looped around. At intervals there were heaps of stones for maintenance and regraveling; they had now sprouted grass. All around, as far as the horizon, the vast plain gleamed with rice fields like a slab of metal.

Where were the villages? Hard to say. In the copses floating here and there in the distance? No doubt. Sometimes at the edge of a lagoon there might be two or three straw huts raised on piles, the sun devouring them on their perches, the paltry shade beneath removing them, as it were, from the ground and providing a place for a pig to wallow. The barren solitude through which the road stretched would turn harsh and weird, as if some vast, palpable thing were readying itself, vibrating. But what? Do not press the human mind to divine all things. Let it sense, and fear, and hope.

Here the sun toils, digs, searches, overlying the muddy waters like a gigantic, fiery male. A tenuous, delicate mist is already gathering. With the pale green of unfurling leaves it tempers the plain, varying in hue within the regular limits of a checkerboard.

This is sprouting paddy, spare and darling in its frailty, tentative in this furnace of a plain. It begins at the road's embankment and, mirrored in its thin sheet of underlying water, continues on to the horizon, a horizon that travels along with you. The peasant grazes the soil with his primitive cart, scarcely disturbing it, at the propitious season of the first storms. That is enough. The soil germinates. Now the germ is rising, breaking the surface of the warm waters, and turning green. And now the land is deserted and silent, and man once more invisible.

Enter the road. Into semicircles it parts fertile regions that for centuries, indefatigably, have germinated in the same manner. Enter the brand-new road, slender and hard, set like a blade upon the pan of a scale, straight and imperative like a fine idea. Other men have come to lay it down, balancing nature's forces against their own. The road is order and discipline; it passes, and to it all things converge and cling. Toward the road, tomorrow, every sprig of paddy will bow its rice-laden head and every human hope, hanging just like the grain from that grassy shaft, will turn.

How lovely a thoroughfare, this road bequeathed by one country to another, blazed by the strong for the weak. You will make your road, commands the one to the other. For ten centuries you have been dreaming and degenerating. The time for dreaming is over. Today we forge. Gather your tools, if you please, as the others do, as I do in my country. Think this road is meant for me? You will pass on this road a thousand Cambodians before running across a single Frenchman.

The tons of sandstone you ground and sculpted in times past, when building your temples, prove you capable of working toward an idea. Well, then, this road goes as far as the temple—and is straighter. Look at it: level, metaled,[48] precisely surveyed, and admirably plain. It is mistress to a hitherto untamed wilderness, where for so many centuries men of all races have died without getting the cord round the unbroken beast. Now that the worst is over, now that you have struggled at our side, take the beast in hand.

The semicircles of the land, one to either side of the road, looked deserted. There was nothing but a russet eagle in the radiant

---

48 Metaling (the term derives from the Latin for *mine* or *quarry*) is the laying of gravel to surface a road.

sky, dominating from above this seemingly uninhabited land, scrutinizing with a keen eye every clump of mud, every ripple in the water, tacking, diving, scooping, climbing once more. And yet the driver kept slowing and calling out. Like gray-scaled reptiles, convoys of carts veered off to their right, ox-drivers hastening to the yokes to encourage their oxen. Beneath the cart roofs somnolent women sat up amid the merchandise to find out what was going on.

They had not been on the road an hour before encountering or passing twenty trucks; automobiles with old, leprous bodies and flaking paint; amorphous machines patched together with planks, panting and out of tune, their vaporous radiators boiling and sizzling with droplets of water; degraded runabouts rolling on bald tires, their sides strung up to the hood with baskets; the unlikeliest trucks, crushed beneath heaped-up sacks or rattling with hanks of rusted iron rods of the sort used for reinforced concrete; tractors running on half their cylinders and moving no faster than a man can walk; and the big, comfortable, brown-painted coaches of the post and other government agencies.

Vehicles of all kinds, perhaps fresh from the garage the day before, or perhaps purchased third-hand, by metal weight, by some consortium of ten or twenty Chinese transport entrepreneurs; bric-a-brac cars held together with wire and bamboo, their bodies refurbished and expanded with planks; ridiculous aggregates of scrap iron that one is astonished to see move under their own power. Vehicles that the natives indiscriminately storm, cramming aboard after a roadside wait. Bonzes squeezed between crates and a pack of dried fish. Chinamen wedged in. Winsome Annamite women, heads swathed in silk foulards, raising their parasols and bundles and slithering their way into the gaps in a pyramid. Big-bosomed Cambodian women yapping away in their sashes and white tunics. Children scattered among the packages. An old four-seater runabout with three Cambodians sitting beside the driver, five more crouched on the running board, and another eight piled atop the rear. Clamped aboard and settled and inserted and coagulated and clinging and snugly canned they ride along for two hundred kilometers, at thirty an hour, breakdowns excluded. And placid and merry they remain throughout, munching on their betel, trying to find their own hands so as to have a smoke, faces windblown with the extraordinary speed, and beaming with the scarcely credible notion that within five or six hours they will complete a journey that only yesterday would have cost them five days. Now even the humble and obscure can kick up some dust!

❖ ❖ ❖

But why do they bother?

Time is of no consequence to them. Why should a man with a cart and a good pair of oxen climb aboard this infernal machine and contort himself like a frightened spider when he could instead make his way peaceably, stage by stage, like his forefathers before him? What hurry can a bushman, who can barely reckon his own age, possibly have? None whatsoever, and yet there he is.

What will he say to his friends in the village when he gets back? He will say: "There is a road; there are mechanical vehicles." "Yoke your oxen, brothers," will not be his counsel to those who wish to set out in turn. Instead, he will say, "Walk straight on southwest. Stop when you reach the road and wait." For he knows that within an hour a cloud of dust will rise in the distance and a strange noise begin to sound.

The man is bleary-eyed still from centuries of art and contemplation, but a road white and straight comes to exist nearby, brushing past his liberty and his wisdom, his disdain for time and his poverty, and in a mere few days he has set out to meet it. There is no discussion. He spares no thought for his gods or for all that separates him from the road. Off he goes. A road needed only pass by for him to go to it—a bare, burning road, whose stones, in fact, he and his brothers in the region were pressed into service to break.

The road has him spellbound. He had watched the new divinity hasten up from the south and glide on north, and now he has come to its edge, scaled the slope of its shoulder, set his bare foot upon this white flesh, struck it with his heel. This heel had left a print on every ground it had trodden, but here it rebounds. And the man advances. Ah! Never has walking seemed so effortless, or so rapid, as along this straight line. No more grasses to cut. No more trees to get around or copses to penetrate. No thorns on this path, or bogs to sink to one's thighs in and emerge from covered in leeches.

Then other men—men who have never thought to lay down a hard band of bare earth through these wilds—make their way to the road, from all points of the horizon, and take possession. And the region has soon coalesced into a long file of hopes and desires. What had been unknown has come to be known. The man who could sell nothing is brought together with twenty buyers. The wifeless man goes out in search of a wife. But the road runs solitary through thousands of hectares of land, where the man's traditions hang, as it were, from the palm trees. Let him take the road if he so desires. Has he no need for it? Let him lean on the central pillar of his hut and put it out of mind with the monotone song of his guitar.

⚜ ⚜ ⚜

"You cannot imagine the traffic between Sangkae and Sisophone," said Ternier. "It is by the dozen that we grant new licenses every month for collective transport. And note that this is just the first stretch, covering a mere quarter of the region."

"You're not counting the carts," said the doctor, "with their dirty oxen that veer off and plop down in the middle of the road, forcing the poor little autos to swerve into the rice fields if they can't stop fast enough."

"Ingratitude on your part, Doctor. Do not badmouth the carts, for you are their fervent admirer."

"Out in the brush, on paths, yes. Most admirable. For one thing, I get a roof over my head. But on the road I prefer autos."

"And where would you have the poor carts pass?" asked Hélène.

"Off to the side, Madame. Off to the side," the doctor gravely replied. "A certain Siamese prince I once had the honor of accompanying opened new vistas for me on the topic. The utmost stupor would spread across his face whenever he saw a Cambodian's cart on the road. He could never believe his eyes whenever he saw one, and would exclaim: 'You give them the right to take the road!' I am certain the affable man left Cambodia convinced that he had been the butt of a joke, and that we had dispatched the carts along the road as extras in our little play."

"Indeed," said Ternier to Hélène, "you must keep in mind that the territory you are in belonged until 1907 to the Siamese, who hold the Cambodians to be no better than slaves."

"The fact remains," gibed the doctor, "when you build a fine house you make stairs for the residents and stairs for the help."

"Well, the service road does in fact exist. In sandy regions, and when their carts are empty, Cambodians prefer to travel alongside the road. But they are constantly obliged to get onto the road, to cross the bridges."

Ternier continued after a pause: "This entire region lay fallow three years back. It was nothing but glades ravaged every year by fire."

Jagged little dykes divided the water into regular checks, the whole forming a vast decorative panel set in the leaden net of a stained-glass window, but the painter of this scene had forgotten to include a horizon line, making it impossible to say where or how things came to an end.

Off in the distance ahead something began suddenly to take shape above a cloud of dust: a black arc surmounting shifting masses of a matte violet. The driver depressed the clutch and, as the car rolled along in silence, Hélène made out the cry of an oboe, so feeble and pining before the mass came clearly into view that it seemed to die out as soon as the ear took note.

"Elephants, Madame," said the doctor, turning to face her.

They were returning from a long journey. Mindful mahouts[49] were keeping weariness at bay by playing minor-key melodies on oboes. In no time the elephants were crossing paths with the car, their soft, cautious legs making not a sound to signal their passing. Some were bare; others carried a saddle on which a traveler lay beneath a circular roof. The musician, astride the lead elephant's neck, had set aside his flute to take up his goad and a long whip with a lead ball at the tip. With these he curbed his beast, which had gone skittish at the sight of the car and the Europeans.

Thus the parade. It seemed to issue from the sun and brush against the sky—a decorative panel, mirage-like behind the magisterial silhouettes and their shifting architecture, that turned to crystal. The troop having just forded a river, only the flanks and lumpen heads the elephants were still pale gray with dust; the legs gleamed like black basalt. Hélène caught an astonishing glimpse of another age: the nervous thigh of a mahout fanned by the great, tattered flap of a pink-lined, black-speckled ear; an unfurled trunk; men in silhouette, their heads swathed in their sashes, their bodies immobile in their rocking mounts. Seen from below, they had a princely bearing, and an air of augury. The convoy had doubtless come across an elephant's remains or lost one of its own, for dangling from one of the saddles was an enormous femur, knotty as a stump and delicately white.

"From that bone," said Ternier, "a craftsman will fashion finely sculpted guitar frames."

The car set off once more.

"Do you grant them passage on the road, Doctor?"

---

49 Elephant drivers.

"I do, Madame. I have long felt a sort of—how shall I say it?—anxious tenderness, yes, for elephants. They are a courageous people. When I was at Darlac[50] I traveled with them quite a bit. Had no choice in the matter, as there were no other means of transport. Remarkably fragile, you know. The horseflies would make their skin bleed. There'd be a fire built for them at every halt to keep the mosquitoes away, they were so sensitive to them. Ah, but how affable at bath time, how grateful for the mahout's massage! And the marquis-like caution with which they set down a foot on dubious terrain! They would stop of their own accord to wait for us to collect a fallen bag that no one had noticed."

"Really!" said Hélène, astonished.

"I assure you, Madame. A steady stream of connected thought beneath the stony bumps of those foreheads, a sort of permanent philosophy that readily deigns to concern itself with man's trivialities and aid in our enterprises with an obeisance that quickly shades into protectiveness."

Added Ternier:

"The elephant is a venerated animal. Mahouts recite certain prayers before securing the saddle-cloth of bark that underlies the pack-saddle itself. There are special flute songs dedicated to the elephant. But all of this belongs to the old, vanishing Cambodia. There are now a mere forty domestic elephants registered within my territory. The king has another forty. Add another fifty for the rest of the country, and there you have the sum total."

❖ ❖ ❖

The horizon came to life. The palm tufts grew more numerous and started to clump. Sisophon, with its river, its junks, its launches. They found the governor's house in one of its squares, within a park of mango trees and coconut palms.

---

50 A Westernized spelling of Đắk Lắk, a province in Vietnam's Central Highlands where George's father Antoine worked in the colonial service.

On the governor's order, the carriage gate had been bedecked with cut banana stipes. It looked to be made of ivory beneath its vault of interlaced palm fronds. The governor was a small, puny man, but keen of eye. He dressed in European clothes and spoke a highly correct French. The worthies ranged behind him to greet the *résident*. There was a profusion of foliage, fruit trees with a thousand glittering palms in them. A few native women passed by in the dazzle of an opalescent sky.

"The governor has prepared a room for you at his house, Madame," said Ternier. "Ask him for anything you need. I will be next door, in that house there, which is in fact the courthouse, but I have a room there. As for you, Doctor, you are familiar with your lodgings."

"Take a guess, Madame, what my lodgings consist of."

"Tell me."

"My lodgings are the in-fir-ma-ry."

"Here?"

"Right here. A fine infirmary, built last year. Three rooms, iron bedsteads, showers—and actual medicines, if you can believe it."

"Why, that's marvelous!"

"And a nurse, certified by the school in Hanoi! It's a hundred meters from here. Take a rest and come see, if you like. I will vaccinate you against cholera, plague, smallpox."

⚜ ⚜ ⚜

The governor led Hélène to a large room lit as if for a catafalque by two acetylene lamps, their valves fully open. A threadbare carpet lay in the center. Two ox heads of painted plaster, with current-pink snouts, haggard eyes, and genuine horns, sprouted from the wooden partition. There were framed, yellowed photographs mounted on a big piece of cardboard; some patient hand had clipped the photographs of French actresses from cigarette packs and glued them there in neat juxtaposition. On a table Hélène saw a carafe, a glass, cigarettes in a silver cup, a sugar bowl of blue glass, a tin of crackers, an Annamite flower pot filled with flowers. A large bed made up with Résidence linen stood in a corner of the room. In another corner stood a phonograph.

The *boy* brought in Hélène's bags. The governor's wife, her mother, and her children gathered in another doorway, knelt in greeting, and proffered pomegranates. A naked little boy, belly protruding and arm outstretched, tottered over to deliver a ragged gloriosa flower.

The room was thus open to the four winds, but once all was in order and the introductions had been made it emptied out as if by enchantment. The swish of bare feet on the planking died away, and Madame Gassin was left alone, the windows of her room wide open onto a darkening verdure where fireflies had begun to glow. The place was so kindly, so naively sincere, that Hélène sat down and let her tenderness for these people well up inside her. They were obliging and dutiful, timid and ceremonious. She was grateful to them, for they had welcomed her into their lives and collected for her pleasure what they considered to be their finest possessions. Now she could hear only the distant babble of the village and the nearby rustle of fronds rubbing together. Emerging from her torpor, she went into a second room. In the center stood a great earthenware jar of water, with jasmine flowers afloat on the surface. On a chair had been set a silver bowl for ablutions.

The woman with the burning secret stretched out on the bed and crossed her arms.

"What a wonderful place!" she murmured.

And she wept in stillness, without a sob. The tears ran down her temples and wandered into her hair. They were cool tears. Through them she saw a sort of circular pendant hanging from the ceiling and rotating, a fine lattice of rattan interwoven with flowers: a sample of the lovely craftwork that Cambodian women do with their small fingers and hang in pagodas on feast days.

XI

The Elephant
Swings His Trunk

M adame Gassin awakened slowly, with a growing sense of noises and the dawn. She saw first the open windows and the morning mist outside. There were countless cocks crowing, and the incipient poundings of a rice mortar, and then an inexplicable creaking. Soft and pitched low, it would approach from various directions and fall silent near the house. Then male voices would speak, and the silence would return. Carts, in fact, were gathering in the square. Hélène dressed and went down. Ternier emerged at the same time.

These carts, which were always drawing Hélène's eye, are forever crisscrossing the country. Today they were going to sing for her. They are elegant vehicles, put together like living bodies. Their axles hiss and grind, changing their inflection with every change in the turn of the wheels. On and on they cry, for as long as the road lasts. They are loudest in the forest, grumble in the morning, and shriek in broad sunlight.

They follow one another, all driving in the same ruts, alternating with yoked oxen. Between the cart and the oxen rides the driver, perched on the draft-shaft. Together cart, oxen, and driver are as one body, crawling and gliding, pitching and rolling, riding the furrowed paths, floating through the savannahs, clambering with a jolt over stumps. Each such body is a unique creature, with three heads and a numberless muddle of legs: the inverted Vs of the oxen, the dangling feet of the man, the whirling wheel-spokes, polished to a sheen by high grasses. The slats that form the sides are curved in the manner of a cradle and decoratively sculpted at the joints. Upon them rests a woven roof with the rounded profile of a pachyderm back and the advancing jut of a bird beak. To ford a river the oxen swim and the vehicle floats. Over the deepest ruts the entire assemblage slides along on its sledge-like framework, and the whole is held together by wooden joints or rattan, with no recourse to iron. The axle itself is the core of a hardwood trunk. The cart is man and forest joined together for transport.

This morning there were eight such carts in file—sixteen wheels: a choir. At the outset two axles broke into song, and as each cart shuddered into motion two new singers joined in, until finally all their tunes were rising with the dust. For hours and hours, rustling like the silken train of a garment, the convoy would snake through the torpor of the wilderness, from village to village, from one source of water to the next, from dawn to dusk, from south to north.

⚜ ⚜ ⚜

While the baggage was being loaded up, Ternier spoke Khmer with the ox-drivers, diligent and affably familiar in his use of their rustic language.

"All right, men. Ready? Where'd you get that helmet, man? Did you cross a cucumber with a potato and a hag's bosom?"

Every mouth agape and black in laughter.

"You, there! My word, what lovely oxen! Looks like you've saffroned their backs and varnished their legs! Mean draft animals—steadfast beneath the yoke and frank in the eye. Fine beasts—you and the oxen both. And you, my lad, standing there like a ninny, looks like you're setting out with a split hub! Huh? What's that you say? Been that way six months? Well, I don't intend to be around to see it fail, thank you very much. And your wheel! Why, it's a veritable polygon, that thing! Have you no shame showing up with a cart like that? Off with you! O Khmer! Khmer! Birdbrains to the end! And you, old man, with the salt-and-pepper head—how goes it?"

The governor whispered into the *résident's* ear.

"Your wife gave birth yesterday? At your age! Hope your friends are *good* friends!"

The man slapped his bare thigh with a guffaw. Ternier turned to Hélène.

"There you have it, my dear. Cambodia. Word of our coming has been spreading for a week. Everyone putting his best foot forward. Six of the eight carts we have called for are usable, and it is going to cost us an hour to find replacements."

The governor smiled and shook his head:

"The Khmer know nothing."

"A governor ought to know for them," Ternier brutally chimed in. "One does not summon a man who has just become a father. And furthermore, Governor, when requisitioning a cart one examines the wheels. Let this be a warning to you."

The governor bowed.

"You see, Madame," continued Ternier, stepping away with Hélène, "these men are peaceable in the extreme. Observe how they follow us about. What are they supposed to do? They do not know, so they walk. They were quite comfortable at home. They are setting out with us now because we have asked them to set out, because that is the way it is. They will eat anything at all, anywhere, or simply go without food. Perhaps one of their oxen, a chunk of their fortune, will up and die. Such is the will of Western man, whose purposes are not theirs, whose reasons are alien to a people lagging behind by centuries. We will pay them, of course, and they will have to submit to certain ground rules. What is certain is that the mandarins are unsparing in their treatment of the Khmer and more often than not exacerbate the rigors of Khmer servitude. Eight times out of ten a native would rather to deal with the *résident* than with the governor. Ah, here comes the doctor."

"What's this?" exclaimed Hélène, stupefied. "Are you going dressed like that?"

The doctor was clad in blue-striped pajamas and shod in old, bowless pumps. There was a rifle slung over his shoulder. His sleep-ridden eyes were but slits behind a pince-nez fogged with morning mist.

"My respects and apologies, Madame. This, in fact, is my explorer's costume. This rifle, which I always bring along, is for hunting, when the occasion arises. I hand it to a Cambodian and am thus guaranteed to injure no one and to bag some game, for I am a poor shot indeed. Now, then, take to your horses, you and the *résident*. I loathe the animals. One is exposed to the sun when riding, and I loathe the sun even more than I loathe horses. So I go by cart. Governor, where is my cart?"

"Here, Doctor."

"Come see, Madame. Isn't it lovely? A brand-new roof, finely woven and coated with resin. What more could one ask for?"

"But there's nowhere to sit in there!"

"One lies down, Madame; one lies down, and that is the beauty of it. Feel this kapok mattress. A marvel! And this excellent little pillow! Ah, you will envy me, you will be positively green with envy, atop your horse."

The doctor suddenly exclaimed:

"God in heaven! What have they fastened to the top of the roof, and with a good ten meters of rattan at least? My bag!"

He turned to the driver, who was wearing an uncomprehending smile, for the doctor was still speaking French:

"You wish me dead! Do you know what I have in that bag? My pad and handkerchief, my quinine, my antipyrine,[51] my watch, my magnifying glass, my pen, small change to throw to village children, my penknife, my cigarettes, my twine—and my Horace! My Horace[52] is in there! And that's not even the half of it, numbskull! And you go and tie it all up!"

The man remained stony faced.

"He doesn't give a damn! I beg your pardon, Madame, but that Cambodian doesn't give a damn!"

The *boy* came and put things to rights, the two new carts arrived, and everything was at last ready. The doctor took his place like a Merovingian king.[53]

Eight carts and sixteen wheels: amounting to a choir. With every cart that jolted into motion a new pair of singers joined in song. Dust was raised, and with it rose all the tunes.

⚜ ⚜ ⚜

By late morning they emerged from the rice fields and the path began twisting through glades. Hélène and Ternier rode up front, gaiter to gaiter, she slender as a young boy, he too big for his horse. So as not to wear out the horsewoman, it was agreed that they would gallop for only ten kilometers before the next stage. Up ahead walked two or three Cambodians, with long, elastic strides.

---

51 A non-steroidal anti-inflammatory and analgesic (painkiller and fever reducer) first synthesized in 1883.

52 Quintus Horatius Flaccus (65 BC – 8 BC), commonly known as Horace, Roman poet.

53 The Merovingian dynasty established a three-hundred-year rule over the Franks in the fifth century AD. The most famous of its kings, Clovis I (481–511), is remembered as the man who united Gaul (ancient France). The kingdom also included Belgium, Luxembourg, the Netherlands, and parts of Germany.

They were almost nude, having gathered their sampots very high on the thigh.

The plant life was so varied and shifting that their nudity did not so much stand out as blend in and take part. The polish of their skin was propitious to the play of light, which set the magnificent pedestrians agleam and bound them to the surroundings, for there is no dance more beautiful than the walk of bare-skinned man.

His changeable architecture is prestigious through and through. The shield-like convexity of the thorax and back, the twin weaponry of the arms, the legs propelling the marvelous machine. Attack, defense, and flight: of these elementary principles of human life naked man is the synthesis, and thus he belies wholesale the vain philosophy that issues from his brain. In the natural world, where in truth he amounts to no more than a stem, naked man need only appear, and all the primordial truths—initial happiness and the battles that secure it or ensue—people his shadow. Confidence and temerity clap a cuirass around the chest of naked man, though he suffer the scrapes of the forest's slightest vines. What sincerity, what loyalty can be more earnest and forthright than frank nudity? The weapon is plainly visible, gleaming in the sun. No deceitful finery, no cowardly protections, no hypocritical snares. In every way the adversary is faced with something elemental. At the center of his enemy's chest he can observe a beating heart. Framing the fragile chest is the defense and force of the limbs. Attack rolls like a wave through the muscles. The feet find silent purchase on the ground, with the slight expansion of suction cups, and stability quickly turns tenacious. An expedient foresight lies dormant in the hollows of the deft hands. And something else as well, liberty, radiates from the whole, which the very air sustains and smiles upon.

Ternier, seeing Hélène observe these men, said:

"These Cambodians are admirably built for paths and forests. They are the true bushmen—the *têtes noirs*, as urban Cambodians call them. They sniff out the cardinal points, observe the sky, point with a seemingly magnetic finger, and set out on foot. Their eyes can pick out the significant leaf among the leaves and spot the fleeing beast that you have failed even to notice. Where I see nothing they infallibly point out coiling rattan, vines that would make good rope, honeybee hives, the tracks of beasts whose names and shapes are unknown to us, trees that can provide hardwood or oil or resin, the leaves of edible or poisonous tubers. One spots them on the road pinpointing mysteries or scrutinizing a copse for things that serve them as clues. Their vigilant machetes are always in motion. To avoid getting lost they cut regular marks into trees. From the shape and color of clods of earth they can tell when it last rained. From color again they can tell the depth of a pond and how recently a caravan has used it as a watering hole. The shape of every kind of tree is fixed in their memory, with the season of the tree's flourishing, the bird species that feed on its fruit, and the medicinal properties of its leaves. They will not lift two stones in the same way, for one surely hides a scorpion and the other not...."

Thirty meters ahead a doe crossed the path, bounded a bit, stopped, lifted its head, watched the convoy approach, and, with a flap of its great ears, sprang off.

"Your rifle, Doctor! Your rifle!" cried Ternier.

"*Ohé, ohé!*" came a reply from the first cart. An arm brandishing the weapon raised the handkerchief that hung as a blind on the front edge of the roof. Ternier passed the rifle to one of the guides.

"And the cartridges?"

"The cartridges as well!" came the protest from the first cart. "Where the devil are the cartridges? *Boy! Boy!*"

"Yes, M'sieur!"

"Where put cartridges?"

"No cartridges."

"What do you mean no cartridges?"

"No, M'sieur. M'sieur no give."

⚜ ⚜ ⚜

Though the path wound through the wilds of a glade, men were constantly appearing by the group to enliven the scene. They would emerge in the distance and take up a post, as it were, grandly greeting the travelers as they passed. News of the *résident's* tour had spread for twenty kilometers all around, and the scattered villages had sent emissaries, in case they were needed. Here and there stood the idle, unhitched cart or two, and horses with rattan bridles. Elsewhere stood the chieftain of some circle of huts, come himself to offer the humble traditional tribute: a chicken, eggs, a bunch of bananas, or some coconuts. Ternier would accept, shake hands with the dignitary, and, if women and children were present, distribute new silver pieces. Hands would join and foreheads bow in thanks. Almost everywhere the emissaries would ask for quinine, in which case the doctor, still in his cart, would dispense the pills from bottles he had previously filled.

"They'll be the ruin of the state, these buggers. You there, take two or three more. There. And now off you go."

Ten times the same patriarchal ritual took place, in silence and peace. There was a curious confidence in the faces, a patient conscientiousness to the salaams. Each man had come to see, had waited, and now set off again. The caravan was already reaching the highlands, deep within the country, its sole defense a hunting rifle with no cartridges. But who was thinking of such things? Why think of them? The *résident* is inspecting the path. The order spreads by word of mouth. It is right and proper and sensible. Let's go see the *résident!* It seems there's a lady with him. And the forest was sunny and the path in good repair, for as soon as the order had spread they had filled the potholes, returned to their road tamping, pulled up the weeds, lest the *résident* raise a fuss.

They wait, rubbing their feet after a four-hour walk. Is it him? Not yet. A horseman will come ahead with the news. We can sleep. There he is! He's riding a horse! Is that the lady? No. It's a boy. I'm telling you it's the lady! Not so loud. Stand up straight! And the village chief, at the head of the group, drops to his knees, or, if a snob, doffs his soft hat and bends at the waist like a Frenchman. Well! Then the muddle of arrival. Noise and dust. The *résident's* said something. What did he say? The chant of the carts fades. It's all over. We've seen him. He's seen us. Those were our orders.

Each man puts his four or five quinine pills in a tin box, with his tobacco. Let's go! And they return to the village, in single file, the chieftain or group elder leading the way. Life is wonderful. Every conscience is at peace. Through the trees a nasal voice says:

OEung oeuy oeung oeuy...

The elephant swings his trunk,

And rocks the palanquin to and fro.

Swing your breasts, woman, to and fro!

The quivering breasts beneath your tunic.

Glades, nothing but glades. No rest for the eyes, no feature to bring them a little joy. Scattered trees, stunted and knotty. They have gray bark, no branches to speak of, and long, broad, thick leaves, wavy and firm, and covered in dust. A third of these leaves are turning green, a third are turning yellow, and a third are dropping off. Here and there, bleached trunks, knocked aslant against their neighbors by lightning. Termite-built cupolas of dried mud. Everywhere, young trees splitting the parched earth and culminating in downy or gummy buds. An unbroken carpet of dead leaves on a ground half-sand and half-clay, white or yellow as the case may be. Bitter sadness, harsh sunlight, shadows too small, too fleeting, and tattered. Every year a fire burns through the young growth and twists the trees that have achieved great height, stripping them down and clipping their momentum. Few birds, but bucks and does by the herd. No big cats; they would find insufficient cover. No coconut palms, or fronds of any kind. An interminable trek to the rich regions of the north, the great and sonorous forests of perpetual humidity, villages huddled onto some less-arid patch of earth, with a watercourse. And, out of nowhere, a gleaming rice field, and trees rising happy and tall.

Yet the hardy, supple path knows where it is going. Its discerning head has persevered through the desert, for its objective lies further on. It has snaked through this wasteland, mowing down the small trees in its way. It veers off to get around a bridge under construction. Like a tentacle it feels out the landscape, evading sand, hugging the marshlands, bypassing rock. At times it hesitates and doubles back. Error acknowledged, a felled tree bars the false start and the path sets out once more. It sinks to a hollow, swells to a ridge, merges with the surface of the earth. It retains as yet the relief of the terrain, though in time, when it has become stone, it will drive its way through the land with more authority, cutting through the obstacles that today it skirts. The sandstone blocks that the stone breakers will reduce to pebbles already stand at intervals at the roadside. Carts by the hundred will deliver more. These bridges are temporary, made as they are of scarcely planed trunks that sometimes sprout anew when replanted. In time a white arch, a span of iron and cement, will cross the stream. Metal wires, higher than the stunted trees of the glade, will line the path. Every thousand meters a stone will mark a stage of human progress. Already, in the friable matter of its indifferent body, the path contains the germ of the future.

⚜ ⚜ ⚜

It is one thing for the *résident* and the engineers to gather beneath a fan, iced lemon sode within reach, and trace a red line across a fanciful, incomplete map of regions as yet quite unknown. It is another to reproduce said line, in a five-meter swath, across the land itself. District after district the inhabitants turn out to fell trees and tamp down the earth. But who takes up the surveyor's glass to scope out the spot and lay down at the proper interval a red and white milestone? Who lives in this parched wilderness for as long as the path requires and will return to build the road? What man has already come through here, clasping a government order, to clear this astonishing trail?

Rummage through the files. Signature added to signature from office to office. The *résident*, having conducted a survey on horseback and questioned the inhabitant, has brought to light the needs of the region. He has ticked off the villages, located the rivers and quarries. Which *résident*? Tomorrow Ternier will be dead and his name effaced. Engineers have relied on bad maps for their studies. Since when? Since time unknown. Names are beside the point. Who in the litany will see the road? This road or another like it, nice and neat and flat, takes shape on a table. The map is folded in octavo and branded with the word APPROVED.

⚜ ⚜ ⚜

Hélène spotted a hut, the first since morning. It was built flush on the ground, with an adjoining courtyard. Piles of tools gleamed in the sunlight. At the foot of a tree was a wheel-mounted barrel, with a mongoose delousing itself upon one of its draft arms. There was linen laid out to dry on shrubs. Farther on stood the trestles of a forty-meter bridge, which spanned the ravine of a dry streambed. Natives were laying the bridge's planks. The ground around the construction site and the house was covered with woodchips and bark. The coolies had pitched their camp a hundred meters off. Chickens wandered sadly about in search of shade.

A Frenchwoman came before the *résident*. She was somewhat stout, with brown hair. A flounce hung free at the back of her faded blue peignoir. She wore espadrilles on her otherwise bare feet and a dirty helmet on her head.

"Well, now, Madame Carlaguet, how are you getting along?"

"Slow and steady, Monsieur le Résident."

She turned toward the house.

"Hey, Émile! Monsieur le Résident's here!"

Émile appeared, hatless and fastening the belt of his khakis. He was a strapping fellow with a haggard face and gentle blue eyes, his red hair aflame in the full-on sunlight. He made his way over to Ternier in a long-striding lope and proffered a hairy, freckled hand. Ternier introduced him:

"Monsieur Carlaguet, overseer of public works. It was Monsieur Carlaguet who made the path."

"That's the honest truth, Monsieur le Résident! Gadzooks. It ain't so much the path. We've got no water. Ever since we got to this damned bridge we have to go seven kilometers to fetch it."

"No rains yet?"

"A few storms, yes, but the land's too dry, drinks it all up. Not coming in for a spell?"

"No, no, Carlaguet. Thank you. We want to arrive before nightfall."

"Come on in, just for minute. It ain't going to hold you up. Just have yourselves some coconut milk. Ah, look who's here. Things still going your way, Doctor?"

"Greetings, Carlaguet."

"Good thing, you coming along. We've got no more quinine. It's not that we've got the fever, but it's touch and go sometimes, you know."

They entered the dwelling. Packed earth. A few items hanging from the bamboo partitions. Two shabby chests, with rounded lids, set on bricks in a corner. A bed beneath a dirty, raised mosquito net. A photograph in a seashell frame strung up at the bedside. It showed a little girl and two little boys, all dressed up in their Sunday best. On the table were bottles of Picon, Dubonnet, and

Cap Corse wine,[54] along with great stemmed glasses. A sugar bowl added a note of blue. The table legs stood in water-filled tins, on account of the ants. Carlaguet, a hunter, and evidently preparing souvenirs for his retirement, had hung up the legs of a wading bird, a python skin, a toucan head, deer antlers bundled like a fagot, and boar tusks.

"Not much of a castle," said Madame Carlaguet with an uncertain, bashful little smile. "Have a seat, Madame."

"We've only got two chairs, but no squabbling, now. *Boy! Boy!* Where's that scullion got to this time?" said the man, adding: "It's not like there's entertainments round these parts."

The *boy* came in.

"Chop the coconuts, slow poke! And don't be sticking your fingers in 'em!"

"And do you live here as well?" a terrified Hélène asked of Madame Carlaguet.

"Where else, Madame? What would I do with myself all alone at Sangkae? This way Émile and I are together. He don't get so bored, and neither do I."

"It's a filthy spot, as filthy spots go. It's on account of the bridge, Madame. Ain't it a sad business, building a bridge where there ain't no water? No way to sink the piles, the ground's so hard. And two months from now the water'll be flowing like the devil! Darned if it ain't galling."

"How long have you been working on the road?" asked the doctor.

"This one here, Doctor, we've been working at for eleventh months. But it ain't like this everywhere, and it gets better once it rains."

---

54 Picon is a bitters made of oranges, gentian (extract of the gentian flower), and quinine and traditionally added to beer. Dubonnet is a wine-based aperitif made with herbs and quinine. Cap Corse wine is wine from the northern cape of the island of Corsica.

"Indeed, Carlaguet," said Ternier in a soft voice, "that's more or less how things always are. If it isn't one thing, it's another. Why not drop by Sangkae every now and again?"

"What for, Monsieur le Résident? To drag the trunks along, and dress up in a white suit, and spend our money? The money's needed for the kids."

"We've got three children in France, Madame," said the overseer's wife. "It's expensive these days."

"Besides, we've grown accustomed—ain't that right, old girl! If only there was some water."

"Is it easy to get supplies?"

"Can't complain on that score. There's a cart from Sisophon twice a week. But, by God, to be building a bridge for more than a month and not have water enough to fill a thimble! If that don't beat all!"

"And the construction?"

"Moving along. But I'm almost out of bolts. Time they sent me some. And some empty drums. It's all on this paper here, the full list."

The *résident* took up the paper and asked:

"And the coolies?"

"They're all right, but they sure ain't in a hurry, them Cambodian sods. When it comes to moving dirt around no need to yell yourself hoarse, but the rest of the time...!"

"And you, Madame Carlaguet. Are you finding enough to keep you busy?"

"Well, Monsieur le Résident, it ain't exactly a courtly life, but I keep busy round the house. It passes the time, sure enough. If only we had a little water we could wash. And do the laundry!"

"Laundry's downright filthy," added her husband.

"If you need anything else, we'll be passing through again in four or five days. Think it over."

The convoy set out once more.

"What hearty people," said Hélène.

"There are many like them, toiling in anonymity. Not always easy to lead, but win them over and they will do as you please. They're nomads, almost always outdoors, camped out. They lead harsh lives, and that excuses much about them. It is they who really make the road…"

After a pause Ternier continued:

"…by hand, with their hands. They lodge in *salas*, or else in shelters like this one. Many of them, Madame, trade the road for the hospital. Their wives rarely follow them out here. In fact, most overseers are bachelors. They bring along a *congai*—a meager amusement. Thus they endure months of privation, in isolation, working in reflected heat on heaps of earth or stones, their needs approximately met in terms of supplies. They live a bit off the land, and off chicken and tinned food, and they spend almost nothing. And when they head back into town or to Phnom Penh, on leave, they go on a spree. Who could blame them? But in a week they've frittered away their savings. When you talk with them nothing is going right and everything is impossible, but in truth they can overcome anything. You think at first you're dealing with a mule, but in no time he's eating out of your hand. Had you run across him at a sumptuous villa, in some enchanted place, the valiant Carlaguet would have complained just as he does in this inferno. Had the stream been flowing Carlaguet would have complained of the water, maintained that we had started in on the bridge too late, and so on."

"Lousy water!" said Hélène, laughing.

"Lousy water, mucking up the construction of his bridge! And beneath those readily raised hackles: hearts of gold. Courageous people who would get down on their own hands and knees and work the bridge over with sandpaper, if necessary. They slave away and deprive themselves of every comfort for the sake of their children, to make sure they are properly brought up in France. Devoted servants who repudiate authority of any kind. No question, there are some dubious elements among them: ruffians and schemers who need watching. But ten Carlaguets suffice to redeem the whole guild. There is an obscure hint of the conqueror in their marrow. They have a lively intelligence, ingenuity, daring. In the great divide of life, however, fate sees them born on the side of obeisance. If they obey, they grumble subconsciously. They believe engineers are imbeciles, and that conviction eases their task. They take pride in the skill of their hands and their practical sense, and the fact is that they are quite often rather expert in their work. The studies for certain difficult roads were undertaken by one such man. He did it in the field, walking through the forest or on a mountainside. He would find the only possible passes and thus set down a remarkable route."

⚜ ⚜ ⚜

A further two hours' progress through the changeless landscape brought this stage of the travelers' journey to a close. The *sala* came into view in the middle of a meticulously weeded, well-packed plot. A path lined with young, freshly planted cycas led up to the vast, cross-roofed structure. It was open at the center and built directly on the ground, but flanked left and right with bedrooms built on piles. These bedrooms were made entirely of bamboo, rattan, and thick thatch. Their partitions were finely woven and bound with ligature to the columns. The doors turned in wooden sockets. In each room a forked, bark-covered bough served as a coatrack and an earthen jar held water for washing. At the center was a framed trellis and four vertical posts on which to hang a mosquito net, the whole forming a more than sufficient bed.

The inhabitants of the village that lay some five hundred meters ahead were hurrying over. Coolies brought bundles of grass, for the horses, and water in resin-caulked baskets. While the carts were unloaded Ternier extended the customary greetings and accepted the chickens, coconuts, and eggs. Two men, led by the village chief, came to offer a roe deer that had been snared in a net, its throat slit and its legs bound to a spit. The doctor handed out quinine and set off a footrace among the children by tossing coins every which way. Indigenous women, drawn by the first European woman they had ever seen, formed a circle around Hélène. An old, bare-chested woman, dusty and pathetic, with a shaven head, hanging pouches for breasts, and hollows beneath her cheeks, took a seat before her, smiled, and cautiously took her hand. She turned the fine, long, milk-white hand in her own hands, which were gray and as knotty as vine cuttings.

Entering her room Hélène saw that the folding mattress had been covered with a fine mat, her trunk had been set on a rack, towels had been hung, her bag had been laid on a table, and a bunch of orchids, with winged flowers, had been hung from one of the columns. The woven shutter of a window opened like a skylight pane, and the light of a low afternoon sun filtered in. A coral-tailed lizard scampered off.

The two men settled in the other wing. Madame Gassin could hear the perpetually cheerful doctor in full-throated song:

Madame à sa tour monte

Mironton, mironton, mirontaine...[55]

He paused to reassure his audience through the partitions:

---

55 Lyrics to the French folk tune *"Malbrough s'en va-t-en guerre."* "Madame" here is the wife of John Churchill, first Duke of Marlborough, who has gone to fight in Flanders, never to return. She climbs to the top of her watchtower to scan the horizon for him. Marlborough died at the Battle of Malplaquet, in the War of the Spanish Succession, which pitted Spain and France against Great Britain, the United Provinces (the old Dutch Republic), and Prussia. The tune is thus a burlesque recounting the death of an enemy nobleman.

"Have no fear, Madame. I sing in the bath. It is a pathognomonic[56] phenomenon whose cause has always been unknown to me. And it's always the same tune!"

He soon stopped singing, signaling thereby that he was cleansed.

✤ ✤ ✤

Such was the way station. The humblest, most remote, most wretched village keeps a house open for wayfarers. It is often the loveliest and cleanest of the houses, the *sala*, completely refurbished once word of the *résident*'s coming arrives. The site is carefully selected. It must enjoy the shade of lovely trees and be near some water, whether pond, well, or watercourse. The hotter the day and the wearier the journey on the road, the greater its charms ought to appear. Happy are those who abide by tradition and work toward the soothing congeniality of that house for which the traveler yearns after a full day's hike.

The traveler spies the house suddenly. The gate, the bamboos, the trodden earth where the oxen linger. His eyes burn from the savannah; his body aches from the lurch of the vehicles, his back from the jolt of the horse. His soul is fraught with the sadness of the glades, and suddenly there is a grassy lawn, an open house, still water in a jar for a relaxing bath. The village chief has laid his best mat on the planking. What is this calm, this quiet? The carts have come to rest, their steady orison reduced at last to silence. Cockcrows, the cooing of turtledoves. Axe blows amid the palms, clangs in the sky, detach coconuts that are brought to you in tribute. Voices…

One scarcely takes note of this envelopment before the unyoked carts blur and fade, and the moon's glow, if it is "moonshine week," washes over the trees. The ox-drivers make their rounds, and in turn each tired ox lies to the side, legs drawn up close, just as

---

56 I.e., typical of a given disease.

the skilled Khmer of the heroic age sculpted them for Shiva to straddle.[57] And night falls.

❖ ❖ ❖

When she emerged from her room Madame Gassin found an acetylene lamp in the middle of the *sala*. The tableau it lit up filled her with surprise. Aluminum utensils gleamed like silver upon an orchid-fringed tablecloth. There were champagne glasses paired with tumblers and a written menu. Mustard, pickles, toothpicks— no accessory had been neglected. The folded napkins rose to a point like a bishop's mitre. From a tie-beam above the table hung a broad, woven punkah, its cord dangling. The two men, dressed in white tuxedos, each with a propeller of frangipani for a boutonnière, rose ceremoniously to their feet.

"We wished, the doctor and I, to give you a surprise, Madame. Just as you knew to pack that charming dress, we wished not to spend all our time in khaki."

"Or in pajamas, Madame," added the doctor, "especially this evening."

"Especially this evening, for today you take your first steps into the wilderness, the true wilderness, and are going to spend your first night in it. An inaugural dinner, then. I hope you are not too tired."

"Not at all, but I am taken aback."

"This is a very simple affair. The trappings that so surprise you have caused us no trouble, nor required a single additional trunk. The order was quite simply given to the *boy*. I insisted for other reasons. As you will be returning to France, you will be able to say that you have penetrated the remotest and most deserted regions of Cambodia, and will thus be in a position to rebut all the nonsense

---

57 In Khmer Hindu mythology, deities are associated with a mount or Vahana (literally "that which carries or pulls") for mobility. The reference above refers to Shiva's mount, Nandi the bull, while Vishnu rode upon the legendary humanoid bird Garuda, and Brahma rode on Hamsa the sacred goose.

going around over there about the wilderness of Indochina in general and of Cambodia in particular. Above all, know that you are taking part in nothing unusual. Like me, an ordinary citizen can find a *sala*, anywhere, open to him free of charge. Like me, he can hire all the carts he needs, and at the same price. Like me, he has a *boy* and a cook. Like the doctor, he can go about in pajamas, with or without a rifle. For any citizen who comes to my province, be he a civil servant or not, I give the same instructions for his welcome. There are, no doubt, some arduous, tiresome treks; there are violent storms, depending on the season; in certain places there are mosquitoes and leeches. Absolutely. It is nevertheless true that in France, in France's forests, it rains and it snows, and one can be stung by bees or annoyed by bugs…"

"At any rate," interrupted the doctor, "I prefer this *sala* to an inn, even one with a Touring plaque.[58] Look at that tablecloth! Look at those orchids! They grow in abundance on the trunks of the sugar palms."

"And the Cambodian night!" added Ternier.

"And that perpetual sense of tranquility among these dedicated people."

"Just as you say, Madame. Look at them setting up their camp. Think those cart drivers are going to sleep, though from morning they have spent their day driving a beast from the precarious perch of a draft shaft?"

"I think it more likely they doze while doing that," said Maillard, "to judge by certain jolts we must endure…"

"Their race is not subject to time the way ours is. The nights are too beauteous and delectable to miss, and these people live them— at least until it gets too late and the mist rolls in."

In the light of woodchip-and-resin torches Hélène could but vaguely make out the camp. The instant an ox stirred a reassuring

---

58 A recommendation from the old Touring Club of France.

human whistle would sound. A flagging fire was revived with the
insertion of a branch between the three surrounding hearth stones.
Now and again the men exchanged remarks, rose, went for a drink,
ate a dried fish breaded in ash, and smoked. They rose to their silent
bare feet and walked around with the air of priests or confidants,
their bodies haloed in ochre or lit by the glacial luminary, which,
round and domed like a breast, poured its mystic milk over the
contours of their muscles.

⚜ ⚜ ⚜

The three travelers daydreamed, waiting for dinner to be ready;
all three communing, whatever the difference in the state of their
souls; each lost in an exotic moment that eclipses all others, in the
solemn beneficence of the twilight divinities, who rise together
from the trees and land to lay their hands on the sun. It is in places
like this, in the tropics, far from the rest of the world, that one must
lend an ear to what these divinities say.

You have escaped your routine. You have slipped your yoke. You
have set aside convention to see something else. You have come
to grips with your own poverty. You have freed yourself from
clasping arms, so as to grow. Free! You have sought to be free! You
have understood that your talent, whatever it is, breathes the same
atmosphere as all the other talents of your generation. Nature lies
dead between your cities; here it reigns supreme. In your world man
remains forever remote beneath the many masks he borrows; here
man is naked, and in the richness of his nudity stands in opposition
to you, who are so often void beneath your artifice. Here bitter,
violent day prepares the way for sweet, fresh night better than
the shadow of your prisons ever could. All is logically sound that
follows the rhythm of the land and the light, and you seek only to
befoul that rhythm. But here at least the rhythm reproves you, and
by taking it up you can gauge the cost of your repudiation.

Look yonder at your "evening star," which here they call the
"village star." Have you ever seen it so bright? That sound just

beginning to build and just reaching your ear is the song of an orchestra, for on moonlit nights the village turns to music and breathes out the tenderness in its heart. How many ten-house villages back where you come from sing in this manner, even on a fine summer night? How many greet the traveler by opening a house prepared and meant just for him? Take heed if you scrutinize your knowledge and wisdom here, at this hour, amid this ambiance, lest you by your own hand cause cracks to appear. Take heed if you compare what the centuries have wrought here against what those same centuries have wrought back home, where you were raised. Are you sure it has been all that wise forever to be adding and expanding, rather than cutting back, stripping away, paring down? Whoever you are, and whatever your god, here, at these hours, you are inescapably a man of God. You are not the man of some other man.

Hélène turned to look at Ternier, who was placidly smoking his short pipe. Well ensconced in his seat, legs crossed, hair still wet from his bath, he looked like a modern athlete at rest—and not one whose nose had been busted by a punch worth twenty-five thousand dollars gold. The builder, the creator, the already graying man who can spend a day on horseback or aboard a junk, or swim across an arroyo. An athlete at rest upon a track laid down on his order. Satisfied, prideful, steeling his resolve and replenishing his forces for the morrow in the beneficence of this vast hour. He struggles unarmed against an entire country. Better than armed, he is zealous. He has erected house after house, one beside the next, and thus raised a city, and is preparing now to raise another, when the time comes, at the terminus of this road. He awaits that moment, hungers for it, and he will prompt it, juxtaposing our civilized ways and the magisterial liberty of the country, daring to attempt the blend, the double transfusion of blood. He is taking the lesson and applying it, and seeks not to be the only one. He has no wish to advance alone into the realms of force and new cultures. He wants to be followed in. But, being of a generous breed, and made more generous still by nights like this, he wants us to advance faster than he, with greater confidence, more easily. And he is clearing the way.

Ternier looked at Madame Gassin, but she closed her eyes at the same instant.

"Let's dine," he said, and rose.

❧

XII
Nature, Civilization, and Death

At midday on the morrow they entered Svay Chèk, the next to last town on the itinerary. A broad river crept drowsily over a sandy bottom. With breakfast being prepared and Ternier transacting some business with the governor, Hélène and the doctor walked through the village. A dozen Chinese merchants had already set up shop along the future road. Among the establishments was a cookshop at the junction of the river and the wooden bridge, half of it rooted to the embankment, the other half cantilevered over the river.

Hélène entered the lair. Having come in from the dazzle of the sunlight, she could at first make out only luminous yellow water, visible through the gaps in the plank floor. Later, growing accustomed to the darkness of the hut, with its patina of kitchen smoke and luster of genuine Chinese grime, she took stock with her companion of what lay within. On a shelf, bottles of beer and lemon soda framed a display of soaps, small spoons, and tinned preserves. Like a besieging army the red and black creepy-crawlies of written Chinese scaled the packages of tea. Bundles of propitiatory incense sticks, sheathed in vermillion, sat next to stacks of piss-colored tumblers, boxes sown shut with garters and peppered with fly droppings, and a few jugs of rice alcohol. There were yet corkscrews, sticks of chalk, porcelain saucers embellished with blue designs, cigarettes, several cans of California fruits. A rare bird in a jar, preserved as it was like a serpent on a museum shelf, caught the doctor's fancy. All of this lay behind doors destined someday to receive their panes of glass; for the moment they were mere shut frames. On the ground, separating the shop from the bridge, was a stand arrayed with mushrooms, chewing lime, onions, peppers, fruits, and crudely colored cakes, the whole of it humming beneath a shroud of flies.

The proprietor was preparing meals for natives, and for travelers as well. All of them were squatting in wait on bamboo chairs. He writhed about in silhouette between the chopping block and the pots. So diaphanous against the light of day was his little blue- and black-checked loincloth that the shade of tremulous testicles came into view with every parting of his legs. The man bled a cock onto the parquet, amid scraps sent flying by the flapping of the death throes. After the plucking and the gutting he prepared the cock with a knife and hung it on a hook. Against the incoming light the carcass seemed a hunk of coral.

A common crow with a broken wing wobbled atop the bamboo pinnacle of another shop, the wind pushing it off balance and ruffling its feathers. Some children had gathered on the bridge to observe the two Europeans. One of them, a boy sitting astride a girl's hip, was hollering on account of the burning, suppurating wound on his leg, where flies had settled for a drink.

The cook's wife, a Sino-Cambodian mix with a loose chignon on her nape, followed Hélène around like a sleepwalker, her eyes half-closed and her triangular face set in a sad, sphinxlike expression. Two pendulous breasts would sag into the silk of her tunic when she leaned forward. A cat stretched and scampered off, and the Chinaman wiped his chopping block and cleavers. The grayish, balled-up rag he used was damp with greasy water and looked like a tripe *paquet.*[59]

---

59 As in the French dish *pieds et paquets* (literally feet and pouches), usually comprising sheep shank and sheep offal wrapped in tripe.

"Antisepsis[60] will be long in coming," lamented the doctor.

As they emerged from the shop their eyes were drawn to the far bank, where they followed a climbing bougainvillea to the roof of a vast house. The flowers, as plentiful as the leaves, lay like a cloth of madder violet, glacial and profoundly sad, however luxuriant and sunlit. In the background, against the white sky, stood a curtain of arecas and bamboos.

⚜ ⚜ ⚜

Mixture of races and eras. A familial humanity spilling out into the street, and half living there. Interiors permeated by the landscape. A centuries-old commingling of everything with everything else. A traditional Chinese sign, in gold-flecked, vermillion paper, and beside it a patent letter with the arms of the French Republic on its seal. Khmer eating Chinese cuisine. Annamites. Siamese. Where are we? Deep inside Cambodia. What do we see? A sordid shop where European merchandise will not sell. A cholera-dispensing shop. Men and women of various races siring children in a garden greenery fit for legend, where the light of the heavens threads its way through palm fronds.

Out in the wilderness, far from the most inconsequential hut, while everything—sand, grass, tree in bloom—faints in the delirious sun, and the cicadas rend their brass, and an eagle wheels at the zenith, there can arise the deep, pungent reek of carrion rotting somewhere nearby. Nature, civilization, and death. It is a commonplace phenomenon, with a well-sifted philosophy behind it, but you urge your horse past the effluvium, past the morbid mixture; you look to the treetops and exclaim: No wonder you're so tall and green, and lovelier than the rest of us, you stoics you!

⚜ ⚜ ⚜

An hour later the glade had once again overtaken the convoy on the still-northbound path. The land developed a mild relief,

---

60 Any procedure to promote the destruction of pathogenic organisms causing infection.

which began ranging the trees into stages. They crossed a patch of laterite.[61] The path turned red and rough, strewn as it was with blocks of spongy rock. It next ran alongside a wall of thick forest, into which a herd of deer melted away. The screech of the cicadas grew louder still. Below gleamed a pond. Ternier pointed out to Hélène a path that linked the pond and the forest through the tall grass, and had been laid down by big cats in the night. White specks, motionless egrets, peppered the water. Then the big trees thinned out and the glade retook the landscape.

That evening's stop, Thma Pouok, was much like the previous one: the big *sala*, the curtain of coconut palms, the women filing to the well with lacquered, leaf-covered baskets, the nocturnal orchestra, and the constellated, troat-filled[62] night.

____

61 Laterite is a type of rock that appears red because it is rich in oxides of iron and hydroxide of aluminum. When mined below the water table, moist laterite can easily be cut into blocks with a spade. On exposure to air and sun the blocks harden making them ideal for construction. The Khmer used the stone extensively for walls and temple structures, then covering the rougher laterite blocks with sandstone for a finished appearance.
62 I.e., filled with the troating, the guttural call, of deer and stags.

XIII
The End of the Path

The doctor, chatting with her as they set out on the morrow, noticed something: an expression of anguish washing over Hélène's features as she saw that her horse was being led over. She walked to it and was soon in the saddle.

The party stopped for lunch at the gates of the great temple of Banteay Chhmar,[63] abandoned centuries ago to the forest, and ravaged by it. They were to visit the temple the following day, on the way back, for the end of the path, with its *sala* for the night, lay no more than three hours off.

They soon reached the great forest and went in. The trunks of felled trees lined the path on both sides. Soft, covered with dead leaves, and but speckled with sunlight, the path itself seemed to be at rest, reveling in the humidity and cool toward which it had so long been tending. With a ten-minute gallop the song of the carts

---

63 One of the largest temples built under the reign of Jayavarman VII in the late 12th or early 13th century. Groslier first visited the site in 1914 and made the first trip there by auto in 1924 giving him the first-hand knowledge needed for this book. Groslier also completed the first detailed surveys of the site and his research there was unparalleled until modern efforts began in 2007.

See *In the shadow of Angkor: unknown temples of ancient Cambodia*, DatAsia Press, 1914, which includes Darryl Collins' article "Banteay Chhmar: First Automobile Visit by Groslier in 1924." Devata.org features an online translation of Groslier's 1937 article, "Une merveilleuse cité khmere–Banteay Chhmar." For a comprehensive look at the temple see Peter Sharrock's 2015 book, *Banteay Chhmar: garrison-temple of the Khmer empire.*

dwindled to silence. To quiet the squeak of hooves on the dead leaves as well, Ternier brought his horse to a halt. Motionless, he and Hélène listened.

The trees, most with white trunks, had grown fast and straight in their struggle for sky. Vines chained them together. One does not at first notice the great silence of the forest, but once "heard" it becomes monumental, astonishing. It seems to flow in through all the senses at once. It becomes an imponderable walled citadel around every thing and every creature, gigantic tree and creeping ant alike. It is not the land fallen into silence, nor an absence of birds or a stillness. No. The silence is positive, a presence. It saturates the atmosphere and molds one's steps. It seems one might part it like a curtain and suddenly hear the forest speak its huge, rational murmur, as if one were emerging from a cave into a crowd.

To be present amid this formidable, incessant life, at the center of an orchestra churning out this most tumultuous of scores, at the heart of a world where birth, death, and digestion grind and chew, where creature and plant snatch like hands; to be right nearby as a tree makes its myriad gestures to reach skyward and combat fellow tree, while at its feet, on its trunk, in the pasty humus through which it drives its roots, the insects work with pincer, leg, wing, and oviduct; to suppose here or there the coiling-uncoiling menace of a reptile or perhaps the skulking of a great cat as it prepares to pounce—and to hear none of it! To perceive a rumble with the mind while cries of joy, pain, and terror fade and die out on the rim of every pore, on the lips of every mouth…

What sort of place is this vacant forest? Birds are rare. Every movement is hidden or vanishes into the surroundings. Nowhere here does the sun manifest that *joie de vivre* in which the glades and the riverbanks and the plains bathe. Disquieting stillness. It seems a cathedral of peace and beatitude, whereas in fact it is a battleground atop a charnel house. In addition to curved thorns the hanging bough carries ants, red and warlike. The tree trunk, dead or alive, is gnawed at. On close inspection a piece of brushwood and a dead leaf are each revealed to bear an insect lying in wait, one shaped like brushwood, the other ruddy like the dry leaf.

In these season-less climes autumn leaves meet springtime. Bedecked with flowers and seeds, the trees simply shed. Dead branches and red leaves fall at every time of year from a vibrant greenery. There is, moreover, a battle raging between vine and tree. One sees the latter twisted by an octopus, bent into a flying buttress. It swells where it is free and doubles its trunk to get away, then is snared once more and tied up by tender green cords that sink into the bark and make the resin spurt. The cords follow the tree if they cannot kill it, go as high as the tree does, and from that height fall in victory, fragile and decked out in white-veined leaves, limp and peaceably spiraling. And the tree, undergoing its death throes or repelling the assault of its tenacious adversary, recalls a woman twisting her hair in lamentation.

No sunlight, or, at best, scattered patches of it sullied by lichen, the blackish rot of the ground. No way out. Everywhere a changeless horizon, a senseless horizon, for lack of a sky, and because the top is as thick as the bottom. An interminable, chaotic colonnade of trees in the distorted clarity of an aquarium. Vines and shrubs entwined; ragged spider webs weighed down with their detritus; a rope-yard of dead rattan and branches haunted by no bird, as it brooks no flight.

Nothing in this staggering greenhouse suggests the time of day or separates dawn from twilight. It is baffling to think that the immutable day bathing the atmosphere could emanate from the sky, a sky mottled by a thousand leaves when glimpsed at all. Everything glitters with a dew that never evaporates, and which wets the legs like a marshland. Few flowers, and most of them white, with tissue-paper petals. But the orchid is everywhere, radiant on the ground, dangling lacy[64] leaves, clamping monstrous

---

64 Groslier writes of orchid leaves *à badrbe d'écrevisse* (literally "in the manner of crawfish barbels"). The term once denoted a frilly shoe popular in the time of French humanist and writer François Rabelais (*c.* 1494–1553) and mentioned in his novels.

baptismal fonts onto tree trunks. At brief intervals it displays pale, clustered blooms, chalices in the shape of galley hulls, brown-speckled clogs stagnant with larvae-filled water.

❖ ❖ ❖

The horses set out once more. And suddenly the path came to an end. A tree trunk had been felled across the way. A red and white milestone marked the axis of the last surveyor sighting. Opaque forest lay ahead. A footpath led off to the *sala*, visible in a clearing some thirty meters to the right. Ternier alighted. Pale and bent double over her horse, her eyes sunken, Hélène said:

"So we've come to the end of the path!"

"Of this stretch, yes. This is where we stopped this year. Next year we will push on."

"So everything comes to an end here," Hélène repeated in a spent voice, eyes fixed on the curtain of trees.

She turned around with difficulty. The path behind her had cut a tunnel through the forest. The Cambodians who had come along were squatting in wait. The horses were still, heads low. Twilight fell.

Pointing with his crop toward the forest the path had run up against, Ternier said, "Here an effort comes to an end. Carlaguet came here to set up that sign. The place is heavy with significance, is it not, Madame? I see from your distress that you have seized upon them. In sum, we have reached the end of our ideas. The twenty centuries of our civilization come to a dead stop here, at this milestone. But they form a buttress. Beyond lies the unknown—everything we seek and desire, and thus what we must obtain. We will go! The mind hesitates still, but along the open path the reinforcements of intelligence are coming up behind us. And with them: action. The scout will take a further leap forward once action has caught up. And we will enter new territories, territories that correspond to our present ignorance.

"Having reached this hinterland…," said Hélène, who seemed not be listening, "what if we cannot go farther?"

"What would prevent us from going farther?"

"What if the unknown lay not in front of the road, in the forest that's barring the way…but…to the right and left of the road…? Yes, in the land that the road's already crossed…without your having…"

"But, what's the matter, Madame?"

Hélène was unsteady in the saddle. Her face was a mask of suffering. She bent forward and pressed her hands to her belly. Ternier leapt to her side and caught her in his arms.

He held her like a child. She thanked him with a pitiable smile.

"It's nothing… I'm just tired, a bit tired…"

With great strides Ternier made his way to the *sala*. Cambodians had gathered there, with flutes and a tom-tom. When they saw him emerge from the footpath the orchestra started up. He sought to silence it.

"Let them," said Hélène.

He laid Hélène out on a rattan bed and placed a damp handkerchief on her forehead. She said nothing and lay motionless, hands still crossed over her belly. The flute sang tenderly. The tom-tom, regularly and softly struck, provided a buzzing accompaniment to the rather tart melody. At last the carts arrived with the doctor. Ternier went out.

"What's this? Are we not being a good girl?"

"No, Doctor."

He examined her at length, saying nothing. A fever of 39.5°,[65] nose pinched, eyes sunken and ringed, abdomen hard to the touch,

---

65 About 103° Fahrenheit.

sharp pain in the right pelvic cavity, McBurney's sign, pastiness under the fingers.

"You felt nothing on our departure from Sangkae?"

"No, Doctor."

"Tell me everything, Madame, I beg you. No knot of pain on the right before we set out?"

"No, Doctor."

"You felt the first pains while riding the horse?"

"Yes."

"When?"

"This morning."

"And you stayed in the saddle all day? Utterly careless! Why didn't you say anything?"

"Because."

Madame Gassin lay by the light of a portable lamp, eyes closed and face twisted into a grimace. The doctor thought it pointless to torment her and gently removed her clothes. The slightest movement put her in agony. She said:

"My God, what a burden I've become to you…! You won't be singing *"Malbrough s'en va-t-en guerre"* this evening, my poor friend…"[66]

A bed was prepared in another room of the *sala*, and the doctor carried her there wrapped in a bathrobe. She asked for her big, green leather bag and placed it between her pillow and the partition. The interpreter brought the first-aid kit.

"Madame, you must remain absolutely still, on your back. Let nothing in the world entice you to move. No cause for alarm."

---

66 "Marlborough Has Left for the War", also known as *Mort et convoi de l'invincible Malbrough* ("The Death and Burial of the Invincible Marlbrough"), is one of the most popular folk songs in French since its appearance the end of the 18th century.

"I know what I have, Doctor."

"Fatigue, some soreness," he said, trying to reassure her.

"No, Doctor. Appendicitis. I'm not afraid."

"You've already been through a bout, then?"

"Yes, when I was seventeen. They didn't operate."

"And they didn't warn you not to tire yourself out, and especially not to ride horses?"

"Yes, Doctor."

"Well, then, you know the treatment. You're going to be a good little girl there and not move an inch. No ice to be had out here, so we're going to apply the opposite: a cataplasm of very hot rice. It'll be nothing at all, just like last time, and tomorrow it'll all be over, eh?"

"Yes, Doctor. It'll all be over, perhaps."

The doctor went to find Ternier.

"Very serious, my friend. Easy diagnosis: acute appendicitis, a relapse. We'll see tomorrow. To be frank, I fear we have a case of peritonitis[67] on our hands. She's been in pain since this morning. Tomorrow it'll be two days; the next, three. The aggravation, if it's going to occur, won't make itself known until tomorrow at the earliest. It's just that I don't like the look of her features, and her temperature's too high for plain-old appendicitis. How could she have stayed on her horse since this morning? I wonder. She's evidently made a superhuman effort to get through the day, and thereby aggravated the crisis…if she hasn't added complications. What's she got under her skin, that little woman?

"Can we move her?"

---

67 A painful inflammation of the peritoneum, the tissue that lines the inside of the abdomen and covers the abdominal organs, caused by infection from bacteria or fungi. If untreated, peritonitis can rapidly spread into the blood (sepsis) and to other organs, resulting in multiple organ failure and death..

"No. If all she has is appendicitis, let's allow it to settle down by keeping her on a strict fast and absolutely immobile. There's nothing better we can do. If there are complications, going back won't change anything."

"What are you saying?"

"I'm saying what I'm saying. Because otherwise we'll have no choice but to operate immediately. And all I've got with me is an absurd little first-aid kit. Let's be reasonable. Today is Thursday. If all goes well, we can set out tomorrow night, with a well-suspended stretcher. It's easy enough. We march day and night, arrive at Sangkae two days later; that's Sunday afternoon. There we operate or not. But transport her now and she might develop complications on the way, and surgery will be impossible, for lack of water. That is not the solution, my friend."

"What, then?"

"It wouldn't take you any longer to get to Sangkae and back, would it?"

"No, certainly not. If I change horses midway, I could get there by noon tomorrow and be back in the evening two days from now."

"Then off you go. I'm going to give you a list of the instruments I'll need. You'll bring them to me. That way we'll save ourselves transport and a day, and we'll be ready to intervene."

❖ ❖ ❖

Night fell. At about eleven o'clock Maillard went to see Hélène. Not asleep, she was gazing upward. Her fever had worsened.

"Listen to me, Doctor. I assure you I'm perfectly lucid. If I die, bury me here, here in this wonderful forest, by the side of the road. I don't wish to be taken away. Swear to me…"

"That I swear, Madame. Now, *you* swear to *me* that you will keep your spirits up."

"I have more spirit than you suppose."

After a moment's silence she asked:

"Where is Monsieur Ternier?"

"He'll be back. He's been called away to…"

"Yes. That's right. And he'll be back soon, no?"

"Yes, Madame, of course. Don't speak, now."

"In an hour, say?" She looked at the doctor with a desperate smile. "What a lousy doctor you make. Don't even know how to lie. Besides, you can hear everything through these partitions, you know…"

She cut herself off to reflect carefully, then spoke once more, closing her eyes:

"Everything. You can hear everything. One day, two days. So many kilometers. We'll do this, that. Not a word of compassion. And he's up and gone…!"

She spoke plaintively, in a monotone. She opened her eyes, revealing a gleam of fright.

"Is he sure to find me still alive when he gets back? And yet he's left without even saying goodbye. The minutes are too precious. Mustn't lose one pressing a hand. Wouldn't be a man of action anymore, would we, if we gave in to a little tenderness. Must act! Act! As if we always knew where action led…"

"You are mistaken. On the contrary, Ternier wanted to spare you the anguish that an explanation of his urgent departure might cause…"

"Couldn't he have come see me without mentioning it? No. It didn't even cross his mind. He just left. That's all. Nothing more…"

The doctor was going to reply. She stopped him with a wave of her hand. So he opened his kit, sterilized a syringe with a flame, broke open a phial.

"What's that?"

"A little morphine to help settle you down and calm that feverish brain."

Afterwards he buckled the straps of his medical bag and pushed it up against the partition. Gazing strangely through half-closed eyelids, Hélène had watched his every move.

XIV
A Philosopher Turned God

A triumphal dawn prompted long, plaintive cries from the howler monkeys. The veils of morning mist dropped away, and the sunlight crept down to the ground from the treetops. The clearing and the *sala* were filled with a ravishing light. Pastel-blue smoke rose from the hearths. Men awoke, stretching their brass-hued nakedness in the lush morning cool. All was promise and youth.

Ternier spurred his new mount, acquired at Thma Pouok. Peacocks and wild roosters fled at his approach. In the glade as in the forest the enchanted morning spread her violets. Paphnutius too once hastened thus, because Thaïs lay dying.[68]

The leaves had a nacreous sheen under the plenteous dew of the tropics. On every side there was sweetness and nonchalance,

---

68 I.e., the Egyptian Anchorite hermit Paphnutius and the courtesan Thaïs, both of fourth-century Roman Egypt and both since beatified. It is said that Thaïs was converted to Christianity by a monk who visited her in disguise. He is identified variously as St. Paphnutius, St. Bessarion, or St. Serapion. (The supposed remains of Thaïs and Serapion were exhibited at the Musée Guimet, in Paris, at the turn of the twentieth century.) Thaïs spent the next few years in a convent and died shortly after reemerging into the world. In the tenth-century play *Paphnutius*, by Benedictine canoness Hrotsvitha of Gandersheim, Paphnutius is the instrument of conversion and Thaïs repents by burning four hundred pounds of gold and treasure. In Anatole France's novel *Thaïs*, however, Paphnuce (gallicised spelling) effects the conversion but is captivated by the beauty of Thaïs and undergoes a reverse conversion himself. As she lies dying and begins to glimpse heaven he tells her that faith is an illusion.

all of it indifferent to the galloping horse. Just about everywhere in these parts death had paid a visit this night. The panther had disemboweled a stag, the python had strangled an agouti,[69] and the toad had had its fill of grasshoppers. Sap had stopped rising in branches, causing flowers to fall. Clouds of mayflies had lost their wings, and night herself, with all her celestial bodies, had perished.

Speed along your road, then, conqueror. At this moment the doctor is measuring in the patient's damp armpit forty degrees[70] of fever. She has begun to vomit, and he no longer doubts that the dreaded aggravation has developed. Why? Because human acts have unforeseen consequences. Your manful pride goaded you south to north along that path, to conquer, and now look at you, scurrying north to south to make amends. Amends for what, exactly? I who am telling this story, who know the ins and outs of these matters, the cause and the end of the events that you are struggling through, I who know what "that little woman's got under her skin"—I tell you that Hélène is going to die.

It is she who will die today, and who perhaps ought logically to take her leave. She is an effort that has overcome another effort— the fall after creation. Indeed, she is perhaps the very soul, the secret flower, of the region that your plowshare has cleared. Who knows? Can you claim with certainty that nothing in your path has been trampled or destroyed? No, you cannot. So with your conscience clean and your scruples intact and your lofty sense of duty, with your noble projects and clairvoyance, you have in fact killed the woman, killed her with your bare hands. Is that not so? For tonight she will die. These are the facts. If you refuse to accept what I am leading you to intuit, you will soon understand these causes for yourself, when you in turn learn the way of things. We think we act in isolation, but we are all symbols. Think back on something Hélène told you one day: that a woman is not always

---

69 A type of rodent, similar to but larger than a guinea pig.
70 104° Fahrenheit.

her own mistress. And, often, events that we think are isolated and unrelated turn out to be one another's cause.

Your road crosses a region, and like an arrow pierces to the heart. Onto the road the automobile manufacturer will dispatch his machines. But the crossed region will strike at his heart as well. The first Roland-Gassin to roll past, northbound, will drive toward a tomb, and there will no doubt be a widower at the wheel. At every one of those bridges a toll has been and will be exacted.

A philosopher turned god rules over these parts. He instructs his bonzes to watch where they set their feet, lest they crush an insect; to drink through muslin at the spring, lest they swallow the animalcules. Illusions! Vain and puerile injunctions! Walk as carefully as you like; you will still crush the cricket hid away in a burrow you do not see. Animalcules too tiny for the mesh of your muslin will slip through. Step aside, as you advance, to avoid the ant; you will set your foot on the caterpillar instead. I am the civilization necessary to man, you say, the civilization dictated and desired by man. Perhaps you are. I think, in fact, that you are correct, but this entails something else: that you, one way or another, and as you yourself said atop the hill, are the strong. However gently you set your broad hand upon the world, whatever the saving certainties you set loose upon it, you will kill. There is nothing to be done about it, I agree, but face the facts.

⚜ ⚜ ⚜

Night fell anew. As the sun went down the patient's fever was just above forty degrees. At about nine o'clock, however, it waned slightly and Hélène seemed to doze off. The exhausted doctor retired to his room: that is, to the other side of a mere partition. A frightened voice awakened him:

"M'sieur! Madame gone!"

"What do you mean gone?"

"Yes, M'sieur. He[71] no there!"

The bed was empty, the first-aid kit open on the table. Terrified, Maillard took a lamp and went out, calling. Cambodians searched by torchlight around the *sala*. The doctor cried out into the night, his calls flashing with the lights through the trees. A man's voice hailed him from the west. There he went, tripping over the vines. At the feet of the native, who held his torch aloft like some ancient statue of bronze, Maillard saw Hélène, a compact patch of white, lying on her side. Her peignoir was open, revealing the little-girl chest.

❖ ❖ ❖

When he had finished cleansing the corpse the doctor put the room in order. He noticed that the phial of strychnine was missing from his medical bag and that the green bag Madame Gassin had asked for two days earlier and jealously kept nearby ever since was no longer on the bed. After searching the room in vain he returned to the spot in the forest where Hélène had fallen. He found the bag, open, with her powder case, a handkerchief, keys, jewels, and money inside. A few paces off he saw a box of matches, and a little farther on the ashes of paper burned along with dry leaves, some half-charred sprigs, and the empty phial.

Red ants were exploring the ground where the dead woman's flesh had touched the humus. Abdomens erect, they looked by the light of the lantern like dripping honey.

71 The gender of this pronoun in the original text is in fact masculine. This could be a mistake by the original editor or typesetter, or it could be an error of speech Groslier attributed to the character, who, of course, is not a native speaker of French.

XV
Two Letters

In accord with her wishes, Madame Gassin was interred in the forest, near the path. Immediately on his return to Sangkae Ternier wired Roland Gassin. The telegram came back stamped RECIPIENT UNKNOWN. Ternier launched a quick investigation and learned that the carmaker had never gone to Saigon and that his famous company had no plans to set up a subsidiary in that city. The Messageries Maritimes could find no Gassin on any passenger manifest for a ship arriving from France over the previous six months.

From the bungalow manager and the postmaster the *résident* learned that Hélène had received no letters and had herself sent a single letter, by return-receipt, to Madame Annie Belgrand, her sister. An inventory of the deceased's baggage, before they were officially sealed, provided no clues, no scrap of paper. Ternier thereupon sent two cables: one to Roland Gassin, at his factory in Levallois-Perret, and another to Madame Belgrand. The latter wired back: "Am desperate. Send details by post." The husband did not reply.

All these obscurities compelled Ternier to pursue his unofficial inquiry further, that he might ease his conscience and at the least determine how to discharge the duties incumbent upon him in his office. He summoned Captain Thévenet and asked him, man to man, to reveal what he knew about the dead woman. The captain did not know her. Come, now! She had gone to his house one night. The captain knew nothing. There had been witnesses. The witnesses could have been mistaken. Legion of Honor, three *palmes*,[72] five wounds, four years of battle in the infantry, thirty-two years of age.

"Madame Gassin admitted to me that she had gone to your house."

"Madame Gassin declared what she saw fit to declare."

"Do keep in mind the gravity of the situation. I am caught between a dozen equally frightful conjectures. I could draw any conclusion at all. What happened? Why did Madame Gassin tell me that she had left her husband at Saigon if in fact he was never there at all? Why did she admit, in my presence, that she had gone to your house one night if you deny it? Suppose it is a serious matter. I will have no choice but to disclose what I know, and you will be an accomplice."

"Then I will be an accomplice."

"The most summary inquiry will reveal whether you knew Madame Gassin."

"Perhaps, but I have only one word to give."

Ternier approached the man and laid a hand on his shoulder.

"I see. I see. And there is but one person who can relieve you of this obligation. Or, rather, there *was* only one?"

The two men looked at each other. The officer made no reply. Ternier shook his hand, firmly.

That evening Ternier drafted a routine report on the death of Madame Gassin, lone traveler. He attested that he had met her in Paris. All the legal formalities had been seen to. The grave was

---

72 French Army citations in the shape of palm fronds, which are ancient symbols of victory. The bronze *palme* signifies one citation; the silver *palme*, five. The *palme* would be pinned to the ribbon of the *croix de guerre* (war cross) or the *croix de valeur militaire* (cross of military valor).

located at kilometer 118 of Colonial Route No. 1, two hundred meters west of the shelter known as "Sala Prei Thom." The deceased had burned her papers. Her baggage, under seal, would be made available to the family, who had been informed by cable. Could the *résident de France* say in good conscience that he knew anything else? No. In good conscience he knew nothing else. He signed. Secretary Tri affixed the seal, then registered the doctor's report and attached it. A woman had died. End of story.

⚜ ⚜ ⚜

Three months later, however, Ternier received an envelope bordered in black. It contained two letters. The first, in mourning like the envelope, was from Hélène's sister. The other was folded in four, written on blue-tinted paper, and initialed in dark-blue ink. Ternier, chilled to the bone, recognized the paper, the initials, and the writing. Here are the contents of those letters:

Paris, 26 June 19—

Monsieur,

You can imagine my stupor and despair on receiving your cable and learning of the death of my poor Hélène. Since then I have lived in anguish waiting for your letter. It arrived yesterday. Fate has decidedly not spared me. I had no one left on this earth to cherish except my sister, and she has died far away from me, after a long calvary. I see from your letter that Hélène's arrival in Indochina has given rise to many suppositions in your mind. I will answer your questions plainly. In doing so I will no doubt hurt you. I hope you will not hold this against me. Seeing where it has gotten us to keep a pointless secret, I am convinced that it would be best to bring everything out into the light of day.

Your appearance upset my sister down to her very soul. She was pent up, willful, and sensitive by nature. She found your temperament, your station, and your line of work seductive.

Her love for you was so imperative and sudden that by the time she tried to get hold of herself it was too late. In the meantime you departed for the East, and your absence stirred the pot. Desperate, Hélène came to me and confided everything, and I have been aware of events ever since then. For several months she tried to devote herself once more to her husband, but in vain. It became intolerable for her to remain by the side of a man she no longer loved. She told him so, and they agreed to a divorce. Hélène then came to live with me and began a new life—quite a sad life, I assure you.

Monsieur Gassin, an innocent victim, fell into deep despair. He knew his wife too well to think that they could continue living a life that even he could no longer accept. The divorce came through quickly. We saw no more of him. We lived in isolation. Monsieur Gassin left his business in the hands of a proxy and set out on an interminable series of travels, seeking oblivion and refusing even to receive any mail. I do not know where he is or whether he knows as yet that Hélène is dead.

Little by little the desire to see you again grew within Hélène. She devoured a pile of colonial books to form some picture of your life and follow you about in her mind. She would doubtless have set out as soon as she had secured her liberty if not for the fear of how you might judge her. She thought up a hundred ways she might do it. I advised her to wait for your next holiday in France, but she could not stand the thought of living in doubt for another two years before she saw you again. At last she dreamed up the dangerous fable you came to know.

She could not say that she had divorced because she loved you. That would have amounted to going to Cambodia to offer herself to you. She hoped nonetheless that subterfuge would preserve her pride and give rise to some eventuality that would open your eyes along the way. Above all, she had to see you again and seize the sole chance she thought she had to win your love. To that end, she would emerge into your solitude, share your enthusiasms. She would not adopt an attitude that was foreign to her, for she was incapable of disingenuousness, but, rather, show herself to be just as she loved you. I repeat that what she feared most of all was that if you learned of her divorce you would suspect her motives. My dear sister was not one to make skillful use of her charms, and I see that she was in fact unable to seize her chance as easily as a woman of lesser pride and scruple might have managed it. The objective of her mad journey to Cambodia was triumph. Otherwise, to cover her withdrawal, she would say that her husband had called her back to Saigon, that plans had changed. And thus she would have stepped out of your life.

I who had already been broken by life, and had found some spark of joy in her folly, considered that Hélène was at an impasse, that she was complicating the situation, and that only a miracle would see her through it. I told her so every which way. Her reply was always the same: "I want to see him again. The rest is immaterial. So much the worse. I have nothing to lose." There you have the whole story, Monsieur. Indeed, she has nothing left to lose, the poor dear.

So she set out. You know the rest. All I received from her afterwards were hasty notes scribbled at waystations. In a letter from Saigon she said that things were going marvelously well and that she was off for Cambodia the following day. A few days after her arrival at Sangkae she posted the last letter she would ever send me. It speaks of nothing but you. I have enclosed it. She will explain better than I (who know nothing more and have no way to judge any of it) how Hélène herself saw things. It is at times a grave misfortune that human nature is so complex and so simple, that man's perspicacity, subtle as it is, should walk right past profound and beautiful things without even a hint of recognition.

As for the papers Hélène burned, I suppose she did not want to leave behind any evidence of her flight, and make sure even from beyond the grave that you never knew she loved you. That pride, or, more properly, that nobility of spirit with respect to your peace of mind or to her own modesty, is perhaps something I lack, for I am now going to reveal the secret that she sealed tight with her dying breath. I have laid out my reasons. I must banish the doubts now obsessing you, and I must especially forestall any inquiry prompted by the suspicious presence of a woman traveling alone and by what must seem, at first blush, her inexplicable acts. I am aware, too, of the nobility of your own character. You have gone down your own road, Monsieur. The only guilty party in this sad tale is fate.

I pray you will express my heartfelt thanks to Dr. Maillard. If possible, if it doesn't seem out of place, extend my heartfelt thanks also to the captain Hélène speaks of. Believe me when I say, Monsieur, that grief has etched into my mind an indelible memory of you.

Anne Balgrand

⚜ ⚜ ⚜

Sangkae, 19 May —

Dear Sister,

For seven days I've been at his side. I've been seeing him, and he's been talking to me and killing me. I was mad to come, and it's getting plainer all the time. Everything he says shows that my dream is impossible. Not even out of pity would he tolerate my love if I revealed it to him. It would mortify him, because he'd be giving nothing in return, and he'd work to cure me of my love by endeavoring to break my heart. I am fallen fruit, as he told me yesterday, the fruit on offer for any old passer-by, and with that kind he wants no truck. He has conquered me, unwittingly, and that conquest, neither decided nor pursued by him, cannot hide the fact that I am giving myself to him. It is a gift he does not wish to accept, as it would demean me in his estimation. Yes, you are reading that correctly. I heard it all straight from his mouth. His pride is on a par with his humility.

Perhaps I ought to allow myself to be conquered, offer myself modestly, let my intentions be glimpsed. But I can't do it. I'm terrified he'll see right through the attempt and disdain the easy conquest. At least this other way I can have him in some measure, stay by his side. My passion devours itself but finds some consolation in contemplating him. He wheedles me as if I were his sister, or a little girl—the blind wretch!

I'm one of the provinces he's penetrated. I keep thinking that thought, keep reviewing that comparison, obsessively. Like the province, I was peaceable and happy, limited in my habits; I had chosen my life. And he made his advance into me, knocked me for a loop with a world of ideas and new passions. I found myself thirsting for riches I'd never even suspected. Like those villages that his road drives back and draws in, my poor little thoughts, my plans, and even my memories are changed beyond recognition. And despite all the suffering in me, despite the deep furrow that's cutting me in two, I feel I've grown. I am defeated, I am the weak, and the authority of the strong has me fearful and weeping. But I love Pierre. Though the reckoning for new joys be a disaster that will make me wish for death, I wouldn't trade a single one of these hours for my past.

I know, sweetheart. I know what you're going to say. But what would you have me do? I've got *my* pride, too. There's nothing more I can do, nothing, and I'm miserable. Once again you'll say that I'm overestimating the steeliness of his conscience and that he's a man just like any other. I don't believe it. If only you could see him here; he's like a lord! Besides, I'd spoil my love if I demeaned its object. I want *him* to love and desire *me* as well! In his company, to honor his constant presence in me for as long as I've loved him, to make myself worthy of him, a lovely exemplar of the virtues he prefers, I have hardened my heart. So much the worse for me. But for as long as I draw breath I want to keep up the hope that he will love me. I want to be ready and keep myself lovely.

I must recount an incident that almost ruined me and has upset the whole enterprise. Among the passengers I met aboard the ship was a certain Captain Thévenet. Imagine my panic when I saw him suddenly appear one evening at Pierre's house. This captain, whom I thought I'd said goodbye to forever at Saigon, had been posted to Sangkae. By some miracle he understood from my attitude that I did not wish to be recognized. This happened at about seven o'clock in the evening, as I was dining at Pierre's. The captain was supposed to go somewhere or other with Pierre the next day, at dawn. I was in anguish when I left and had only one thing on my mind. I had to inform the captain, cook up a story if necessary, but ask for his silence, because he knew quite well that I was traveling alone, that Roland was not in Saigon. So I hurried to his house, in the middle of the night. He was the soul of discretion, didn't even ask for an explanation, and swore, soldier's honor, that he'd keep quiet. What a lovely character. You wouldn't believe the good it did me, in my distress, to meet somebody like that!

Alas, my sweet, I wasn't yet out of danger. My nocturnal visit came to be known, and in this tiny village I now pass for the captain's mistress. Pierre was informed right away, and an hour later he had a dagger in me. How could I deny the visit? How could I reveal its purpose? And imagine the frightful torment I was in. True, Pierre is convinced that I am not what village rumor says I am, but he also knows that I went at night to the house of a man whom I had seen a few hours earlier at the Résidence and appeared not to know. What is he supposed to think? It was in fact during the baleful conversation he and I had on the subject that I understood the extent of my misfortune. I realized that what until then I had believed was my liberation (the divorce) could in his eyes be nothing other than a downfall, even if he was the cause, and that, in my madness, though I detached myself from the tree, I became fallen fruit, the kind of fruit no one wants, the kind you have to clean off… I thought I'd saved myself, but my method of salvation was my undoing in another way, and words perhaps did a better job of hitting me where it hurts than any events I averted.

I'm sorry, dearie, to sadden you with the tale of my torments. It does do me some good to recount it. Just think that I have to watch myself every instant, weigh my words, and be careful what I even look at. I'd love to curl up in his arms and feel that rude mustache of his on my lips forever! And yet I have to play the role of an aloof passer-by, of a tourist! My life is at stake. And he suspects nothing. He's in action, like some powerful machine. Off he goes, devoted to his task, his own master, with the egotism of the strong, the ponderousness of the logically minded. He forges ahead, laying down his road! His senses are satisfied: he has a native wife, young and pretty. I saw her one morning, as I was leaving the Résidence. And I'm jealous of her!

I've got to stop. I'm in good health, but I'm terribly weary. Everything I see is wondrous. How will it all end? Well, we'll talk soon, Annie. I'll write you in a week, by the next post. Receive all the tenderness of your poor devoted

Hélène

⚜ ⚜ ⚜

We know how it all ended, and why, by the next post, Madame Gassin did not write her sister.

Friday, 2 May 1924 – Phnom Penh

Fin

Appendices

George GROSLIER Profile –1928
by Paul E. BOUDET

Book review: *Revue des lectures*
15 January, 1926

The Works of George Groslier

Publisher's Notes
by Kent DAVIS

Colonial Battambang Today
**Revisiting George Groslier's Setting
for "The Road of the Strong"**
by Tom KRAMER

Le Route du plus fort
1925
Complete original French text
Avant-propos moderne par Henri COPIN

George GROSLIER Profile – 1928

Extrême-Asie - NOTRE INDOCHINE

– No. 20, February 1928 –

By Paul E. Boudet

GEORGE GROSLIER, a smiling, hospitable man who welcomes you with the sort of joyous voice one does not employ on the importunate. The Cambodian house is so very un-colonial, more like a Pompeian villa, with its flagstone peristyle and an impluvium[1] crawling with new leaves. The den of the lord of the manor is in a shady far corner of the gallery, its double doors closing without a sound. Books all along the walls, sometimes jostling for space with a polished, attractive grey block: the head of a Khmer with contemplative eyes. Higher up and all around, the scintillation of Cambodian silks, old sampots of faded lamé, still sumptuous despite the gentle effacement of time. The entirety of Khmer art, the imperishable stones, the extinguished silks, and the lasting jewels, heavy with precious cabochons.

Before he has said a word we have understood George Groslier's whole history: fifteen years in the life of this still-young man are writ here, and each has left its mark around one who, like no one else, can condense and collect the many scattered and disparate traits of a potent personality.

---

1   In Greece and Rome this was the sunken part of an atrium that carried away rainwater that fell through the *compluvium* of the roof. An apt description of Groslier's home, as seen in photos on pp. vi, viii and 198.

On the walls, canvases, already old, from the writer's brush; in boxes, a trove of ink drawings. All of them attest to the artist's first years, his first vision of the Angkorean forest, of the temples still buried within, romantic like the wellspring of his inspiration, which had initially made him into an artist of the line and color variety, a man devoted to his visual existence as artist-explorer.

He has since been months in the Cambodian forest. When scarcely adolescent he had not yet acquired the means of externalization that would later transform him into both a visionary archeologist and a writer.

Instantly his artistic temperament found his most immediate means of expression: painting. One of the canvases, among his oldest (a temple in a forest), which I chanced on at a friend's house, seems already to harbor the secret of what the man would become.

But it was a long preparation that George Groslier was obliged to undertake—years of solitude in the forest, years of research and tent-bound meditative life, leisure in which a paintbrush strives to express what the man seeks, and then, once more, dogged work to extirpate an active intellectuality from the passive nature depicted by a dazzled artist...

For he is exceedingly young, this artist, and has not yet forged his own temperament before this invasive variety of nature. But he is driven by an obscure force of will that with astonishing speed will unfetter him from lines and matter, lead him to an intellectual and no longer sentimental comprehension of Khmer art; he will pass from things to living beings and on to souls.

In those boxes of ink drawings are the inspiration for his first book: *Cambodian Dancers: Ancient and Modern*. Long before they were described the dancers and poses were captured as they are depicted in that box. The author always proceeds from sensible forms to spirit.

In the Shadow of Angkor is a lovely and already long-published book, which Groslier's early manner cloaks in romantic charm: temples in the wilderness that cluster around ancient Khmer cities—Ta Phrom, Prah Vihear, Beng Méala, Banteay-Chhmar. He spent interminable days traveling by ox cart between them, sleeping nights in the forest, writing when the dense tropical deluge forced him to take shelter.

Recent years have matured him further: the artist no longer paints. *In the Shadow of Angkor,* which seemingly paved the way for him to become a new "Pèlerin d'Angkor,"[2] has no future. His form, increasingly intellectual, has led to that first-rate work *Recherches sur les Cambodgiens d'après les textes et les monuments depuis les premiers siècles de noire **ère*** (1921) and to the creation of a collection, *Art et Archéologie Khmers; Revue des recherches sur les arts, les monuments et l'ethnographie du Cambodge, depuis les origines jusqu'à nos jours* (1921-25), in which, for the first time, the author has rendered the entirety of Cambodian artistic life.

It was thus a surprise in 1925, ten years after a purely literary work like *In the Shadow of Angkor,* when the author drew from his boxes to produce a lovely novel titled *The Road of the Strong.*

An unforgettable, palpitating read—the temperament of George Groslier had returned to its primitive, purely intuitive form. In reading *The Road of the Strong* those who had been loath to see him absorbed in the probing of a lost art's traditions, in the painstaking exhumation of a slow, skillful craftsmanship, so as to revive what time had buried, suddenly had the sense that the man had bided his time before revealing certain aspects of his personality, aspects that until then he had purposely kept dormant…

Edmond Jaloux, better placed than any other publisher to judge the flavor of this evocation of the Cambodian forest, enthusiastically retained the book for his collection, and the

---

2   Referring to Pierre Loti's popular 1912 travel book, *Un Pélerin d'Angkor (A Pilgrimage to Angkor),* which was issued in English in 1913 under the title *Siam.*

literary critics were grateful. As Jaloux himself said in *Nouvelles Littéraires* and his much-appreciated chronicles:

> "All of the descriptions are worthy of note. They are
> not descriptions in the rhetorical and banal sense that
> we have given the word; they are recreations, a series of
> living, stirring poems scattered throughout the book,
> making us feel all the beauty of a little-known land...."

And this from the *Gazelle de Lausanne*, which reaches to the very depths of the work:

> "The new perspective M. Groslier has managed to take on
> the enduring conflict of Orient versus Occident is evident.
> His book is troubling, sad in its beauty, like Hindu music."

And next we have *Le Singe qui montre la lanterne magique*, which M. Groslier has just entrusted to Extrême-Asie.[3] This latest work is no less surprising than *The Road of the Strong*, or, rather, confirms us in our surprise at seeing the full manifestation of a writerly temperament from which the rigors of pure science had momentarily removed our attention.

Here, then, is the new novel, hardy and vigorous, its unexpected youthfulness drawn from a new way of life. A new world opens up, a world that steely resolve creates within a hostile forest. From this effort, it seems, a different sort of existence has arisen, one that demands a vaster field in which to exert its resolve, that escapes in every direction from fragile fetters. It is man conquering his domain, and emerging from the conquest, as he inevitably must, with a conqueror's heart—that is, with simple appetites that will overcome all worldly resistance, for brutal, absurd resolve is victorious more often than one might think.

---

3   Groslier's little-known work appeared as a series in *Extrême-Asie*, with Boudet's biographical here published with the first installment. DatAsia Press has a French edition of this title in preparation. Groslier released his next novel, *Le retour à l'argile* (*Return to Clay*), shortly after this article. In 2014, DatAsia Press issued an English translation, including the original French text.

Here, then, is the new rubber-tree plantation claimed since yesterday from the forest. It fully symbolizes the new world where man, with his elemental personality, makes an appearance only when he has occasion to provide some unexpected resolution to events. *Le Singe qui montre la lanterne magique*: a title of old-fashioned charm, so felicitously paired with epigraphs from Florian or La Fontaine, thereby to temper the at first disconcerting, though in time unsuspectedly elegant, act! How enigmatic and curious the skeptical narrator, who smiles as he recounts the most disturbing events! Readers in the Far East will certainly be carried along by the daring imagination of a man who questions the entire moral edifice of marriage.

If we asked him this instant, would G. Groslier not speak to the profound unity of his work? Is not the hero of *The Road of the Strong*, like the hero of *Le Singe qui montre la lanterne magique*, the creature of resolve, partly unaware of, or at least closed to, all external suggestion, who follows his road in the blindness of his own personality?

Does M. Groslier deliberately seek out men who are dead set on a single thought or act, something so simplified as to be a machine launched on its course and never deviating from its objective? Is it a superb contradiction if the saddening solitude of the forest and the indolent skepticism one acquires in it have led the author to this unheard-of concentration of resolve, which willingly impoverishes a personality so as to substitute strength for lost diversity?

The memory returns of charming hours spent with G. Groslier, spent listening to him read other works, some that the author will perhaps jealously keep forever in his boxes. Deep intuitions of a complex psychology where other characters live, but only within!

I see the nervous hand quickly put the pages away, and I wonder what aspect of this artistic temperament will come to dominate in the long run: the novelist of new men, elemental and deep like all that is intimately bound up with action, or other aspects entirely, diverse and nuanced and open to the outside world?

What surprises lie in store for us as this artistic, archeological, writerly temperament that can already externalize itself in so many ways reaches fruition?

Paul E. Boudet

Director of the Archives Department
and the Libraries of Indochina

February 1928

Paul E. Boudet

July 18, 1888–November 11, 1948

Paul Boudet arrived in Hanoi in 1917, and would then spend his entire career in French Indochina. Before the end of his first year, Governor Albert Sarraut charged him with an archival mission to found what would become the National Library of Vietnam. After establishing the Central Library of Indochina in Hanoi, he set up a lending program for students, a public reading room (including materials for young readers), and even organized a  system of bookmobiles to take books to rural locations.

Boudet went on to supervise the construction and modernization of archival libraries throughout the region—including Saigon and Phnom Penh—while implementing rigorous library staff training programs. In a work that benefits scholars and readers to this day, he created the Boudet Classification System in 1918 to organize the collections. In 1945, he detailed his final revision of the system in his *Manuel de l'Archiviste.* The National Archives of Cambodia (NAC) still uses the Boudet Classification System, as do the repositories of French colonial records in Aix-en-Provence (France), Hanoi and Ho Chi Minh City (Vietnam).

N° 1 (DE LA XIV° ANNÉE).   15 JANVIER 1926.

Revue des Lectures

Fondée en 1908
sous le nom de Romans-Revue | **DIRECTEUR**
Louis BETHLEEM

paraissant le 15 de chaque mois

SOMMAIRE

PARIS (6°)
77, rue de Vaugirard, 77

ABONNEMENTS

FRANCE : 25 fr. (le numéro, 2 fr. 50).

ETRANGER : 30 fr. (le numéro, 3 fr.).

35 fr. pour les pays n'ayant pas adhéré à l'accord de Stockholm
(le numéro, 3 fr. 50).

TÉL. : FLEURUS 35-93. — C.-C. : PARIS 180-42.   R. C. : SEINE 260.194.

卐 卐 卐

La Route du plus fort, titre que M. George Groslier a choisi
pour son dernier roman, est sans doute une expression figurée.
Pas tout à fait cependant. La route terrestre, celle où circulent
les hommes, les animaux, les voitures, tient sa place et sa large
place en cette histoire. Il ne s'agit pas de nos routes de France,
aussi anciennes que la nation, mais de celles que l'effort humain
ouvre maintenant à grand'peine, en de lointaines contrées, à
travers les terres vierges et les forêts impénétrables du Cambodge.
Ce livre est l'hymne à la route.

C'est aussi un hymne à la nature. L'auteur, professeur en
Indo-Chine, connaît à merveille le pays qu'il décrit. Il en évoque,
en artiste, toute sa splendeur. Il donne le goût des randonnées
et des explorations lointaines.

Malheureusement, en son livre, les personnages attirent moins
que le cadre. Sans doute, le traceur de voies nouvelles, l'inspira-
teur de la tâche obstinée des défricheurs, Ternier, le Résident de
Sangké, est une nature ardente et énergique. En taillant la route
dans la brousse, il suit aussi la sienne, « la route du plus fort. »

Mais ce fort a de singulières faiblesses, trop courantes, hélas!
aux colonies, présentées, excusées comme toutes naturelles, et
sur lesquelles il est préférable de ne point insister.

Quant à l'héroïne, quant à l'intrigue qui gravite autour d'elle,
intrigue obscure, qu'il s'agit de deviner peu à peu, l'une et
l'autre sont invraisemblables. C'est l'éternelle histoire de l'infidé-
lité conjugale, sans l'ombre d'un prétexte, d'une explication ou
d'une excuse, la poursuite de la chimère, en marge du devoir et
du droit chemin. On nous dit, il est vrai, qu' « en ce triste
roman, la fatalité demeure seule coupable. » Cette fatalité a
vraiment bon dos.

L'auteur n'insiste pas outre mesure sur les détails réalistes. Il
ne les évite pas non plus. Son livre ne s'adresse donc qu'à ceux
qui ont la pleine expérience de la vie. S'il leur fait goûter le
charme des choses, il ne leur fera pas aimer les hommes.

卐 卐 卐

"Revue des Lectures" Magazine Review

January 15, 1926

The Road of the Strong (*La Route du plus fort*), as Mr. George Groslier has titled his latest novel, is undoubtedly a figurative expression, but not quite entirely. The earthly road, on which men, animals, and cars circulate, plays a role, a large role, in the story. It does not concern our roads in France, which are as old as the nation itself, but the roads that human effort is now painstakingly laying down in distant lands, through the virgin terrain and impenetrable forests of Cambodia. The book is a hymn to the road.

It is also a hymn to nature. The author, a professor in Indochina, has deep knowledge of the country he describes. As an artist, he evokes it in all its splendor. He gives us a taste for hikes and far-ranging explorations.

Unfortunately, the book's characters are less attractive than its setting. The planner of new thoroughfares and inspirer of land-clearers in their obstinate task, Ternier, Résident of Sangkae, is without a doubt a fervent and energetic man. In cutting the swath through the wilderness he follows his own path, the "road of the strong."

But this strength has singular weaknesses, which, alas, are all too common in the colonies. They are presented and excused as perfectly natural, as if it were better not too insist on the matter.

As for the heroine and the intrigue surrounding her, the obscure intrigue that we are invited gradually to infer, both are improbable. It's the same old story of conjugal infidelity, without the shadow of a pretext, an explanation, or an excuse—the pursuit of a chimera, with its departure from duty and the straight and narrow. We are told, it is true, that "the only guilty party in this sad tale is fate." Fate truly makes a good whipping boy.

The author does not insist too much on realistic details, but neither does he avoid them. His book is thus addressed only to those who have had a full experience of life. He provides a taste of the charm of things, but he will not inspire any love for humanity.

The Works of George Groslier

George Groslier in his study - 1922.

Creative, passionate and prolific, George Groslier was a visionary man of many talents. First trained in fine arts by Parisian master painter Albert Maignan, George returned to his Cambodian birthplace in 1911. There, he devoted his life to documenting, preserving, promoting and celebrating Khmer art, culture and history.

Groslier expressed himself visually as a painter, intellectually as an archaeologist, museum curator and essayist, and emotionally as a creative writer. He championed Khmer patrimony in every endeavor, infusing his artistic works with his unique love, respect and sensitivity for Cambodia that ensure the timeless validity of his contributions.

Modern French & English Language Editions

- ❖ *La Route du plus fort.* Paris: Kailash, 1994.
- ❖ *Le Retour à l'argile.* Paris: Kailash, 1994.
- ❖ *Cambodian Dancers – Ancient & Modern.* Holmes Beach, FL: DatAsia Press, 2010; and Phnom Penh, Cambodia: DatAsia Press, 2011.
- ❖ *In the Shadow of Angkor – Unknown Temples of Ancient Cambodia.* Holmes Beach, FL: DatAsia Press, 2014.
- ❖ *Return to Clay – A Romance of Cambodia.* Holmes Beach, FL: DatAsia Press, 2014.
- ❖ *Water and Light – A Travel Journal of the Cambodian Mekong.* Holmes Beach, FL: DatAsia Press, 2015.
- ❖ *The Road of the Strong – A Romance of Cambodia.* Holmes Beach, FL: DatAsia Press, 2017.
- ❖ *Danseuses cambodgiennes – Anciennes & Modernes.* Holmes Beach, FL: DatAsia Press. In Preparation.

Books

- ❖ *La Chanson d'un Jeune.* Self-published. 1904.
- ❖ *Danseuses cambodgiennes anciennes et modernes.* Paris : A. Challamel, 1913.

- ❖ *A l'ombre d'Angkor; notes et impressions sur les temples inconnus de l'ancien Cambodge.* Paris : A. Challamel, 1913.
- ❖ *Angkor...Ouvrage orné de 103 gravures et de 5 cartes et plans.* Paris: H. Laurens, 1924.
- ❖ *Arts et Archéologie khmères, 2 vol.* Paris : A. Challamel, 1921-1926.
- ❖ *Recherches sur les Cambodgiens d'après les textes et les monuments depuis les premiers siècles de notre ère.* Paris : A. Challamel, 1921.
- ❖ *Arts et Archéologie Khmers. Revue des Recherches sur les Art, les Monuments et l'Ethnographie du Cambodge, depuis les Origines jusqu'à nos Jours.* Paris: Société d' Editions Géographiques, Maritimes et Coloniales, 1925.
- ❖ *La sculpture Khmère ancienne ; illustrée de 175 reproductions hors texte en similigravure.* Paris : G. Crès, 1925.
- ❖ *Les collections khmères du Musée Albert Sarraut à Phnom-Penh.* Paris: G. van Oest, 1931.
- ❖ *Eaux et lumières; journal de route sur le Mékong cambodgien.* Paris: Société d'éditions géographiques, maritimes et coloniales, 1931.
- ❖ *L'enseignement et la mise en pratique des arts indigènes au Cambodge (1918-1930).* Paris: Sté d'éditions géographiques, maritimes et coloniales, 1931.
- ❖ *Angkor, with 103 illustrations, 5 maps and plans. Translated from the French by Paule Fercoq Du Leslay.* Evreux: impr. Hérissey, 1933.
- ❖ *Ankooru iseki.* Japanese translation of *Angkor.* Tokyo: Shinkigensha, 1943.

Novels

- ❖ *La Route du plus fort.* Paris, Emile-Paul frères, 1926.
- ❖ *Le Retour à l'argile.* Paris : Emile-Paul frères, 1928.
- ❖ *Monsieur De La Garde, Roi: Roman, Inspiré Des Chroniques Royales Du Cambodge,* 1934, Paris: *L'Illustration.*
- ❖ *Les Donneurs de Sang, Phnom Penh et Saigon.* Saigon : Albert Portail, 1941.
- ❖ *Le Christ Byzentine,* 1953, Ellery Queen Mystère Magazine, N°69 and N°70.

Graphic Works

- ❖ *Les Ruines d'Angkor.* Indochine, 1911.

Archeological Publications

- ❖ "Objets anciens trouvés au Cambodge." *Revue archéologique,* 1916, 5e Série, vol. 4, pp. 129-139.
- ❖ "La batellerie cambodgienne du VIIIe au XIIIe siècles." *Revue archéologique,* 1917, 5e Série, vol. 5, pp. 198-204.
- ❖ "Objets cultuels en bronze dans l'ancien Cambodge." *Arts et Archéologie khmers,* 1921-3, vol. 1, fasc. 3, pp. 221-228.
- ❖ "Le temple de Phnom Chisor." Ibid, vol. 1, fasc. 1, pp. 65-81.
- ❖ "Le temple de Ta Prohm (Ba Ti)." Ibid, vol. 1. fasc. 2, pp. 139-148.
- ❖ "Le temple de Preah Vihear". Ibid, 1921-1922, vol. 1. fasc. 3, pp. 275-294.
- ❖ "Essai sur l'architecture classique khmère." *Arts et Archéologie khmers,* 1923, vol. 1, fasc. 3. pp. 229-273.
- ❖ "L'art khmèr." Paris, *Arts et Décoration,* août 1923. vol. 27. N° 260, pp. 34-40.
- ❖ "L'art du bronze au Cambodge." *Arts et Archéologie khmers,* 1923. vol. 1, fasc., pp. 413-423.
- ❖ "L'Art khmèr." Paris, *Arts et Décoration,* August 1923, vol. 1, pp. 413-423.
- ❖ "Amarendrapura dans Amoghapura." *Bulletin de l'Ecole Française d'Extrême-Orient,* Hanoï, 1924, vol. 24, pp. 359-372.

- *Angkor, Les Villes d'Art célèbres*. Paris, Laurens, 1924.
- *Catalogue du Musée de Phnom Penh*. Hanoï, IDEO, 1924.
- "La céramique dans l'ancien Cambodge." *Arts et Archéologie khmers*, 1924, vol. 2, fasc. 1, pp. 31-64.
- "La vie à Angkor au XIe siècle." Saigon, *Pages Indochinoises*, 15-1-1924, N.S., vol. 1, pp. 9-17.
- "Les empreintes du 'Pied du Buddha' d'Angkor Vat." *Arts et Archéologie khmers*, 1924, vol. 2, fasc. 2. pp. 65-80.
- "La région d'Angkor." *Arts et Archéologie khmers*, 1924, vol. 2, fasc. 2, pp. 113-130.
- "La région du Nord-Est du Cambodge et son art." Ibid., pp. 131-141.
- "L'Asram Maha Rosei." *Arts et Archéologie khmers*, 1924, vol. 2. fasc. 2. pp. 141-146.
- "L'Art hindou au Cambodge." *Arts et Archéologie khmers*, 1924. vol. 2, fasc. 1, pp. 81-93.
- "Essai sur le Buddha khmèr." Ibid, pp. 93-112.
- "Sur les origines de l'Art khmèr." *Mercure de France*, 1-xii-1924, vol. 176, N° 365, pp. 382-404.
- "Les influences grecques au Cambodge et l'art pré khmèr." Paris, *L'Art Vivant*, 1925.
- "Sur la route d'Angkor : le Prasat Phum Prasat." Saigon, *Extrême-Asie*, déc. 1925, N° 14, vol. 12, pp. 493-494.
- "Introduction à l'étude des arts khmèrs." *Arts et Archéologie khmers*, 1925, vol. 2. fasc. 2, pp. 167-234.
- "La femme dans la sculpture khmère ancienne." Paris, *Revue des Arts asiatiques*, 1925, vol. 2, fasc. 1, pp. 35-41.
- "La fin d'Angkor." Saigon, *Extrême-Asie*, Sept. 1925.
- "Note sur la sculpture khmère ancienne." Hanoï, *Études asiatiques, École Française d'Extrême-Orient*, 1925. vol. I, pp. 297-314.
- "A propos d'art hindou et d'art khmèr." *Arts et Archéologie khmers*, 1926, vol. 2, fasc. 3, pp. 329-348.
- "Les collections khmères du Musée Albert Sarraut." *Ars Asiatica*, XVI, Paris, G. Van Oest, 1931.
- "Les Temples inconnus du Cambodge." Paris, *Toute la terre*, June 1931.
- *Angkor, Les Villes d'Art célèbres*. Paris. Laurens, 1932 (English translation).
- "Troisième recherche sur les Cambodgiens." *Bulletin de l'Ecole Française d'Extrême-Orient*, Hanoi, 1935, vol. 35, pp. 159-206.
- "Une merveilleuse cité khmère. Banteai Chhma, ville ancienne du Cambodge." Paris, *L'Illustration*, April 3, 1937, N° 4909, pp. 352-357.
- "Les Monuments khmers sont-ils des tombeaux?" Saigon. Bulletin de la Société des Eudes Indochinoises.1941, N.S., vol. 16. N°1 pp. 121-126.

Publications on the Indigenous Arts of Cambodia

- "La Convalescence des Arts cambodgiens." Hanoï, *Revue Indochinoise*, Imprimerie d'Extrême-Orient, 2e sem. 1918, p. 207; 1er sem. 1919, pp. 871-890, 22 p. ill. p. 16, fig. 21.
- "L'agonie des Arts cambodgiens." Hanoï, *Revue Indochinoise*, 2e sem. 1918, p.207.
- "Question d'art indigène." Hué, *Bulletin des Amis du Vieux-Hué*, Oct.-Dec. déc. 1920, pp. 444-452.
- "Étude sur la psychologie de l'artisan cambodgien." *Arts et Archéologie khmers*, 1921, vol. 1, fasc. 2, pp. 125-137.
- "Seconde étude sur la psychologie de l'artisan cambodgien." *Arts et Archéologie khmers*, 1921, vol. 1. fasc. 2, pp. 205-220.

- ❖ "Royal Dancers of Cambodia." *Asia*, 1922, vol. 22, N° 1, pp. 47-55, 74-75.
- ❖ "Soixante-seize dessins cambodgiens tracés par l'oknha Tep Nimit Mak et l'oknha Reachna Prasor Mao, Arts et Archéologie khmers." Paris: *Société d'Edition Géographique, Maritime et Coloniale*, 1923. 331-386 p.
- ❖ "The Oldest Living Monarch." *Asia*,1923. vol. 23. pp. 587-589.
- ❖ "La reprise des arts khmèrs." *La Revue de Paris*, Nov. 15, 1925. pp. 395-422.
- ❖ "Avec les danseuses royales du Cambodge." Mercure de France, May 1, 1928, pp. 536-565.
- ❖ "La mort de S.M. Sisowath." *L'Illustration*, Oct. 1927.
- ❖ "Les cérémonies d'incinérations de S.M. Sisowath." *L'Illustration*, April 1928. 86è année, n°4443. Samedi 28 Avril 1928. pp. 410-415.
- ❖ "Die Kunst der Kambodschanischen tànzerinn." Munich, *Atlantis*, Jan.-Mar. 1929, vol. 1,pp. 10-16.
- ❖ "Die Tanzerinnen des Konigs." [Miscellanea], p 16. 2 plates (1 col.) *Atlantis*, Jan 1929.
- ❖ "Le théâtre et la danse au Cambodge." Paris, *Journal Asiatique*, Jan.-Mar. 1929. vol. 214, pp. 125-143. (See Appendix for English translation)
- ❖ "Contemporary Cambodian art studied in the Light of the Past Forms." Boston, *Eastern Art*, 1930. vol. 2, pp. 127-141.
- ❖ "La Direction des Arts cambodgiens et l'École des Arts cambodgiens." Saigon, *Extrême-Asie*, March 1930, N° 45, pp. 119-127.
- ❖ "La fin d'un art." Paris, *Revue des Arts Asiatiques*, 1929-1930, vol. 6, fasc. 3., pp. 176-186; p. 184 et 251, fasc. 4, pp. 244-254.
- ❖ "La fin d'une tradition d'art : les pagodes cambodgiennes et le ciment armé." *L'Illustration*, January 11, 1930, vol. 175, pp. 50-53.
- ❖ "De Pagode en Pagode." Paris. *Toute la Terre*, July 1931.
- ❖ "L'Orfèvrerie cambodgienne à l'Exposition Coloniale." Paris, *La Perle*, 1931.
- ❖ "Rapport sur les arts indigènes au Cambodge." Congrès International et Intercolonial de la Société Indigène, Paris. 1931.
- ❖ "L'Enseignement et la mise en pratique des Arts indigènes au Cambodge." *Bulletin de Académie des Sciences Coloniales*, Paris, 1931.
- ❖ "Les Arts indigènes au Cambodge." *Exp. int. des Arts et Techniques*, Indochine Française, Paris, 1937.
- ❖ "Les Arts indigènes au Cambodge." 10th *Congress of the Far-Eastern Association of Tropical Medicine*, Hanoi, 1938, pp. 161-181.

Narratives

- ❖ "Propos sur la maison coloniale." Saigon, *Extrême-Asie*, 3° trim. 1926, pp. 2-10; March 1927, pp. 307-366.
- ❖ "Le Singe qui montre la Lanterne magique." Saigon, *Extrême-Asie* , Feb. 1928, pp. 347-366; mars 1928, pp. 435-450; avril 1928, pp. 499-505; mai 1928, pp. 546-554.
- ❖ "C'est une idylle...." Paris, *Mercure de France*, July 1929.
- ❖ *La Mode masculine aux colonies.* Paris : Adam, 1931.
- ❖ "Nos boys." Saigon, *Extrême-Asie*, August 1931, N° 55, pp. 69-76.

❖ ❖ ❖

Publisher's Notes

Kent Davis

Completing George Groslier's first novel, *The Road of the Strong*, is such an important personal step forward that I'm adding these notes to give readers a "behind-the-scenes" look at my work as the literary archaeologist behind DatAsia Press. Further, it clarifies our approach to restoring extraordinary lost, out-of-print and forgotten books about Southeast Asian history.

This Groslier book has been a long time coming. In early 2016, I began having health issues that ultimately stopped me from progressing on all my books for more than a year. Dozens of projects stalled as I lost my clarity and energy. During this hiatus, DatAsia was still able to bring four important titles to print, but only because the authors had their manuscripts so well-polished:

Customs of Cambodia

Zhou Daguan

A new translation of the most important eye-witness account of the Khmer Empire from the year 1296 AD. Born in Cambodia and China respectively, Solang and Beling Uk based their translation on personal knowledge of both cultures and languages, thereby clarifying linguistic puzzles that have been unresolved for centuries. For the first time, they bring unidentified places, titles, plants, animals and other details to life in this full color edition, featuring a foreword by renowned author Amir D. Aczel.

Cambodia Past
Explaining the Present

Étienne-François Aymonier's 1875 book, *Notice sur le Cambodge*, in an original English language translation by Marie-Hélène Arnauld. This edition includes 59 illustrations, featuring images by photographer Émile Gsell taken from 1866–1875. Joel Montague edited the book with photographer Jim Mizerski, who restored the images and designed the text.

The Khmer Kings and the History of Cambodia
Book I–1st Century to 1595:
Funan, Chenla, Angkor and Longvek Periods
Book II–1595 to the Contemporary Period

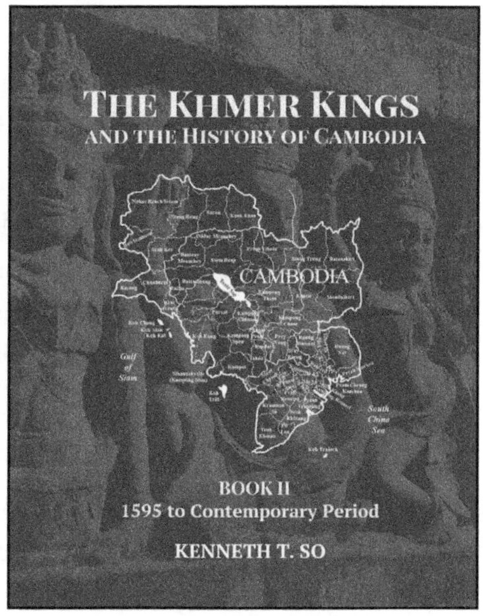

Cambodian scholar and retired scientist Kenneth T. So spent ten years creating the most comprehensive study of the origins and evolution of the Khmer civilization available. His two-volume, 804-page set covers every significant Cambodian event, place, temple and person from the 1st century to modern times, supplemented by hundreds of full-color illustrations including genealogical charts, photos and diagrams. The books include detailed appendices with additional notes, references, bibliography and full index.

Working with these talented authors inspired me during my down period, but dozens of unfinished books still languished—including this one. Thanks to finding a new doctor in May, my clarity and energy began returning. On October 7th, I wrote in my diary "Best editing day in a year and a half." Now, one productive week later, I am grateful to see *The Road* going to print after years of effort from many dear friends.

The idea for DatAsia Press began in the 1990s when I returned to the United States after five years working in Thailand. I missed Southeast Asia and soon began collecting antique books on the topic. I still returned annually and, despite my growing familiarity, every Asian visit revealed new wonders. I knew then, as I know now, that a lifetime of secrets and surprises awaits there. My growing archive confirmed that many who preceded me felt the same, and those rare men and women in my library put their extraordinary dreams and adventures into print.

One of my frustrations with older editions is that the authors, their motivation, their personal relationships with the topics, and events leading to the subsequent publication of their work are usually shrouded in mystery. Many are now little more than obscure names whose lives have vanished along with the books they created.

Though I had dabbled with the idea of restoring some old titles, it was reading Paul Cravath's 1985 doctoral thesis on Cambodian dance in 2006 that inspired me to begin publishing in earnest. How could such an essential piece of scholarship on Cambodian history have been forgotten for more than two decades? Well, you'll have to read my Publisher's Notes in that edition for the full story. The point is that by 2008 we had put the author's now award-winning book into print: *Earth in Flower–The Divine Mystery of the Cambodian Dance Drama.*

Thanks to Cravath's extensive research, *Earth in Flower* became the blueprint for my future in publishing. It was he who introduced me to George Groslier, Roland Meyer and Jean Despujols, three men to whom I will devote many more years of my life. As Groslier published the first book on Cambodian dance in 1912, I chose that as my next major project to complement *Earth in Flower.* It was in preparing the first English edition of *Cambodian Dancers–Ancient &* *Modern* that I defined many editorial techniques that I now use in all DatAsia publications.

Paul Cravath's *Earth in Flower*—**limited-edition 2008 hardcover (left) and 2012 paperback (right)— led me to know Jean Despujols (1886–1965), whose art we featured on the cover.**

In 1936, Despujols embarked on an extensive two-year tour of French Indochina, painting, sketching, photographing and recording a life and time that has long since vanished. The historic miracle is that his entire collection of works from that journey remain intact, preserved by the Meadows Museum and the artist's family in Shreveport, LA.

A panorama showing part of François Doré's Librairie du Siam et des Colonies in Bangkok, Thailand.

My mission became taking the content of worthwhile, but forgotten, books and bringing them back to life for future generations. There were already services that scanned originals to reprint them, but I had no interest in doing that. A "new old book" is still an old book. The entire world had changed since the originals were published. Words, news, events, mores and people familiar to the author and readers at the time are mostly long forgotten, or were never known to readers far removed from the Southeast Asian settings in the first place. How could we make these books relevant and accessible again?

First, by resetting the text. Older editions are often poorly typeset with small fonts on cheap paper. Many originals were produced on a shoestring budget, often by printers far removed from the authors. Time, costs, technology, poor communications, distance and the printer's lack of familiarity with the subject matter limited the quality of most works right from the start. My mission was to fix all that and much more.

Our unbreakable rule is that every word of the original text must be included. This commitment, by the way, has made republishing

a translation of Roland Meyer's 180,000 word, 1919 epic, *Saramani*, into an unfinished 8 year project…thus far! With living authors, on the other hand, editing and revision are up for grabs until the ink hits the paper. In the case of *Earth in Flower*, Paul Cravath and I spent more than a year crafting a superb first edition based on his thesis… then in 2012 we went back to spend months redoing the photos and polishing the entire text with hundreds of small improvements for the paperback edition. The limited edition, hand-sewn original hardcover is a rare collectable, but the paperback has cleaner content.

This is a good place to bring language into the equation. DatAsia publishes in English and French, with a touch of Khmer, Thai, Chinese and Latin added from time to time. I'm proud to re-publish rare American contributions by Helen Churchill Candee and Harry Hervey, but the breadth and depth of French experiences in Asia go far beyond what most Anglophones can imagine. Over the course of a century, French colonial writers created a library filled with adventures, romances, hardships and bravery.

Though many titles are long forgotten—even in France—a shrine to this genre exists in Bangkok, Thailand. There, curator François Doré presides over the Librairie du Siam et des Colonies,

**François Doré, the library's
knowledgeable founder and curator.**

preserving one of the world's most complete collections of colonial literature. With his guidance, I have come to appreciate that the stories of French Indochina are every bit as thrilling as American tales of the "Wild West" (that are read in every language). Yet, almost none of these exotic French tales have come into English. Therefore, a major DatAsia goal is to continue translating and publishing works of early 20th century French colonial fiction.

In the case of George Groslier, a grant from the National Endowment for the Arts enabled us to work with the highly skilled translator Pedro Rodríguez on four books (including this one). The grant and translator are gone, but we still have many excellent titles ready to translate. One thing I've learned in 10 years is that literary translation is an art that has very little to do with fluency in two languages. With the caveat that the glory of this job far exceeds the pay, please email me if you are interested in helping. An undiscovered world of French Southeast Asian adventure literature awaits new English language readers.

The next task for our antique book restorations is to make the long-gone author's immutable text become intelligible to modern readers. We do this by adding detailed footnotes, illustrations and supplemental articles in the appendices. Obscure terms and places are explained on the spot, rather than sending readers off to hunt for answers. Appendix articles from sources contemporary with the original, as well as from modern scholars, add context and outside views. For some translated editions, such as this one, we include the original French text to create a complete record of the original work.

For some titles, adding period photos of the places and events makes a huge difference in helping readers see *exactly* what the authors describe. A few original books included low quality photos, but modern software and access to photo archives allows us to add many more images, further enlivening the story.

Now we get to one of the most critical tasks; bringing the authors themselves back to life along with their works. To me, respecting authors with biographical details is essential. Who was he/she? Why did he/she write this? Is it pure fiction or was the author personally involved in the story? The questions stand for both non-fiction and fiction.

Since 2006, I have worked on translations of Roland Meyer's epic novel, *Saramani*. I always suspected that his book was more fact than fiction, then something happened as surprising as finding Nicole Groslier living near my home. In 2012, Jean Courtois introduced himself to me as the grandson of Roland Meyer *and Saramani*. His astounding revalation finally proved that Saramani (above with Roland and three of their children) was a real historical figure. On August 25, 2017, the *Phnom Penh Post* covered the news in a front page article, "A history written in plain sight" by Rinith Taing.

I've gone to great lengths to learn about my authors, with a few uncanny coincidences along the way. Finding George Groslier's daughter, Nicole, living just 20 minutes from my home was the most serendipitous blessing, and I treasure my years working with her and her family. For others, like Helen Churchill Candee and Harry Hervey, I found researchers already working on detailed biographical profiles. Direct contact with the families of Charles Gravelle, Roland Meyer, Jean Despujols and Makhali-Phal provided a wealth of primary data, as it did with Groslier. Though the facts can be elusive, we continue building biographies for authors that are, or soon will be, in print again, including: Guillaume Henri Monod, Nguyen Phan Long, Pierre Rey, André Joyeux, Alexander MacDonald, Elizabeth McIntosh, Pierre Dassier, Jean d'Esme, Jean d'Estray and Réginald d'Auxion de Ruffé.

That leaves just one component left to explore: the cover! It's funny, but explaining the cover design was the *original* intent of this article. Somehow, the other thoughts above found their way in. For me, new book editions only come alive when I have a striking vision for the cover in mind. For some, I've found modern illustrations that capture the mood or action of the original text. For others, I seek images and inspiration contemporary with the original publication. Such is the case with *The Road of the Strong*.

Working with Becca Klein, a brilliant graphic designer, I prepared a menu of antique images that she blended into the cover you hold. Groslier opens his story in France with the chance encounter of Cambodian official, Pierre Ternier, driving his *Roland Gassin* automobile on a visit to the French countryside of Auvergne. He encounters a broken-down car, *also* a *Roland Gassin*. Coincidentally, the car manufacturer—Roland Gassin himself— is in the disabled vehicle, accompanied by his young, intelligent and attractive wife Hélène. That sets the stage for what follows in Cambodia.

Don't bother Googling to see what a *Roland Gassin* looks like. This imaginary marque for a luxury touring car came from Groslier's imagination. So, Becca and I had to set about creating one, drawing from images of popular cars of the time. Note the marque emblazoned on the grill, as well as the license plate PV465, copied from Groslier's car seen on the first trip to Banteay Chhmar on p. 202.

Grand touring cars in early 20th century French Indochina.

Next, for the gorgeous Cambodian background we must thank the 1931 *Exposition coloniale internationale* in Paris. This six-month exhibition was the most ambitious display of the cultures and resources of France's colonial possessions ever organized. Apparently, that inspired Lincoln to create this stunning advertisement.

Last, but not least, we have the image of Hélène Gassin herself, conjured from a selection of models and fashions of the mid-1920s. As a final touch, she wears a handwoven Cambodian silk *krama* scarf.

So, with the cover, translated text, foreword, footnotes, photos, appendix articles, reviews, maps and French text, we finally come to the end of George Groslier's *Road of the Strong*. I hope you've enjoyed this article and will explore the books it is based on. Now you know how they came to be and, if you have the inclination, I invite you to help us create more.

Above left, a very fashionable Suzanne Groslier on her first visit to Angkor Wat in January 1918. Above right, *haute couture* from Hélène's home in Paris. Below, American fashions in the mid-1920s

Statue of Ta Dambong on Rt. 5, entering from Phnom Penh.

Myself, and my trusty "Crocodile" brand bike.

Colonial Battambang Today
Revisiting George Groslier's Setting
for *The Road of the Strong*

Tom Kramer

"George Groslier was a man whose pen could strike that singular balance between things he saw, encountered, and felt, within his own dreams embodied by the foreign land he explored.

"No other writer has concentrated so many disparate and complementary qualities, all in the service of the gaze and prose of a poet. Painting Cambodia in words was an act of sharing his innermost feelings, his ideals and his aspirations."

Prof. Henri Copin, University of Nantes
Foreword to George Groslier's *Water and Light*. P. xix.

It was in 1998 that Chamroeun, my spouse, and I had the first opportunity to safely return to his birthplace in the town of Battambang. Since then, we've had many extended stays visiting Chamroeun's family and exploring the countryside in the surrounding area.

Fifteen years later, I was delighted to learn that the renowned Khmérophile George Groslier himself had written his first novel set in Battambang in 1926. As I don't read French, I eagerly anticipated the first English translation of his work from DatAsia Press. I was not disappointed!

It was thrilling to follow Groslier's protagonists on the same roads, bridges and river, to visit the same rice fields and temples that I had grown to love. While I've seen many changes over the past two decades, his words affirm that the essence of life there remains the same.

As there are few modern works about the history and legends of Battambang, the publisher approached me to create this personal account to give readers better context into Groslier's setting for his book. We will follow the sequence of his novel to explore places and ideas he mentions, as they were and compared with how they are today. Page references from this edition of *The Road of the Strong* appear in brackets [ ] following my quotes from the text.

Finally, I offer my special thanks to scholar Dr. Lia Genovese and to DatAsia editor Kent Davis for their considerable efforts editing and expanding my article with citations and historic photos.

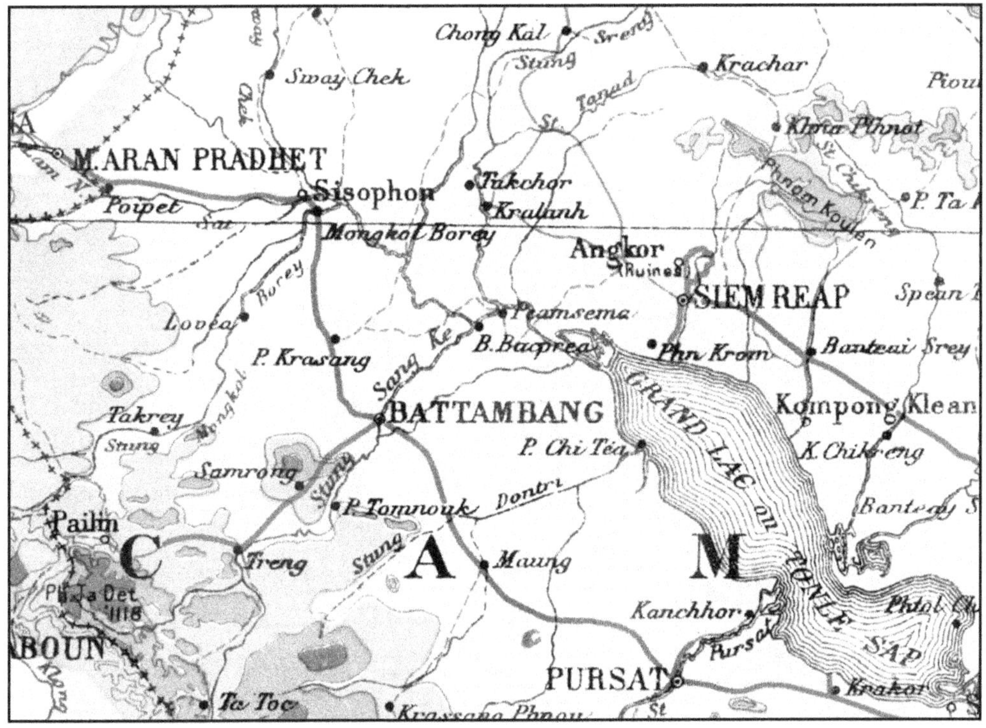

The Battambang area in 1928.

A Brief History of the Battambang Area

Located on the Southeast Asian peninsula, Cambodia rests squarely on the crossroads of maritime commerce between China and India. Goods, religions, wealth, power and knowledge have all traversed this place since time immemorial, so it is not surprising that traces of civilization found here date back to at least the 5th millennium BC. The first detailed records of local nation states appear in Chinese annals from the 1st to 6th centuries. Beginning with Funan, at the southernmost part of the peninsula, centered on the lower Mekong River, power expanded northwards. By the early 9th century, rulers established their capital cities just north of the Tonlé Sap, a massive fresh water lake that provided sustenance for a rapidly growing population. By the end of the 12th century, the Khmer Empire finally became the region's most dominant power.

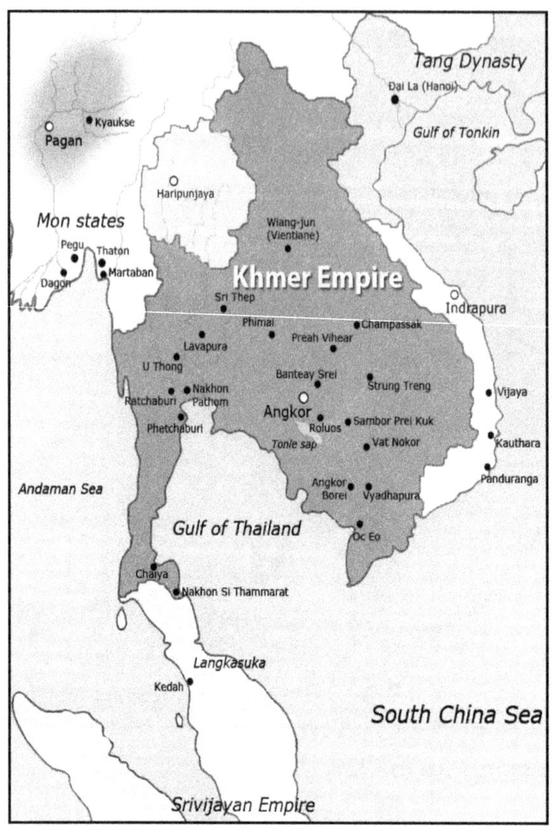

**The extent of the Khmer Empire
in the 9th to the 13th centuries CE.**

Battambang province—our area of interest—is situated about 60 miles (96.5 km) due west of the ancient Khmer capital of Yasodharapura, now known as Angkor. The region is framed by the nearly impassable Dângrêk mountain chain to the north, and the wild Cardamom Mountains to the south. This margin of geographical isolation has afforded the area and its residents a degree of autonomy through the ages. In his day, George Groslier described its "Wild West" allure in his account of Banteay Chhmar temple:

If one ventures to the north-western borders of Cambodia, one arrives in a region surrounded at right angles by the extreme western end of the Dângrêk mountain chain. Beyond them lies Siam. Occupying 2 or 3,000 square kilometers, this area is nearly deserted. Consisting of soil made of clay and sand, crossed by some dry rivers six months of the year, it offers nothing to the traveler but uncultivated plains and sparsely wooded forests whose trees remain stunted due to fires that rage in the dry season. In the summer, there is no game and torrid heat; in winter, the area is subjected to violent storms deflected by the mountains.

Villages, increasingly rare, finally disappear completely; this place is the most desolate in Cambodia. However, ruins are found there;

The region from Bangkok to Battambang in 1928.

an imposing array of monuments from an ancient empire. Among these ruins is not only one of the largest Khmer temples that we know of (including those of the Angkor group), but also one of largest temples in the world. This temple is known as Banteay Chhmar.[1]

Indeed, as Groslier notes, these western areas attained prosperity and power for reasons that are still debated today. But one thing is certain: the Khmer Empire began to unravel sometime in the 13th century, culminating with the sack of Angkor by the Siamese in 1431, the onset of centuries of Siamese rule over the northwestern provinces of Cambodia. With its new rulers nearly 200 miles (322 km) to the west, in Bangkok, the area practically became a land that time forgot, until the arrival of the French in the late 19th century. For the sake of Cambodia, it seems they arrived just in time.

---

1 Translated to English from "Une merveilleuse cité khmère. Banteai Chhma, ville ancienne du Cambodge." Paris, *L'Illustration*, April 3, 1937, N° 4909, pp. 352-357.

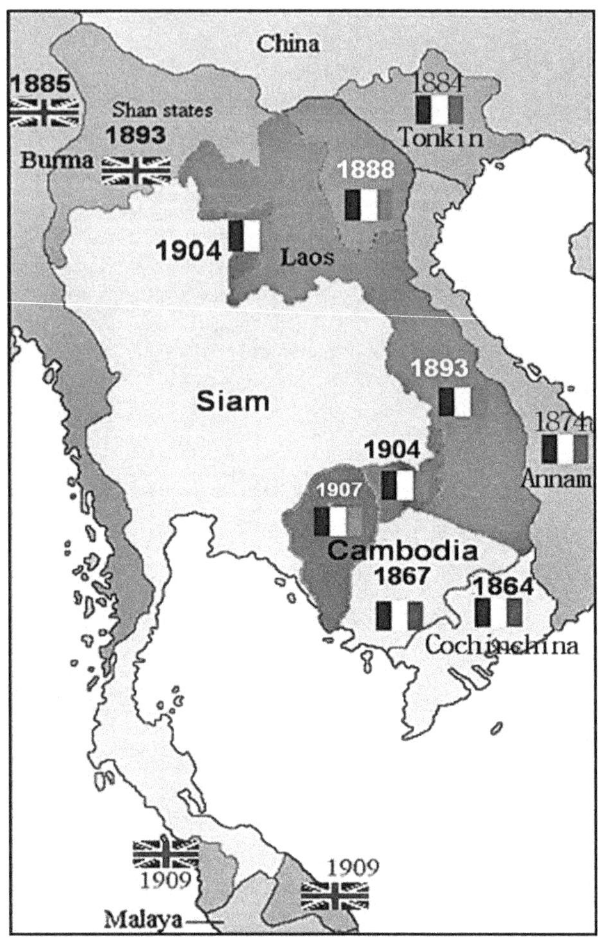

Colonial aquisition dates for France and England

The Siamese neighbors to the north and west, and Vietnamese neighbors to the east, continued overrunning weakened Khmer territories. King Norodom of Cambodia (r. 1860-1904), therefore, saw a relationship with the French as a way of preserving his kingdom.

Despite King Norodom granting France suzerainty over Cambodia in June 1863, on December 1, 1863 he secretly also devolved his country's suzerainty to Siam, with similar terms! The December 1863 secret pact between Cambodia and Siam was declared null and void in April 1865, when France negotiated a new treaty with Siam, with the latter acknowledging French protectorate over Cambodia. The April 1865 treaty was widely criticised in France and did not come into force as it was never ratified by the French government. More negotiations ensued until July 15, 1867, when a new treaty was concluded in Paris where in return for Siam's nullification of the 1863 secret treaty with Cambodia and its recognition of France's protectorate over

Cambodia, "France recognized Siam's claim to Battambang and Angkor and guaranteed Cambodia's observance of the treaty".[2]

This is especially surprising in light of the rediscovery of the fabulous temples of Angkor by French naturalist and explorer Henri Mouhot (1826-1861) in 1859. While French diplomats may not have appreciated the scope of cultural and artistic treasures in the western provinces of Battambang and Siem Reap, King Norodom himself was deeply troubled. Soon, the diplomats caught up.

A Franco-Siamese Treaty reached thirty year later, placed the provinces of Battambang and Siem Reap in a "special situation", which expressly forbade the Siamese government to build "any fortified posts or military establishments in the provinces of Battambang and Siemreap and within a radius of twenty-five kilometers on the right bank of the Mekong".[3]

From this period we have an account by L.B. Rochedragon, nom de plume for Marie-Louis Bazangeon (?-1892), a French legal scholar[4] who traveled to Southeast Asia when Siem Reap and Battambang were under Siamese influence while the rest of Cambodia was a French protectorate. Bazangeon mentioned the Oath of Allegiance, an important state ceremony where court officials drink water previously hallowed by monks while reciting mantras. This ceremony, detailed by H.G.Q. Wales (1900-1981),[5] was carried out twice a year in Siam at specific times and was incumbent on various classes of officials. During the reign of King Rama V (r. 1873-1910), around two thousand officials were required to drink the contents of a small cup of hallowed water "to the last drop",[6] while a priest read out the Oath of Allegiance to the monarch. The practice was in force in ancient Cambodia, as attested to by the eight inscriptions detailing the names of

---

2 Briggs 1946: 444.
3 Article 3, Annex to the Franco-Siamese Treaty of 3 October 1893.
4 In France, Bazangeon served as state attorney at Embrun (Hautes-Alpes, southeast France) and later as court judge in Isère, a department in the Rhône-Alpes region.
5 Serving in the Lord Chamberlain's Department at the Court of Siam, 1924-1928.
6 Wales 1931: 193.

This monument at Wat Phnom shows King Sisowath receiving three classically dressed royal women. They and their offerings—a stupa, a lotus and a royal scepter—represent the provinces of Battambang, Siem Reap and Sisophon returned to Cambodia after the 1907 Franco-Siamese treaty.

numerous officials "who swore allegiance to "Sūryavarman I, each inscription being preceded by the Oath of Allegiance in Khmer".[7] Briggs reports that as many as "4,000 names may be counted"[8] on the gopura of Suryavarman's Royal Palace, where the officials convened to swear the oath of allegiance.

Bazangeon recounts that it was rare for the viceroy of Battambang to take the oath in Bangkok, preferring instead to perform the ceremony in Battambang "in the presence of all his mandarins, who would drink after him".[9] During the ceremony, the

---

7   Wales 1931: 195.
8   Briggs 1951: 151.
9   Rochedragon 1890: 15-16.

viceroy would wear a casquette anglaise, decorated with a large gold band, and a silk sampot.

In 1904, France pulled northern border lands (including the temple of Preah Vihear, perched atop the Dângrêk Mountains) back under Cambodian rule. Finally, on March 23, 1907, Siem Reap and Battambang provinces reverted to Cambodia and, by extension, fell under French protection. Groslier arrived on the scene soon after, so that all of his explorations, and the novel at hand, take place on French Cambodian soil.

After World War II, Vietnam, Laos and Cambodia sought, and gained, independence from French colonial rule. King Norodom Sihanouk (r. 1941-1955 and 1993-2004) declared independence from France on November 9, 1953, but independence became official only with the signing of the Geneva Accords in July 1954, when Cambodia became a constitutional monarchy. But new struggles were already brewing as Communist ideologies destabilized the region, vying for political control.

For years, French troops fought unsuccessfully against communist forces, until the Americans took over the fight in the late-1950s. While intent on fighting communism in Vietnam, the US secretly conducted extensive but unofficial military operations in Laos and Cambodia. This included large-scale and highly destructive bombing campaigns that scar landscapes and people in Laos and Cambodia to this day. The sheer quantity of munitions dropped on Laos, divided by a sparse population, has bestowed on the country the unenviable accolade of being the most bombed country in the world, per capita.[10]

America's wholesale destruction seems to have actually helped communist groups to successfully recruit adherents from the wider population. America first withdrew from Vietnam and then Laos,

---

10 Data by Nobel-prize winners MAG (Mines Advisory Group), www.maginternational.org/where-mag-works/where-we-work/mag-in-laos/ (accessed September 8, 2017).

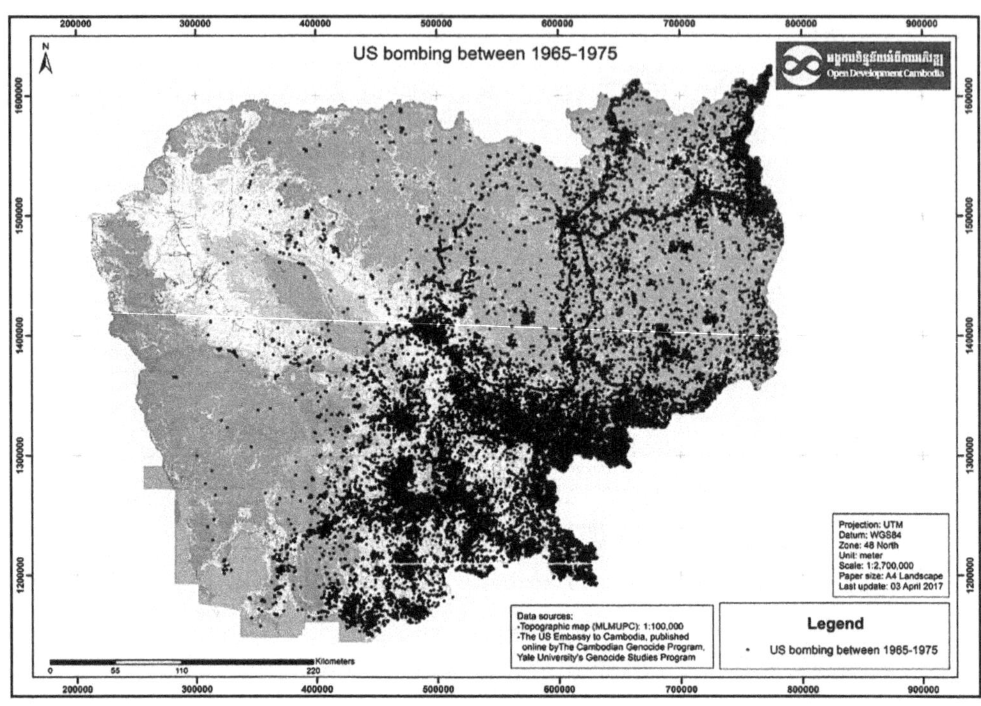

Map of US bombing in Cambodia.
Open Development Cambodia, licensed under CC-BY-SA.

allowing the communists to assume control of both countries. While there were officially no American troops in Cambodia, the country had been supporting the pro-American minister of defense, General Lon Nol, in his fight against the communists. The Khmer Rouge (literally, the 'Red Khmer'), quickly took control of most of Cambodia, with the exception of Phnom Penh. In April 1975, the capital city fell to the Khmer Rouge, a communist faction that imposed their radical ideologies on the entire population.

The Khmer Rouge abolished money, property ownership, the postal service, travel and all communications outside the country. In one of the worst documented cases of genocide in modern history, the regime systematically murdered and enslaved a large percentage of the trapped population. For nearly two decades, Cambodia remained largely cut off from the world. first due to the oppressive nature of the Khmer Rouge government, and then due to civil war and instability following the Vietnamese invasion in 1979.

The tyrannical ideology of the Khmer Rouge sought to emulate the mastery of Cambodia's ancient water engineers by dispensing with modern excavation machinery and tools. In January 2004, during a year-long tour of archaeological sites in Southeast Asia, Lia Genovese travelled to Kamping Puoy, to the west of Battambang. Kamping Puoy is the site of a Khmer-rouge era project to build a dam entirely by hand, a utopian construction effort that is thought to have exacted a death toll of 10,000 people. Today's weekend visitors may be forgiven for being unaware of the dam's tragic past, as they relax in simple straw huts by the cooling waters of the reservoir, which thankfully now resonates with joyful laughter.

Not until the early 1990s did the United Nations sanctions help Cambodia in implementing a new government. Until the very end, the remote Battambang area was the scene of seasonal fighting between government forces, Khmer Rouge and other military factions. Other travelers told me that access to Battambang was safer via Thailand in the west than from the eastern road (National Road 5) that ran from the Cambodian capital of Phnom Penh. In the late 1990s, the remaining Khmer Rouge troops surrendered and the country's western region began admitting foreign travelers like me. What my companion, Chamroeun, and I found 70 years after George Groslier's first visit would have been, in many ways, strangely familiar to him.

George Groslier in his home office on December 5, 1922,
working beneath a bust of his daughter Nicole.

Groslier on the Road to Battambang

While *The Road of the Strong* was Groslier's first novel, he drew from decades of Cambodian experience in coloring its pages. Indeed, after 14 years of academic writing, it seems clear that he savored the opportunity of breaking free of those restraints to relate what he truly saw and felt.

In February 1887, future artist, author and historian George Groslier was one of the first children born in Cambodia to French parents. When Groslier was two years old, his mother decided that colonial life in the tropics was too dangerous and she returned to France so that young George could receive a French education. In essence, he grew up fatherless but his scholarly dedication guaranteed him a place at the École des Beaux Arts in Paris. However, as his biographer Kent Davis observes, "the die was cast. The soul of the Khmer land had infused itself into the child and by the age of 23 he was drawn back to his birthplace."[11]

In 1910, Groslier returned to Cambodia on assignment from the French Ministry of Public Education, in what would be the beginning of his life-long commitment to the arts, culture and people of the Kingdom. In 1912, he gave Westerners their first in-depth look at the kingdom's ancient sacred dance with *Cambodian Dancers – Ancient and Modern*. WWI delayed his next book, a documentary account of his solitary exploration of Khmer monuments—*In the Shadow of Angkor–Unknown Temples of Ancient Cambodia*—which included visits to the Battambang area. Following his service in WWI, he returned to Cambodia in 1918 to design, build and establish both the Albert Sarraut Museum (now the National Museum of Cambodia) and the School of Fine Arts. Both institutions still thrive in their mission of preserving and perpetuating the history and culture of the land.

---

11 Kent Davis, "Le Khmérophile: The Art and Life of George Groslier," in *Cambodian Dancers-Ancient and Modern*, George Groslier (Holmes Beach, FL: DatAsia Press, 2012), p. 208.

Groslier's map showing his journeys in 1912-1913,
including his first trip to Battambang.

Through his scholarly articles and publications, Groslier came
to be recognized as a quintessential witness to colonial life in
Cambodia in his lifetime. Tragically, on June 18, 1945, just weeks
before the end of WWII, Groslier died in Phnom Penh under
Japanese interrogation because an informer connected him to
activities supporting the liberation of Cambodia. Though his death

Colonials in Phnom Penh preparing for a road trip in 1912.

certificate honored him with the legal designation "Mort pour la France" recognizing his service to his country, Groslier's entire catalog of rare books about Southeast Asia fell into obscurity after his murder. In 2008, historian Kent Davis—literary archaeologist at DatAsia Press—began working with the author's daughter, Nicole Groslier Rea (1918-2015), to revive her father's legacy and to restore his creative works missing for more than half a century.

The Road of the Strong is one of their modern restorations, appearing in English for the first time in 2017. In it, Groslier describes the lives, challenges and romances of colonial residents in a remote corner of the protectorate of Cambodia in the early 20th century. My enthusiasm for the book grew even stronger when I realized that I, too, had traveled the same roads he described. His words inspired this article, exploring his setting then and now.

Groslier group arrival of the first cars at Banteay Chhmar; March 9, 1924.
© Copyright - The National Museum of Cambodia

Groslier's Early 20th Century Road

Though he traveled by oxcart in 1911, Groslier broke new ground in 1924 when he made one of the first recorded visits to the area north of Battambang, by automobile.[12] He was headed to Banteay Chhmar, when Route Coloniale No. 1 afforded the only viable motoring option from the capital of Phnom Penh to Battambang in the west. Present-day National Road No. 5 replicates the route followed by this historical road, stretching from Phnom Penh via Poursat to Battambang and thence to Banteay Meanchey, on its westward section towards the Thai border.

---

12 Collins, Darryl. "Banteay Chhmar: First Automobile Visit." Appendix article, *In the shadow of Angkor: unknown temples of ancient Cambodia* by George Groslier. DatAsia Press, 2014. Pp. 139-147.

Four-wheeled transport sharing the road with four-legged transport in 1912.

In his novel, Groslier describes the Phnom Penh-Battambang route as being a five-hour trip:

> "Thereupon a car equipped at Saigon crossed Cochin China, switched to Cambodian roads, stopped for a night at Phnom Penh, set out once more at dawn, and five hours later, hot and dusty, pulled up beneath the porch of the Résidence of Sangkae." [p. 10]

Later, he continues with a discussion between Pierre Ternier, résident de France in Indochina, and Hélène Gassin:

> "It is the main thing. You made the trip from Phnom Penh in five hours."

> "Upon a magnificent road."

> "Ten years ago you would have been five days crossing the savannah, on a horse or in a cart. It is worthwhile for a *résident* to watch over the roads. He sees to their every need." [P. 46.]

Five hours is approximately the length of time required to travel today from Phnom Penh to Battambang. Not long ago, however, poor road conditions made this trip nearly twice as long, due to the neglect caused by thirty years of civil unrest, which left roads and other infrastructure in a dire state of disrepair.

In Groslier's story, Ternier plans to extend Route Coloniale No. 1 to Sisophon ("Srey Saophon", or "Beautiful Lady" in Khmer), directly to the north of Battambang.

> "It has just been resurfaced. It goes all the way to Sisophon, eighty kilometers from here, and past that a path has been cleared for more than a hundred kilometers. In three years there will be cars at the foot of the Dângrêk Mountains. The northernmost reaches of Cambodia and, through the passes, the nether regions of Laos will be opened up. On our side, we will also have opened up the northeast provinces of Siam." [Pg. 50]

This road network was of strategic importance to the Union of French Indochina as a counter to the commercial advantage

A primitive colonial road in 1912.

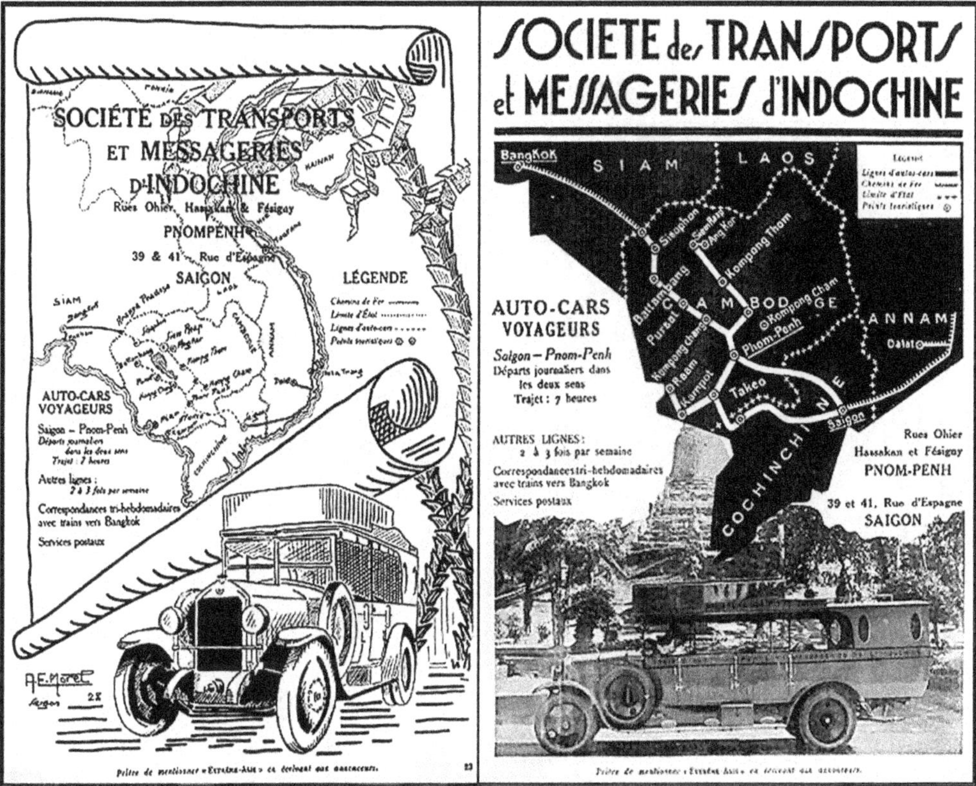

and economic threat posed by Siam, and its port of Bangkok. For
Governor-general Albert Sarraut (1872-1962), later Minister for
Colonies, a road network connecting Vietnam, Laos and Cambodia
was crucial to French interests.

Route Coloniale No. 1, also known as the Mandarin Road,
was the backbone for the highway infrastructure of Indochina.
Since its construction by the Chinese around 2,000 years ago,
Route Mandarine has evoked romantic notions of the Orient and
its rich splendors, with the odd exception, however. The French
novelist Roland Dorgelès (1886-1973), for instance, could scarcely
understand the appeal of "a wide, badly paved highway, skirting
the railroad."[13]

---

13 Dorgelès 1926: 7.

Colonial bus service.

Vietnamese emperors' expansion extended it to the south, from Hanoi to Saigon, and the French stretched its length further, into Cambodia and to Battambang on the border with Siam at Aranya Prathet. It was this route that Chamroeun and I followed on our journey from Thailand to Battambang.

In the September 1928 issue of *National Geographic* magazine, Robert J. Casey writes:

> "Splendid automobile roads, cut through what was once a thicket of bamboo and is now an endless rice field, bring the traveler, on schedule and with little personal discomfort, from Saigon, at the foot of Asia, to the bungalow on the edge of the Angkor moat, in a few hours."

Another early account of the Mandarin Road dates to 1931, when W. Robert Moore left Bangkok by train bound for Aranya Prathet, from where he crossed into Cambodian territory at Poipet and thence to Sisophon, for a car adventure that took him to the gates of China.[14]

---

14 Moore, Robert. "Along the Old Mandarin Road of Indochina." National Geographic 8/1931. P. 157.

A UN truck in the mid-1990s.

The Road in Modern Times

These early accounts are remarkable, considering that this same trip had become a challenging journey as recently as our first visit in 1998.

Having travelled overland to India in the mid-1970s, I had some prior experience with roads in developing countries. On entering Cambodia from Thailand during our first visit, the transition was stark. Given that the ongoing conflict had rendered much of that area effectively off-limits, particularly to foreigners, the experience was akin to stepping into a time capsule. It soon became apparent that Cambodia had suffered greatly from the war. If, as I had been informed, National Road 5 eastwards to Battambang was the 'better road', the mind wandered as to what awaited drivers on the even poorer westbound route from Phnom Penh.

After reaching the Thai-Cambodian border in mid-afternoon, we doubted our ability to reach Battambang by nightfall, our

Heading east from Poipet.

apprehension heightened by informal reports that outlaws roamed the roads. At Poipet, a Cambodian border town, we haggled for a ride to Battambang via the ubiquitous Toyota Camry "taxi". Other means of public transport—buses or trains—were at the time not available and a sturdy Toyota was the mode of travel, in preference to a journey in the back of a pickup truck.

Crossing the border from Thailand felt like being transported back in time to another century. Humans joined animals pulling overloaded old wooden carts, as masses of people trudged along the dusty road. In Thailand we experienced some of the trappings of relative modernity, such as ATM machines, but just across the border, in Cambodia, we saw poverty and simplicity. Despite this, I perceived a sense of happiness and contentment on people's faces, especially when contrasted with the hurried bustling of modern Thailand. I speculated that musings about the romanticism of a simpler way of life are easily entertained by people in a position of privilege, but rarely by those actually living it on a daily basis. Yet, there seemed to be something there that I could not deny.

The road to Sisophon had deteriorated badly by the time this photo was taken on May 10, 1947.

Leaving Poipet, we headed east towards Sisophon and thence south to Battambang on National Highway 5, which was very likely the same road Groslier describes here:

> They set off for Sisophon in the afternoon two days later. Riding in the Roland-Gassin were Hélène, the doctor, and Ternier, and riding in the Résidence car a secretary, the cook, and a boy. The baggage had been dispatched that morning on one of the service trucks that shuttle between Sangkae and Sisophon. At that final outpost, where the gravel road came to an end, they would have to switch to horses and make their way north along a path cleared through the glades, a first stage of seventy kilometers. Beyond that the future road pushed on as a mere swath, veering northwest for some twenty-five kilometers more to the edge of the great Chong Kal forest. With Hélène along, Ternier had limited the daily trek to twenty-five kilometers. This put them three days from their destination. [P. 94.]

In the distance we saw large overloaded trucks disappear into massive craters in the road and then resurface. I wondered how well the suspension on our Toyota would handle these roads, which appeared better suited to tanks or lunar vehicles.

At several informal checkpoints, soldiers would stop vehicles and gratefully accept a cigarette or two or a few Thai baht to facilitate our passage. Nevertheless, despite the calm exterior, as the sun set we became anxious for any unpleasant developments that might stem from a perceived lawless ambiance.

Small, one-lane bridges backed up traffic in both directions and were spanned by wooden planks barely the width of tires. As vehicles and animal-drawn carts jostled for position on both sides, I looked on and thought to myself "we can't possibly be going over that!" Yet, we waited our turn and did indeed.

Implausible looking vehicles rigged up with engines, driveshafts and makeshift seats puttered along the road, old Russian and

Chinese trucks sans cabs or body sputtering along, with drivers looking on intently… everyone dodging chickens, cows, children, bicycles and small 100cc motorcycles. Passing through tiny villages, some dwellings were patently far too close to all this traffic. The red dust, raised by passing vehicles, would have been reason enough to relocate further back from the road, if circumstances had allowed.

Thankfully, traffic velocity was largely curtailed by the road's poor condition. Yet sadly today, with the roads in much better repair, accidents are recorded on a daily basis on these very roads. Economic growth and modernization have had unintended, and often tragic, consequences.

We arrived after dark at Chamroeun's family's house, which at the time was little more than a wooden shack along the banks of the Sangker River, just north of Battambang town.

Stepping out of the car into the darkness, after a five-hour bone-jarring journey from the Thai border, I was struck by the number of stars visible in the night sky. Electricity was relatively scarce in this part of town at that time and, through the darkness, we could barely discern a crowd of neighbors starting to gather at this rare presence of a vehicle in their village. Chamroeun had not been back home in 30 years, since fleeing the country after the Vietnamese invasion (which allowed for thousands to escape when the Khmer Rouge were put on the defensive). Our visit was unannounced and a complete surprise.

Amid the weeping of Chamroeun's mother and surviving relatives, a festive atmosphere ensued. It seemed that the whole village gathered to witness our arrival. We had arrived in the legendary city of Battambang…which brings us to the legend itself.

The Legend of Ta Dambong

The best-known local legend relates to the origin of Battambang's name. In Khmer, 'bat tambang' means 'lost stick'. One version of the tale involves a poor cattle herder who found a magical staff that gave him great powers that he used to usurp the throne from the king. The king's son escapes to the forest and later, aided by the Hindu god Indra, returns to his father's kingdom on a mythical white horse to challenge 'King Dambong', who foresaw his impending demise. King Dambong threw his magic stick at his challenger, the prince, but when he missed, the magic stick was lost, reputedly in the Battambang area, and still waiting to be found.

**Ta Dambong Kranhoung statue on Highway 5
entering Battambang from Phnom Penh.**

Today, 'King Dambong' (affectionately known as 'Ta Dambong' or 'grandfather stick') is revered by the locals, who place incense at the foot of his large statue which greets travelers as they enter Battambang on National Highway 5 from Phnom Penh. A larger representation has since replaced the original, smaller statue at the roundabout approaching the town. It seems that King Dambong's following has grown in recent times. Replicas of Ta Dambong Kranhoung, where 'Kranhoung' is a tree whose wood is said to be exceptionally hard, are on sale in carving shops in the town. There are three prominent statues in Battambang based on this legend.

1859 view of Battambang from Henri Mouhot.

Sangkae: A History of the Town

Historian O.W. Wolters offers a succinct introduction:

The modern town of Battambang is on the Sangke River, about ten miles south-west of the Vat Baset hill. According to an account written in 1882 by the renowned army officer, explorer and diplomat Auguste Pavie (1847-1925), before 1835 the present Battambang site was occupied by the small village of Sangke, while 'Old Battambang' was in the immediate neighborhood of 'Baset'. Pavie's account explains why Mouhot, visiting the area in 1859-60, believed that a numerous population had lived a century earlier around the ruins of "Bassette" and why, some years later, Louis Delaporte (1842-1925), quoting the explorer Félix Gaspard

**An engraving of Phnom Banon from Delaporte's 1880
"Voyage au Cambodge, L'Architecture khmer.".**

Faraut (1846-1944), refers to the "former capital of Basset" and to the remains of the towns ramparts and moats. During the nineteenth century, north-western Cambodia was ruled as a Siamese dependency and old Battambang was originally the provincial capital. In 1835, and again according to Pavie, the Vietnamese invaded Cambodia, and the decision was taken in Bangkok to pull down the old town of Battambang and rebuild it on the site of the Sangke village. The provincial capital was now transferred to its present site, and the Dambang River, an arm of the Sangke River flowing by Vat Baset and entering the Tonlé Sap south of the present Sangke estuary, was blocked.[15]

---

15 Wolters, O. W. 1974. "North-Western Cambodia in the Seventh Century". *Bulletin of the School of Oriental and African Studies, University of London.* 37 (2): 367.

Cambodian historian Tauch Chhuong expands on Wolters closing comment:

> "At the time of the rivers blockage, a dike was built at the point where the river branched, near Wat Khvaeng. But the dike could not contain the water so it was often breached. Later, a large thvae boat was placed across the canal and filled with soil to create a dike. Many elders who remembered the incident recalled that they had conducted a ritual offering by killing a pregnant woman and offering her to the sacred beings protecting the dike. That place was called Prek Ponnareay"

> "Subsequently, the dike was never breached and water flowed between the river banks of Battambang, increasing in size. The river flowing along the Aur Dambang gradually became smaller and more shallow"[16]

Battambang Under Thai Rule

Before the French restored Battambang to Cambodian control, the province was under Thai sovereignty for more than a century. By the time of Groslier's arrival, it had been governed by Cambodian and French authorities for less than 20 years.

Under Thai rule, the Abhaiwongse family governed the area for six generations. The last Siamese governor was Lok Mchas Chhum (or Choom) Abhaiwongse, upon whom King Rama V bestowed the title "Chaophraya Abhaibhubejhr."

According to American historian David Chandler, the Siamese appeared to have no long-range plan for Battambang and Siem Reap when they were first brought under Thai control, but Rama I (r. 1782-1809) was obliged to grant the two provinces to Ta-la-ha

---

16 Tức, Jhuan. 1994. *Battambang during the time of the lord governor.* Phnom Penh: Cedoreck. P. 24.

Lok Mchas Chhum Abhaiwongse.

(the prime minister) Baen for his years of faithful service to the Bangkok court. Thai suzerainty over the Battambang region meant only that Baen had to send tributary gifts to Bangkok from time to time.[17]

---

17 Chandler, David P. 2000. *Cambodia before the French: politics in a tributary kingdom, 1794-1848*. Ann Arbor, Mich: UMI Dissertation Services, p. 78-79.

Musicians at the Governor's mansion in 1889.

Khmer Classical Dance in Battambang

Battambang's connection to Cambodia's sacred dance tradition may have also attracted Groslier to the region. Some of the earliest photographs and descriptions shared with Europe originated in this area.

In 1883 Moura claimed that Norodom's rung ram or "dancing shed" was the only theatre in Cambodia. In this he was possibly mistaken since photos of a theatre in Battambang were published by August Pavie in 1898—a theatre he had seen sometime between 1879 and 1895. Pavie's pictures of a rehearsal in the Battambang theatre are the oldest available photographs of Khmer classical dancers. ...One traveler to Cambodia between 1880 and 1884 attended a theatre in Battambang which may have been the same as that mentioned by Pavie. [18]

---

18 Cravath, Paul. *Earth in Flower – The Divine Mystery of the Cambodian Dance Drama.* DatAsia Press, 2008. P. 120.

Tauch Chhuong also provides a detailed description of the Lord Governor's dance troupes:

> "The governor owned two theater troupes, a male troupe and a female troupe. ....The men's theater troupe was a large group composed of more than 100 actors. Their office and rehearsal hall was located south of present-day Loe Market. The troupe used male actors alone, even for the role of Seta. This was a masked troupe, the giant, Hanuman, the monkey, all wore the masks. The masks were made from paper hardened with lacquer and covered with beautiful decorations.

> Each actor danced to the rhythm of the music gesturing to the song being played. During that era, they sang primarily in Thai, explaining the story in both Thai and Khmer. The use of Thai was a custom among the nobles. The principal actors were Putrea as Preah Ream, Man as Preah Leaks, Tuot as Reap, and Pech as Hanuman. Popular clown were names Daor and Krang. This was reported by the elder, Kuang Pheak. In this male theater troupe, Kim portrayed the role of Seta. The elderly woman, Um living at Wat Kantoeng village reported that the governor enjoyed Kim very much because he had the face, body, arms, and legs of a beautiful girl. The governor said that if anyone so much as broke a single finger on Kim's hand, that person would pay a fine of one hundred tamloeng. The governor allowed only Kim to act with the female troupe, in which all the principal actresses were wives of the governor.

> The female troupe had fewer actors than the male troupe. Men were not allowed to mingle with the women's troupe either during rehearsals or public performances. The governor allowed only one male actor to dance with the women; this was Kim, already described in the section above. The women's troupe was selected when Kathathan Chhum first came to power. The actresses were chosen from among beautiful thirteen and fourteen year old girls. Most of the actresses were Khmer, but a few were Chinese or Vietnamese. No Thai actresses were reported.

Dance Drama Rehearsal at Battambang, ca. 1885. Pavie. Probably the dancers of Lok Muccha, who was Lord Governor of the province at that time.

From the information we have, many parents with beautiful daughters hid them when the actresses were being selected in order to prevent them from being seen. Some parents were found guilty of trying to hide their daughters or of refusing to allow their daughters to become actresses. This does not mean that the people of Battambang did not appreciate the arts, but rather, becoming the governor's actresses meant the loss of their freedom, which was already limited. Actresses had to live on the premises of the governor's home under strict regulation and control. They were forbidden to contact anyone outside the fort. If an actress secretly contacted a man, she was sentenced to death along with her lover. The lord governor absolutely prohibited actresses from having husbands. Actresses were mere tools to be used for the passions of the governor"

... "In earlier times, the women's troupes like the men's troupe performed only the Reamke story"[19]

That said, it is unlikely that the dance troupe Groslier mentions are those described by Tauch Chhuong:

> "Ternier and Hélène took a street that ran beneath a vault of trees. It led between sidewalks and compartments to a square with a grand theater, where every evening Siamese and Cambodian actors played The Ramayana." [P. 21]"

This is because most of the relatives (numbering in the thousands) of Chhum Abhaiwongse, the last lord governor, moved to the Thai province of Prachinburi shortly before this time. According to eyewitnesses, when Lord Chhum moved to Thailand, he took with him about 100 cartloads of gold and assets, taxed from Khmer farmers in Battambang. However, though likely Chhum took most of his dancers with him, it is quite possible that some may have remained in Battambang.

A final point of interest is that Lord Chhum, who had more than 40 wives, had a Thai wife among them. She bore him a son named

---

19 Tưc, Jhuan. 1994. *Battambang during the time of the lord governor.* Phnom Penh: Cedoreck.

The Lok Mchas family stupa at Wat Kdol.

Khuang who took the surname of Aphaiwong. Khuang Aphaiwong was born in Battambang on May 17, 1902 and died on March 15, 1968 in Bangkok. He served three times as the prime minister of Thailand, a fact that Cambodians take great pride in. Khuang was one of the most important leaders of the 1932 coup that reformed the Thai kingdom from an absolute monarchy to a constitutional monarchy, under the reign of King Rama VII (r. 1925-1934).

Spean Thmar Chas bridge, with the Residence top left.

Arriving in Groslier's Sangkae

Since we met in 1987, Chamroeun has recounted many tales from this area's rich oral history, and Battambang is featured in many popular Cambodian songs. All this inspired me to deepen my knowledge of the area's culture and history. Finally, in 1998 we had the opportunity to return together to experience the river, the trees and the temples featured in the songs and folklore of his place of birth. Groslier's early account of the city fascinated me because the places and scenes he described were immediately familiar.

Wat Sangker, 1936.

To my knowledge, this is the only novel focused on the Sangkae (Sangker) district of Cambodia. The novel's protagonist, Pierre Ternier, is the *résident*, the region's chief administrator acting on behalf of the French government from its largest town. Today, the town is known as Battambang, from which the province takes its name. Sangkae is still a district in the town, named after the Sangker River, which flows through it. It is a peaceful town, despite the presence, in rice fields and on undeveloped land, of unexploded ordnances (UXO), remnants of the recent conflict.

Sangker is a type of tree (Combretum Quadrangulare Kurz) that grows in the sparse local forests. Since ancient times, the Khmer people have used Sangker leaves as paper for cigarette wrappers, they have burnt its trunk for firewood and extracted potash water from its ashes. As early as 500 CE, communities around the world have extracted potash from land- and sea-plants, with hardwoods like the sangker being a particularly viable source. Potash is critical for bleaching textiles and for the production of glass and soap.

A legend recounts that the river was named after a large sangker tree was cut down so that villagers could cross on its trunk. A wat was built in that precise location. Today, Wat Sangker still stands on the east bank of the river, where the original large tree stood, just across from the water and to the north of the "old stone bridge".

> "The door clattered shut, and the car made its way over a bridge of reinforced concrete across from the Résidence." [P. 14.]

The bridge of reinforced concrete across from the Résidence (now called Sala Khaet), which Groslier mentions, probably corresponds to modern Spean Thmar Chas (Old Stone Bridge), the oldest bridge in Battambang. Built in 1916 by the French administration, the bridge emphasizes the main axis from the east of Battambang to the Provincial Hall (Sala Khaet). One can still see the French road kilometer stone (with the inscription "0 kilometre à Battambang") and the traditional pair of lions on the west bank of the river. The bridge was damaged by military vehicles in 1997 and is now only

Colonial mile marker. Walter Koditek Archive.

accessible by motorbike and pedestrian traffic. Colonial-era cannons are still positioned in front of Sala Khaet.

As detailed earlier, the Siamese controlled the Battambang region from the late 18th to the early 20th century under the rule of the Khmer Chaofa Baen family (later known as the Aphaiwong Family). Chaofa Baen was a high-ranking military official in Ouddong (the Cambodian capital at the time) who enjoyed the support of the Siamese king (Rama I). The family ruled the area as "Lord Governor" (Lok Mchas) for six generations, until 1907.

The last Lord Governor of Battambang was Lok Mchas Kathathon Chhum (Chhum Aphaiwong). In 1905, Lok Mchas Chhum hired Italian architects from Bangkok to construct a new residence inside his fort ("Kamphaeng"). This residence is known today as Sala Khaet. The fort itself was destroyed in 1911 with only a small part of the north wall remaining. Nearby a temple and a school still carry the name Kamphaeng.

The city's fortified north gate (Kamphaeng) in the 1890s and early 1900s.

The Residence in the early 1900s. Joel Montague Archive.

While the Lord Governor's Residence (Sala Khaet) is still a prominent feature in Battambang, in fact Lok Mchas Chhum never lived in it. Lord Chhum and his descendants moved to Thailand in 1907, when France insisted that Battambang province and several other provinces be returned to Cambodia as a result of the Franco-Siamese Treaty of March 23, 1907. When Lord Chhum moved to Prachinburi, he built another mansion nearly identical to the one in Battambang (now known as the Chaophraya Abhaibhubejhr building). He is said to have hired some of the same craftsmen. The cost was estimated at about a million baht, equivalent to 0.5 million US dollars in today's terms.[20] This building in Prachinburi now houses a museum of traditional Thai medicine.

---

20 Early in the 20th century, the rate of exchange was 55 Thai baht to 1 US dollar. The approximate value of 0.5 million dollars has been arrived at by using the Consumer Price Index (CPI) provided in the MeasuringWorth.com website.

BATTAMBANG — *Vue des bureaux de la Résidence - Ancienne habitation du Phya-Kathathor*

**The Residence in the early 1900s (above) and in the 1920s (below),
contemporary with Groslier's novel. Joel Montague Archive.**

203   CAMBODGE — *BATTAMBANG* — *Bureaux de la Sala-Ket*

Modern photo of Spean Thmar Chas leading the the Residence.

It is erroneously believed that Sala Khaet was built by the French Colonial administration. It would seem likely that, after Chhum's departure, it accommodated the "Résident-supérieur Français" and was used by the French administration under the Protectorate. It is currently the seat of the Provincial Governor.

Over the years, Sala Khaet has undergone several restorations, losing some of its original architectural features — roof pediments, windows, doors, etc. — in the process. In the 1990s, the main gate was replaced with a new gate in the style of Banteay Srei temple. This was initiated by the then Governor of Battambang, a former Governor of Siem Reap Province. The new gate has since been removed, perhaps in an attempt to return it to a more original appearance.

Thus, the evidence suggests that Sala Khaet, also known as the former "Lord Governor's residence", is the building Groslier refers to as the "Résidence of Sangkae", where Pierre Ternier resides

The Residence, Sala Khaet, in the 1990s.

in our story. A fascinating account of the Thai colonial period is given in a book called "Battambang during the time of the Lord Governor" by Tauch Chhoung.

Madame Gassin's initial impressions of Battambang describe activity on the Sangker River, the "New Town" being built by the French on the east side of the river. Groslier contrasts this with the rural, village-like west side that, to an extent, existed during our first visits in 1998.

> "It is all yours, Madame. It is a particularly lovely time of day, and I do believe that the land of Sangkae has turned itself out for you. The new town, the one we are building, is on this side of the river. I will give you a proper tour tomorrow. If you would like to observe native life, cross the river and make your way beneath those trees on the far side, the ones the sun is shining on right now. [P. 13.]

The riverside in the early 1900s (above) and in 1926 (below),
contemporary with Groslier's novel. Jim Mizerski Archive.

Their tour of the town begins on the western side of the river, with observations of "village life" that do not seem terribly removed from my own first impressions.

> "Oxen passed. She saw and recognized open watermelons in a basket. There was a steady thump from a paddy mortar, operated by a woman standing atop its pestle. Farther off young men sat idle in daydreams, staring off toward the river before them. Two bare-necked cocks, standing tall on their madder-colored legs, made a sudden, mad scramble for some fish guts and came to blows. Small children had gathered around the car. Then a decrepit old carriage, with the stuffing coming out and rattan patchwork and two rope-harnessed horses to draw it, came rattling along the road, transporting Chinese women with baskets in their laps. Bonzes advancing in Indian file and draped like Romans crossed its path. Flowers with a pale-yellow core were coating the ground at the roadside, the last of them dropping from a barren tree, its trunk and branches grey, twisted, and scaly." [P. 15.]

The riverfront in 1948.

Madame Gassin's tour continues in the "new town" on the eastern side of the river, with M. Ternier proudly describing landmarks such as the post office, bus depot and hospital:

> "Yesterday, Madame, on the far bank, you saw native life, with its calm and its liberty. Places once isolated by days and days of travel we have now linked to the rest of the country by roads. Here in this square, behind those trees and between the blue walls, stands the post office, with its telegraph and telephone lines. It serves also as a depot for the buses, which depart in all directions. [P. 20.]

According to Tauch Chhuon, French improvements like the hospital were not favorably received under Thai rule:

> "During the lord governor's era, people were miserable and they experienced many physical difficulties. Contagious diseases caused almost half the people to die annually, the majority of whom were children... The lord governor never conceived of building a public hospital to assist people... One disappointment concerned the hospital located at the French Consulate. The lord governor forbade people from having any contact with it. He threatened that anyone who attempted to do so would be shot."[21]

---

21 Tưc, Jhuan. 1994. *Battambang during the time of the lord governor.* Phnom Penh: Cedoreck. P. 34.

The riverfront in 2009 with colonial buildings intact.

The post office in 1948. Walter Koditek Archive.

BATTAMBANG — *Bâtiment principal de l'école résidentielle*

"Our schools were no sooner opened than they were filled to capacity. " [P. 20.]

BATTAMBANG   *Habitation des Sous-officiers Européens, en face le camp des tirailleurs*

The residence hall for non-commissioned officers.

"Dying children? We will presently be passing in front of the hospital, with a maternity ward for natives and pavilions scattered in a park." [P. 20.]

As Ternier describes, French administration quickly brought the region into the 20th century with many conveniences:

> We have also built the safe, hygienic market where the Cambodian buys and sells; the guarded roads where he need no longer fear highwaymen; the hospital that heals him free of charge; the school his children freely attend; the offices where he need no longer be under the mandarin's thumb; the bridges he can cross with his carts, without unmooring a sampan that the current can carry off; the factory that provides his pure water and his light. [Pg. 21]

The center of activity in every town was the marketplace, seen on the following pages in Groslier's time, accompanied by photos of the new "art-deco" version built in 1937 on the same spot.

Battambang Market in the early 1900s, 1912 and 1925.

Views of the modern Phsar Nath Market built in 1937. Walter Koditek Archive.

Battambang colonial cemetery, circa 1950.

Passenger car service in Groslier's time.

Finally, for many French, the road ended in Battambang's colonial cemetery:

> In the past or at present, wittingly or not, unbidden or compelled by an order, all these people—every half-family short a father, mother, or child; every exile, doubtless a volunteer; every errant soul, though he err to earn a living—had played an eminent role... In the colonies there are but laborers—indeed, to judge by the scope of their task, good laborers.

> Names like theirs are etched into the stones of Sangkae cemetery. The bearers of those names would doubtless be satisfied to see straight roads, a school, a dispensary, and a hygienic market in the town where only sixteen years earlier they were leveling the land and breathing in its pestilence. [P. 89]

Walking through Battambang today, visitors can still see many sites with fascinating vestiges of colonial and pre-colonial times.

Lok Mchas Chhum family stupa at Wat Kdol.

Wat Kdol

Following the Sangker River north of the city, we find the temple of Wat Kdol, where the Thai Lord Governor built a stupa to house remains of his ancestors before moving to Thailand. There, many unusual sculptures reflect the colonial past. Though Groslier didn't mention this pagoda in *The Road of the Strong*, its unusual style of statuary caught his eye in his 1929 journeys on the Mekong.

> The entrance alone is an omen. It is flanked by two French soldiers — life size, thank you very much — each sporting a moustache, a jacket pinched back with a half-belt over his lower back, a melon atop his head, a rifle, and a toothy expression. Over the past eight days I have seen more French soldiers at pagoda doors than are stationed at the Phnom Penh garrison. Of course, one should not harbor prejudices. Such statues can be amusing, and the idea of flanking temple entrances with two threatening guardian statues goes back a thousand years. The sanctuaries of Angkor were guarded by dvarapalas.[22] Well, today the dvarapalas have become French soldiers. So what? But these — these are jumping jacks, stupid, sadly grotesque, devoid of verve, utterly lacking even in rancor! [23]

Groslier's characters did, however, journey to another nearby pagoda that's still popular today:

> "Well, then. It's four o'clock. Let's venture another thirty kilometers from here and take a look at a well-situated pagoda: Wat Romduol. The road through the rice fields is not too bad. How about it?" [P. 26.]

Named for the romduol, a fragrant flower that is, in fact, the national flower of Cambodia), the temple is about 3 km north of the city along the river very close to Chamroeun's family home.

---

22 *Dvarapalas* are powerful human or demonic figures flanking temple and palace doorways to protect the holy places inside. They are often fierce looking and armed.
23 Groslier, George. *Water and light: A travel journal of the Cambodian Mekong.* Holmes Beach, FL: DatAsia Press. 2016. P. 49.

French soldier as *dvarapala* guardian at Wat Kdol.

French official as *dvarapala* guardian at Wat Kdol.

Wat Ek in 1871. Jim Mizerski Archive.

Outside the city

Groslier takes us on several excursions outside the town, including the dramatic climax to his tale. Continuing 13 km north of the city from Wat Romdual one arrives at Wat Ek Phnom, another 11th century Hindu temple built by King Suryavarman I. Battambang is permeated by this history. During all of our visits, we travelled the surrounding area mostly on foot or by bicycle, experiencing the area in ways motor vehicles do not allow. The quiet and leisurely pace, though sometimes a test of endurance on account of the heat and dust, allowed us to venture through rice paddies and into villages and areas not otherwise accessible. There, we saw a side of Cambodia that was still relatively untouched, its pre-conflict isolation exacerbated by the civil war.

I recollect an old villager asking Chamroeun, in French, if he could touch my skin, because he could scarcely believe what he was seeing. I also recall another elderly villager, a school teacher

Engraving of Phnom Banon from Henri Mouhot's book, *Voyage dans les royaumes de Siam, de Cambodge, de Laos et autres parties centrales de l'Indo-Chine,* **1858-1861.**

from the outskirts of Battambang, wearing a costume which was a mixture of Khmer and French colonial: a French military-style jacket with epaulets, a sampot, a top hat and a long ornate cigarette holder (sans cigarette). Wherever we went, surprises awaited us and the Cambodians we met. Villagers were invariably welcoming and friendly to a fault. Pausing at small villages, people would stop to talk to us, sending a youngster to scurry up a tree to grab some coconuts as our refreshment. There is nothing quite like fresh coconut water to quench one's thirst. Incidently, Chamroeun told me that during wartime, locals used coconut water in emergency transfusions to approximate saline solution, and even plasma, that were in short supply.[24]

Phnom Banon

One of our favorite day trips by bicycle took us south along the Stung Sangker to Phnom Banon, a hilltop Angkor-era temple with nearby caves that has been a destination for French explorers since Henri Mouhot first visited in 1858. In his 1872 book, *Voyage dans les royaumes de Siam, de Cambodge, de Laos et autre parties centrales de l'Indo-Chine*, he describes a quantity of Buddha statues inside the temples, as well as significant carvings of smaller deities. Mouhot also offers one of the earliest descriptions of Khmer dvarapalas, which he called "a guardian with an iron stick" flanking the entrances. Many Cambodian temples, ancient and modern, have frightening guardians with magic weapons, including French soldiers like at Wat Kdol! Sadly, the Banon statues and stone guardians have long since been looted and only the bare edifice remains.

---

24 This article from NPR.org substantiates Chamroeun's memory: "Coconut Water To The Rescue? Parsing The Medical Claims." [www.npr.org/sections/health-shots/2011/08/15/]

Phnom Banon in 1871. Jim Mizerski Archive.

Lintels at Phnom Banon in 1871. Jim Mizerski Archive.

In his book, Groslier describes a picnic there in the mid-1920s:

> The doctor and his guests went up to the temple courtyard to take their own lunch, settling beneath a tree of gleaming leaves. The picnic chest was set down and opened near a gutter stone in the shape of a monster, through whose elephant trunk, a thousand years earlier, water had flowed for the ablutions of the idols. The arrival of the three Europeans disrupted the banquet in the sala, and part of the crowd drained off in curious pursuit. The Europeans suddenly had twenty-odd servants making themselves useful just to get a closer look at the dishes and the forks. The rest of the audience took a seat on the steps or in the gaps of the surrounding galleries. Children in file and women by the bunch had gathered round, and soon bonzes added their sunflower splashes to the tableau. [P. 61.]

The peaceful temple site is still popular with locals and tourists. In Groslier's novel, the temple provides a dramatic backdrop to a conversation about conflicts between the ancient culture and modernity in Cambodia, as Pierre Ternier, his bachelor friend Doctor Maillard, and Hélène Gassin climb up to visit Phnom Banon:

> "From here, Madame," said the doctor, "you can once again see what has so forcibly struck you already: human life wedded harmoniously to the land, with no intellect to speculate in the name of progress or introduce its instruments or impose its will. Reptiles leave a lustrous trace in the sand; behold now the lustrous trace of man, all that you discover of human life."
>
> "You're headed for a scolding from Monsieur Ternier."
>
> "Oh, he agrees deep down, and when he's not off on his roads."
>
> "Especially since the doctor is talking such sleep-inducing poppycock and has you looking down, where there is nothing to see," interrupted Ternier. "Take a look instead at this quite visible temple, with its five crowning towers—the art and intelligence of those same, allegedly nature-bound men. As for my roads, keep in mind that ten centuries ago, when they built this temple and six hundred others just like it, those same men laid down a great many roads, on levees. We find traces of them everywhere. Their length, were we to add it up, would equal that of the roads that we Frenchmen are laying down now. Would you have us believe, Maillard, that the near-vanishing of all this is a good thing? I am of your same opinion. That what we have before us are a people and a country that can make do without? I concur. Do you intend to linger atop your mountain and observe? I won't begrudge you your contemplation. But I, dear friend, prefer to rebuild what has been destroyed, to make better roads than those that have failed to last. I would rebuild temples if I could. There are ten of us who think this way, whereas you are alone in your philosophizing." [Pp. 57-58.]

Phnom Sampov
and the
Legend of Sovann Machha

Though Groslier did not mention Phnom Sampov, the extraordinary story associated with this site made it an irresistible pilgrimage point for Chamroeun and I. Located 12 km. west of town this became another favored biking destination. Its name, Phnom Sampov, means "Ship mountain." In Khmer, "phnom" applies to mountains and hills, whether big or small.

The local legend recounts the friendship of the mythical maiden, Sovannn Machha, and a talking crocodile. Cambodian dance scholar Paul Cravath gives us some background:

> Hanumān—a more child-like aspect of Rām— seduces another
> daughter of Rāb, Sovannn Maccha. The two stories present both

Chamroeun and his nephew, Arit, who rode on the back for the 24 km trip!

the comic and serious sides of the eternal father-daughter-hero triangle.

The Khmer heroine's association with the subterranean nāga realm is totally undisguised in the favorite and most frequently performed episode in the Khmer dance repertoire, the story of the fish-maiden, Sovannn Machha.[25]

---

25 Cravath. *Earth in Flower.* P. 210.

Sovannn Machha's prominence in the Cambodian dance drama makes this local legend even more significant.

> The seduction of Sovannn Machha, Queen of the Fish and daughter of Rāb (corresponding to the Sanskrit Rāvana), by Rām's white monkey general Hanumān is the single most popular dramatic piece in the entire dance drama repertoire. Eighteen of the twenty-one times it appeared in the random sample of palace programs, it opened the performance. Categorized here as a drama because of its place in the Rāmker, the piece is fundamentally a dance duet. Significantly, it is not found in the Sanskrit Rāmāyana.[26]

With the help of Cambodian scholar Solang Uk, here is a refined version of the legend based on the work of Bou Saroeun.[27]

In legendary times, when much of Cambodia was under a sea, the Khmer capital was in the Dângrêk Mountains to the north. To the south, a poor maiden named Neang Sovannn Machha was renowned for her beauty, and was also known for her close friendship with a talking crocodile named Athon. Her friendship grew, literally, from her finding an egg while she was in the fields. She took the egg home and when it hatched she cared for the crocodile from birth. As it grew she found that the crocodile could speak human language and would obey everything she commanded.

In the capital, Prince Reach Kol heard of her beauty and was determined to make her his bride. He made his interest known to her but, just as with contemporary royal families, relatives were concerned that this common woman was not suitable for a royal marriage. Her unusual friendship with the intelligent crocodile Athon did not help!

Heeding his parents, Prince Kol told Sovann Machha that he could not marry her. To insure an end to the relationship, Prince Kol's father asked his court to find a princess for his son to marry.

---

26 Ibid. P. 223.
27 Bou, Saoreun. "The crocodile tears of Phnom Sampov". Phnom Penh Post, July 20, 2001.

A woman named Princess Rom Say Sork from a neighboring kingdom was deemed appropriate for the royal blood that flowed in her veins. Though perhaps not as beautiful as the maiden Sovann, Princess Say Sork had one exceptional attribute; a head of divine hair that allowed her to grant any wish upon a single stroke of her silky locks.

With the betrothal finalized, Prince Reach Kol ordered his people to load his engagement presents onto a ship in which he would travel to retrieve his new wife. Upon hearing of this Sovann Machha flew into a jealous rage. She ordered her trusted crocodile Athon to block the prince's ship from leaving port.

The desperate prince attempted to reason with Athon, but to no avail. The crocodile responded to his pleas with a stubborn reply: "I serve only those who feed me."

Prince Kol then had his retinue throw a bounty of vegetables, fruits, chickens and ducks into the harbor, in the hope that Athon would switch his allegiance to them. The crocodile, however, was steadfast. He ignored the barrage of tempting edibles raining down around him and continued to blockade the ship. The distraught Prince Kol then began praying for divine intervention to allow him to reach his beloved.

A helpful spirit passed the news of his predicament onto Princess Rom Say Sork in her homeland. She herself chose to break the crocodile's control that was stopping her marriage, so she began stroking her hair while wishing that the sea would recede.

Soon, her magic worked and the waters began to subside. Athon quickly found himself floundering on the muddy sea bottom, surrounded by the remains of the food he had declined. Without water, Athon died soon after and his body became Crocodile Mountain (Phnom Kroh Peu), within sight of Phnom Sampov, where a monument to Athon exists today. Chicken and duck carcasses in the area became the smaller mountains that sprang up nearby Crocodile Mountain.

Phnom Sompov view and statues in the inner sanctuary.

Cave entrance at Phnom Sampov.

As odd at the legend sounds, there are a number of ancient Khmer tales that suggest much of the land was underwater in the remote past. The view across the plain from the top of Phnom Sampov does actually resemble looking out on a vast sea.

Inside the mountain there is a temple, small stupas and caves. Sadly, the caves— Laang Teng Kloun, Lang Lkoun, Laang Pka Sla—became known as the "killing caves" as they were used by the Khmer Rouge to dispose of bodies during the genocide.

Solang Uk leaves us with a happier memory from his visit in 1959: "A friend and I crawled through a narrow hole into the mountain cave with just a small kerosene lamp. A hermit monk presided over the site and he had placed a thin jute rope on the floor as guide to help silly explorers like me to find the way out again. Thinking back, we were lucky to get out alive because our kerosene lamp kept going out due to lack of oxygen!"

An echo of colonial roads in the early 1900s, and Battambang's historic charm today.

The "off the grid experience" is still alive and well
in Cambodia as this 2007 trip illustrates. Photo Meng Dy.

The End of the Road

On each of our subsequent visits in the decade that followed, we witnessed improvements in road conditions, and other infrastructures like electricity and communications. The odd television set could now be seen in the homes of a fortunate few, sometimes even accompanied by video-cassette recorders (VCRs). Cambodians finally experienced a slow but steady process of modernization, just as seen in neighboring countries, and before long adding these comforts became a collective aspiration among the people. But Battambang retained its charm.

Again, we return to the idea that those in positions of privilege can be prone to wistfully romanticizing simple lifestyles, especially when they can return to their comforts at will. But for me, I am forever grateful for the opportunity to have experienced a

Chamroeun, his mother, myself, his sister Sunnary, and her daughter Sokunthea. On the far right is my "Crocodile" brand bike that took me on my adventures.

Cambodia in transition, when peace had just returned and the inexorable pace of modernization had yet to leave its imprint on the country. Many travelers, including myself, still seek these wonderful 'off the grid' experiences that are getting harder and harder to find.

Many French Indochina authors explored these conflicts between old and new, ancient and modern, primitive and civilized, East and West, but few of these works have come into the English language. In *The Road of the Strong*, Groslier also touches on the theme of French colonials who 'go native', abandoning French values, lifestyles (and women) for local mores. The idea must have appealed to him because he made it the central theme of his second novel, *Return to Clay*, for which he was awarded the Grand Prix de Littérature Coloniale in 1929:

> Doorways to the past were closing behind him. Despite his efforts, all his ties with the West were snapping one by one like so many strings, cut by the very hands he most cherished. Meanwhile everything he once thought would be hostile and impenetrable was in fact welcoming, waiting with open arms. The country offered him nothing but kindness and decorum. Claude's Western riches, the fruit of his sweat and a lifetime's probity, were being stripped away or proving useless. And here, all around him, were piling up other riches: great construction works, the joy of creation, the beauty of the land, the fertile riverbanks, the smiling acquiescence of the inhabitants. He had thought himself a blind, transient foreigner, bound to his past by roots that one simply did not sever... and these roots were drying out. [28]

When I discovered Cambodia I shared those feelings and Groslier stimulated my views of how disparate cultures influence one another for mutual benefit. Modern Cambodia has certainly adopted many western and foreign customs, sometimes it seems overwhelmingly. Yet something subtle, peaceful, ancient and vibrant remains untouched.

Cambodia is where my heart is, as it was for George Groslier. It feels good to walk in his footsteps seeking the next magical experience on the country roads less traveled.

To be continued...

---

28 Groslier, George, Henri Copin, and Kent Davis. 2014. *Return to Clay: A Romance of Colonial Cambodia*. P. 32.

BIBLIOGRAPHY

Briggs, Lawrence Palmer. 1946. The Treaty of March 23, 1907 between France and Siam and the Return of Battambang and Angkor to Cambodia, in *The Far Eastern Quarterly*, Vol. 5, No. 4 (Aug., 1946), pp. 439-454, http://www.jstor.org/stable/2049791

Briggs, Lawrence Palmer 1951. *The Ancient Khmer Empire*, Transactions of the American Philosophical Society, New Series, Vol.41, Part I, Philadelphia.

Dorgelès, Roland. 1926. *On the Mandarin Road* (Gertrude Emerson tr.). New York: The Century Co.

Mouhot, Henri. 1878. *Voyage dans les Royaumes de Siam, de Camboge, de Laos et Autres Parties Centrales de l'Indo-Chine*. Paris, Librairie Hachette.

Rochedragon , L.B. 1890. Voyage à Siam, in *Bulletin de la Société de Géographie de Rochefort*, Tome XII, No. 1, July-August-September, 1890-1891, pp. 11-33.

Wales, Horace Geoffrey Quaritch. 1931. *Siamese State Ceremonies: Their History and Function*. London: Bernard Quaritch.

La Route du plus fort

George GROSLIER

C'est parfois un bien grand malheur que la nature humaine soit si complexe et si simple et que la perspicacité de l'homme, pourtant si subtile, passe à côté de belles et profondes choses sans même les pressentir.

Avant-propos moderne par
Henri COPIN

Édition originale par
Éditions Émile-Paul Frères
14, Rue de l'Abbàye, 14
1925

Le plus fort, et la belle fille
à l'écharpe couleur
« graisse de crabe »

« *Nous sommes tous des symboles… *»

La Route du plus fort, qui paraît en 1926, est le premier roman de George Groslier, écrivain cambodgien. Cambodgien ? Oui Cambodgien ! Certes, Groslier n'est pas Cambodgien pour l'état-civil, mais il l'est par sa naissance en 1887, sans doute le premier Français né dans le pays des Khmers. Et il l'est encore bien plus par la véritable passion qu'il porte à sa terre natale, une passion que l'on pourrait appeler raisonnée, si ces mots allaient ensemble, car elle résulte d'une construction de connaissances savantes, combinées avec la fascination pour l'histoire et la culture d'un pays qui avait été, dix siècles plus tôt, le plus grand Empire de l'Asie, au temps du rayonnement d'Angkor.

Aujourd'hui, huit décennies après la publication de *La Route du plus fort*, l'auteur, l'époque où il écrit, le contexte colonial et le cadre du Cambodge nous apparaissent bien lointaines, dans l'espace et surtout dans le temps. La plupart d'entre nous en ignorent presque tout. Il est donc nécessaire de prendre quelques instants pour les resituer dans leur histoire, et pouvoir ainsi apprécier ce livre singulier, et riche des contradictions d'un homme et d'une époque.

Un Français Cambodgien…

L'auteur, tout d'abord. George Groslier, né en 1887, approche donc la quarantaine quand paraît son premier roman, et, bien sûr, il ignore qu'il lui reste moins de vingt ans à vivre, dans ce pays qui l'a vu naître, puis le verra mourir, en 1945, en cette fin de Deuxième Guerre Mondiale, alors que l'Indochine est encore occupée par le Japon. George meurt tragiquement, sous les coups de la terrible police militaire japonaise.

La *Kempetaï* l'avait arrêté parce qu'il utilisait une installation de radio-amateur, elle le soupçonnait de communiquer ainsi des informations à la Résistance. « *Mort pour la France* », peut-on lire sur sa tombe. Pour la France, et pour le Cambodge, doit-on ajouter, tant son destin se révèle aimanté par cette seconde patrie.

George est le fils d'un fonctionnaire français, arrivé en 1886 au Cambodge au service du Protectorat instauré en 1863. A cette date, le roi d'un petit pays en déclin, presque dépecé par des voisins trop gourmands, le Siam (actuelle Thaïlande) et l'Annam (actuel Vietnam), signe avec la France, depuis peu installée en Cochinchine (sud du Vietnam actuel), un traité de Protectorat qui assure sa survie. Cette alliance arrange les deux parties : le Cambodge y trouve un protecteur contre les appétits des puissants riverains, tandis que la France consolide sa récente installation en Cochinchine, autour du grand port de Saïgon. Elle s'adosse ainsi à un arrière-pays khmer que traverse le Mékong, voie possible croit-on alors, vers l'immense marché de la Chine. Dans les faits, le Cambodge devient assez vite une colonie gouvernée par la France plutôt qu'un protectorat. La date de 1887, naissance de George, marque également la naissance de l'Union Indochinoise, incluant le Cambodge. Désormais on n'écrit plus Indochine, mais Indochine, façon de souligner son unité.

George passe ses deux premières années au Cambodge. Puis sa mère, ne supportant plus ses conditions de vie, rentre en France en emmenant son fils. Son mari poursuit sa carrière dans l'administration sur place. Elle ne reviendra jamais au Cambodge. George y retourne, vingt et un ans plus tard, en 1910. Entre temps, il a fait ses études, à Marseille puis à Paris, à l'Ecole des Beaux-Arts, où il devient peintre. Il faut garder en mémoire cette formation artistique, ses efforts pour décrocher un Grand Prix de Rome, son échec aussi qui le détourne d'une carrière de peintre. Cette partie de sa vie a fait de lui un homme épris de l'art, et qui déguste le spectacle du monde comme s'il était une palette de peintre. Son écriture reflète sa vision d'artiste.

« La reprise des Arts khmers »

Lorsqu'il revient sur sa terre natale, et qu'il la découvre, il reçoit un choc. On dirait presque une seconde naissance. Il fait connaissance avec un petit pays qui porte les traces grandioses de l'empire disparu d'Angkor, avec sa civilisation raffinée, ses temples imposants, ses vestiges, ses références mythologiques et religieuses, ses énigmes aussi. Il séjourne à Angkor, découvre et étudie l'art khmer ancien, puis présente en France et en Belgique une série de conférences sur cette civilisation disparue. Par la famille de son épouse il bénéficie d'appuis politiques, et lorsque le Gouvernement Général du Cambodge décide de lancer une réforme de l'enseignement artistique du Cambodge, il confie cette mission à George Groslier, que sa formation aux Beaux-Arts et ses connaissances qualifient, ainsi que ses propres conceptions sur les arts. Groslier a en effet rédigé de nombreux textes sur le sujet, dès 1913, avec *Danseuses cambodgiennes anciennes et modernes*, suivi en 1916 de *A l'ombre d'Angkor*. En 1918, il publie successivement dans la *Revue Indochinoise*, *La Convalescence des Arts cambodgiens*, puis *L'agonie des Arts cambodgiens*. Plus tard, en 1925, ce sera *La Reprise des Arts Khmers*.

Les enjeux de ce projet de réforme dépassent le simple cadre d'un enseignement des Arts. Il doit servir le Cambodge, l'aider à reconstruire une identité, et contribuer en même temps au prestige de la France, tout en produisant des retombées économiques liées au développement du tourisme, et à la promotion de l'Indochine par celle du patrimoine khmer. L'œuvre à laquelle Groslier va se consacrer à partir de 1917, au service de ses deux patries, est riche et complexe. Il s'agit de créer une institution qui impulse une véritable rénovation des Arts khmers, pour poursuivre les réformes initiées dans ce domaine par le Roi Sisowath, à la suite de son voyage en France en 1906. Cette rénovation, projet commun à la Cour et aux autorités du Protectorat, a besoin d'un élan nouveau. Ce sera la mission de Groslier, la création d'une Ecole des Arts, indépendante, et reflétant sa propre vision d'un peuple résigné à une obscurité souriante, tout en gardant le souvenir d'un passé glorieux, mais comme amputé de son identité culturelle.

Pour Groslier, les pratiques artistiques des Khmers répondent à des nécessités d'abord utilitaires et fonctionnelles (avant d'être esthétiques), ainsi qu'il l'écrit dans une *Etude de la psychologie de l'artisan cambodgien*, titre d'un article qu'il publiera plus tard, en 1921, ou encore dans d'autres *Etudes sur l'Art khmer*, en 1923. Groslier met donc en place un enseignement dont le premier principe est « *Ne faire que de l'art cambodgien et le faire en cambodgien* », afin d'éviter toute influence étrangère. On pourra par la suite reprocher à cette doctrine de former des artistes dépourvus d'originalité créatrice. « *Mon rôle est de défendre, par tous les moyens en mon pouvoir, la tradition cambodgienne* »écrit-il encore[1]. Notons que le projet qui sous-tend la création de l'Ecole supérieure des Beaux-Arts d'Indochine, à Hanoï en 1925, sous la direction de Victor Tardieu et de Nguyen Nam Son, était au contraire de rénover les arts traditionnels tout en les ouvrant sur les influences occidentales, choix inverse donc et couronné d'un remarquable succès. Dans le cas des Arts cambodgiens, l'opération de rénovation dépend d'abord des conceptions de Groslier sur les arts khmers. Il joue donc un rôle décisif comme responsable de l'Ecole des Arts, puis du Musée Albert Sarraut qu'il dessine, réalise et dirige, et enfin de la Direction des Arts (de 1920 à 1944) qui coordonne le tout.

Telle est donc la situation de Groslier quand paraît son premier roman en 1926 : artiste et savant, acteur central du dispositif de protection et de rénovation du patrimoine artistique du Cambodge, et d'inspection des antiquités historiques et ar-

---

1 Cité par Gabrielle Abbe dans « Le Développement des Arts au Cambodge à l'époque coloniale, George Groslier et l'Ecole des Arts cambodgiens (1917-1945) », *UDAYA, Journal of Khmer Studies*, 12, 2014 (paru en 2015).

chéologiques. Il est de ce fait conduit à jouer un rôle actif dans l'arrestation et le procès d'un jeune homme qui n'est pas encore connu comme le grand écrivain André Malraux, futur ministre du Général de Gaulle, mais plutôt comme un aventurier voleur de statues dans le merveilleux petit temple de Banteay Sreï. Mais au-delà de cette affaire retentissante, il faut voir dans l'action de George un engagement profond et efficace en faveur de la restauration de l'identité culturelle du Cambodge, autour du passé angkorien. Il œuvre au service de la France et de son prestige colonial, et tout autant au service de sa vision du Cambodge. A cette date, il a publié près de 35 savants articles sur l'archéologie, et près de 12 sur les arts « indigènes », le tout dans des revues prestigieuses. Et donc surgit une question : qu'est-ce qui pousse cet homme reconnu dans le domaine du savoir et de l'action à se risquer dans l'écriture d'une œuvre de fiction, *La Route du plus fort* ?

Un mythe colonial

La réponse, ou les réponses, car ce n'est pas simple, se trouve dans une lecture attentive du livre. Disons tout de suite notre hypothèse : au contraire de l'écriture scientifique ou documentaire, la fiction permet de juxtaposer des émotions ou des points de vue différentes, voire contradictoires, reflétant ainsi les ambiguïtés du réel. Dans *La Route du plus fort*, George Groslier célèbre l'action de la France colonisatrice, en même temps qu'il chante la séduction d'un art de vivre à la Khmer… Cette tension s'accentuera dans son deuxième roman, *Retour à l'argile*. On y découvrira une apologie de la « décivilisation », célébrant un art de vivre khmer comme retour à l'état de nature, contre une « pseudo-civilisation » occidentale, présentée elle-même, comme un forme de « décivilisation »… Ce sera un véritable renversement des valeurs de la doctrine coloniale fondée sur la « mission civilisatrice » de la France. *White man's burden*, disait Kipling ! Les deux romans s'éclairent, car *La Route* contient en germe la révolution du *Retour à l'argile*. Tentons d'y voir plus clair – sans toutefois dévoiler le récit au lecteur qui s'aventure ici…

Il faut d'abord rappeler que *La Route du plus fort* se rattache au genre alors naissant appelé « littérature coloniale », qui peut se définir (entre autres) par son rapport à l'idéologie coloniale. Certains ouvrages glorifient cette idéologie, en sortant les clairons du salut aux couleurs. D'autres expriment un soutien plus subtil. Ici, le titre signifie une apologie du « plus fort », c'est à dire du colonisateur face au peuple assoupi du Cambodge. C'est la force occidentale, avec sa maîtrise technique, face au fatalisme attribué aux Asiatique, c'est la route symbole de supériorité technique. Mais ce n'est pas seulement l'expression d'une domination, puisque la route est « donnée par le plus fort au plus faible », par la France au Cambodge. Le héros, le Résident Ternier, fonctionnaire supérieur de Protectorat, vit tout entier engagé pour cette mission, cette route qui relie les êtres, désenclave les villages, ouvre les marchés économiques, et garantit la sécurité et la paix.

« *Nous sommes donc venus et en quelques années, nous bâtîmes une ville neuve entre des jardins couverts de manguiers centenaires. [...] Nous avons relié par des routes au reste du pays ce qui en était isolé par des jours et des jours de voyage* », déclare-t-il, par exemple. La route traverse tout le roman, structure le récit, et distribue les personnages. Autour de Ternier apparaissent un constructeur automobile français et sa femme Hélène, rencontrés lors d'un congé. La route coloniale, l'automobile métropolitaine, le message est clair : la colonie et la mère-patrie sont complémentaires. Une vision pragmatique de l'idéologie coloniale veut y voir un bénéfice réciproque pour les deux parties.

Cette représentation correspond d'ailleurs à l'air du temps. L'entre-deux guerres voit le développement des transports maritimes, aériens, terrestres accompagnant la naissance d'un tourisme encore réservé à une élite. Les colonies devenant moins lointaines, on y construit des palaces, autour de la Méditerranée, en Indochine, à Angkor. Déjà en 1908 le duc de Montpensier reliait Saïgon et Angkor en automobile, sans perdre un boulon ! Tirée de plusieurs mauvais pas par des buffles, sa « *Lorraine Diétrich 24/30 HP à châssis américain renforcé* » escalade plusieurs marches d'Angkor Wat pour en parcourir la chaussée monumentale ! Plus tard, la Croisière Noire, puis la Croisière Jaune illustreront les pouvoirs de l'automobile pour la connaissance du vaste monde. L'architecture métallique de Eiffel permet de construire des ponts, comme celui de Hanoï, ou de lancer une voie ferrée aux innombrables ouvrages d'art, jusqu'en Chine du Sud. Le journal *L'Illustration* diffuse, avec ses reportages photographiques, une vision de l'aménagement des colonies, associée à l'efficacité et à la modernité. 1920 est une année de progrès économique dans toute l'Indochine (et de lourde fiscalité sur les paysans), et en 1930 le Cambodge (bien changé depuis 1863) peut compter sur quelques 9000 km de routes, en grande partie construites avec la main d'œuvre des corvées, et bientôt sur une voie ferrée vers le Siam. En 1931, l'Exposition Coloniale internationale de Paris mettra en scène l'apogée du système colonial (bientôt suivie de son déclin), autour de la reproduction en plein Paris du temple d'Angkor Wat.

Ainsi Groslier bâtit sa fiction sur son expérience du réel et sa vision de l'œuvre coloniale. D'autres écrivains, Roland Dorgelès avec son reportage *Sur la route mandarine*, ou le romancier Henry Daguerches avec *Le kilomètre 83*, qui imagine un épisode de construction de voie ferrée au Cambodge, illustrent eux aussi, à leur façon, ces représentations. Bref, à l'époque le consensus est général, coloniser est faire œuvre de progrès, et la route en est un symbole indiscutable...

Voici qui permet donc une première lecture du roman, comme reflet d'une certaine réalité : le Résident Ternier, en charge de la route, fait découvrir à une femme d'industriel venue de France son propre Cambodge, ses paysages, ses villes, sa brousse, ses forêts, ses pagodes, ses habitants, et ses Français expatriés. Ce faisant, le bâtisseur colonial explique à la métropolitaine fraîche arrivée le sens de son œuvre, utile à la France et au Cambodge. Chapitre après chapitre, il montre la tâche quotidienne et la valeur d'une mission qui dépasse les individus et les transfigure : « *Ils ont, à la fois, enrichi deux civilisations. Ils travaillent à une route, non seulement au bénéfice de leur pays ou de leur clan, mais aussi à celui d'un autre peuple* »[2].

Ce récit colonial culmine avec une réception officielle qui regroupe autour du Résident Ternier une petite société française en smoking, avec argenterie, grands vins, cuisine à la française, décorum et protocole, vieux coloniaux aux anecdotes pittoresques, et un Gouverneur cambodgien inutile et décoratif. Groslier décrit avec un humour acéré ce microcosme qui en brousse et au milieu de la nuit fait briller les lumières de la civilisation, autour du Résident, véritable phare : « *De cet homme [...] des routes rayonnaient, blanches de lune, à travers sa province, comme le symbole de la main pacificatrice qu'il y avait posée. Dans cette étoile [...] plus de trois cent mille vies humaines sommeillaient. Et chacun de ceux qui levaient leur verre de cristal en cette atmosphère de prospérité avaient accompli aussi leur tâche* ». On retrouve tout au long du roman des références à l'œuvre, à ses acteurs, à ses bénéficiaires. Parfois inutilement insistantes, elles vont jusqu'à suggérer que le Résident Ternier (et donc la France) prolonge l'œuvre des grands anciens, créateurs d'Angkor et de ses voies royales... « *Tu feras ta route, ordonne celui-là à celui-ci. Tu rêves et dégénères depuis dix siècles. On ne rêve plus à l'heure présente : on forge* ». C'est à cela que sert la création romanesque : à élaborer ces mythes qui prennent appui sur le réel et l'éclairent.

Sous le regard des femmes

Pourtant, si le personnage du Résident Ternier apparaît parfois monolithique tel une statue dans son monde idéal, et peu accessible au doute, la fiction de Groslier laisse en même temps entrevoir un autre monde, parallèle, et différent. A côté du Cambodge montré (et démontré) par le Résident, une autre lecture apparaît alors, plus complexe, plus humaine aussi, grâce au regard de deux femmes, Hélène et Vétônéa.

C'est d'abord Hélène, la métropolitaine qui, avec son œil neuf, donne à voir, au fil de ses découvertes, le charme des villages, les scènes bucoliques quotidiennes, les lentes charrettes, les jonques pansues, les marchés, les enfants qui jouent, les hommes en marche, les bruits, les parfums, les odeurs. C'est elle qui vante, après la réception officielle, le charme de la simple *sala*[3] villageoise, avec son accueil sans apprêt mais non sans attentions. Elle qui entend le chant des charrettes, « *ces charrettes qui sillonnent le pays, qui allaient aujourd'hui chanter pour elle, véhicules élégants,*

---

2 Il va d'ailleurs jusqu'à ajouter que « *si à la base de toute colonisation il y a un principe faux, ou du moins discutable, et dans certains cas inopportun, ils n'en sont pas responsables* ». L'apologie de la route entraine une réflexion sur la légitimité de l'acte de force à la base de toute colonisation. La réflexion sera reprise par Albert Sarraut dans Grandeur et servitude coloniales, en 1931.
3 Maison de passage pour les voyageurs.

organisés comme un corps vivant et dont la voix des essieux susurre, gémit et module au moindre mouvement des roues et qui aussi longtemps que la route s'allonge, gémit, module et susurre, plus sonore en forêt, grave le matin, aiguë dans le soleil ». C'est par ses yeux encore que Groslier dépeint le ballet parfait des corps nus marchant dans la forêt : « *tout est prestigieux dans cette architecture mouvante : ces deux armes, les bras et les jambes, propulseurs de la merveilleuse machine [...]. Quelle sincérité, quel loyalisme peuvent être plus affirmés que cette franchise de la nudité [...] Autre chose enfin rayonne de cet ensemble que l'air soutient et favorise : la liberté* ».

Or cet hymne à l'état de nature, à la beauté originelle des corps et des êtres, à la liberté qui en émane, c'est le sujet même du second roman de Groslier, *Retour à l'argile*, ici posé en germe, et en contrepoint à l'hymne à la *civilisation... L'homme nu*, ce n'est pas tout à fait le même symbole que *la route*. Groslier se découvre plus encore, par la suite. Alors que ses personnages se livrent à une paisible méditation dans la douceur de la nuit commençante, l'auteur prend la parole pour s'adresser, à qui ? on ne sait pas bien, à lui-même peut être : « *Tu as quitté tes habitudes. Tu as dégagé ta tête du joug. Tu as laissé les conventions pour voir autre chose [...] Libre, tu as voulu être libre ! La nature est morte entre tes villes, ici, elle règne. L'homme de chez toi est inaccessible sous les masques qu'il emprunte ; ici l'homme est nu, et riche sous sa nudité* ». Et cette étrange faille dans l'armure du rude Ternier, cet aveu de faiblesse pour la liberté épanouie au sein de la nature du Cambodge, s'élargit à mesure que le récit avance, jusqu'à ce troublant aveu : « *Tu dis : je suis la civilisation nécessaire, dictée, désirée par les hommes. [...] Cela signifie que tu es le plus fort [...] Et quelle que soit la douceur avec laquelle tu poses ta large main sur le monde, et les certitudes salvatrices que tu y déverses – tu tues !* ». Voici le civilisé devenu accessible au doute.

Cette fille subtile et orgueilleuse

C'est donc par les yeux d'une femme, Hélène, que cette réalité s'impose, autre que celle du discours idéologique. Une autre femme joue encore un rôle clé dans ce roman : Vétônéa, la *prâpôn*, la petite épouse indigène de Ternier, une « *fille subtile et orgueilleuse, au teint ocre clair* ». Sur la masse indistincte des Cambodgiens qui figurent dans le livre, où aucun n'est traité comme un individu à part entière, elle est la seule à être dessinée avec plus de précision, au fil d'un portrait contrasté et singulier. Personnage secondaire ? oui, certes, car elle est la petite épouse qui n'a pas le droit de se montrer, « *cet être déroutant qu'est la compagne indigène d'un Européen, émanation du pays dont elle concrétise tous les charmes* ». Mais elle apparaît au pivot du livre, et réoriente l'histoire. Et si elle était le vrai personnage principal du roman ? Mais je n'en dirai pas plus, ô lecteur ! fais ta découverte par toi-même, et observe bien la jeune Vétônéa « *fraiche, sèche et douce comme l'ivoire* », petite idole que Ternier prétend pouvoir « dompter », pour toutes sortes de bonnes raisons du plus fort...

Elle est pour moi la vraie cause de la faiblesse inavouable du si fort Résident, et le vrai symbole d'un Cambodge dont Groslier est follement épris, par tous les sens, et qu'il dépeint à merveille en maintes aquarelles jetées au fil du récit, selon les lieux évoqués, où formes et couleurs éclatent dans leur luxuriance : « *nœuds du gingembre, fleurs de nénuphar, marrons de Chine, chair effilochée de poisson sec, haricots germés pareils à des agglomérats de larves,* écheveaux de vermicelle transparent, piles de petites jarres pleines de sauces fermentées, pots de chaux rouge comme une pâte de corail, tabac noir, rangées régulières de feuilles de bétel aux formes d'as de pique, *arachides, safran brun…* ». Groslier le peintre ne saurait résister aux couleurs et aux formes, allant jusqu'à peindre « *les tas d'ordures presqu'aussi beaux que les éventaires […] qui se désagrégeaient avant de pourrir, avec une coquetterie brillante* ».

Je relis ce livre plusieurs années après l'avoir découvert, et je suis frappé par cette merveilleuse possibilité qu'offre le roman de pouvoir agencer des symboles, voire de créer des mythes, qui coexistent avec leurs différences, et leurs contradictions, leurs significations opposées. La route, contre la piste. La civilisation, contre la nature. Le progrès, contre la liberté. On peut en même temps tenir un discours volontariste, fondé sur l'action et la transformation du réel, et laisser transparaitre une violente attirance vers tout ce qui va disparaître du fait de cette action. Une attirance, une préférence ? Chacun apportera à ces tensions opposées le sens qui lui conviendra. Groslier, lui, clôt ses dernières pages sur cette magnifique ambiguïté : » *ta route passe à travers une région et, comme une flèche, va la toucher au cœur. Mais la région traversée te frappe aussi au cœur* ».

Henri Copin
Nantes, France
31 octobre, 2017

La Route du Plus Fort

George GROSLIER

I

Sur la route, entre Royat et Fontanat, dans la belle Auvergne. D'un côté, les prés en pente douce ; de l'autre, les roches d'où suintent des sources vives et froides. Le soleil oblique se mêle au bruissement de l'eau et un minuscule arc-en-ciel frôle les mousses.

Privée de chauffeur, capot ouvert, une automobile stationnait. Un couple résigné l'occupait ; lui, grand garçon ayant passé la trentaine ; elle, mince, blonde, avec ces mains longues et fines qu'on voit souvent aux Italiennes depuis les Quattrocentistes. La voiture était une Roland-Gassin, équipée pour la route et poudreuse comme elle.

La belle soirée de juin poussait sur cette même route une seconde voiture, Roland-Gassin aussi et de même type. Derrière un chauffeur annamite qui conduisait avec une extrême lenteur, un homme à la moustache forte et tombante, une courte pipe sous cette moustache, se carrait avec désinvolture, tout au paysage et au bien-être de l'heure. Lorsqu'il aperçut la voiture désemparée, il se redressa, fit arrêter et s'adressa au couple :

— Vous est-il arrivé quelque chose de fâcheux ?

— Panne sèche de magnéto, monsieur.

Alors il descendit et se présenta :

— Pierre Ternier, Résident de France en Indochine.

— Roland Gassin, constructeur d'automobiles. Ma femme.

Ternier s'inclina et tournant un sourire vers le capot ouvert :

— Mauvaise réclame, monsieur, mais je connais la marque.

Les sources fraîches eurent un bruissement nouveau : c'était madame Gassin qui riait. Et puisque les voitures s'étaient reconnues, chacun fut à l'aise.

— Le chauffeur est parti à Royat chercher une autre voiture et nous l'attendons.

— Je descends moi-même à Royat. Je vous en prie, n'attendez pas ici et permettez-moi de vous y conduire.

On s'installa et l'automobile valide continua sa route.

On communique aisément entre gens du même monde, en pleine campagne et dans de telles circonstances. Les Gassin comptaient arriver à Clermont le soir et continuer sur Saint-Etienne le lendemain. Ternier, lui, stationnait à Royat pour les eaux et surtout vagabonder aux pieds des Dômes avant de retourner achever son congé à Paris. Les coloniaux, même éminents, sont peu connus en France, mais le ménage comprit bientôt qu'il était en présence d'un homme distingué. Et, le client rencontrait son fournisseur sur une route d'Auvergne, le possesseur de cette marque si réputée, alors en pleine vogue.

La soirée se poursuivit à l'Hôtel du Parc, où était descendu Ternier, tandis que sa voiture retournait sur la route guetter le chauffeur des Gassin. Le dépannage demanda plusieurs heures. Il faisait frais. Dans le hall qui domine le parc et d'où l'on entrevoit les montagnes, on dressa une petite table que des bruyères, dans une large coupe de cristal, ornèrent d'améthyste. Ainsi et là, l'amitié qui devait lier les Gassin et Ternier prit naissance en raison de cette sympathie rapide que suscitent la franchise des regards, le son des voix et la quiétude des âmes sans détour.

Ils se retrouvèrent bientôt à Paris.

Roland Gassin était un esprit actif. Dans l'usine de Levallois-Perret qu'il tenait de son père, entouré d'un personnel de choix, sa sûreté d'homme d'affaires avait rapidement conduit à un succès durable les trouvailles de l'ingénieur. Il avait de la vie cette notion souvent hautaine de ceux qui suivent une voie bien tracée, y triomphent et concluent volontiers que celui qui échoue est un maladroit. L'effort constant qu'ils savent accomplir efface peu à peu, à leurs yeux, la part de chance qui les sert. Ils ne connaissent ni la misère, ni la trahison. Et Roland Gassin fonctionnait comme l'un de ses moteurs dans une action complexe et sévèrement concertée où tout se commande et s'enchaîne avec précision.

Sa femme, qu'il avait rencontrée une dizaine d'années auparavant dans son milieu industriel, était d'une nature plus difficile à définir. Nous tenterons de la comprendre en la regardant vivre. Ses vertus mondaines et la simplicité de ses allures déjouaient l'examen. Elle semblait éminemment souple et féminine. Les femmes féminines sont si rares maintenant. Rien en celle-ci n'était saisissable, non pas qu'elle dissimulât, bien au contraire : un émail uni la recouvrait avec régularité, sans craquelure et d'une belle couleur pure. Mais on ne savait si cette couleur était celle de l'émail ou si l'émail transparent laissait voir la couleur de la matière qu'il enveloppait. Dès qu'elle se confiait, elle devenait une sorte de camarade ayant l'air de se mettre sous votre protection. Peut-être que son charme était d'avoir une volonté puissante et de n'en pas user, comme si elle estimait ne pas en avoir besoin puisqu'elle était femme et vous jugeait galant homme. Madame Gassin disait : je ferai ceci, cela et elle le faisait. Je pars, elle se levait et partait. Demain, dix heures ; le lendemain, à dix heures, elle paraissait. J'écrirai ; elle écrivait. Ces petites résolutions sont dans la vie courante d'un pouvoir lâche et l'on s'en libère à tout propos. C'est à manier pourtant ces poids légers, et souvent bien mieux qu'à s'arcbouter inutilement aux rochers, que la volonté se décèle. Et sans doute est-ce la forme vraiment féminine de la volonté, puisqu'ainsi elle suit subtilement sa carrière sans que l'homme y prenne garde. Un jour il s'y soumet malgré la barre de fer dont il s'arme trop tard pour la vaincre.

Madame Gassin aimait son mari. Chez celui-ci perçait une tendre admiration pour cette compagne d'une rare qualité. La confiance heureuse que son mari lui témoignait, la communauté de leurs goûts, les attentions délicates et toujours opportunes qu'ils échangeaient prouvaient du moins que Gassin était fixé sur ce qui aiguisait notre curiosité.

Est-ce que madame Gassin, par une pudeur attentive, entendait à tout prix celer les qualités de son cœur, afin d'en disposer complètement ; considérait-elle que sa sentimentalité, comme les formes secrètes de son corps, eût été souillée par des voiles transparents ; avait-elle l'orgueil ou le souci de ne rien livrer de ce qu'elle considérait comme une faiblesse ; supposait-elle, par un scrupule opiniâtre, que toute sa passion offerte à son mari ne lui appartenait plus et qu'elle devait en conserver d'autant plus l'intégralité ; s'était-elle fait, de son amour, un rituel secret et s'imaginait-elle que parler même de l'amour eût risqué de divulguer le sien — aimait-elle, même ? Voilà toutes les questions auxquelles nous pouvions, dans le même instant, répondre par l'affirmative ou la négative, soit qu'aux allusions que nous tentions dans l'intimité, la bouche de madame Gassin s'entrouvrît avec candeur, soit que son regard se perdît au-delà de nos paroles afin d'en suspendre le cours.

Entendez bien qu'elle n'était point pimbêche, ni bigote. Les mots ne l'épouvantaient pas et son rire résonnait au choc des allusions plaisantes. Il semblait que ce fût dans les régions élevées ou profondes des sentiments que sa sensibilité s'effarouchait, lorsque l'investigation approchait de certains domaines où madame Gassin devait se tenir, telle ces oiseaux qui ne vivent que dans les parties reculées des forêts ou aux grandes hauteurs. Elle avait, d'autre part, une affection profonde pour sa sœur, Annie Belgrand, plus âgée qu'elle. On connaissait peu celle-ci, car à la suite d'une catastrophe de chemin de fer qui lui avait broyé, dans la même seconde, son mari et un garçonnet de dix ans, elle vivait très retirée.

Je préciserai suffisamment le portrait de madame Gassin en ajoutant ici un dernier trait que le récit du drame qui va suivre ne laisserait pas transparaître. Elle était une de ces femmes qui savent écouter et dont il semble qu'on voie l'intelligence saisissable et épandue sur leur visage comme un masque lumineux. Droite dans son fauteuil, les pieds croisés, les yeux bien ouverts sur les vôtres, elle vous posait, par son maintien et la curiosité qu'elle vous accordait, une question latente et, filtrant tout ce que votre parole pouvait contenir de valable, elle faisait naître en vous le besoin de vous exprimer. Les allusions de ces femmes attentives sont discrètes et leurs questions insidieuses. Vous vous trouvez vous-même à mesure que vous vous découvrez à elles. Si l'imbécile ne fuit pas lorsqu'elles apparaissent, elles savent lui soutirer des paroles sensées. Elles ont une vie intérieure profonde et brillante car, aussi bien, doivent-elles savoir, dans la méditation, s'écouter elles-mêmes. Leur pouvoir « d'assister » ainsi à toutes sortes d'hommes les enrichit de connaissances variées, fleuries et châtiées par le talent ou la conscience de ceux qui les leur transmettent et qu'elles savent choisir. Aussi sont-elles reconnues profondes et supérieures d'autant plus volontiers par les hommes que ceux-ci, la vanité satisfaite d'être attentivement écoutés, se convainquent de l'intérêt des paroles qu'ils dispensent.

Ternier n'échappa pas à ce charme, d'autant que madame Gassin témoigna plus de curiosité que de coutume à ce passant désœuvré, hautain et courtois. Les familiers du ménage, ingénieurs, hommes d'affaires, industriels et de bonne société, formaient un cercle brillant où quelques- uns, et les femmes surtout, donnaient dans l'esprit nouveau. Ou bien, les conversations se nourrissaient de questions dont madame Gassin avait acquis l'habitude. Quelques littérateurs passaient avec des artistes. On donnait des dîners fins où des paroles ailées traversaient l'arôme des plats. Cependant, l'invité nouveau ne s'opposait pas au convive de la veille. Sa tournure d'esprit, son érudition ou ses qualités morales se mêlaient, au contraire, sans imprévu, à toutes celles qui formaient ce milieu égal et choisi.

Le colonial s'imposa donc avec le prestige du lointain et de l'inconnu d'où il venait. Sa conviction, la rudesse parfois de son verbe, la liberté de ses paradoxes donnaient des sons nouveaux sur des thèmes inédits. Soit qu'il décrivît l'administration coloniale, soit qu'il peignît la vie indigène, soit encore qu'il développât tel programme de civilisation instauré ou à appliquer, soit enfin qu'il s'en tînt à l'épisode ou à ses propres souvenirs, une atmosphère jamais respirée et qui sentait les épices, enveloppait madame Gassin. Plus et mieux que tout autre, elle s'y abandonna, bien que Ternier se fût appliqué à détruire en elle toute idée romanesque et tout esprit d'aventure. Il attaqua surtout de front cette tenace et saugrenue légende coloniale dans laquelle tant de gens mal informés se complaisaient. Et sa parole prit d'autant plus de force dans l'esprit de madame Gassin que, jusqu'alors, des romans dit « coloniaux » ou « exotiques » ne lui avaient laissé que des impressions douteuses et des tableaux artificiels. Si les révélations et les touches sobres du Résident la déroutaient encore, elles l'invitaient à s'avancer désormais dans tout cet inconnu en démarches logiques, sur des routes bien établies, éclairée d'un tranquille bon sens et surtout entraînée par la conviction profonde du défricheur qu'il était.

Voilà pourquoi, il y eut au 27 de l'avenue d'Eylau, chez les Gassin et à la fin de cette année-là, une saison coloniale, jusqu'au moment où Ternier partit rejoindre son poste, la province de Sangkè, dans le Cambodge septentrional.

II

— Mon cher docteur, me le répéteriez-vous toutes les heures, nous sommes réduits à ce que nous avons.

— Nous ne parvenons qu'à grand-peine à faire nos tournées de vaccine.

— Eh ! je ne le sais que trop ! À toute occasion, je demande à la Résidence supérieure et au Chef du service local de la santé un médecin de plus, dans mes rapports, dans mes lettres privées, officielles, verbalement. Il n'y en a pas. On en manque partout.

— Notez, monsieur le Résident, que le service est assuré.

— Je le sais, Maillard, je le sais.

— Seulement, assurer le service est insuffisant. De la besogne utile pourrait être faite dans toute la province et nous demeurons rivés à Sangkè et aux environs.

— Ce que vous me dites là, l'ingénieur des Travaux Publics, le directeur des écoles, le forestier me le répètent pour leur propre compte à chacune de leurs audiences. Le personnel manque partout. Il faut en prendre notre parti.

Le docteur Maillard offrait cet aspect jovial des petits hommes bien nourris, des yeux vifs derrière un lorgnon, une face rasée, les cheveux poivre et sel, coupés à l'ordonnance. Il avait vu grandir le centre sous l'impulsion de Ternier. Les deux hommes s'entendaient d'ailleurs étroitement, l'un et l'autre célibataires, épris de leur métier et du pays, associés à la même œuvre. Depuis plus de cinq ans, le docteur demeurait à Sangkè sans prendre de congé, toutes attaches rompues avec la France, père et mère disparus de bonne heure. Tel est le sort de beaucoup de coloniaux qui, peu à peu, cessent ainsi de regarder vers l'Occident. Son abord bon enfant et sa bonté, qu'une voix bourrue ne parvenait pas à masquer, avaient plus fait, près des indigènes, que le prestige d'une science qui n'a pas encore assez leur confiance, les intimide et les soumet à des conditions dont ils ne comprennent pas la portée. L'incroyable pudeur des femmes entre pour une grande part dans cette répugnance et la visite médicale, les attouchements du praticien demeurent encore pour elles des formalités insurmontables.

Un planton apporta un télégramme.

— Ah ! par exemple ! s'exclama Ternier en le parcourant.

— Vous êtes décoré ? demanda le docteur.

— Je vous ai souvent parlé des Gassin, ce couple aimable que j'ai connu à Paris durant mon dernier congé.

— Le constructeur d'autos ?

Ternier tendit le télégramme au docteur : « Sommes Saigon pour monter succursale. Pensons aller vous voir bientôt. Lettre suit. Amitiés et bons souvenirs des Gassin. ».

— Ils ne vous avaient pas laissé entrevoir ce voyage ?

— Jamais, et du diable si je pensais à eux ! Nous avions échangé quelques lettres banales depuis mon retour ici. Bonne affaire, cette visite. Vous verrez un ménage extrêmement agréable.

— Elle surtout, m'avez-vous dit ?

— Elle surtout, femme intelligente. Lui, c'est l'ingénieur-homme d'affaires, gros travailleur, moins ouvert peut-être sur l'extérieur. Excellente chose d'ailleurs pour la colonie qu'il ait pensé à venir établir sa firme en Cochinchine. Ses clients seront autant de pris aux marques américaines.

— Un Français de France qui vient ici ; qui ose venir ici, lui-même, tenter des affaires, je propose qu'on l'empaille.

Le lendemain soir, la lettre annoncée arrivait. Madame Gassin l'avait écrite et excusait son mari. Il avait à faire plus qu'il ne prévoyait avec les banques, cherchait un local ou des terrains à bâtir, étudiait la main-d'œuvre et les moyens d'action locaux ; bref, il semblait devoir être immobilisé plus d'une quinzaine. Quant à madame Gassin, la ville de Saigon lui produisait une impression des plus fâcheuses, elle y étouffait et ne savait qu'y faire. Ennui noir. Aussi, envisageait-elle la possibilité d'y laisser son mari organiser son entreprise, de prendre les devants et de venir l'attendre à Sangkè, en ce Cambodge dont Ternier avait si bien su lui vanter les charmes. Pouvait-il lui télégraphier qu'elle ne serait pas indiscrète et si elle trouverait une chambre à l'hôtel ? Ternier le lui télégraphia.

Aussitôt une auto équipée à Saigon traversa la Cochinchine, pénétra sur les routes du Cambodge, s'arrêta la nuit à Phnom Penh, repartit à l'aube et cinq heures après, poudreuse et brûlante, stationnait sous le porche de la Résidence de Sangkè. Madame Gassin en descendit, une flamme heureuse dans les yeux, les joues fouettées par le vent de la course. Mais il parut à Ternier qu'elle avait légèrement maigri et que ses traits n'offraient plus cette expression de quiétude et de détachement spirituel dont ils se paraient naguère. Peu habitué et malhabile à lire sur le visage des femmes, il ne poussa pas son examen plus avant.

Et d'ailleurs qui peut prétendre lire avec succès sur le visage d'une femme ?

Le soir même, madame Gassin s'installait au bungalow, dans une grande pièce d'angle donnant par de larges vérandas, à l'est, sur la rivière et, au sud, sur des arbres d'une propriété voisine. Le Résident avait complété le mobilier par une table pesante faite d'une loupe pareille à du marbre rouge, une berceuse, des fleurs, quelques soieries pour effacer la nudité des murs, du linge fin sur la coiffeuse. Il vint lui-même vérifier l'installation et recommander de nouveau la voyageuse au gérant adjudicataire du bungalow, un Chinois plein de bonne volonté et qui portait à sa chaîne de montre, en breloque, un petit cochon d'or serti d'éclats de diamant.

III

Sans doute Ternier eût préféré recevoir madame Gassin à la Résidence. Il ne le lui proposa pas en raison de convenances qu'elle eût peut-être invoquées, avec sa liberté.

— Je n'ai pas d'inquiétude à savoir que vous logerez ici, avait-il dit à Hélène, car l'exposition de votre chambre est excellente, la vue admirable et le gérant, qui m'est dévoué, a tout intérêt à bien vous soigner. J'y veillerai.

La vue se déroulait sous les yeux de madame Gassin, ordonnée comme un décor, dans une chaude opulence. L'ombre baignait cette rive et le soleil flambait sur l'autre. Entre elles, la rivière roulait ses moyennes eaux déjà rapides en drainant des sables d'acajou. On la voyait venir de loin, atteindre plus de deux cents mètres de largeur à la hauteur du bungalow. Puis, au nord, elle tournait. Hélène s'accouda.

Il y avait d'abord, à ses pieds, des embarcations de tous tonnages, depuis la fine pirogue jusqu'à la haute jonque chinoise qui s'abaisse à l'avant entre ses deux yeux peints ; toute une cité balançant se désagrégeant et se reformant dans l'activité paisible d'une population de toutes races.

Sur la berge d'or, les pieds nus des femmes venant puiser l'eau avaient lustré les chemins. Au-dessus, parmi les cases, deux façades de pagodes dressaient de scintillants frontons et, du sud au nord, couronnant les hommes, la terre et les eaux, un rideau profond de verdure fermait l'horizon.

Le regard se perdait dans la gamme des essences. D'abord, par bouquets, les larges feuilles déchirées des bananiers, puis le pointillé des citronniers où des *champas* faisaient des boules claires ; au-dessus, par masses déchiquetées, inconsistantes, légères, les tamariniers ; de ci, de là, des jaquiers arrondissaient un feuillage foncé et lustré. À travers ces hauts taillis serrés et continus, la colonnade des aréquiers aux stipes gris s'insinuait. Et partout où la vue parvenait, les cocotiers, éclatant à toutes hauteurs, isolés, par groupes ou pressés sur un pan d'horizon, imposaient leurs palmes de métal. Il s'y mêlait les panaches des bambous. Et Hélène distinguait d'autres arbres qu'elle ne connaissait pas encore, parmi eux des géants opaques et d'un vert noir où le soleil luisait comme un vernis, organisés et massifs ainsi que des rochers : les manguiers.

Par endroit, entre les jonques et au pied de la berge, où la rivière s'alanguissait en perdant les reflets du ciel et les moires du courant, le rideau des arbres se renversait et des pirogues baignaient dans ces frondaisons. La voyageuse, peu à peu, se sentait subjuguée par l'intime mélange des choses et des êtres. Comme si sa chair, absorbée aussi, se fût diluée dans la lumière, Hélène descendait à la rivière, devenait nonchalante et multiple, et en elle comme dans les eaux courantes, le ciel et l'œuvre de la terre se doublaient.

Ternier respecta un moment sa contemplation et dit :

— Tout cela est à vous, madame. L'heure est particulièrement belle et je crois que la terre de Sangkè s'en est parée pour vous. Sur cette rive se trouve la ville nouvelle, celle que nous bâtissons. Je vous en ferai les honneurs demain. Lorsque vous voudrez observer la vie indigène, franchissez la rivière, allez en face sous ces arbres que vous voyez maintenant au soleil. Vous pourrez demander un sampan au gérant si vous craignez de faire le tour qu'imposent les ponts ou plutôt, téléphonez-moi, et je vous enverrai une voiture. J'aimerais rester avec vous ce soir, malheureusement une commission que je préside se réunit dans quelques instants. En tout cas, nous dînons ensemble, à huit heures, sans cérémonie. Je vous ferai connaître le docteur Maillard.

— Entendu. Allez vite. Merci. Vous m'avez installée comme une princesse.

Ternier se retirait.

— Oh ! dites ! La voiture, envoyez-la-moi tout de suite.

❖ ❖ ❖

Ce fut la Roland-Gassin dans laquelle, un an et demi plus tôt, Hélène et son mari étaient revenus des cascades de Fontanat. La portière claqua et la voiture passa un pont en ciment armé en face de la Résidence, puis, prenant à gauche la route de berge, elle roula à l'allure du pas humain.

Madame Gassin pénétrait au cœur de cet horizon de verdure dont elle venait d'embrasser le déploiement ; elle en foulait la terre rouge sous des voûtes que le soleil horizontal éclairait de côté. Autour de chaque maison, des jardins en fête portaient l'architecture des grands arbres. Les hibiscus aux fleurs en flammes, quelques touffes jaunes et rouges de cannas devant une case ou la chevelure blanche d'une amaryllis, des lauriers roses ; en bordure des propriétés, le long du chemin, des lignes de cactus piqués de fleurettes comme des volants posés sur des raquettes, un buisson de jasmin ; près d'une porte, sous un petit toit, une jarre d'eau pour le passant assoiffé : voilà donc où des hommes vivent tandis que nous souffrons, nous autres.

Hélène cherchait ces hommes. Trop de choses révélées déroutaient ses regards, trop de choses qu'elle ne connaissait pas, qu'elle ne comprenait point. Elle voulut isoler les êtres, l'expression de leurs visages, les détails de leurs vêtements, y fixer son esprit — impossible. De même que ses yeux restaient impressionnés par la splendeur de l'arbre en découvrant le rythme d'un mouvement humain, le bombé d'un torse couvert du bleu céleste ; de même qu'elle distinguait autour d'un poignet tantôt un bracelet de fleurs tressées, tantôt un anneau d'or ; de même qu'il lui semblait que cette terre sanglante passait dans le rougeoiement des hibiscus, comme si le rouge de ces fleurs eût été celui de cette terre devenu plus clair et plus ardent à mesure qu'il montait et qu'elles fleurissaient ; de même qu'aux visions que ses yeux embrassaient se mêlaient la perception parfumée d'un air ponctué de fruits et la mollesse un peu lourde d'une ombre perpétuelle — Hélène ne pouvait séparer les êtres des choses.

Ses regards glissaient avec une égale jouissance sur un pli d'étoffe, dans les couleurs de ce pli, autour du geste qui les animait. Et aussitôt, à travers sa pensée, un palmier lançait sa trajectoire et continuait le geste humain par-dessus la rue de ce village ombragé comme un bois.

Elle fit arrêter la voiture et, tapie dans son coin de cuir, elle ouvrait son intelligence à cette fécondité.

— Je suis toute petite... murmura-t-elle.

Des bœufs passèrent. Elle reconnut dans une corbeille des pastèques ouvertes. Un battement sourd et régulier venait d'un mortier à paddy qu'une femme, debout sur le pilon, actionnait. Au-delà, des jeunes hommes, immobiles sur un banc, rêvassaient en regardant devant eux, vers la rivière. Tout à coup, deux coqs aux cous pelés, haut perchés sur des pattes garance, foncèrent et se disputèrent les entrailles d'un poisson. Des petits enfants s'étaient immobilisés autour de l'automobile. Puis une lamentable calèche, bavant son crin, réparée au rotin et traînée par deux chevaux harnachés de cordes, bouleversa la rue : des Chinoises s'y trouvaient tenant des paniers sur leurs genoux. Des bonzes, en file, croisèrent l'équipage, drapés comme des Romains. Au bord de la route, un arbre aux branches et à tronc gris, tordus, écailleux, sans une feuille, perdait des fleurs blanches à cœur jaune pâle qui couvraient le sol.

— Marche, chauffeur, dit madame Gassin.

Elle passa devant une pagode chinoise vétuste qui présentait deux cercles décoratifs ajourés, chaque côté de sa porte ; d'autres cases où des femmes préparaient le repas autour de foyers d'argile et elle vit soudain une vieille maison abandonnée, bâtie en brique, percée de trois arches en plein cintre, reposant sur des chapiteaux à feuillages. On accédait à l'étage par deux escaliers latéraux, formant fer à cheval. La toiture à lourds solins s'était noircie au soleil et aux pluies. On voyait des balustres en faïence vert émeraude et les restes d'un décor en stuc, le tout désuet et mélancolique, lézardé, marbré de lichens ; maison construite depuis plus d'un siècle dans cette architecture candide que les jésuites introduisirent en Chine dès le XVIe siècle et qui se propagea jusqu'à Manille et jusqu'à Singapore, mêlant la grâce savante d'un décor chinois à des lignes Louis XIV abâtardies. Tout à coup, elle suggère à l'Occidental, stupéfait de sa découverte, de vieilles grand-mères à robe puce. Et il cherche dans la courette où l'herbe pousse entre les briques, la berline dételée, là, sous des aréquiers, entre ces cases cambodgiennes, au bord de cette rivière où des pirogues se balancent.

— Arrête ! commanda Hélène à voix basse, et elle se pencha comme à une fenêtre.

Deux enfants se trouvaient là, tout petits, nus, rouges de la poussière où ils se traînaient. Ventres bombés à gros nombril, faces déjà dessinées, très sérieux. L'un, assis au pied d'une haie, regardait l'autre. L'autre parlait ou plutôt s'occupait à une absorbante besogne et parfois disait un mot, désignant ce qu'il faisait. Ce tableau, cette méthode pouvaient se placer à l'origine du monde. L'enfant assis tournait le dos à la rue et n'avait pas entendu la silencieuse voiture s'arrêter, l'autre, trop occupé, ne voyait rien.

Le travailleur avait raclé la poussière d'une petite aire carrée et disposé à chaque angle une feuille d'arbre.

— Phtéa, dit-il.

— Phtéa, répéta l'autre.

— Que disent-ils ? demanda tout bas Hélène au chauffeur.

— Maison.

Hélène vit la maison au bord de l'herbe.

— Stoung, dit le premier enfant.

— Stoung, approuva le second et il ouvrit la bouche, le bras levé, ses petits doigts écartés.

— Rivière, souffla le chauffeur.

Sur cette rivière, le maître du jeu posa un tesson d'écuelle bleu, en disant « Touk ».

— Hœu ! fit le spectateur satisfait en laissant retomber son bras que la préoccupation ne soutenait plus. « Bateau », avait traduit le chauffeur. L'action prenait de l'ampleur. Et, chose singulière, la voyageuse voyait aussi. Elle voyait autour d'elle le paysage que recréait l'enfant. Des mandarines mûres luisaient. Un merle, ayant éventré une papaye, voletait sur place pour se maintenir à la hauteur du fruit et sa noirceur, violette dans l'ombre, se juxtaposait au jaune de la pulpe ouverte.

Tout le Cambodge s'assoupissait là, contenu, symbolisé en un coin de son territoire. Le fleuve le traverse en entier, toutes ses cases pareilles se groupent, ainsi enrichies et protégées par ces mêmes arbres, unifiées en des traditions séculaires. C'est partout cette même volupté immobile et simple, la même poésie qu'enveloppe l'immédiat horizon, une pénétrante emprise des choses sur les âmes ignorant les tourments de la pensée. Mais alors, ces enfants, tout à l'heure ?

Eh bien, oui, ces enfants étaient déjà des hommes : la maison, le fleuve, le sampan, aussi bien que le jeu, limiteront la durée de leur vie. À deux ans, ils connaissent leurs destinées et l'épuisent sans se soucier beaucoup de l'étranger qui passe, ni des races qui s'entremêlent autour d'eux. Aucune complication, rien de nouveau ne surgira. Ils ne mettront, plus tard, qu'une étoffe sur leur nudité pour aviver les désirs de l'amour.

La voiture repassa la rivière. Pressant l'allure dans la ville française, elle parvint au bungalow au moment où l'électricité traça d'un seul coup, le long de l'avenue, un cordon de points lumineux. Un gros camion postal, traînant sa remorque, couvert de poussière, rempli d'indigènes et parti le matin de Phnom Penh passa en trombe. À peine madame Gassin eut-elle le temps de monter à sa chambre et d'y déposer son chapeau que le crépuscule y pénétrait. La rivière s'enfonça entre ses rives. Et lorsque la voyageuse s'accouda pour songer à tout ce qui venait de l'envahir, ce fut la nuit qui la reçut.

IV

Dès l'aube, afin de profiter de sa fraîcheur, Ternier vint prendre madame Gassin et l'emmena visiter à pied la ville française.

⚜ ⚜ ⚜

La berge d'une rivière avec des cases dans la verdure où somnole une population trop vieille, immobile depuis dix siècles et asservie. La terre est ravinée et les immondices y stagnent. Le moustique pullule. De temps à autre, un choléra endémique prend son homme. Un enfant sur trois meurt. Bêtes et gens boivent à la rivière. Les pagodes luisent au soleil et des chants montent dans les nuits. Les arbres ploient sous les fruits au bord des eaux poissonneuses et, s'étendant sur les terres aussi loin que l'homme veut pousser son soc, les rizières brillent. La population paie l'impôt au mandarin siamois.

Et tout à coup, dans cet état de choses, dont il semblait que rien ne devait pouvoir changer, sur ce tuf gras et profond où les cendres de cent générations se dispersèrent pareillement, dans ce paysage immobile, parmi cette population où la fille se mariait à la même place que sa trisaïeule et à la faveur de rites identiques, entre ces pagodes où depuis plus de treize cents ans d'invariables paroles se prononçaient, nous sommes venus, nous, Français.

Ternier a dit : nous, Français, et il parut à Hélène qu'en spécifiant cela, il dressa un peu sa taille. Il n'a pas dit : Occidentaux, parce qu'il fallait que ce fût nous et pas d'autres qui vinssions, afin que ce qui se passa pût se passer sans que les pagodes cessassent de méditer, les chants de monter dans les nuits et les filles de se marier comme leurs trisaïeules, dans des pavillons légers, décorés d'étoffes blanches et de troncs de bananiers sculptés. Nous sommes donc venus et en quelques années, nous bâtîmes une ville neuve entre des jardins couverts de manguiers centenaires.

— Vous avez vu, madame, hier, sur l'autre rive, la vie indigène, son calme et sa liberté. Nous avons relié par des routes au reste du pays ce qui en était isolé par des jours et des jours de voyages. Voici, sur cette place, derrière ces arbres et entre des murs bleus, la Poste, tête de ligne des autocars qui partent dans toutes les directions, la Poste et ses fils télégraphiques et téléphoniques. Les enfants mouraient ? Nous passerons, dans un instant, devant l'hôpital, sa maternité indigène et ses pavillons disséminés dans un parc. Au-delà, c'est la banque. Nos écoles n'étaient pas ouvertes qu'il fallut les agrandir : nous les agrandîmes. Plus d'un millier de Chinois vivaient à Sangkè, forces actives et commerciales de la région ? Nous leur traçâmes des rues larges, bordées de maisons solides, claires et salubres. Dans ces jardins, longeant cette avenue, voyez les villas et les offices des Français, créateurs de la jeune cité. Puis, un jour, l'électricité a jailli et la glace fut sur toutes les tables. Tous les marécages asséchés, nous pouvons maintenant, la plupart des nuits, dormir sans moustiquaire. Demain, la gare apparaîtra. À droite de la route venant de Phnom Penh, vous avez pu voir le terrain d'aviation et ses hangars.

« Sur trois kilomètres de longueur, coquettement répartie le long des méandres de cette rivière, nous bâtîmes donc notre ville, une ville sans caserne, car les quelques soldats français qu'on y avait appelés à l'origine repartirent : ils étaient inutiles. Nous installâmes notre ville et notre autorité sans tirer un coup de fusil. Ces maisons, ces boulevards furent créés à l'aide d'une main-d'œuvre chinoise et annamite et les dix piastres d'impôt que chaque Cambodgien mâle paye par an ; ainsi que le marché où il vient vendre et acheter dans la sécurité et l'hygiène, ces rues surveillées où il ne craint plus la piraterie, cet hôpital où il est soigné gratuitement, cette école que ses enfants fréquentent librement, tous ces bureaux dans lesquels il ne peut plus subir la pression du mandarin, ces ponts qu'il franchit avec ses charrettes sans détacher de la berge un sampan que le courant emporte au loin, cette usine qui lui distribue l'eau pure et la lumière. Nous avons circonscrit ses propriétés qui appartiennent maintenant au plus faible sans qu'il ait à redouter le plus fort. Nous appelâmes des vétérinaires qui surveillent son bétail. Et le long de ces berges, les chaloupes à vapeur ont décuplé son commerce.

« Il n'en avait pas besoin ? Pourquoi n'est-il pas parti ? Il était libre. Pourquoi, en cinq ans, la population a-t-elle quintuplé ? Pourquoi nos sacs postaux sont-ils pleins de ses lettres, nos chaloupes et nos autos bondées de voyageurs ? Pourquoi tous les terrains urbains libres sont-ils achetés ? Pourquoi, sortant de l'école traditionnelle des pagodes, les petits enfants viennent-ils dans nos écoles primaires et pourquoi nos dispensaires sont-ils pleins, chaque matin, à l'heure de la visite, puisque, à peine à cinq kilomètres d'ici, c'est la brousse et la liberté ; puisque, aussi bien, dans les limites rigides de ce centre urbain, les pagodes continuent leurs prières et que, dans toutes ces cases, chacun respecte toujours les vieilles traditions ?

⚜ ⚜ ⚜

Ternier et Hélène prirent une rue que des arbres recouvraient d'une voûte. Entre ses trottoirs et ses compartiments, elle aboutissait à une place où un grand théâtre se dressait dans lequel, chaque soir, des acteurs siamois et cambodgiens jouent le Râmâyana.

De chaque côté de la rue, presque entièrement habitée d'Annamites, dans les logements ouverts ainsi que des boutiques, des taches carminées se précisent, s'allongent, où Hélène distingue ces dessins bizarres et mouvants qui sont l'écriture : les tablettes de famille. Ou bien, faites de bois noir, elles s'effacent, de sorte que les lettres d'or ou de nacre miroitent, soutenues par on ne sait quoi. Entre ces panneaux renouvelés de maison en maison, change aussi l'autel ancestral pieusement entretenu au fond du logis.

À la porte, des êtres en haillons, femmes sales qui se grattent la tête minutieusement, un ongle long entre les cheveux et derrière elles, au cœur de l'ombre, accrochant les aventureux reflets du jour, scintillent les deux chandeliers, le brûle-parfums, le vase à cendre, tout le bronze mystique d'une chapelle en arrière d'une chienlit. Au premier plan, une humanité chassieuse, et au-delà, un rituel soigné et rutilant, le saut du dragon contre l'angle d'un socle ou bien le vol décoratif d'une chauve-souris sculptée.

— C'est un phénomène curieux, dit Ternier, auquel on ne prend pas assez garde, que le mélange des races asiatiques dans ces centres cambodgiens et que ces races se côtoient et demeurent libéralement chacune avec ses coutumes, ses croyances et ses hardes. En cette petite ville, telles sont les rues chinoises et annamites ; l'Hindou en pagne blanc passe après des Malais en toques de velours. Et tandis que les étrangers s'établissent dans des maisons maçonnées, en plein centre, le Cambodgien reste aux faubourgs. Il n'a aucun goût pour les affaires et préfère ses jardins et ses cases légères.

Des étalages hétéroclites dévalaient sur les trottoirs, balles de coton ou sacs de riz, piles de poissons secs, monceaux de peaux et, dans les boutiques, tablées de Célestes aux torses nus, mangeant une soupe commune entre deux déchargements de chaloupes ou de camions. On entendait, dans le matin léger, le bruit sec des abaques, le cliquetis des porcelaines au déballage et puis, deux cents mètres plus loin, tout s'effaça instantanément.

La rue agitée et bruyante devint une route déserte entre des bananiers et des files d'aréquiers. À droite et à gauche, ce n'était que charmilles et petits bocages où madame Gassin retrouvait les tableaux de la veille. De ce qui vivait là, rien ne pouvait se comparer à ce qui vivait ici. Ils traversèrent une place, terrains à bâtir. Les hautes herbes en faisaient une savane où du sable arrondissait des dunes blanches. Une rue y débouchait sous un flamboyant énorme, régulier comme une gerbe arrangée dans un vase et bombant sur un tronc multiple le dôme de ses fleurs. La terre était rouge des pétales tombés. À son ombre, un Cambodgien dormait dans sa charrette dont le timon se redressait en col de cygne. À l'est, un cinéma était en construction. Plus loin, des voix d'enfants, ânonnant l'alphabet sur un air de cantique, franchissaient un mur d'école. De rares passants : un trio de bonzes aux crânes bleus ; un Chinois, marchand de soupe, rapide et glissant sous la palanche à laquelle se balançait sa cuisine portative. Sur un des tas de sable, des dindons somnolaient, le poitrail ouvert et portant leurs entrailles à leur bec.

Le Résident fit traverser à Hélène le marché. Il débordait du hall métallique sur de larges trottoirs. C'est un enchantement que ce voyage dans le chaos des couleurs opulentes de la nourriture extrême orientale. Les éventaires dessinent des mosaïques peintes et vernies par les feux du soleil. Et le hasard des arrangements y est parfois si heureux, tel panier de piments rutile si opportunément sur un monceau de courges que la marchande semble en avoir sciemment réglé l'ordonnance à la faveur d'une science picturale subtile.

Hélène traversait des zones d'odeurs aussi nettement séparées que des nappes d'ombre et de soleil. Des jasmins s'annoncèrent à vingt mètres à la ronde par-dessus une pyramide de courges, prêtant à ces énormes fruits leurs exhalaisons de fleurs. Les ananas s'empilaient en de grands couffins et la lumière, arrêtée par les facettes de leurs écailles, refroidissait leur bronze doré et le glaçait au bleu du ciel. Et puis ce furent des paniers d'aubergines au violet luisant, les fleurs de bananiers en fuseaux garance qui se violacent à la pointe, et partout, des piments cabossés sous leur vernis profond dont le vert incisif où le violent carmin sont, aux regards, ce que leur pulpe est au goût.

Après, Ternier guida Hélène entre des petites boutiques légères dont les cloisons disparaissaient sous les régimes de bananes et ils avançaient entre des murailles hérissées de mille cornes versicolores à travers lesquelles passait un soleil déchiqueté comme du coton dans une carde. Les étalages se rapprochèrent, plus gris et très compliqués : nœuds du gingembre, fleurs de nénuphar, marrons de Chine, chair effilochée de poissons secs, haricots germés pareils à des agglomérats de larves, écheveaux de vermicelle transparent, piles de petites jarres pleines de sauces fermentées, pots de chaux rouge comme une pâte de corail, tabac noir, rangée régulière de feuilles de bétel aux formes d'as de pique, arachides, safran brun ; cuisines avec leurs quartiers de lard, leurs poulets écartelés et des canards laqués.

Dans ce labyrinthe, à travers cette chimie déconcertante dont tous les sens s'effarent, parmi cette vie ardente de choses qui semblaient protéiformes sous les mains qui offraient ou choisissaient, une foule caqueteuse se mouvait. Chinois aux torses clairs, Annamites en fourreau noir, des Cambodgiennes de toute qualité, de robustes paysans portant des charges de pastèques, des Chinois, encore, déchargeant des quartiers de porcs et le corps taché de sang, agents de police indigènes, quelques Tonkinoises en turban noir et robe cachou, des enfants de tous âges, nus, à cheval sur des hanches, l'un jouant avec un crabe.

Et tous les acheteurs se hâtaient avant la chaleur, criaillaient, se glissaient entre les piles de fruits et dans la vapeur des cuisines, la hanche saillante sous le panier circulaire qui s'appesantissait ou portant, au bout d'un lien de rotin, un poisson.

Par terre, sur le bord des trottoirs, ce furent enfin les tas d'ordures presque aussi beaux que les éventaires et que le soleil déjà ardent mélangeait, fouillait, reprenant de la vie dans cette mort des choses, de toutes ces choses nées de lui et qui se désagrégeaient avant de pourrir avec une coquetterie brillante : demi-noix de coco dont l'intérieur aux blancheurs d'albâtre et la tignasse rousse font qu'elles ressemblent à des crânes de poupées cassées, noyaux de mangues sur lesquels des milliers de mouches vertes ajoutaient une pulpe d'émeraude, opercules en cornet des pousses de bambou, viscères ambrés de poissons, pelures d'ananas : ces dépouilles de reptiles écorchés vifs, toupies vert amande des nénuphars — toutes sortes de choses polychromes, enchevêtrées, poussées par le balai comme des confettis et des serpentins aux portes d'un théâtre, après un veglione.

V

Ternier fit appeler le chauffeur et demanda à madame Gassin :

— Vous avez tout votre temps, n'est-ce pas ?

— Libre comme l'air.

— Eh bien ! Il est quatre heures. Allons à une trentaine de kilomètres d'ici voir une pagode bien placée : Vat Romduol. La route n'est pas vilaine à travers les rizières. Vous voulez bien ?

— Pouvez-vous le demander ? Allons.

Hélène semblait fatiguée, mais ses yeux resplendissaient sous son chapeau de daim gris orné de perles d'acier et qu'une bride maintenait sous le menton — militairement. Sa robe droite et simple soulignait la minceur de son corps. La blancheur de ses mains, le mauve qui ombrait ses yeux, l'imperceptible langueur dont elle était pénétrée contrastaient avec le mordant de ses gestes, l'activité de sa voix et surtout la floraison de ses regards.

— Les rivières débordantes et les premières pluies ont inondé une partie des campagnes. C'est l'époque du repiquage du paddy et des plus beaux couchers du soleil. Pas trop vite, chauffeur.

Dès qu'ils eurent quitté les frondaisons du centre, ils virent autour d'eux la plaine immense dans le soleil. La route droite et blanche finissait à un point où la rejoignaient les fils du télégraphe. La Roland-Gassin y glissait aussi, son volant immobile, à travers le souffle tiède de la mousson de suroît.

— La bonne route !

— Elle vient d'être rechargée. Elle atteint Sisophon, à quatre-vingts kilomètres d'ici. Au-delà, plus de cent kilomètres de piste sont déjà percés et, dans trois années, les automobiles arriveront au pied des monts Dangrèk. Les régions les plus reculées du Cambodge nord et, par les cols, le bas Laos seront alors débloqués. Nous aurons, de plus, ouvert de notre côté les provinces du nord-est siamois.

— Et cette piste est-elle accessible aux autos ?

— Pas encore, car les premiers orages l'ont ravinée et les ponts ne sont pas terminés. Je dois aller voir les travaux la semaine prochaine.

— Vous m'emmènerez ?

— Oh ! oh ! il ne s'agit pas d'une promenade.

On ne peut circuler qu'à cheval ou en charrette. L'eau est rare en cette saison et la région sablonneuse. La tournée durera cinq ou six jours.

— N'augmentez pas mon désir de vous accompagner.

— Vous y viendrez avec votre mari.

— Il ne sera pas encore arrivé.

— Il vous abandonne, dites-moi.

— Je ne suis pas à plaindre. C'est moi, plutôt, qui l'ai abandonné ! Saigon est une ville étouffante. En deux jours, le voyageur en a épuisé tous les charmes et n'y trouve plus que de l'ennui.

Dans les rizières, les Cambodgiens repiquaient le paddy, de l'eau jusqu'aux mollets, une eau figée qui miroitait à travers les jeunes tiges. Le ciel s'y reflétait, de sorte que le riz semblait pousser dans les nuages. Des femmes aux vêtements boueux liaient par bottes ruisselantes l'herbe nourricière. Quelques enfants péchaient au panier des poissons qui, pareils à ceux de la fable, quittent en cette saison les cours d'eau débordants pour s'égarer dans les campagnes. Debout sur des herses d'où giclait une vase gluante, les hommes guidaient en cercle leur couple de bœufs que des merles mandarins escortaient.

Hélène posa machinalement sa main sur la portière. La patte en cuir de la sacoche percée dans l'épaisseur de la carrosserie portait, frappées en fort relief, les initiales de la marque : RG, enlacées au centre d'une double circonférence. Lorsqu'elle les sentit sous ses doigts, elle éprouva une commotion. Ses paupières battirent et, vivement, elle retira sa main. Aussitôt, pour masquer son geste et son trouble, elle redemanda :

— Vous m'emmènerez ?

— Songez-vous à ma responsabilité ?

— En avez-vous peur ?

— J'ai peur de la rudesse de l'expédition qui n'est pas faite pour une femme et au cours de laquelle il faudra redouter des orages, des contretemps pénibles.

— Vous ne voulez pas vous embarrasser ?

— Je ne veux pas vous voir privée de tout confort.

— Ne m'avez-vous pas souvent dit, à Paris, il m'en souvient, qu'une tournée pouvait parfaitement s'organiser ; qu'en pleine forêt, vous aviez une nappe sur la table et, qu'en deux heures, les indigènes savaient élever un abri parfait ? Je vous dispenserai de la nappe.

— Tout cela est vrai pour un homme et non pour une Parisienne qui arrive tout droit de l'avenue d'Eylau.

— Bien.

Madame Gassin songea une minute. Aux fils du télégraphe des couples de martins-pêcheurs lustraient le saphir de leurs ailes en gonflant un jabot léché de feu.

— Alors, j'irai toute seule, conclut-elle en souriant.

— Je vous le défends bien !

— Vos pouvoirs résidentiels ne vont pas jusque-là. Et puis on ne me défend rien.

— Est-ce un entêtement de femme auquel vous voulez me voir souscrire ?

— Est-ce un parti pris d'homme que vous m'opposez ? Tenez, vous allez comprendre tout de suite mon désir. Vous m'avez tant parlé de la brousse ! Une occasion unique m'est offerte d'y aller en compagnie du meilleur guide qui soit, sans trop le déranger et vous voulez que je ne saisisse pas cette occasion ?

— Cela revient à dire que cette randonnée, c'est moi qui vous ai poussée à la faire.

— C'est vous. Voulez-vous une preuve de ma mémoire, une preuve qu'il ne faut rien dire devant les enfants ? Nous sommes avenue d'Eylau. Il y a madame Gassin, son mari, deux ou trois comparses et puis un Résident en congé. Il raconte de belles histoires et les indigènes de Paris le suivent, par la pensée, en forêt. Il dit quelque chose comme ceci : « Des colonnes de fourmis noires serpentent durant des heures, sans interruption, brillantes et sinueuses comme des coulées de laque. Sous certains arbres, si l'on tend la main, on sent tomber des petites graines pressées et régulières comme une giboulée de grêlons, et cela dure une matinée. Le sentier, que l'on ouvre en coupant, en arrachant et en écrasant, est introuvable quelques jours après : la tige laissée pour morte a ressuscité, des rejets apparaissent déjà sur les blessures faites au coupe-coupe, le nid de guêpes est reconstruit, la bête que l'on avait tuée, dépecée... ». Est-ce cela ?

— Il n'y a pas là de quoi se monter l'imagination.

— Voulez-vous que je continue ?

— Du tout — ou bien, changez d'auteur.

— Il n'y a pas lieu de se monter l'imagination, dites-vous ? Non. Mais est-on maîtresse de cette imagination, doit-on la brider, lorsqu'on trouve à la vie un peu trop de monotonie ? Sans médire de cette vie, comprenez-moi bien, tout en étant comblée par elle, on éprouve cependant des curiosités ardentes et légitimes que les occasions réveillent. C'est mon cas. Et puis le hasard me conduit ici. Les quelques jours seulement que j'y ai vécus dépassent toutes mes idées et vos paroles. Ne me laissez pas à mi-chemin, mon ami. Me mesureriez-vous les beaux souvenirs que je veux emporter et qui pourraient m'être si précieux, lorsque je vivrai de nouveau en France ? Tout ce qui vous entoure ici ne vous frappe plus, le pays vous a incorporé en lui. Mais moi, je passe, étrangère, voyageuse, et je vis dans l'enchantement. Tenez, les préparatifs de cette tournée, cela seulement, les caisses pour les charrettes, le cheval qui attend : me voilà petite fille.

— Appelons Robinson.

— Appelons Robinson ! Il vit des traces de pied humain sur le sable — et sa solitude cessa.

— Le vent les efface et il n'en reste plus rien.

— Je veux les voir, avant.

— Vous le verrez donc.

Dans un bruit de trompe, ils traversaient un village. Madame Gassin entrevit des touffes de palmiers à sucre, des boutiques chinoises en paillote, une haie de cactus, des cases dispersées dans une colonnade serrée de palmiers. Puis, d'autres arbres grandirent, entourèrent une place d'ombre et une mare de lotus roses : la pagode sous son toit à antéfixes dorées, quelques toges jaunes de bonzes. Et de nouveau le soleil inonda d'autres rizières à perte de vue.

Hélène se tourna un peu vers Ternier.

— Vous verrez, je serai bien sage. Vous n'aurez pas à vous occuper de moi. À cheval lorsqu'il le faudra et aussi longtemps qu'il le faudra. Vous ne pouvez évaluer ce qu'est pour moi cette simple perspective et ce que sera ce voyage... Et puis, je serai si fière de suivre votre route, de voir et de bien comprendre comment elle s'avance dans ces régions qu'elle va réveiller... L'admiration que votre œuvre m'inspire ne peut pas vous importuner, dites ?

Ternier se départit de sa brusquerie coutumière et répondit d'une voix assouplie :

— Elle m'est précieuse, madame, dans mon isolement. Mais songez à ce que ma courtoisie et mon affection vous doivent. La garde de cette province m'échoit, non pas parce que je suis Pierre Ternier, mais parce que mon tour est d'être là. Je dois la sécurité à la plus misérable paillote, le guet à ce riz qui pousse et si des oiseaux en volent le grain, je suis un mauvais gardien. Vous passez. Aussi bien veillé-je sur vous. Vous devenez mon invitée. Je vous dois la santé, la réalisation de vos désirs et accepte ce devoir avec joie. Or, ma conscience, d'une voix plus profonde, me dit : « Prends garde surtout à celle-là qui est seule et qui compte sur toi. ». Et je suis d'autant plus intéressé à votre quiétude que vous êtes ici, ainsi que vous venez de me le rappeler, surtout en raison des promesses que je vous ai faites. Il faut, madame, que ces promesses soient tenues. Si vous subissez un accident, je vous aurais menti. Si une calomnie vous frôle, je vous aurais menti. Si votre mari est effleuré de l'ombre d'un soupçon, je vous aurais menti. Vous ne comprenez pas. Vous ouvrez de grands yeux étonnés, parce que, femme, vous avez l'habitude d'être portée. Mais l'homme qui porte, lui, ne voit pas les choses sous le même angle. S'il a accepté un fardeau, même léger, il doit à son semblable ou se doit à lui-même de porter ce fardeau d'un point à un autre, intact — sinon, il ment. Mais oui, il ment. Oh ! je sais bien qu'on a l'habitude, maintenant, de donner des noms divers à chaque chose. Et s'il refuse le fardeau, cet homme, c'est qu'il en a peur ou se sent incapable de l'accepter.

— Il n'y a pas de déshonneur...

— Non. Seulement, que cet homme s'en aille d'une place qu'il usurpe.

Tout à coup, dans le grincement des freins, la voiture s'arrêta court. C'était, à travers la route, une statue énorme en bronze mal coulé, squameuse, gluante de boue, le mufle tendu et l'œil en flamme. Allait-elle bondir sur les voyageurs ? Non, elle tourna pesamment, se sauva et se jeta dans une mare : un buffle. Des crabiers s'envolèrent.

— Puisque nous parlons de projets, continua Ternier, en voici un autre : dans trois jours, je donne un grand dîner pour fêter la rosette de la Légion d'honneur qu'on vient d'octroyer au Gouverneur de la province. C'est un vieux serviteur du Protectorat. Vous verrez, à ce dîner, à peu près tout le centre réuni : une quarantaine de convives.

— Mais c'est une aubaine ! J'aurai ainsi le spectacle de la population coloniale et du luxe des réceptions officielles.

— Préparez vos tablettes. Ne vous attendez pas toutefois à ce qu'il y ait un nègre derrière chaque convive et des almées au fond de la salle. Cette population que vous allez voir, toute de fonctionnaires, est une population tranquille et bourgeoise qui ne correspond nullement à ces tableaux aux couleurs trop poussées que certaines chroniques se plaisent à en tracer. Je vous donne l'assurance que les hommes ne changeront pas d'épouses au cours du repas et que la Résidence ne comporte pas de lits « profonds comme des tombeaux ». Nous perdrons en pittoresque.

— Je tâcherai de m'en consoler.

— Vous pourrez vous convaincre qu'en France, aux colonies et, du reste, dans tous les pays, les milieux correspondants se ressemblent. Ce qui fait dire souvent que notre société d'expatriés est dissolue et gaspilleuse, âpre à l'avancement, c'est qu'on ne la compare pas à des éléments de même nature pris ailleurs. On dirait vraiment, qu'en Europe, le milieu des hauts fonctionnaires, du grand négoce, en un mot tout ce qui constitue le « dessus du panier », n'est que pureté et intégrité, ordre et harmonie, élégance et érudition ; que chacun est à sa place et qu'il est impossible d'y trouver l'ombre d'une intrigue, un seul désir d'adultère, un soupçon d'ambition ! Pourquoi l'individu transporté ici, dans les mêmes conditions sociales, verrait-il tous ses vices augmenter et pas une de ses vertus ; pourquoi, mettant à Marseille le pied sur un bateau, dépouillerait-il aussitôt ses facultés morales, intellectuelles et professionnelles ?

— Je vous le concède bien volontiers. Pourtant, à la longue, le climat, certaines occasions qu'offrent la colonie, les soldes avantageuses, dit-on, et même...

— Arrêtez ! Que je puisse vous répondre à mesure. Vous n'avez pas ici de main-d'œuvre européenne. Le plus modeste expatrié est déjà un chef de chantier ou de magasin. Vous ne trouvez pas, non plus, de classe aristocratique, pas de rentiers ni de politiciens. Vous chercheriez en vain un milieu libéral, j'entends d'écrivains, d'artistes, de savants, de professeurs libres, un monde des théâtres. La population où vous pénétrez — exceptée celle de Saigon et de Hanoi — correspond donc exactement à la partie de notre bourgeoisie française, aux mains de qui sont placées les choses de l'État et du commerce. L'indépendance est fictive, car il n'y a pas de commerçant, d'avocat qui, à un moment donné, ne soit obligé d'accrocher son wagon au train administratif. Il est aisé de comprendre qu'une discipline avouée ou non, sourdement combattue, maladroitement admise ou plus ou moins discrètement imposée, règne du haut en bas de l'échelle. Il en résulte une ambiance puissante que rien ne peut disperser, dont nul ne songe à se retrancher et qui agit. Ceci posé, il conviendrait, lorsqu'on veut juger le milieu colonial, de départager cette influence et celle du pays proprement dit et de savoir si les miasmes que l'on respire, de la Cochinchine au Yun-Nan, montent de la terre ou bien n'ont pas été simplement importés par nous et, par conséquent, ne se retrouveraient pas aussi bien dans le département de l'Indre-et-Loire ou de l'Allier, si on les y cherchait.

— Il me semble pourtant que la chaleur, l'humidité doivent, dans certains cas, modifier les tempéraments.

— C'est exact. Au cours des deux ou trois mois de l'été, la chaleur combat l'énergie et diminue l'effort. Nul ne songe à le contester, mais là, nous changeons d'idées et, vous avez dit le mot, atteignons le tempérament. Le tempérament n'est pas la mentalité. Remarquez toutefois que nous disposons de plus en plus de bons moyens pour lutter contre cette chaleur et nous parviendrions à en supprimer les effets si la sainte routine ne nous entravait pas, si nous apportions des mesures rationnelles à notre architecture et à notre urbanisme, à nos heures de travail, à nos régimes alimentaires. En fait, nous luttons mal contre les conditions du climat. Il nous atteint, c'est notre faute. Du point de vue humain, social plutôt, le tout est de savoir si la quantité de travail salubre, nécessaire à notre rôle colonial, correspond à tout ce que nous pouvons produire. Si, en France, valant dix et produisant dix, je suis en équilibre, ici valant huit, si je produis huit, l'équilibre n'est pas rompu. Eh bien, j'ai l'impression de produire ici autant qu'en France, vous pouvez voir que ma Résidence fonctionne comme une Préfecture et que le médecin soigne ses malades quand il le faut. En conséquence, je ne suis pas éloigné de penser que beaucoup de coloniaux produisent plus à leur poste que s'ils étaient chez eux, en un poste semblable, puisqu'ils sont appelés à fournir plus d'efforts, tout en surmontant plus d'obstacles.

— Donc, vous vous usez plus vite. On voit beaucoup de mauvaises mines ici.

— N'en voit-on pas de bonnes ? D'où vient la différence ? On a pris l'habitude d'attribuer au climat beaucoup de maladies que le colonial porte en lui et dont il aurait aussi bien souffert à Dijon. On ne fait partir théoriquement de la métropole que des gens parfaitement sains. Il n'en va pas ainsi. Dans nos jugements, ne faisons pas intervenir, non plus, le passé. Depuis cinquante ans, beaucoup des nôtres sont morts à préparer le présent déjà si salubre que nous vivons. Songeons à ces sacrifiés et ne calomnions pas les résultats de leur abnégation. Les maladies reculent avec les marécages. Considérez mille individus en France et les mille Français qui peuplent actuellement le Cambodge. Eh bien ! L'état sanitaire est supérieur ici à ce qu'il est en France.

— Ce n'est pas croyable.

— C'est tout naturel, et si vous en doutez, je vous fournirai les statistiques les plus précises. Les mauvaises mines que vous remarquez, ne vous y attardez pas trop. La plupart disparaissent après un mois de terroir. Cherchez-en souvent les causes, surtout chez les femmes, non dans la rigueur du climat, mais dans leur inertie, leur mauvaise alimentation, leur crainte du mouvement et, précisément, de ce grand air et de ce soleil qu'elles évitent par tous les moyens possibles. En France, sur cent femmes, sous le fard et la poudre, combien de visages pâlots, de traits tirés ?

— De personnes pâles pour pilules Pink !

— Par exemple ! Vous-même, n'êtes-vous pas un peu pâlotte aujourd'hui ? Et vous n'avez pas quinze jours de séjour.

— Je suis déjà une victime du climat ! Tout cela ne se sait pas en France. Je me rends compte, à chaque minute, que nous n'avons que des idées fausses et souvent absurdes sur la vie des nôtres, aux colonies.

— Disons tout de suite qu'elles ne sont pas toutes comme notre Indochine, les colonies.

— Que l'Indochine soit à mettre à part, n'est-ce pas trop de l'ignorer ? Si j'avais un fils, maintenant que j'ai vu, un peu vu ! Il est certain que je n'éprouverais aucune appréhension à le voir venir se fixer ici.

— Vous seriez comme toutes les mamans, la séparation...

— Peut-être, mais il n'y aurait que la séparation. Il est vrai...

— C'est beaucoup. Je vous disais donc, il y a un instant, que vous verrez, au dîner projeté, toute la société du poste.

— Un échantillonnage.

— Mêlé, car j'invite tout le monde et à peu près tout le monde vient.

— Le placement à table doit faire l'objet d'une véritable stratégie.

— C'est en effet un travail complexe. Je voudrais vous placer à ma droite, mais vous vous y ennuieriez et je ne pourrais pas m'occuper de vous comme je le désire. Aussi je vous mettrai entre M. Barrois, le Trésorier-payeur et notre national et célèbre Garde général des forêts Tubinque. Tubinque est probablement l'un des derniers types marqués qui subsistent des temps héroïques de la colonie. Les histoires humoristiques ou truculentes, cent arlequinades dont les héros sont encore connus et dont on remplirait un recueil bien curieux subsistent dans la mémoire des vieux coloniaux. Il convient que vous en ayez quelques échos.

— Et vous n'avez qu'un de ces représentants des âges révolus ?

— Vous saurez qu'il suffit. Les générations nouvelles sont plus complexes, plus tranquilles et souvent plus sournoises. La grosse blague avait son prix. Parmi le reste de nos convives, je ne vois rien de saillant à vous recommander.

— Les dames ?

— Vous verrez vous-même. Quelques-unes gentillettes, malheureusement casanières. Trop de peignoirs alanguis sous le ventilateur. Pas de cavalières. Nos tennis sont presque déserts. Aucune, d'une façon générale, ne s'intéresse à l'indigène. La femme française devrait jouer un rôle charmant et utile près des Cambodgiennes. Elle serait accueillie avec une grande sympathie, une curiosité enfantine et discrète. Au contraire, il y a même trop souvent chez celle-là une sorte de dédain pour celles-ci, ces jaunes, ces petites guenons, ces *congaïs*, comme elles disent volontiers. On ne fait exception que pour les princesses endiamantées, d'ailleurs les femmes indigènes les moins intéressantes du pays.

— En aurons-nous de ces princesses, au dîner ?

— Non, pas de princesse, on n'en voit qu'à Phnom Penh, au palais royal et autour. Nous aurons la fille aînée du Gouverneur, lequel a brûlé sa femme l'année dernière.

— Oh ! mon Dieu !

— Je veux dire qu'il est veuf et vous savez qu'ici on brûle les morts.

— Ah ! j'aime mieux ça, surtout pour un homme décoré !

⚜ ⚜ ⚜

Ils arrivèrent à la pagode de Romduol, au bord de la rivière. À leurs pieds, le troupeau des jonques se pressait. À l'ouest, le couchant suspendait son faste et la rivière en mêlait les reflets à des fleurs flottantes d'un mauve de jacinthe. Une femme annamite, les cuisses illuminées, s'aspergeait. D'autres femmes venaient du bain, un vase plat sur la hanche. Chaque sampan allumait un foyer d'où la fumée montait droite et mince comme un mât. La paillote des roofs se glaçait d'une ombre lumineuse et les rayons du soleil, sur le point de disparaître, les lamaient par endroits d'amarante, cependant que le sommet des arbres émergeait encore dans la fournaise : sérénité des soirs toujours nouveaux dans laquelle on ne sait plus que l'on est citoyen, père, époux ; où s'abolissent les devoirs de l'homme, son souvenir le plus frais et ses plus obsédants projets. Tout le déserte et ne lui laisse plus que le regard pour contempler cet irrésistible épanchement, cette transmutation du plomb en or.

Ils passèrent la porte charpentée de la pagode. Celle-ci scintillait par-delà un groupe de banians. Quelques jeunes hommes jouaient au volant, le pagne ramené entre les jambes et le torse nu. Ils se passaient une balle de rotin et lorsque l'un d'eux s'apprêtait à renvoyer le hochet qu'un autre prenait à sa place, ses muscles tressaillaient et s'apaisaient dans l'effort devenu inutile aussitôt que préparé. Puis le regard suivait, à gauche, une ligne de cellules sur pilotis, où des bonzes méditaient. Et entre quelques stoupas en forme de cloches et verdis de mousses, le temple levait les courbes de sa toiture et s'en couronnait.

Cette toiture, comme toutes celles des pagodes du pays, avait la grâce et le rythme d'un poème dédié au ciel. Leurs deux rampants abrupts, très larges, s'incurvent afin que le soleil y glisse avec mollesse. Les tuiles vernissées brillent des deux couleurs filles de la lumière : le jaune et le vert, et le faîte de ce toit d'or, bordé d'émeraude, soulevé par le double essor des deux pans obliques, s'insinue dans l'air où il luit comme un sabre. Il monte et aussitôt un deuxième toit paraît, plus petit, supporté à la façon d'une selle par l'étalon. Voilà la première strophe du poème. La deuxième strophe est la flèche. La double toiture tend l'arc de son profil et la décoche. Elle est à étages pyramidaux emboîtés les uns dans les autres, ainsi que des gobelets ciselés. Minceur de stipe, élégance dorée.

Ces aériennes charpentes symbolisent le génie artistique de ce peuple. Ses motifs décoratifs, sa musique ont cette même netteté souple. Il somnole et son art, seule manifestation de son existence, est ardent. Ainsi le serpent indolent au soleil devient lanière de fouet lorsqu'il se meut. La courbe, qui éveille une idée alanguie entre deux points d'appui, change de sens dans ce pays. Une seule de ses extrémités touche à la matière et tout le reste file vers le zénith dans une activité, une nervosité, une détente surprenantes, une fuite. Courbes vivantes et dressées : le timon de la charrette, le croissant de la jonque, les épaulières de la danseuse, la poignée de l'outil, les manches des guitares, toutes les courbes que trace le Cambodgien et que lui ont dictées l'élancement du reptile et celui du palmier. Or, c'est à toutes ces courbes exagérées et comme exprimées à l'octave que se suspend la toiture de la pagode. Chacune est alors à l'œil ce qu'un cri de cigale est à l'oreille. Elle entraîne le regard de bas en haut, quel que soit le point où il se pose. Ainsi que la femme heureuse ouvre ses bras à l'amant, la pagode ouvre ses toits au ciel.

Madame Gassin dit :

— On devine que les hommes qui conçoivent cette architecture aiment le ciel. Je les ai déjà observés au crépuscule, accroupis et regardant béatement le couchant.

— Vous dites bien. À peine marche-t-il, l'enfant y lance son cerf-volant et lui offre sa nudité. Chaque quartier de lune est fêté. C'est, en somme, entre l'homme et les astres, un dialogue ininterrompu. Regardez un Cambodgien accomplir sa journée : la moindre action dont le sens vous échappe aura son mobile dans la présence du soleil. La pagode, la maison seront orientées vers l'est et, afin que l'astre ne se souille jamais à la plante des pieds de l'homme qu'il endort et réveille, le lit, dans la maison, est tourné du nord au sud. Il faut attendre un jour propice pour partir en voyage, se marier, enterrer les siens. Nous n'avons pas cet amour des astres, nous autres, ce commerce permanent avec les lumières célestes.

— Nos maîtres sont plus bas, ajouta madame Gassin.

Elle se retourna vers la pagode dont ils s'éloignaient. Les dorures de son fronton s'éteignaient. Mais pour offrir quand même quelque chose d'elle et de plus léger que ses courbes, des clochettes éoliennes, suspendues à son chéneau, en jetaient des tintements. Lorsque les visiteurs furent de nouveau en marche vers Sangkè, les ultimes clartés du jour dispersaient une cendre de perle autour d'eux.

— Quel étrange contraste ! dit Hélène. Je vois s'encadrer dans le pare-brise et entre ces deux phares toute une vie d'un autre âge, ces cases paisibles y défilent semblables entre elles et à elles-mêmes, m'avez-vous dit, depuis des siècles. Tout à l'heure, notre lumière électrique éclairera littéralement la vie d'il y a je ne sais combien d'années. Voici une heure, j'étais dans ma chambre où aboutit le téléphone et dans laquelle notre civilisation se résume et il nous suffit de quelques tours de roues pour pénétrer en un monde où tout diffère du nôtre, où tout m'est étranger, où je ne reconnais rien, où je suis perdue et pourtant empoignée par une poésie irrésistible et une quiétude immense. Oui, quelle étrange chose.

— La profonde voix de la terre, sans doute, entendue de tous.

— Peut-être et qui parle avec sa simplicité primitive. Et il me semble en effet la comprendre.

— Malgré ces frondaisons où pas un arbre ne vous est connu, malgré des êtres nouveaux pour vous, les formes surprenantes des choses.

— Malgré tout cela.

Qui dira la beauté des fins de journées ici, sur les berges de la rivière de Sangkè, le long de toutes les rivières du pays. Un peu de fraîcheur monte de l'eau, si reposante, par contraste au flamboiement du jour, qu'elle ajoute à la paix de l'heure une douceur inconnue aux crépuscules d'Occident. C'est alors qu'il faut sortir des maisons noires. L'apaisement commence dès l'indécis moment où le soleil se prépare à rougir et tient encore la terre par le sommet des arbres et le penchant des monts.

Au cours de la journée, il a suscité à travers le pays une action puissante. La lumière et les ombres s'étalaient avec violence et l'on devinait un ardent travail jusque dans la feuille immobile. Puis, l'orchestre s'est tu après l'enthousiasme de la finale et le silence devient poignant dans la salle de spectacle. La terre s'ouate sous les pieds ; tout s'estompe comme dans un lointain progressif. Et les sensations s'imposent si moelleuses qu'on les perçoit comme le fruit mûr doit se sentir enveloppé par le fleuri qu'il élabore.

Les enfants s'assagissent. Les hommes ont encore les cheveux humides des ablutions. De lui-même, le bétail regagne ses abris près des cases et l'on entend, au loin, l'appel des paons juchés. De minute en minute, des tranches de ciel glissent et s'effondrent coupées par des flèches de lumière. Un vent léger, intermittent comme le souffle expiré d'une poitrine, prend les feuilles des bananiers si larges qu'elles se déchirent, les lève et les repose et on le suit sur les futaies, on le voit qui s'élève, écarte les palmes des cocotiers. Il pénètre enfin dans la masse noire des manguiers et se perd.

Les phares s'allumèrent car la nuit s'était rapidement étendue. Les yeux des bœufs luisaient comme des flammes jumelles de phosphore, ou ceux d'oiseaux posés sur la route qui, éblouis, ne s'enlevaient qu'à la dernière seconde. Un peu de fumée se mêlait à l'air, venue des cases où les indigènes brûlaient des herbes aromatiques afin d'éloigner les moustiques. De ci, de là, une lampe révélait dans l'intérieur d'un logis des familles réunies, ou bien quelque chose de fluide et de rythmé glissait, enlaçait la voiture, s'en déroulait, puis s'effaçait : un chant de flûte.

⚜ ⚜ ⚜

Si Ternier avait regardé madame Gassin, il eût vu qu'elle avait renversé sa tête et que, les yeux fermés et la figure tendue vers le ciel, elle paraissait morte.

VI

— Bonjour. Vous êtes seul ?

Madame Gassin se montrait à la porte du bureau de Ternier,

— Entrez ! Entrez donc !

— Je passais. Voilà donc le Résident dans son bureau.

— Voilà le Résident dans son bureau.

— Vous m'intimidez et je vous dérange.

— Je vous intimide, vous me dérangez, bien ! Mais asseyez-vous.

— J'entre et je sors.

— Alors, au revoir !

La pièce mesurait plus de huit mètres de côté et les vérandas l'agrandissaient encore. Au fond, une double porte battait sur le secrétariat. Le ventilateur tournait au plafond, balançant un bouquet de lampes. Hautes armoires le long des murs. Au centre, la table de Ternier, en bois massif, de ce style Henri II rectifié par des ébénistes chinois et dont l'Indochine ne sera pas débarrassée à l'heure du Jugement dernier. Les fils du téléphone et d'une lampe de table à réflecteur de porcelaine verte tombaient du plafond en torsades multicolores. Les dossiers administratifs s'étalaient avec cette arrogance des parvenus chez eux, lorsqu'ils reçoivent les petites gens. Deux grandes défenses d'éléphant montées sur une tête de monstre sculptée dressaient leur croissant entre deux portes. Quelques chaises perdues flottaient à la dérive sur un carrelage polychrome et luisant. Et un opulent fauteuil de cuir destiné au visiteur, bâillait en abîme en face de Ternier.

— Vous viendrez m'y repêcher, s'écria Hélène en y tombant.

Un planton entrait et sortait, glissant sur ses pieds nus, portant des papiers que Ternier signait en les parcourant du regard.

— Vous êtes gentille de venir me surprendre dans les paperasses.

— Je ne vous avais pas encore vu dans votre ministère.

— Ministère ? Ministère ? Mais on travaille ici !

— Je n'en doute pas et retire ministère.

Ternier s'arrêta sur un dossier de télégrammes jaunes.

— Vous permettez ?

— Je ne suis pas là.

— Tri ! appela-t-il.

Un secrétaire apparut, ses cheveux gris en chignon sous un turban de pongé et le torse gainé d'une tunique noire que maintenaient, sous un bras, de petits boutons d'or. Son large pantalon de soie laissait voir les becs de canard de ses souliers jaunes. Il avait relevé ses lunettes sur son front et s'approcha avec componction en se tenant les mains.

— Tous les renseignements de circulation sont là ?

— Oui, m'sieur R'sdent.

— Écrivez.

L'annamite fit tomber ses lunettes à leur place et partit en sautillant sur la pointe des pieds chercher un bloc.

— Télégramme à Résuper. Avis de circulation. État route coloniale 1 bis a souffert dans ensemble pluies hier et fort orage cette nuit. Délégué Siem Reap m'informe : 1° De Kompong Kdei à Damdèk, remblais récemment faits pour fermer coupures sont presque tous emportés mais déviations restent solides… Vous y êtes ?

— Oui, m'sieur R'sdent.

— 2° De Damdèk à Siem Reap, route praticable sans difficulté sauf secteur 200 mètres au point kilométrique 278 où remblais récents sont profondément… non, mettez : assez profondément.

— assez profondément…

— détrempés. Toutes coupures ont été condamnées et flèches indiquant dérivations sont placées 150 m. en avant. C'est tout. Relisez.

L'interprète chantonna quelque chose qui tenait de la litanie et de la vocalise, tantôt de la gorge et tantôt des narines. Lorsqu'il eut fini, il regarda le Résident par-dessus ses lunettes.

— Bien, faites partir.

Après une légère inclinaison, il alla.

— Comme elles sont bien soignées vos routes, dit Hélène qui avait écouté attentivement.

— Oui, ce sont de bien capricieuses personnes.

— Et tous les jours c'est ainsi ?

— Oui, les pluies commencent et tout le travail fait en saison sèche va être éprouvé, les remblais se tasseront, les eaux s'accumuleront inégalement de chaque côté et chercheront un passage.

— Elles ne le trouveront pas ?

— Si, mais pas toujours aux dalots, ponts et ponceaux qu'on leur réserve. Alors elles coupent la route ou la submergent.

— Et vous êtes prévenu ?

— De jour en jour. D'un bout à l'autre des rubans qui sillonnent ma circonscription, les autorités indigènes surveillent. Au premier incident, leurs émissaires convergent vers le télégraphe le plus proche. Et, en quelques heures, une déviation réunit les deux tronçons coupés. Sur cent kilomètres, au cours des gros orages, on compte cinquante, soixante coupures, dont huit ou dix graves.

— Que d'efforts !

— Non, de soins. On soigne les plaies inévitables qu'un corps vraiment vivant et travailleur reçoit, lui, dans l'effort. Ces routes mouvantes se font aimer. Depuis des années que je le suis, aussi bien dans les parties qu'ont établies mes prédécesseurs que dans celles que j'ai faites moi-même, je connais mon réseau routier, kilomètre par kilomètre. J'en ai appris toutes les souffrances, car si les ingénieurs qui me sont adjoints changent, moi je reste et je suis la mémoire de mes routes. Je sais où l'une fut atteinte l'année précédente et où elle résista. Elles semblent fixes, monotones, nues, lorsque vous y passez. Mais moi, je les vois lutter, changer de formes, osciller parfois dans les insensibles changements qu'il faut apporter à leur tracé primitif. Je les ai vues gagner leurs ponts. Là, on les soulagea dans une situation désespérée. Cinquante voitures et camions passaient par jour, maintenant elles m'en amènent deux cents. Plus je fais rapidement panser leurs déchirures et vais moi-même tâter leur rude échine, plus je les questionne en saison sèche — plus elles m'apportent de voitures. Ah ! ce ne sont pas des ingrates ! Fatiguées, défoncées, crevées de flaques, hachées d'ornières, elles travaillent, les vaillantes ! Les véhicules passent lentement, mais ils passent. Tout est là, voyez-vous, car lorsque deux cents autos et mille charrettes et trois mille piétons et quinze cents bœufs et cent cinquante cavaliers ont foulé, dans une journée, chaque kilomètre de mes routes, je sais que ma province va bien, que son pouls bat normalement et que chaque case a ce qu'il lui faut.

— Oui, tout est là : passer, dit rêveusement Hélène.

— Tout est là. Vous êtes venue de Phnom Penh en cinq heures.

— Sur une route magnifique.

— Il y a dix ans, vous eussiez mis cinq jours, à cheval ou en charrette à travers la savane. Cela vaut la peine qu'un Résident surveille sa route. Il veille à tous ses intérêts.

— Lorsque je venais, je ne me doutais pas que vous aviez ainsi préparé mon voyage.

— Depuis dix années je prépare, le Résident prépare et surveille cent voyages, tous les voyages. Là où vous passez, soixante hommes travaillaient la veille. Ce soir, mon télégramme préviendra toutes les voitures, les cars pleins de voyageurs, les camions bondés de marchandises, qu'ils auront à se méfier à tel endroit. Si l'inondation survient, ou une coupure irrémédiable, je dois, dans les heures qui suivent, en informer les entreprises qui, se fiant à moi, lancent à tout moment une partie de leur capital sur la route. C'est sur cette route que convergent, en fin de compte, toutes les vies humaines et toutes les fortunes, à la santé de la route qu'est soumise celle du pays.

— Et tout cela exige un grand travail.

— Dans ce pays, les trois quarts du travail d'un Résident.

— Les trois quarts de sa responsabilité.

— Cela dépend des Résidents, dit Ternier en souriant, car il n'est pas seul. Il ordonne, contrôle, suggère sous l'autorité de son Résident supérieur. Les Travaux Publics exécutent sous celle de ses chefs de service.

— Je vois. On peut ainsi se passer la balle.

— Vous l'avez dit.

— Depuis le peu de temps que je suis en Indochine, il me semble comprendre que les Travaux Publics ont bon dos.

— Les Résidents aussi. Voulez-vous une confidence ?

— Si je ne suis pas indiscrète.

— Ici comme en France, services administratifs, services techniques sont ou mauvais ou excellents !

— Voilà une confidence peu compromettante.

— Il est vrai. Le tout est de savoir comment les hommes qui composent ces services entendent leur rôle social.

— Il n'y a pas de fonctions.

— Aussi avons-nous ceci : une collectivité minutieusement organisée pour se passer de l'individu et perpétuellement soumise au bon plaisir de celui-ci.

— Là-dessus, je me sauve. Dites donc, est-ce que vous me voyez toujours ?

— Comment, si je vous vois ?

— Dans votre fauteuil ? J'y suis de plus en plus enfoncée. Ouf ! Me voilà. Quand me montrez-vous votre grande route ?

— Je vais organiser cela. Eh quoi ! Une visite si courte ?

— Je m'en veux déjà de tout le temps que je vous ai fait perdre.

⚜ ⚜ ⚜

Comme elle sortait de la Résidence et traversait le parc, elle aperçut une femme indigène qui venait en sens inverse. Toute l'allée ocellée d'ombre et de soleil allongeait derrière elle une queue de paon. Chaque pied nu, en avançant, repoussait sur l'autre les plis du pagne. La bordure rouge et verte de la soie se déroulait et s'enroulait au ras du sol dans une ondulation de reptile. La longue veste nationale, unie, flottait un peu autour des hanches, puis, plus étroite au-dessus, serrant le torse et les bras, elle ouvrait un long triangle d'où le cou délicat de la femme sortait. Cette gaine de soie indigo, le soleil lui donnait un lustre de cuivre verdi et violacé. Les seins la repoussaient deux fois, d'abord de leurs dômes qui vibraient à la marche, puis sur leurs pointes avec je ne sais quoi de brutal, de juvénile et d'insolent. Et la terre s'emparant de leur ombre y mêlait des reflets changeants d'ocre et de violette.

Madame Gassin distingua les très petits plis de la veste aux aisselles et le teint mordoré d'un cou fardé au safran, lorsque la femme la croisa, ainsi que les lourds bijoux de ses mains. Elle avait mis, en masse, son écharpe blanche sur la tête. Comme elle en tenait un pan, sa figure recevait, par transparence, une glaçure mauve. Sous le bord du voile, deux yeux très beaux et somnolents coulèrent sur Hélène un regard appuyé et celle-ci se retourna. La femme, poursuivant sa marche, contourna le porche et entra dans la Résidence par une porte latérale. Un planton qui sortait la salua d'un brusque mouvement d'échine, en tirant son casque. Et comme il salua aussi Hélène en passant à sa hauteur, elle lui demanda :

— Qui est cette jolie Cambodgienne ?

— Madame Résident, répondit le planton.

⚜ ⚜ ⚜

C'était en effet Vétônéa, la femme indigène de Ternier, la *prâpôn*, c'est-à-dire « l'épouse », fille subtile et orgueilleuse. Elle tenait d'une mère cambodgienne l'ocre clair de son teint, sa belle stature et, d'un père siamois, la finesse de ses attaches. Ce père, mandarin sous le gouvernement siamois, retourna dans son pays après la rétrocession des provinces, laissant là son épouse khmère grosse de Vétônéa. Les deux femmes vécurent assez misérablement, la mère tantôt revendeuse, tantôt repiqueuse de paddy ou commissionnaire ; la fille placée pour payer les dettes de la mère jusqu'au jour où Ternier, remarquant celle-là, « la plaça sur son trône ainsi que sur son lit ».

Lorsque, parée d'un *sampot* cassant pareil à de la toile cirée et d'une écharpe teinte au safran, Vétônéa, une fleur sur l'oreille et parfumée au « Cœur de Jeannette » fit son entrée dans les appartements de la Résidence accompagnée de sa mère, d'un petit garçon et de deux vieilles formant escorte, Ternier l'avait prise à part et lui avait dit, en épithalame, dans un cambodgien fleuri qu'il parlait à merveille :

— Vétônéa, belle fille à l'écharpe couleur « graisse de crabe », je te prends à partir d'aujourd'hui pour épouse. Je te donnerai quarante-cinq piastres par mois. Voici, ici, deux chambres et là, une autre, pour se laver. Tu vois, là-bas à l'ouest, l'escalier. Il conduit à une porte par laquelle tu entreras et sortiras à ton gré. Voilà ton domaine. Tu pourras y dormir, fumer, coudre, tresser des fleurs, prendre ta douche dix fois par jour et recommencer. Bien entendu, tu ne cracheras pas par terre et tu ne chiqueras pas le bétel. Tu pourras chiquer le bétel dehors, à condition que je ne m'en aperçoive pas et que tes dents restent blanches. Tu comprends ? Bien ! Ça n'est pas difficile à comprendre. Maintenant, il est absolument défendu d'aller ailleurs qu'où je t'ai dit. Même lorsque la maison sera vide, interdiction de passer par les grands escaliers, de traverser les autres pièces, de te montrer dans les salons, de paraître aux fenêtres de la façade. Si tu désobéis, la première fois je te rappellerai ces prescriptions, la seconde je te punirai, et la troisième nous divorcerons. Tu comprends aussi cela ? Ça n'est pas plus compliqué que le reste. Ta mère est une honorable femme et je l'aime beaucoup. Voici deux cents piastres que tu vas lui donner en la priant de quitter Sangkè et d'aller, par exemple, à Kralanh. J'enverrai des instructions au Gouverneur afin qu'il lui donne un petit terrain et lui construise, à mes frais, une paillote.

Vétônéa joignit les mains, les éleva à hauteur de son front. Ternier continua :

— Ne me remercie pas. Celui qui honore ses parents s'honore lui-même. Ta mère va donc aller à Kralanh. Elle y sera bien et surtout vivra à quatre-vingts kilomètres d'ici, car notre mariage comporte une nouvelle et dernière condition : je ne veux pas voir ici de visiteurs. Je te l'ai dit : tu sortiras comme tu voudras. Mais je ne veux pas que défile à la Résidence toute la province, de vieilles bonnes femmes chaque jour renouvelées et qui seront toujours tes tantes et des gamins de toutes tailles, invariablement tes petits frères. Cela, c'est pour ton bien, d'ailleurs, et t'évitera beaucoup de soucis. Voilà. Ton intérêt est de te tenir tranquille et tu seras heureuse. Regarde, c'est beau, ici, grand. Fumer une cigarette sur ce lit vaut mieux que d'aller pêcher des anguilles dans la vase, au soleil. Si tu es gentille, je t'achèterai des *sampot*s, une ombrelle en dentelle, des parfums et un sac à main, tout ce que tu voudras. Vétônéa, fille chérie, je te trouve belle. Je t'aime déjà beaucoup. Veux-tu, maintenant que je t'ai parlé et que tu connais tout, rester avec moi ?

Il s'était assis et la tenait debout entre ses jambes. La tête baissée, elle tordait l'extrémité de son écharpe, souscrivant bien à toutes ces conventions qui, pour elle, petite malheureuse, étaient splendides. Toutefois, un point restait dans l'ombre, qu'il fallait préciser. Vétônéa, après avoir avalé sa salive, demanda :

— Manger, comment faire pour manger ?

Ternier éclata de rire.

— Comme tu voudras.

Après un nouveau silence :

— Est-ce que le prix de la nourriture est compris dans les quarante-cinq piastres ?

— Allons ! Je payerai la nourriture en plus, combien ?

— Cinq piastres. Je connais une femme qui la préparera et me l'apportera ici.

⚜ ⚜ ⚜

En quelques mois, Vétônéa, belle fille à l'écharpe jaune, était devenue cet être déroutant qu'est la compagne indigène d'un Européen. Elle est là, toujours présente dans ses soies multicolores, émanation du pays dont elle concrétise tous les charmes. Vous parlez, elle répond ; vous méditez, elle demeure immobile et sans voix. À quoi se passe sa vie ? À regarder. Elle observe. Attentive, elle prend toutes vos habitudes et jusqu'à vos manies. Son œil paisible et velouté où veille la flamme noire d'une intelligence certaine vous suit et vous guette. Pourquoi ? Levez les yeux : elle sourit et le sourire est enfantin et confiant. Allongez-vous : elle prend l'éventail et s'approche. Vous sortez : elle vous tend votre casque et a mis dans votre poche le mouchoir et l'étui à cigarettes regarni. Vous arrivez : elle vous attendait. D'où venez-vous ? Elle ne demande rien, elle sait. Si elle ne sait pas, elle saura. Elle a jeté des fleurs dans votre eau de toilette pour la parfumer et tout est en ordre dans la chambre.

Oui ! Qu'on est bien chaque soir, ainsi, dans les bras déliés du pays où l'on vit en exil. C'est une odeur indéfinissable de chair ferme et de peau poivrée, des mains fluettes et des pieds minuscules, un corps glabre soigneusement épilé aux aisselles, frais, sans sueur. Son calme, dans l'étreinte, vous subit avec pudeur et bienveillance. La *prâpôn* est votre chose au sens absolu du mot, souple et si passive qu'elle vous donne votre image comme une empreinte. Tout ce que vous lui dites, elle le saisit. Ignorante et illettrée, ne sachant pas lire sa propre langue, elle connaît vos papiers parce qu'elle sait ceux que vous prenez dans telle ou telle circonstance, la façon dont vous les traitez. Sortez-vous une cigarette de la boîte, cette femme vous présente l'allumette. Elle attend que l'eau de la douche cesse de couler et la voici vous offrant la serviette, car elle écoutait le bruit de l'eau, accroupie derrière la porte. Laisse-moi ! Et elle s'étend sur la natte telle une fleur tombée. Et l'homme égoïste et satisfait s'épanouit. Qu'il prenne garde à lui.

Tout cela est bel et bien, en effet, s'il résiste à cette emprise permanente, d'autant plus sûre et irrésistible qu'elle ne peut trahir son existence, puisqu'elle ne paraît être que passivité et soumission. Elle satisfait les bas instincts de cet homme s'il est vulgaire, et berce son imagination et ses sentiments artistes s'il est supérieur et sensible. Tout cela est bel et bien si la main de cet homme reste ferme et son cerveau lucide, si, à aucun moment, il n'est dupe, s'il fait aussi le guet, s'il n'est pas un timide, s'il maintient l'équilibre de sa vie et se dit à tout moment : demain, cette femme peut partir, je sais qu'une toute semblable la remplacera ; si, sorti de la maison où elle l'attend, il ne songe pas qu'il y a laissé une maîtresse et si, enfin, il lui est indifférent qu'elle profite de son absence pour rejoindre un milicien ou un interprète, l'amant qui recueille sa solde et l'harmonieuse étreinte de la race.

Cet homme, ainsi, comprend le piège. Il discerne que, dans cette conjonction, lui seul peut perdre : ce n'est pas en quelques mois qu'un peuple monte en joindre un autre, bien que leur bras s'entremêlent, et si celui d'en haut ne s'enfonce pas retrouver celui d'en bas. Au fait ! Comme il est tentant de s'enfoncer. Cet homme n'a pas à se mettre en frais : il commande. Toutes les fringales de son égoïsme que parmi ses semblables il doit contenir, il les assouvit sans rencontrer de résistance. Il triomphe sans effort, sans qu'il lui faille être bien tourné, intelligent, ni entreprenant, et les mains roturières s'emparent de l'idole. Quel qu'il soit, il est aimé sans combat, il a un chez lui une femme intelligente qui obéit. Peu à peu, il s'exalte, croyant qu'il élève cette épouse, qu'il s'augmente de tout ce qu'il conquiert.

Pourquoi, en effet, serait-elle inférieure parce que d'une autre race ? Elle a un cœur et une âme. Sont-ils bien les mêmes et en use-t-elle de la même façon que nous ? Cet attachement, cette obéissance, cette discrétion, cette attention étroite dont elle vous entoure et qui, chez elle, sont des qualités femelles qu'elle ne s'impose pas, mais qu'elle dispense ataviquement, prennent lentement à vos yeux couleur d'amour et, de jour en jour, vous perdez pied. Des comparaisons que vous proposez vous justifient bientôt. Ce n'est pas une Française qui serait ainsi ! Certes non. Et la Française vous paraît lourde, épaisse, vulgaire, bruyante, parce que vous avez toujours sous vos yeux ce corps fluet, souple et passif. La toilette occidentale devient compliquée, ridicule, car vous vous accommodez mieux, maintenant, d'un pagne de soie toujours frais et d'une écharpe. La Française souffre du climat, transpire, ses toisons vous répugnent, tandis que cette indigène demeure fraîche, sèche et douce comme l'ivoire. Il est vrai.

Puis, vous faites un pas de plus vers ce qui vous apparaît une libération, l'individualisation salutaire de votre nature masculine. Dès lors, vous vous irritez que la Française, rencontrée chez l'ami où vous allez encore, discute — cette pécore ! Elle ne vous ramasse pas la canne échappée de la main — cette poseuse ! Chez vous, la royauté — ici, toujours la lutte pour la vie. Quelle fatigue ! Là, au moins, vous êtes le paon, vous vous asseyez « à l'aisance royale » sur votre lit — ici, vous risquez de n'être que le geai. Viens ! Ô petite idole à l'âme naïve et aux vertus primitives ! Mets tes mains sur mes yeux et éloignons-nous de la vulgarité et des conventions. Les mains fines et sèches s'abattent sur vos yeux. À tout prendre, ce ne serait pas trop mal.

Or, ce n'est pas du tout cela. À partir de ce moment, tout change. La souple esclave a des a regards durs que vous ne pouvez plus saisir. Elle s'irrite parfois. Vous cédez :

oseriez-vous compromettre tant de félicité en l'instant précis que vous en prenez conscience ? Elle boude, un jour, la *prâpôn*, chère petite enfant et, d'ailleurs, vous l'avez dit, pourquoi n'aurait-elle pas le droit, aussi, d'être femme ? Elle l'a et le prend. Ce que vous redoutiez de votre semblable et qui vous poussa vers l'indigène réapparaît sous d'autres formes et vous trouve enchaîné, Samson aux cheveux coupés.

Vous faites toujours l'esprit fort, car vous ne croyez pas encore à ces chaînes. Attendez un peu : si elles ne suffisent pas, on en trouvera d'autres. Des mains adroites serviront vos vices ou bien la *prâpôn*, un jour, sera enceinte. Par le sexe, par l'habitude, par votre veulerie, par toutes vos faillites, votre orgueil ou votre timidité, par votre devoir enfin, puisque voilà un ventre fécondé par vous — vous serez définitivement fixé. Déchu ? Allons-donc ! Tout cela, vous l'aviez voulu, n'est-ce pas ? Parbleu ! Après des mois de foyer, d'étreintes, de conquêtes et de poésie, près d'un métis né de vous, auriez-vous le front de vous reconnaître sans foyer ? Du reste, la timide indigène, de plus en plus riche des forces que vous lui avez transmises, vous domine cette fois et l'intelligence que vous lui reconnaissiez, réelle en effet, vous tient en échec. Oui ! Vous pouvez affecter des mines dégagées. Regardez l'heure et ne vous attardez pas au cercle ou chez des amis, car si la chose déplaît à votre passive servante, elle refusera ce soir de dénouer son *sampot*.

Elle sait maintenant le montant de votre solde et vous lui avez abandonné les clés de vos armoires, le contrôle des boys. N'est-ce pas elle qui les choisit ? De la sorte, à tout moment, dans tous les coins de l'Indochine, on voit des hommes de tous âges et de toutes situations, des douaniers et des Résidents supérieurs, des chefs d'industries et des savants, des soldats et des banquiers rivés au même déduit, vidés, émasculés par une *prâpôn* cambodgienne ou une *congaï* annamite flétrie par la maternité, dénuée des charmes passagers de sa race, prête à tout et bonne à tout et qui sourit de sa bouche noire en chiquant son bétel, femelle subtile et patiente qui, telle la mante religieuse, achève de dévorer son mâle avec des courbettes respectueuses d'échine et les mains jointes — une pauvre petite indigène de rien du tout.

Ternier, qui n'en était pas à sa première, savait que Vétônéa serait comme les autres. Ainsi avait-il pris les devants. Il dut, bien entendu, bientôt déjouer de premières tentatives. D'abord les repas qu'on apportait de la ville devinrent des prétextes. Un jour, l'enfant préposé à cet office fut remplacé par une femme qui demeura là, tandis que Vétônéa mangeait et qui, le lendemain, assista à sa digestion. Ternier imposa d'autres mesures. Après, Vétônéa démontra qu'il lui faudrait une servante. Bon, dit Ternier, je la choisirai et ce sera ma femme seconde. Vétônéa n'insista pas. Ensuite, il trouva la belle métisse en promenade dans le grand salon de la Résidence, lieu interdit, et Vétônéa fut informée que, le surlendemain, 30 du mois précisément, elle ne toucherait que quarante piastres au lieu de quarante-cinq. Elle se prit à réfléchir et comme, malgré tout, la place était honorifique, rémunératrice par ailleurs — elle n'insista plus.

⚜ ⚜ ⚜

— C'est madame Résident, avait dit le planton.

Hélène fit tourner son ombrelle et poursuivit sa marche. Elle passa la grande porte de la grille, où l'on voyait deux gros canons du XVIII⁰ siècle levés sur des affûts de marine.

Un indigène s'y appuyait et bayait aux corneilles. Lorsque l'Européenne fut à une centaine de mètres, il la suivit.

VII

Le Phnom Banon est un des nombreux monticules qui parsèment le Cambodge. Hauts de cinquante à cent cinquante mètres, ils dominent un pays uniformément plat, de sorte que, malgré la faible élévation à laquelle il se trouve, le voyageur sur le faîte jouit d'un vaste panorama. Ses regards suivent les terres jusqu'en des confins bleuâtres où elles ne cessent jamais avec netteté, mais passent, déjà immatérielles, dans un air épaissi de vapeurs.

Quelques-uns de ces sommets, comme celui-ci, conservent les ruines d'un temple. Sur ses dalles auxquelles on accède, ici, par un escalier monumental d'une centaine de marches, les moines des anciens monastères précédèrent de dix siècles ceux de la pagode actuelle et, comme eux, venaient aux heures propices méditer sur les métamorphoses des dieux, dans la liberté de l'espace découvert.

Le temple de Banon fut bâti sur une plateforme. À l'est, l'entrée principale de l'enceinte, tant est exigu l'emplacement choisi, ouvre sur la dernière marche de l'escalier qui plonge aussitôt, presque à pic, puis s'adoucit, s'incurve, obéissant à la configuration de la croupe, et parvient à la plaine par une molle obliquité. Au-delà, on suit des yeux la tache verte d'un lac. Tout se déroule à la rencontre du soleil levant. Le reste n'est que plaine et forêt.

La mousson de suroît, que madame Gassin, Ternier et le docteur Maillard ne sentaient pas tandis qu'ils montaient, plaqua leurs vêtements sur leur corps dès qu'ils parurent sur le dallage couleur de rouille. Ils la virent, pour ainsi dire, monter à l'escalade sur les mille feuilles des arbres dont l'immobilité lointaine et estompée du panorama augmentait l'ensoleillement et le mouvement, par contraste. Grâce à ce contraste encore, les choses de cette solitude aérienne prenaient des couleurs et des valeurs plus vives. Des laques remplissaient les angles des pierres et c'était de l'ombre. Sa main, que le docteur tendit, se découpa en vermeil sous le soleil. Et les arbres dont les têtes atteignaient la plateforme, tant ils brillaient et verdoyaient, on croyait les voir à travers le cristal jaune d'une lunette solaire.

Au-dessous des visiteurs, l'échiquier des rizières desséchées revêtait une couleur de cendre. L'inondation n'était pas encore parvenue dans cette partie du pays et les premières pluies avaient été bues par une terre avide. Les petites digues restées de l'année précédente la découpaient en carrés de la grandeur d'une main. À travers ce réseau mat et régulier, des lignes plus claires, tortueuses, s'insinuaient et se croisaient. C'étaient les pistes, les mille chemins suivis par les indigènes et qu'ont tracés et polis leurs pieds nus ; la terre caressée par la chair de l'homme ; le labyrinthe que lui confie l'être qu'elle porte de la maison au travail, du travail à l'amour, de la naissance à la mort.

Et la pensée est obsédée par cette terre qui montre dès qu'on la domine d'un monticule quelconque, en premier lieu, l'homme qu'elle recèle. Aucune meurtrissure, pas de route tracée par le fer en cette région, nulle moisson, pas de clocher ni de fumée. Le sol désert avec ses bouquets d'arbres s'écrase, en bas, à la façon d'une toison laineuse de chevreau. Tout s'avère inexploré, inexploité, menaçant. Et cependant, tendue et luisante, voilà la toile complexe de fils ténus qu'a tissée, d'heure en heure, la paisible vie d'hommes qui passent scrupuleusement où passèrent ceux qui les précédèrent et juxtaposent leurs pieds nus aux traces des pieds nus qui les ont devancés.

— Tenez, madame, dit le docteur, vous constatez d'ici, une fois de plus, ce qui vous a déjà tant frappée, cette harmonie de la vie humaine en intime liaison avec celle du sol et sans que la pensée, spéculant au nom du progrès, n'interpose ses appareils et sa volonté. Les reptiles laissent ainsi sur le sable des traces lustrées : or, voilà tout ce que vous découvrez de la vie des hommes.

— Vous allez vous faire faire les gros yeux par monsieur Ternier.

— Il en convient dans l'intimité et lorsqu'il n'est pas sur ses routes à lui.

— D'autant plus volontiers, interrompit Ternier, que le docteur vous raconte des histoires à dormir debout et ne vous fait regarder qu'en bas où il n'y a rien à voir. Voici, ici, un temple bien visible, couronné de cinq tours : l'art et l'intelligence de ces mêmes hommes soi-disant liés à la nature. Quant à mes routes, sachez bien qu'il y a dix siècles, lorsqu'ils construisirent ce temple et plus de six cents autres semblables, ces mêmes hommes tracèrent aussi de nombreuses routes, sur digues. On en retrouve partout les vestiges dont la longueur, si on la calculait, serait la même que celle des routes que, nous Français, traçons à notre tour. Alors, Maillard, que voulez-vous dire ? Vous voulez dire que si tout cela a disparu, c'est bien ? Je suis de votre avis. Que voilà, en effet, des hommes et un pays qui s'en passent ? Je vous l'accorde. Allez-vous demeurer sur votre montagne et regarder ? Je ne vous conteste pas cette contemplation. Mais moi, mon cher, j'aime mieux rebâtir ce qui est détruit ; refaire des routes meilleures que celles qui n'ont pas résisté, des temples, si je le pouvais. Nous sommes dix à penser de la sorte, tandis que vous êtes seul à philosopher comme vous le faites.

— Vous êtes les plus forts.

— Mon dieu, oui ! On pourrait discuter là-dessus. Mais c'est un fait. Il vaut mieux s'en tenir à lui. Nous sommes les plus forts. Il faut que ça serve à quelque chose, hein !

— Votre cynisme est écœurant.

— Non, Maillard. Quand vous avez ficelé votre malade pour lui amputer un membre gangrené, il hurle de douleur. Vous êtes le plus fort à ce moment. Qu'il hurle ; vous sciez. Pourquoi ne tombez-vous pas plutôt en contemplation devant cette jambe en pourriture, œuvre de la nature collaboratrice de l'homme ?

— L'intervention du docteur est justifiée par la maladie et le résultat heureux qui en résultera, dit Hélène d'un air candide.

Ternier la regarda longuement, puis :

— Madame, le docteur m'a accusé, il y a un instant, de cynisme. Permettez-moi de n'être pas de votre avis. Non, lorsqu'il coupe une jambe, le docteur ne sait pas si son opération réussira,

— Je l'espère, je tente les seules chances...

— Lorsque je trace une route, je ne sais pas si elle réussira, je tente la seule chance qu'il me reste de ramener une région à la vie et non pas à la vie précaire, que j'estime précaire tout comme vous estimez la vie de votre malade menacée, de ramener cette région, dis-je, à la vie active et prospère qu'exige l'époque, Voilà. Maintenant, si je me trompe, tant pis ; tant pis pour le malade si le docteur s'est trompé. Nous avons fait pour le mieux et nous avons été les plus forts. S'il y a une autre justice et un autre équilibre que les nôtres, qu'ils interviennent ! Et d'ailleurs, docteur, permet-tez-moi de vous rappeler que nous sommes aujourd'hui vos invités. Vous nous avez promis un excellent déjeuner sur ce mont, déjeuner auquel la glace elle-même ne manquerait pas. Si vous demeurez en contemplation devant ces rizières desséchées, dites-nous au moins où est la caisse aux provisions.

C'était jour de fête et des centaines de pèlerins visitaient le temple et saluaient les Bouddhas aériens. Déjà, les trois Européens en avaient aperçu des groupes, lors de leur ascension. Fatigués sous le poids des offrandes comestibles qu'ils hissaient, ils se reposaient, épars sur les roches. Des mères en profitaient pour donner le sein aux nourrissons, et des hommes, les jambes écartées sur deux pierres, tendaient au soleil leurs écharpes humides de sueur.

Aussi roulait-il dans l'enceinte du temple une foule renouvelée d'heure en heure. À l'est du sanctuaire, des fidèles offraient leurs chevelures aux divinités. De larges rasoirs à lame ronde ouvraient des chemins violets et bleus dans ces têtes noires et, sur le sol, un tapis de cheveux se mêlait aux feuilles mortes. Dans les sanctuaires, devant tous les socles anciens et modernes, les bougies propitiatoires flambaient.

La foule glissait au gré des galeries ou se répandait sur l'esplanade, en plein ciel. Parmi les groupes, les filles robustes des *tchamkars,* parées de gros bijoux, se tenaient par la main. Étaient venues, aussi, des vieilles femmes dont on eût dit qu'elles ne pouvaient plus marcher, tant leur peau était ridée et tant leurs vestes faisaient des angles aigus sur leurs os ; des troupes d'enfants, des mères, leurs petits à cheval sur la hanche et de ces vigoureux hommes qui drapent leurs muscles de laboureurs et leur cuir aduste d'écharpes vaines et chatoyantes.

Le chef de la bonzerie mitoyenne vint saluer le Résident et tint à le conduire à la sala du monastère. C'était un grand vieillard. Tandis qu'il parlait, le vent sculptait son ample toge et couchait sur ses bras, couleur de cannelle, ses poils blancs. Une rumeur profonde venait de cette sala d'où se détachait un air de xylophone. Bien que le hangar fût formé seulement d'un toit reposant sur des colonnes, l'obscurité y régnait, produite par une foule dense. Une chaleur animale vous touchait au visage. L'odeur de tous ces corps, épaissie par celle des fards au santal, et sans trouver d'issues, se mêlait aux vapeurs fades du riz chaud, des cires fondues, aux parfums des fleurs coupées et à l'aigreur des soupes. Les sons des instruments de musique, logés à l'autre bout de l'abri, perçaient à peine cette atmosphère. On y distinguait pourtant, spectacle sain, une longue file de bonzes qui mangeaient, la traînée d'or qu'elle faisait entre les corps mouvants des visiteurs et, parfois, la tache éclatante d'un plat de riz. Un enfant hurlait en serrant des fleurs sur son petit ventre. Des femmes en habit blanc, vieilles bigotes en mal de rédemption, portaient des vases d'eau aux saints hommes qui les prenaient avec des mains gluantes d'aliments, sans regarder, en mastiquant, à grands coups de mâchoires, des purées de citrouilles.

❧ ❧ ❧

Le docteur et ses invités remontèrent pour déjeuner à leur tour, dans la cour du temple, sous un arbre à feuilles luisantes. La caisse aux provisions fut ouverte près d'un caniveau en forme de monstre à trompe d'éléphant par où s'écoulait, il y a mille ans, l'eau d'ablution des idoles. Les trois Européens firent ainsi tort au banquet de la sala, car une partie de la foule les avait suivis. Ils disposèrent soudain de vingt serviteurs qui le furent pour voir de plus près leurs assiettes et les fourchettes. Le reste de l'assistance s'échelonna sur les degrés et dans les crevasses des galeries environnantes. Le regard parcourait des lignes d'enfants, des grappes de femmes, puis des bonzes vinrent mettre des taches de tournesol au tableau.

Cette population avait, par extraordinaire, ce même jour et pour la sainteté du pèlerinage, fait plusieurs lieues à pied ou en charrettes. Aussi, ces deux Français et cette femme blanche et blonde en robe grise leur offraient un spectacle à nul autre pareil, et d'autant plus remarquable que l'homme dont la moustache couvrait les lèvres était le Résident ; qu'il mangeait là, en plein air, sous leurs yeux, sans mystère et sans façon. Ils voyaient donc, ces pauvres campagnards, ce dont ils parlaient entre eux et que racontent d'un air avantageux ceux des leurs qui reviennent des villes, fonctionnaires ou miliciens libérés. Voici ces pains dorés et ronds qui remplacent le riz — et pas de riz sur la table. Ça, c'est curieux ! Il est donc vrai qu'ils boivent en mangeant, les Français !

Soudain, les chuchotements se suspendirent. Le cercle des enfants se resserra. Les hommes tendaient le cou. Le docteur sortait de la sciure de bois la glace à rafraîchir. *Tök kâk*, eau congelée, ô merveille ! Une eau solide qui brûle lorsqu'on la touche, un cristal de roche qui disparaît dans l'heure — est-ce croyable à des hommes sans savoir et fils aimés du soleil !

Ternier en donna un bloc, dans une coupe de cuivre. Tous le prenaient avec la même précaution. Les uns souriaient. Les autres examinaient de près, en tous sens. Un homme chenu et noir y posa le doigt, en regardant dans le vague, incrédule, impénétrable. L'un, plus subtil, s'aperçut que son doigt laissait une trace dans la buée qui couvrait le vase. Et le bloc étincelait entre toutes ces mains stupéfaites et devant la sévère grisaille des murs.

Il devint, aux yeux d'Hélène et dans ce cadre incroyable, une gemme miraculeuse empruntée au giron des dieux et que se passait une foule à qui ce simple attouchement conférait les vertus désirées. Ne vont-ils pas ainsi, tous ces simples, toucher les seins de certaines statues, polis par d'innombrables caresses, afin d'en retirer bonheur et fécondité ?

Or, une jeune voix s'éleva, timbrée par la plus intense stupéfaction, une voix charmante qui se suspendit dans le silence. Ternier traduisit ceci :

— C'est une jeune fille qui découvre que le morceau diminue de grosseur.

Une rumeur avait suivi. Puis quelques-uns burent une gorgée de cette glace fondue. Et l'on voyait sur toutes ces farces tannées par le soleil les grimaces qui les crispaient au passage de l'eau dans des gosiers pourtant corrodés par le bétel, les piments et les carrys.

Ternier, qui demeura un instant pensif, dit au docteur :

— Docteur, je repense à ce que nous avons dit, il y a un instant. Du sommet des monts, les pensées s'élancent plus à l'aise. Et si quelque poète aimant les symboles était avec nous, il nous dirait peut-être, après vous : tant de choses brillantes ou surprenantes fondent ainsi dans des décors immuables, entre nos mains humaines, sans que nul ne puisse dire s'il n'est pas très bien qu'elles fondent, si leur véritable utilité n'est pas différente de celle qu'on leur assigne et si les mains où elles disparaissent sont, de ce fait, frustrées ou enrichies.

Et le docteur, qui tenait au bout de sa fourchette la tranche ambrée et juteuse d'un ananas, la leva, tel Vishnou dans un des sanctuaires voisins brandissait son disque :

— Si le Résident rêve, madame, pardonnez-moi, nous sommes foutus, répondit-il.

VIII

Ternier, qui ne fait jamais la sieste, lit. L'éblouissante méridienne n'entre que par les persiennes closes des vérandas et, dans le luisant du carrelage, le lit double la blancheur de sa moustiquaire relevée. En l'ombre paisible où le ventilateur étale un disque qui miroite ne parvient du dehors, et de temps à autre, que le son du grelot en bois qu'agite un bœuf, au loin.

Vétônéa, assise sur sa natte, torse nu, une écharpe autour des seins, roule des cigarettes à l'aide d'une petite machine faite d'un carton et d'une baguette. Au lieu de les coller, elle les ceinture d'un délicat ruban de papier qu'elle noue. Puis, au ciseau, elle festonne les deux minuscules pans du nœud. Elle travaille posément, les jambes repliées devant elle, flexible sur ses hanches. Sans lever la tête, d'un regard qui monte, elle observe Ternier. Enfin, rebaissant les paupières, une cigarette tournant au bout des doigts, impassible et d'un ton détaché, comme se parlant à elle-même :

— Madame française encore venir, ce matin.

Ternier reste plongé dans sa lecture. Le regard de l'indigène remonte le long de lui, observe, puis redescend. Vétônéa achève cette cigarette et en commence une autre. Ses fines épaules, dans la lumière diffuse et sous la tache noire de ses cheveux courts, verdissent et des touches bistrées soulignent son menton, le pli de ses bras. Elle reprend :

— Nhê... Elle est très jolie...

Puis elle paraît réfléchir en découpant son nœud et, posant la cigarette :

— Elle a de grands pieds, ajoute-t-elle.

— Ah ! fit Ternier qui n'écoute pas mais perçoit que Vétônéa lui parle.

Elle prend une pincée de tabac, l'étire entre ses doigts allongés, lève les yeux, les baisse :

— Elle vient souvent ici, madame française.

Ternier, sans bouger, regarde Vétônéa. Il a compris. Elle noue le lien de papier, le découpe au ciseau, se penchant, souffle les petits triangles blancs tombés sur ses cuisses. Elle s'étire, les bras en croix rejetés en arrière, réajuste son écharpe en offrant à l'air, l'espace d'une seconde, ses deux seins impeccables dont les pointes parurent deux violettes, reprend du tabac, l'étale sur son papier et d'un ton évasif :

— Cette femme est très mauvaise. Je sais.

— Tais-toi, ordonne, laconique, Ternier.

Il boit une gorgée de café où un bloc de glace achève de fondre et reprend sa lecture. Vétônéa se lève, s'approche, puis, décidée, repousse le livre et s'insinue sous le bras de Ternier, onduleuse et charmante.

— Je sais des choses, dit-elle.

Et le Résident apprend avec vingt détails précis que madame Gassin est allée, une des nuits précédentes, coucher chez le capitaine Thévenet.

— Es-tu folle, Néa !

— Je ne suis pas folle, je sais.

— Qui t'a dit ça ?

— Tout le monde connaît, les boys de l'hôtel, le cuisinier de monsieur docteur, et le Chinois Li qui a vu madame monter dans le pousse-pousse.

— Je te défends de dire des choses pareilles, Néa. Ce sont des mensonges.

— Je dis à mon mari.

— Tais-toi. Je te défends d'en reparler. À personne, tu entends bien.

Vétônéa se détache de lui, la figure fermée et retourne à sa natte.

— Si je sais que tu reparles de ces saletés, tu partiras d'ici.

— Pourquoi parler ?... Tout le monde connaît, tout le monde parle.

— Tais-toi, toi.

Elle se tait, souffle délicatement pour séparer deux feuilles de papier à cigarette. Ternier lit, du moins il a repris son livre.

⚜ ⚜ ⚜

L'avant-veille, au crépuscule, après une promenade, Hélène, le docteur et lui s'étaient installés sous la pergola. Une buée semblable à un fleuri de pêche gainait les verres glacés. Les lucioles palpitaient dans les arbres. Un bruit de pas interrompit leur quiétude et une voix demanda :

— Ne suis-je pas indiscret ?

C'était un visiteur, le capitaine Thévenet, affecté tout récemment au commandement de la brigade des tirailleurs.

— Pas du tout, répondit Ternier en se levant.

Et l'officier parut dans la lumière, homme jeune et mince, noir de poil, formé à la guerre. Or, Ternier se rappelait qu'en le présentant, quelque chose d'insolite s'était passé à quoi il n'avait fait aucune attention. Le capitaine Thévenet, qu'il nommait à madame Gassin, s'avançait vers elle. Celle-ci eut un air si hautain et un battement

de paupières si impérieux en tendant la main que le visiteur hésita une seconde —
puis s'inclina sans mot dire. À peine Ternier crût-il saisir ces nuances que madame
Gassin retrouvait son sourire. Tout s'effaça et la conversation courut.

Le visiteur venait préciser l'heure du départ, le lendemain, afin d'aller examiner avec
le Résident la butte de tir en mauvais état. Ils convinrent de s'y rendre à l'aube et,
une demi-heure après, l'officier prit congé. Comme le docteur et Hélène dînaient à
la Résidence, la soirée intime se prolongea jusque vers onze heures. Puis, Maillard
reconduisit madame Gassin à l'hôtel. Ce fut donc, après, qu'elle en ressortit.

Que vaut cette calomnie ? Rien encore, si ce n'est d'avoir été formulée. Ternier la
nie et la repousse, mais elle se mêle aux lignes qu'il lit et la gorgée de café froid
qu'il prend lui laisse un arrière-goût de fer. Il ne veut rien avoir entendu. Il reprend
pourtant le petit fait de l'avant-veille, qu'il n'avait pas noté et auquel il confère une
réalité troublante en y repensant. Il conteste ce contrôle, mais ce contrôle agit. Vétônéa ne pèsera pas lourd si elle a menti !

N'est-ce pas une intrigue nouée par elle afin de se préserver d'une Européenne
apparue brusquement dans l'intimité du Résident ? Cette indigène n'est-elle pas
d'autant plus attentive à surveiller sa fortune qu'elle se sent impuissante à modifier
la moindre décision de Ternier ? Qu'est Hélène ? Elle ne sait pas, ne connaît rien
d'elle — sinon qu'elle est femme et seule. Vétônéa raisonne comme elle peut. Et si
le Résident qui est tout puissant veut madame Gassin pour femme ? Vétônéa n'aura
qu'à s'en aller. Elle prend donc la seule arme dont elle dispose : l'insinuation. Or,
comme elle n'est pas maladroite, pourquoi commettrait-elle cette imprudence, for-
gerait-elle pareille histoire ? Elle doit bien se douter que Ternier vérifiera. Un Résident sait tout dans son centre, lorsqu'il le veut. Non, Vétônéa n'a rien inventé. Elle
n'a rien inventé et il faut au contraire qu'elle soit bien sûre d'elle, pour avoir parlé.

Je m'informerai donc, se dit Ternier. Qu'on invente ou me prouve que madame
Gassin est la maîtresse du capitaine Thévenet, je m'en fiche. Seulement, il importe
que je sois fixé et sache si la fraternelle confiance et les soins dont je l'entoure
s'égarent ou si je dois, au contraire, leur donner plus de signification encore afin de
défendre une malheureuse injustement salie. Désormais, mon doute serait intolérable. Son intelligente curiosité, son enthousiasme, ces désirs qu'elle témoigne de
pénétrer l'œuvre entreprise ici, la spontanéité de ses actes, son aspiration à s'enrichir
l'esprit ne seraient que des masques sous lesquels elle poursuivrait une aventure et
retrouverait un amant ? Il se peut et c'est son droit. J'imagine que c'est aussi le mien
de me pourvoir en conséquence.

Deux jours après, le Résident était définitivement fixé. Ainsi que de coutume, à la
fin de chaque matinée, le planton annonça Hélène. Ternier la trouva balancée dans
un rocking-chair. Comme un homme, elle avait posé son chapeau au porte-manteau en entrant et ses cheveux la casquaient de cuivre. Un trait de rouge avivait
ses lèvres et un collier d'améthystes d'Auvergne rendait ses yeux plus pâles et plus

bleus.

— Madame, dit Ternier, le front dur, notre conversation n'aura pas ce matin son cours habituel.

— Vous avez en effet un air bien grave. Dois-je être inquiète ?

— Nous allons en discuter. Nous sommes à la fois de vieux et de nouveaux amis. Notre rencontre fut fortuite. Vous m'avez reçu à Paris avec un charme et une bienveillance que je ne peux oublier.

— Vous faites bien mieux, à mon égard, depuis mon arrivée ici.

— Je fais donc ce que je dois et ce que je peux, tout ce que je peux. Et je le fais sans arrière-pensée, dans la joie et la satisfaction sans mélange que j'éprouve de vous avoir ici. Pouvez-vous me donner l'assurance qu'il en est de même de votre côté ?

Il la regardait avec insistance. Hélène remua les lèvres. On eût dit que des mots y mouraient et sa main, en tremblant, monta égrainer ses améthystes. Elle effaça sa confusion en l'avouant.

— Vos paroles me troublent. Qu'entendez-vous ?

— En d'autres termes, je vous demande si les raisons de votre présence à Sangkè sont bien celles, je veux dire : sont bien toutes celles que vous m'avez dites ? Et j'ajouterai : à supposer qu'il y en eût d'autres, votre confiance en moi serait-elle assez complète pour vous permettre de me les communiquer ?

Hélène baissa la tête, songea une minute et répondit :

— J'ai assez de confiance en vous pour ne pas vous mentir, mon ami. Non, je ne vous ai pas dit toutes les raisons pour lesquelles je suis ici. Mais si j'ai assez de confiance en vous pour ne pas vous mentir, je n'en ai pas assez, peut-être pas encore assez, ajouta-t-elle avec peine, pour vous confier ces raisons.

— Je vous remercie de parler net. Et me voici plein d'amertume à constater que votre quiétude, à mes côtés, connaît des limites.

— Elle n'en connaissait pas, il y a cinq minutes. Vous les avez tracées vous-mêmes en me questionnant puisque ce que je vous ai laissé voir jusqu'ici ne vous suffit plus.

— Ne faites pas intervenir votre orgueil. Croyez-vous que le père qui voit sa fille mélancolique ou la croit menacée diminue son devoir et la confiance qu'il lui voue en s'inquiétant de la paix de sa fille ?

— C'est un père. Je ne suis pas votre fille. La connaissance que vous avez de moi et tout ce que j'ai pu ou voulu vous laisser voir de mes pensées justifient l'attitude exquise que vous avez toujours prise à mon égard. Du moins, je l'imagine, car je me refuse à supposer que vous soyez de ceux qui se dépensent en toutes occasions et par simple ostentation. Vous êtes l'ami le plus cher que je possède et que cet ami soit vous ne me laisse pas sans orgueil. À votre contact et bien que nous soyons, comme vous venez de le dire, de nouveaux amis, je sais déjà... Comment dirai-je ? Concevoir la valeur d'une action. M'avez-vous mal inspirée ? Me suis-je mal mise en route ? Pour vous le dire, il me faudrait vous devoir des aveux. Je ne vous dois pas d'aveux...

Hélène se replia, fit un effort intense de réflexion :

— Non, je ne le crois pas.

Après une nouvelle pause, elle reprit :

— L'admiration que je peux avoir pour votre nature, l'affection que vous m'inspirez laissent intacte mon indépendance.

— Parlons posément. Dieu me garde d'y toucher. Vous avez aussi votre franchise ?

— Tout entière, je viens de vous en donner la preuve.

— Oui, vous êtes franche. Et c'est pour cela que je vous trouve ambiguë depuis votre arrivée — comme une source troublée. Ne m'interrompez pas. Ce n'est pas une discussion que je veux entre nous, mais vous dire, moi, toute ma pensée, comme à un homme, quoique vous ne puissiez pas me dire toute la vôtre. Et parbleu ! Oui, vous appartenez à votre mari. C'est être indépendant que d'aller à l'aventure. Mais il arrive qu'on se perde. Et lorsqu'on se perd, on n'est plus indépendant. On peut aller à l'aventure lorsqu'on est au bras de son mari, que le rythme de la vie commune, chaque soir, vous ramène autour de la nappe. Il fait bon alors, j'imagine, être indépendant. Or ici, depuis une huitaine, vous êtes seule, à six cents kilomètres de Saigon. Monsieur Gassin doit arriver bientôt, d'accord, mais il n'est pas encore là. Et les heures passent auxquelles on ne prend pas assez garde. Vous êtes donc seule. Je sais ce que vaut l'ambiance où vous êtes seule. Accordez-moi que je ne vous connais pas assez pour savoir ce que vous valez. Ne froncez pas les sourcils. Aimeriez-vous mieux de fades compliments plutôt que l'expression claire d'un homme qui s'attache à vous comme à un ami ? Si je dis que je ne vous connais pas assez pour vous évaluer, j'entends ne rien redouter inutilement de vous, tout en ne manquant pas, dans une quiétude imprudente, aux devoirs qui me sont implicitement échus par le seul fait de votre arrivée dans mon petit royaume, devoirs que je me suis formellement dictés. Sans doute, un homme est ridicule qui veille sur une femme et votre mari qui vous a laissé partir est responsable. Il vous connaît, certes, mieux que moi. Toutefois, vous vous mouvez en ce moment entre nous deux et lorsque nous vous regardons, ce n'est pas du tout la même femme que nous voyons. Lui vous aperçoit à travers sa confiance, votre passé commun, tout ce que vous vous êtes dit de tendre et de solennel, la vertu d'un contrat à laquelle il croit. Il vous aperçoit telle qu'il vous a faite ou telle que vous vous êtes développée durant dix années de vie mêlée. Moi, madame, je vous vois sans que ces conditions interviennent, non comme une femme déterminée, mais comme la femme, comme l'homme, comme l'être humain. Ce que l'on en connaît sèchement, je veux dire : objectivement, ne suffit pas à prévoir ce que deviendra demain cet être éminemment versatile et d'une fragilité telle que son assurance en soi n'est pas seulement une armature insuffisante, mais trop souvent aussi une cause d'aveuglement et d'inexpérience. Votre mari vous croit, vous vous croyez armée : je vous vois désarmée. Il vous a vêtue de son amour. Vous avez puisé dans le vôtre la quiétude avec laquelle vous vous êtes mise en route : prenez garde que cette belle robe et cette arme brillante... À quoi pensez-vous, vous ne semblez pas m'écouter ?

— Si, si, allez, je vous écoute ! Je ne vous écoute que trop ! Vous m'avez dit de ne pas vous interrompre.

— Bref ! Vous n'êtes pas en sécurité ici.

— Je vous sais gré de me le dire.

— Ne persiflez pas. Ce n'est pas un conseil que je désire vous donner. Vous êtes assez intelligente pour vous le donner vous-même s'il en est temps, et trop femme pour qu'il ne devienne inutile du seul fait que je le formule. Ne redoutez pas non plus un sermon.

Il se leva, s'accrocha les mains derrière le dos et vint se planter devant madame Gassin. Renversée dans son fauteuil, elle le voyait d'en bas.

— Ecoutez bien. Il y a ici le capitaine Thévenet. Il est arrivé prendre son poste à Sangkè depuis très peu de temps. Je vous l'ai présenté. Lorsque je dis que je vous l'ai présenté, c'est une façon de parler, car j'ai eu nettement l'impression que vous vous connaissiez. Un geste de lui, un battement de paupière de vous, puis une froideur affectée : voilà ce que j'ai vu. Je ne vous questionne pas, car tout ce que vous estimez devoir me celer ne me regarde pas. Cela dit, autre chose : vous concevez que, dans un poste comme celui-ci, l'arrivée d'une jolie femme, voyageuse solitaire, précédant son mari retenu ailleurs pour affaires, quoique événement tout logique, ne reste pas sans commentaires. Nous sommes enveloppés par la vie indigène qui, sur ses mille pieds nus, dans son désœuvrement et sa curiosité volontiers malicieuse, observe tout ce qui est européen. À l'hôtel, des boys circulent à toute heure du jour et de la nuit, ont l'oreille aiguë et bonne vue. Chaque maison, depuis celle du brigadier de gendarmerie jusqu'à la mienne, n'a que murailles de verre. Ce que nous disons à table se propage, ce que nous faisons se sait à mesure. Vous devinez où je veux en venir ?

— Je vais le savoir.

— C'est donc ainsi que jeudi soir, chacun sait, depuis le tenancier chinois de la fumerie jusqu'au cuisinier du receveur des postes, que, revenant de chez moi, vous êtes entrée à l'hôtel vers onze heures. Vous en êtes aussitôt sortie du côté de la rivière. Vous avez marché quelque cent mètres sur la rive, puis vous avez pris un pousse-pousse, et vous êtes allée chez le capitaine Thévenet. Il est célibataire... Et sans *congaï*. On sait encore qu'il n'y avait pas de lumière chez lui, mais qu'il devait vous attendre car, après que vous eûtes pénétré, il vint lui-même fermer la porte et vérifier s'il y avait quelqu'un dans la rue.

Hélène ferma les yeux et y appuya ses doigts, la bouche entrouverte dans une expression de souffrance indicible. Ternier avait fait demi-tour et marchait de long en large. Elle l'arrêta en lui disant d'une voix calme, mais les mains serrées :

— Et vous a-t-on dit quand j'en étais sortie ?

— Ma chère amie, le ou les observateurs bénévoles qui vous épiaient, vous ayant vu entrer là où vous entriez, en pleine nuit et de la façon dont vous y entriez, en avaient, j'imagine, suffisamment appris. Aussi, l'histoire ne dit point à quel moment vous avez regagné l'hôtel. Elle dit tout crûment que vous êtes la maîtresse du capitaine, que vous êtes venue le rejoindre sous l'œil bienveillant du Résident — car on sait aussi une intimité que nous n'avons pas à cacher. Excusez ce que mes paroles ont de rude : la précision paraît souvent de la brutalité. Je vous ai donné les commentaires européens de la ville d'abord pour que vous en fussiez prévenue, ensuite pour vous assurer qu'il n'est point dans ma nature de croire à des commentaires. Pour moi, je ne m'en tiens qu'aux faits et tout s'arrête où ils cessent. Je n'imagine et ne veux supposer rien au-delà. Encore un coup, c'est un ami qui vous parle. J'ajouterai, afin de ne rien laisser d'obscur, que je suis prêt à vous aider, si besoin est.

— Merci, mon ami. N'êtes-vous pas surpris que je ne proteste pas contre tout ce que vous venez de dire ?

— Je n'en suis pas surpris. Si vous vous étiez insurgée, vous m'eussiez déçu. La comédie ne prévaut pas sur la flagrance des faits. Et j'ai eu soin de vous prévenir que je ne vous demandais aucune explication.

— Il en est qu'on ne peut donner.

— Je suis bien de votre avis et ne me le fîtes-vous pas sentir il y a un moment ?

— Il en est aussi qu'on peut donner.

— Disposez-en pour le mieux.

— Je vous les dois. Je ne suis pas la maîtresse du capitaine, non, je ne suis la maîtresse de personne. J'allai chez lui comme vous le savez. C'était la première fois. Dix minutes après, j'en ressortis. Je n'y suis plus retournée.

— Je vous remercie de préciser ce point et ce que vous me dites me suffit. L'habitude de la vie montre souvent ce qu'ont de fallacieuses certaines apparences. Il est évident qu'une femme seule qui se rend chez un homme seul, la nuit, peut aller y coucher — il est aussi possible qu'il n'en soit rien.

— Tout dépend de la femme.

— Si vous voulez. J'aime pourtant mieux : tout dépend des circonstances.

Hélène eut un sourire douloureux, puis, après un long silence durant lequel Ternier continuait sa promenade :

— Et si j'étais la maîtresse du capitaine Thévenet ?

— Du moins vous n'avez pas peur des mots. Si vous l'étiez, j'aimerais moins cela. Vous êtes mariée.

— Est-ce vous qui parlez ?

— Je réponds comme je peux, seulement ne vous méprenez pas sur le sens de ma réponse. Je ne fais pas appel aux lois générales, ni même aux conventions les plus larges car je ne vois pas, en votre ménage, un vulgaire couple et ne vous tiens pas pour une femme ordinaire. Que votre mari soit trompé, cela n'a aucune importance à mes yeux et me laisse indifférent : il n'avait qu'à veiller au grain, à se rendre indispensable, à être le premier dans vos pensées et selon vos goûts. Je vous reconnais le droit de prendre un amant. Mais voyez-vous, je ne peux accepter de vous la déchéance d'appartenir à deux hommes à la fois. Je vous imagine assez fière pour faire un choix, laisser l'époux s'il a cessé de plaire et prendre l'amant, s'il a su vous asservir. Vous êtes à l'abri du besoin, sans enfant, et assez séduisante pour susciter une passion profonde, une passion semblable à celle dont vous êtes capable. C'est pourquoi il me déplairait que vous fussiez la maîtresse de n'importe quel être, même d'élite, tout en demeurant la femme de Roland Gassin, parce que ça ne serait pas élégant, ni clair. Tout le reste, l'appareil légal et religieux dont on écrase l'adultère au profit de l'égoïsme m'est égal. Vous me déplairiez parce que, obligée de mentir, de calculer, vous seriez réduite à la duplicité et à toutes les sales rouateries habituelles en l'occurrence. Vivre clairement, hardiment, rien n'est plus beau, surtout pour une femme puisque ça lui est plus difficile qu'à l'homme. Voici mon amant ! Bravo à celle qui le proclame au grand jour avec une hardiesse qui n'apparaît insolente qu'à cause de nos conventions étroites. Toutefois, il ne faut pas qu'elle le proclame entre le mari et l'amant. J'arrête, car je n'ai pas à faire ici le procès de l'adultère. C'est de vous qu'il s'agit, vous à qui j'aime à penser sur un plan supérieur, sans malaise, sans désapprobation et sans complicité, fière et nette comme une médaille bien frappée et de pur métal.

Hélène frissonna. Ternier, qui poursuivait sa marche de long en large, ne la voyait pas. Elle le suivit des yeux, les ailes du nez serrées, et une indécision affreuse tendait ses traits.

— Et puis, ce serait trop facile ! Vous vous seriez libérée en mentant, en prétextant l'ennui de Saigon et le désir de venir en plein pays voir l'ami qui vous y invita. Et soit que la fugue eût été concertée, soit que vous eussiez, par hasard, saisi l'occasion, soit même que vous l'eussiez subie — l'amant serait à votre discrétion et le mari réservé. Quelle banale aventure dans un pays où les célibataires sont nombreux et à l'affût, les mœurs faciles et la volupté conseillée ! Il n'y a qu'à se baisser, et l'on se baisse. Oui, vraiment, il me déplairait de vous voir vous baisser de la sorte. Ma rigidité n'a rien d'étroitement timoré. Elle renâcle devant les actions communes. Les fruits qui sont en bas de l'arbre à portée de la main, la poussière de la route les souille. Mais voyez ceux du sommet, ils sont intacts. Toutefois, il faut grimper pour les quérir. Aussi, généralement, les trouve-t-on trop verts...

Hélène, songeuse, dit :

— Sont-ils meilleurs que ceux d'en bas, les fruits du haut ?

— Vous n'avez pas à les essuyer. Que valent les conquêtes faciles ? Que vaut ma *congaï* obéissante, près de la femme que j'eusse connue, méritée, gagnée, prise à elle-même et aux autres, si j'avais pu, si j'avais su peut-être, et si ma vie lointaine ne m'avait pas toujours tenu hors des sociétés riches en belles filles qui ne s'achètent pas avec la monnaie courante comme des courtisanes, mais se donnent à un seul homme : le plus fort ou le plus habile. Faire comme les autres, cueillir le fruit d'en bas, n'est-ce pas toujours possible ? Prendre la femme du voisin, la belle affaire ! On opère sans être vu. Je comprends qu'on aille chez ce voisin et lui dise : ta femme me plaît, garde-toi, je vais tout faire pour m'en emparer. Et la lui prendre, de vive force, par tous les moyens ; ah ! ah ! voilà un adultère qui change de signification. L'homme chasse. Cherchez autour de vous de ces adultères-là : vous les compterez aisément.

— Sans doute, mais si la femme prend les devants, si c'est elle qui décide la conquête et... dans les conditions que vous venez de fixer ?

— Elle est libre. Quant à moi, ce ne serait plus alors le fruit le plus bas de l'arbre, ce serait le fruit tombé. Je n'ai pas d'orgueil. Je m'estime d'un prix moyen et mon physique n'est pas d'un conquérant. Que vaudrait à mes yeux une désœuvrée qui se jette aux pieds de tout homme qui passe ? Celui-ci ne va pas, ses qualités et ses vertus déployées, telle une frégate, toutes voiles dehors et l'équipage sur le pont. Où trouverai-je en telle conjoncture l'assurance que moi, plutôt qu'un autre... Et si la femme s'aperçoit ensuite qu'elle s'est trompée, emballée ? Je crois, puisque vous me questionnez sur ce point précis, que l'amour véritable a une genèse obscure, animale et violente. S'il n'y a pas lutte, attaque de l'homme, défense de la femme surtout, si la loi du plus fort dans tous les sens du terme ne s'impose pas, si la recherche que doit fournir le mâle poussé par l'instinct ne s'exerce pas, s'il ne prend pas conscience qu'il vainc, s'il entre dans l'amour sans orgueil, sans l'impérieux besoin de toutes ses facultés — qu'il prenne garde que son amour soit sans saveur et, l'ayant trop facilement acquis, de n'éprouver aucune ardeur à conserver un bien dont il n'apprécie pas le prix. Mais, revenons à nos moutons. J'ai souci de vous seule. Dans une dizaine de jours, votre mari doit arriver. Comptez-vous toujours l'attendre ?

— Pourquoi me demandez-vous ça ?

— Après ce que je vous ai dit et ce qui s'est passé, je le crois nécessaire.

— Il ne s'est rien passé dont je doive compte à mon mari.

— N'estimez-vous pas que pour couper court aux bruits qui circulent...

Madame Gassin éclata de rire avec nervosité.

— Je m'en fiche des bruits qui circulent !

— Je n'en demande pas plus. Vous trouvez-vous en pleine quiétude ?

— Je ne m'y suis jamais trouvée si bien.

— Alors nous n'avons rien dit.

— Si, vous m'avez dit des choses précieuses... La femme est un pauvre animal toujours traqué, en somme. Qu'est-ce qui n'est pas une attaque, de tout ce qui se dirige vers elle ? Cependant, je me sens apte à me défendre... (Sa voix devint plus amère.) Mais bien malhabile à attaquer. J'avoue que cette sécurité à laquelle vous veillez si étroitement, et que vous osez garantir par tous les moyens, ne me laisse pas indifférente. Mon orgueil n'éprouve aucune irritation à s'en accommoder.

— Vous êtes, madame, une épouse seule, une femme exquise venue chez moi.

— Je suis, avez-vous dit, une médaille bien gravée...

— Et une médaille se porte en vue, sur la poitrine.

— C'est une belle place.

— Il y a le cœur dessous.

— Le cœur où naît la fierté..., ajouta Hélène en se levant.

— Vous l'avez dit, la fierté de battre sous une médaille.

— Vous la perdrez, cette médaille, lorsque je m'en irai.

— J'aurai le souvenir de l'avoir portée.

— Elle n'aura pas été trop gênante ? demanda Hélène en tendant la main.

— Il est peut-être des poids qui s'alourdissent dans le regret qu'on en garde.

— Il est temps que je m'en aille : vous faites le galantin.

— Je m'y prends lourdement. N'avez-vous besoin de rien à l'hôtel ?

— De rien. Je suis comme une reine. Je ne sais plus où mettre vos fleurs.

— À ce soir.

— À ce soir.

❖ ❖ ❖

Ils étaient sous le porche et elle fit quelques pas, après avoir pris congé, rassérénée semblait-il. Elle se retourna tout à coup, revint hâtivement et Ternier eut devant lui sa figure bouleversée. Elle chancelait et s'appuya contre lui.

— Mais qu'avez-vous ? Vous allez tomber ! Rentrez vous reposer...

— Non, non ! Laissez ! Ecoutez-moi. Je suis une malheureuse. Vous venez de me martyriser et j'ai fait ce que j'ai pu pour vous le cacher, le cacher à moi-même.

Croyez-moi, je suis énervée, folle ! Ayez pitié de moi, désemparée ! Voulez-vous que je vous le demande à genoux ? Là, voyez, je ne fais pas de chiqué ! Je voudrais mourir, que ce soit fini ! Il me semble que tout m'abandonne. Mais vous ! Ne m'abandonnez pas. Faut-il vous mendier votre estime ? Pour l'amour de Dieu, ne m'interrogez plus. Oubliez tout ce que vous m'avez dit. C'est incohérent ce que je vous demande là ! Mais vous êtes généreux. Une femme n'est pas toujours maîtresse d'elle-même. Je voudrais, oh oui !, je voudrais vous expliquer tout et c'est la seule chose qui m'est interdite. Me prendriez-vous de force, comme une brute, si vous me vouliez et si je me débattais ? Non. C'est impossible. Vous ne pouvez savoir de moi plus que je vous en ai dit. Laissez-moi quand même votre confiance ; que je sois l'Hélène Gassin dont vous avez fait le portrait. Il est exact. Dites-le moi et je sais que ça sera. Si vous pouviez voir, en moi, tout est en sang, déchiré. Vous voulez des confidences ? Vous les voulez, maintenant, dites ! Les voulez-vous ?

Elle reprenait ses forces. Ses regards fixés sur Ternier perdaient leur expression d'égarement. Elle tamponnait ses lèvres de son mouchoir sur lequel ses doigts se crispaient.

— Non, madame, non. Je vous donne aussi l'assurance que tout ce qui vient d'être dit par vous et par moi est effacé.

Hélène, d'un mouvement violent dont il ne fut pas maître, saisit la main de Ternier et la porta à ses lèvres, puis la rejeta, épouvantée de son geste.

— Merci. Et maintenant, laissez-moi partir, comme d'habitude.

— À ce soir ? répéta Ternier.

— À ce soir.

Du haut du portique où ruisselait le violet éclatant et triste d'une bougainvillée, il la regarda s'éloigner. Ses pas déliés frappaient la terre rouge de l'allée. Traversant l'ombre et le soleil que les arbres laissaient tomber par taches, sa silhouette s'illuminait et s'éteignait. Puis elle passa la grille. Ouvrant alors son ombrelle, elle ne fut plus qu'une petite chose mauve, fine et longue suspendue à un disque. Et bientôt, elle se désagrégea dans la lumière.

... Une femme n'est pas toujours maîtresse d'elle-même, avait-elle dit.

IX

Ternier avait fait décorer le portique, la véranda et le salon central de lotus blancs et roses. Les énormes fleurs aux pétales retournés à la main, ce qui augmentait encore leur volume, enveloppaient les bases des piliers et, étagées en touffes, obstruaient les arcades du fond. Il s'en dégageait un parfum à peine saisissable de citron. Sous les lustres flambant, elles prenaient des nacrures de coquillages et les quatre ventilateurs de plafond en faisaient frémir quelques-unes. Sur le dallage miroitant, des pétales détachés, chassés par des tourbillons d'air, flottaient comme sur un étang.

La salle à manger prolongeait le hall et la table démesurément longue, blanche et rose sous la même vague de fleurs, l'occupait presque tout entière. Par trois grandes fenêtres ouvertes, au fond, l'épanouissement d'un papayer et le tronc d'un caoutchouc géant recevaient un peu de lumière. La nuit était superbe, chaude, mais l'air brassé par dix hélices tournoyantes la rendait légère. On entendit des trompes d'automobiles.

Madame Gassin et le docteur arrivèrent de bonne heure. Elle était vêtue d'une robe en tissu vert amande frappé or, le dos nu, un simple rang de perles au cou. Elle parut à la fois éblouissante et discrète, de cette élégance hardie mais si harmonieusement comprise que l'attitude y collabore, voile la nudité et modère tout éclat. À un moment, le docteur, observant une vague inquiétude dans ses regards, s'informa de sa santé. Elle répondit en souriant, et soit qu'il eût mal vu ou qu'elle se surveillât dans la suite, elle déjoua son attention.

Le Gouverneur cambodgien entra avec sa fille, tous deux drapés pareillement dans le *sampot* national formant culotte ; lui, de ce brocart blanc et or qu'on ne trouve plus maintenant dans le pays ; elle, de soie changeante rose et argent, plissée menu. Il n'avait accroché à son smoking blanc que sa croix de la Légion d'honneur. Elle portait, à la mode siamoise, une sorte de chemisette courte et surchargée de dentelles. Une dizaine de sautoirs se chevauchant et faits de fils ou de mailles d'or finement entrelacés passaient de son épaule gauche à sa hanche droite où brillaient des coulants tubulaires sertis d'éclats de diamants. Ses doigts étaient lourds de bagues, un petit mouchoir brodé pendait à sa ceinture et elle marchait avec hésitation sur des chaussures à talon Louis XV, venues de France.

Sa figure était sans beauté, mais non sans finesse sous des cheveux coupés court comme ceux d'un homme, relevés devant en un rouleau d'un noir profond et luisant d'huile parfumée. Un peu de poudre rendait grise sa peau bistrée.

Tout intimidée, elle s'assit telle une fillette sage, les pieds pendants, sur une chaise européenne trop haute pour elle. Lorsqu'elle saluait, elle souriait avec beaucoup de charme, faisait un petit signe automatique de tête et tendait une main menue, sèche, qui ne serrait pas. Elle était énigmatique et puérile, gracieuse et engoncée, à peine ridicule dans le mélange asiatique et européen de ses atours. Hélène, séduite par cette grâce native et cette timidité, alla s'asseoir près d'elle et les deux femmes échangèrent des sourires, car la jeune fille n'entendait pas un mot de français.

D'ailleurs, le salon se peuplait, chaque ronflement d'auto y jetant un couple nouveau. Le docteur avait déclaré à madame Gassin qu'il tenait à remplir près d'elle les fonctions d'officier d'ordonnance afin de constituer sa maison militaire et de délégué du Résident de France à Sangkè, de manière qu'elle eut aussi une maison civile. Il lui nommait les arrivants en assumant la charge des présentations.

Une dizaine de dames se réunirent en petit comité et par affinité avec une indépendance apparente qui cachait mal un grand souci de hiérarchie. Malgré la longueur des communications entre la France et ce coin perdu au nord du Cambodge, les modes métropolitaines étaient suivies d'assez près et avec ingéniosité. Ce choix d'étoffes brillantes et de toilettes du soir, dans le cadre rose des lotus et l'abondante lumière, ne laissait pas de surprendre Hélène qui ne faisait pas abstraction des deux mois environ au cours desquels elle avait parcouru seize ou dix-huit mille kilomètres, presque la moitié du tour de la terre.

Les hommes, en pantalon noir et smoking blanc, restaient entre eux et, par groupes, consultaient le plan de la table disposé dans la véranda. Le Résident-adjoint, aidé d'un secrétaire, passait à chacun une carte où figurait le nom de la dame qui attendait leurs soins. Quelques invités manquaient encore qui, ne possédant pas d'automobile, attendaient celles de la Résidence et du docteur affectées au va-et-vient. Un brouhaha de bonne humeur flottait déjà et deux boys, les bras écartés par de larges plateaux, servaient les cocktails.

Beaucoup de regards examinaient Hélène avec curiosité, puisqu'elle était étrangère, et quelques-uns la quittaient pour chercher machinalement le capitaine Thévenet. On n'est pas maître de ces alternatives qui ne marquent pas d'intention désobligeante, mais plutôt une sorte de complicité. Le capitaine, qui avait d'ailleurs salué Hélène avec le plus grand naturel comme tous les autres hommes, fut happé par le Directeur de l'usine des eaux et d'électricité et l'Inspecteur de la milice, petit homme à tête si ronde et qu'il levait avec tant d'opiniâtreté qu'il donnait l'impression d'un bilboquet dont la boule, mal ajustée sur son tenon, menaçait de choir.

La femme du banquier et celle de l'agent des Messageries accaparèrent bientôt madame Gassin. La première, maigre et d'allure distante, lui communiquait le peu d'agrément qu'une femme éprouve à vivre dans un poste, loin d'Hanoï ou de Saigon. Là, au moins, on a des facilités, une saison théâtrale et on retrouve tous les chefs de service. Sans doute, lorsqu'on voyage, comme madame, et qu'on arrive de France, l'intérieur du pays est très intéressant. Mais quand on vit depuis huit ans à la colonie, on ne sait plus quoi inventer pour se distraire, et l'on « n'a plus de goût à rien ». La dame des Messageries fit des réserves, car elle s'occupait beaucoup chez elle et ne trouvait jamais le temps de tout faire. Et elle n'avait pas d'enfant, elle ! La dame de la Banque avait, en effet, un garçon et une fille, cinq et huit ans, madame. Elle ne pouvait pas les mettre à l'école avec les petits indigènes et c'était bien ennuyeux pour leur avenir. Ils étaient, en outre, toujours sur son dos. L'instituteur leur donnait des leçons particulières, mais ça ne leur profitait guère...

Ternier survint, accomplissant rondement ses devoirs de maître de maison, cherchant un mot pour chacun et ne le trouvant pas toujours. À ce moment, les cocktails lui donnaient de l'aisance.

— Avez-vous pris un cocktail, madame ? Était-il frais ? Un second ? Boy, viens par ici.

Il parvint ainsi à faire un tour complet du salon et ce fut autant de gagné. Hélène, parfois, à travers toutes ces figures étrangères, ces hommes dont les vestes blanches faisaient des plis cassants et empesaient les torses, le cherchait des yeux. Et lorsqu'elle découvrait ses cheveux grisonnants, sa forte moustache et sa grande taille coupée haut par le spencer, elle se sentait moins seule et reprenait la conversation avec plus d'intérêt. Au moment où une dame en crêpe gris perle rehaussé de grosses fleurs garance lui demandait ses impressions d'arrivée, le docteur toucha le bras d'Hélène. Un monsieur raccompagnait.

— Monsieur Tubinque, qui aura le plaisir de vous conduire à table.

Elle vit un homme de taille moyenne, à bouc pointu et méphistophélique, qui lui déclara d'une voix caverneuse qu'il était très honoré. Et l'on passa à table car, au même moment, le grand boy métis sino-cambodgien, homme de confiance de Ternier et qui faisait les fonctions de maître l'hôtel, se plaçant avec une gravité automatique au milieu du salon, avait dit :

— Monsieur le Résident est servi.

— Non, on dirait un annonciateur des pompes funèbres ! Il en a un air lugubre ! dit Tubinque en conduisant Hélène. Et vous savez, madame, c'est tout ce qu'il peut dire. Il ne sait pas un mot de français. Vous êtes ici, madame ? Non. Bon voilà que je me trompe, c'est plus loin ! Vous parlez !

Il secoua un peu Hélène à cause du flottement et parce qu'il se penchait sur chaque carte pour voir le nom. Enfin, il éloigna une chaise. En s'asseyant, il confia à Hélène, mettant sa main devant sa bouche comme s'il lui révélait un secret :

— Faut que je fasse attention. Une fois comme ça, à la Résidence de Kompong Chhnang où je venais d'arriver, je conduisais une dame à table, c'était la femme de l'Instituteur. Elle s'est remariée depuis avec un Corse et elle est au Tonkin, maintenant. Je ne fais pas attention, je tire la chaise trop loin et voilà la dame le derrière sur le carreau. Je ne savais plus où me fourrer. Dites ! Hein ! Quelle situation. Elle ne voulait plus vivre, la dame.

Les blocs de glace brillaient dans les verres. Sur du bristol le chiffre de la République surmontait l'inscription en encre dorée « Protectorat du Cambodge ». Au-dessous, Hélène lut :

Purée de volaille au carry

Vieille braisée au Chambertin

Filets de canetons en salmis

Gigue de chevreuil rôtie à l'ancienne

Salade d'aréquier

Asperges sauce Chantilly

Glace au corossol en meringues

Fruits et gâteaux

Les vins marqués étaient Gris de Lorraine 1888, Sauternes 1889, Pommard 1893. L'inévitable silence des débuts de repas suspendait les conversations. Elles renaquirent bientôt, ponctuées par le cliquetis de l'argenterie.

— C'est la première fois que vous venez à la colonie, madame ?

À cette question qu'on lui posait à toute minute depuis une demi-heure, Hélène répondit à Tubinque :

— La première, monsieur.

— Ah ! bien ! Moi, il y a vingt-trois ans que je suis en Indochine et je commence à en avoir ma balle. J'ai connu le Résident Ternier en 1904, il débutait. Et même qu'il avait une sacrée frousse sur les grands lacs. Dites ! Il y avait des poissons qui lui crachaient à la figure. Il ne voulait plus vivre. Il me tirait par le paletot et appelait sa mère. La preuve, il y avait le douanier de Kompong Luong qui faisait cuire des crevettes à l'avant du bateau et qui faillit flanquer le feu à tout le bastringue en lui portant secours. C'est pas de la blague, ces poissons. Ils vous suivent — hein ! — ils sortent la tête et ils vous envoient de l'eau à la figure.

Pour appuyer son dire, tantôt Tubinque se penchait vers Hélène avec la main en abat-son sur la bouche ou bien lui donnait des coups de coude.

— On voit de drôles de bêtes, ici. C'est comme une fois, les singes sur la route du Cap. J'étais avec le surveillant des Travaux publics. Dites ! Un pauvre bougre, il est mort empoisonné par du cresson. C'est pas de la blague. Il avait trop mangé de cresson et il s'est baigné tout de suite après. Il se baignait dans un tonneau et il y restait des heures. Sa femme criait comme un putois qu'il mettait de l'eau partout. On ne pouvait plus le sortir du tonneau, avec ça qu'il était gros ! Le boy tirait comme un âne, vous parlez d'une situation. C'était à Pursat. Moi, je partais le lendemain et j'avais mes valises à faire, j'en bavais. On a mis plus d'une heure, — dites ! hein ! — pour le sortir de son tonneau. C'est comme Duston, un journaliste, je l'avais invité à déjeuner. Il logeait chez moi. On l'attendait en bas en prenant le Pernod. Il y avait encore du Pernod en ce temps-là et, tout d'un coup, on voit de l'eau qui dégoulinait par le plafond et qui nous tombait sur la tête. La femme de l'adjoint demandait un parapluie. Elle ne voulait plus vivre parce qu'elle avait une robe en truc... Machin... Oui, quoi ! Qui prenait les taches. Je vais voir ce qui se passait, — dites ! hein ! — je trouve mon type accroupi dans la salle de bain qui s'était endormi sans lâcher la ficelle de la douche ! Vous parlez d'un déluge ! J'en ai eu pour trente piastres de réparation. C'est pas de la blague. Il s'était endormi. Il avait dû biberonner pas mal dans la matinée. Il dormait comme une lanterne et cet imbécile-là s'était assis sur le trou, alors l'eau ne pouvait pas partir.

— Mais les singes, sur la route du Cap ? demanda la dame que Tubinque avait à sa gauche.

— Ah ! oui ! Les singes, ils plumaient une fouine.

Chacun écarquilla les yeux.

— C'est pas de la blague. C'est méchant, ces bêtes-là. Ils avaient attrapé cette fouine sur la route et puis ils la dépiautaient comme un poulet. Les poils volaient partout. Ils la plumaient quoi ! La fouine ne voulait plus vivre, elle gueulait comme un putois. Et les singes tiraient dessus, et je te pèle, et je te décortique. C'était affreux de voir ça, dans les arbres. J'ai raconté cette histoire à machin, chose, là, l'ambassadeur vous savez bien, Froleau. Il était en visite officielle à Angkor. J'avais fait un appontement pour le recevoir et dites ! Les eaux baissaient. Il est arrivé huit jours plus tard qu'on l'avait annoncé, alors l'appontement était à trois cents mètres dans les terres. Il a failli se flanquer dans la vase quand il a débarqué. Ça a manqué provoquer un incident diplomatique. Heureusement que je n'étais pas là ! Le délégué du Gouvernement non plus. Il n'y avait que Noël pour le recevoir.

— Noël ?

— C'était le nègre, le malabar du bungalow, quoi ! Le préposé aux transports. Il était plus noir que nature. L'officier d'ordonnance faisait un foin du diable : « Il n'y a personne ici pour recevoir l'ambassadeur ! » qu'il disait à tout moment. Alors le nègre répondait d'une voix suave : « Je suis là ! Je suis là, mon lieutenant ! ». Mais l'autre ne le voyait pas, dites ! C'était en pleine nuit. Noël ne voulait plus vivre : il en a attrapé la jaunisse. C'est pas de la blague. Elle n'est pas mauvaise cette vieille.

Hélène crut qu'une autre histoire s'accrochait, mais se souvint du menu et comprit qu'il s'agissait du poisson. Le coin de la table faisait à Tubinque son succès habituel. Le voisin de droite de madame Gassin mangeait avec une application qui tenait de la ferveur et du calcul d'un logarithme. En abandonnant le bras de sa voisine, il avait esquissé un petit coup de tête, puis, avant de s'asseoir, refait le même, tourné vers Hélène. Depuis, il paraissait tellement préoccupé que les deux dames n'avaient pas été effleurées par l'idée de le déranger. Il n'osait pas rire des histoires de Tubinque, car il aurait eu l'air d'écouter. Mais, par moments, il mastiquait en se tordant la bouche et les veines de ses tempes saillaient.

Ternier surveillait sa table. La jeune Cambodgienne, toute menue, malhabile à couper ses filets de caneton, jetait autour d'elle un regard craintif, après chacune de ses bouchées. Elle était à côté de l'Inspecteur de la garde indigène qui savait un peu de cambodgien. Lorsqu'il lui parlait, elle l'écoutait attentivement de son joli sourire, et parfois les diamants de ses parures jetaient des lueurs. Tous les visages s'épanouissaient. Les hommes avaient bonnes mines. De jolies notes jaune clair ou noir rouge vibraient au fond des verres et les gobelets d'eau glacée, transpirant, étalaient des disques humides sur la nappe. Au-dessus de la ligne de têtes qu'Hélène voyait en face d'elle, au-delà du chemin de table en lotus et des coupes de fruits, les boys passaient, agiles, si fluets dans leurs vestes blanches empesées, les yeux mi-clos, souples à pencher une bouteille entre deux convives ou à déposer dans un verre un bloc de glace qui scintillait au bout des pinces.

Madame Gassin n'entendait plus que par intermittence Tubinque qui continuait à épancher sa bonne humeur et sa mémoire autour de lui. Un chaud bien-être envahissait la voyageuse. Le docteur lui fit, de loin, un signe d'intelligence et, parfois, un regard de Ternier croisait le sien et lui souriait. Les services se succédaient, bien réglés.

⚜ ⚜ ⚜

Aucune pensée de ces quarante convives ne semblait s'évader de cette salle à la rencontre d'une menace ou à la poursuite d'un regret. Au-delà du parc, la rivière s'éclairait aux feux de ses jonques. Des prières montaient des pagodes avoisinantes et à cinq kilomètres de cette table soignée, de cette France opulente, de cette poignée d'hommes au linge blanc et de femmes joyeuses, la brousse, ses savanes et ses forêts s'étendaient sous la nuit.

En ce lieu, où des fleurs abondaient ce soir, les lotus sacrés des étangs, un homme, dixième venu de ceux de sa race, souriant entre vingt autres hommes, ses collaborateurs, l'âme sans inquiétude, le cœur battant bien, buvait le vin et rompait le pain de son pays. Le télégraphe et le téléphone demeuraient silencieux. De cet homme, par-delà les étangs, jusqu'aux bourgades lointaines et au pied des montagnes frontières, des routes rayonnaient, blanches de lune, à travers sa province, comme le symbole de la main pacificatrice qu'il y avait posée. Dans cette étoile embrassant vingt-huit mille kilomètres carrés de terre, plus de trois cent mille vies humaines sommeillaient. Et chacun de ceux qui levaient leur verre de cristal en cette atmosphère de prospérité avaient accompli aussi leur tâche. Cette femme de banquier qui s'ennuyait ; cette autre, vulgaire, là, obscure femelle qui, entre chaque plat, nettoyait de sa langue ses dents creuses ; l'autre, plus loin, jeune et gentillette et les autres, toutes les autres, vivent en aveugles, entretiennent imprudemment le regret de leur patrie ou exagèrent sans discernement la profondeur de leur exil — mais quand même, elles sont là.

Toutes ces demi-familles auxquelles il manque un père, une femme ou un enfant ; tous ces expatriés, volontaires sans doute ; tous ces errants bien qu'ils errent pour gagner leur vie — n'en ont pas moins, hier et aujourd'hui, conscients ou non, spontanément ou poussés par un ordre, joué un rôle éminent. Ils n'ont pas, en effet, tourné une roue, tenu une place ordinaire, assuré selon leurs moyens la vie courante d'une collectivité. Ils ont à la fois enrichi deux civilisations. Ils travaillent à une route non seulement au bénéfice de leur pays ou de leur clan, mais aussi à celui d'un autre peuple. Leur égoïsme ne les favorise pas seuls. Et si l'on veut prétendre qu'à la base de toute colonisation, il y a un principe faux ou du moins discutable et, dans certains cas, inopportun — ils n'en sont pas responsables. Voyez plus haut — ici, il n'y a que des ouvriers et, si vous tentez d'évaluer l'ampleur de leur tâche, de bons ouvriers.

Dans le cimetière de Sangkè, des noms semblables aux leurs sont gravés. Ceux que ces noms rappellent doivent être satisfaits, s'ils voient les rues droites, l'école, le dispensaire et le marché salubre de cette ville dont, il y a seize ans à peine, ils nivelaient le terrain et respiraient la fièvre. Après ces précurseurs, ceux qui, ce soir, en héritent ne sont peut-être pas tous de bons esprits, des natures supérieures ni des âmes généreuses : ils obéissent néanmoins. Il y a aussi autre chose. Lorsqu'ils posent leurs regards sur le Résident, leur chef direct et commun, ces regards s'avivent d'une lueur imperceptible. Quelle que soit la complexité de leurs sentiments ou la loyauté de leur nature, leur attention converge manifestement vers lui. Dans sa rigueur professionnelle et par la fermeté d'un devoir qu'il impose et l'ampleur d'une conviction qui s'échappe de lui, il exprime plus qu'une idée d'autorité. L'importance de son grade n'apparaît pas. Il n'est pas seulement celui qui met des notes individuelles sur des dossiers. Il est surtout celui qui a bâti la maison que chacun retrouvera tout à l'heure dans la fraîcheur nocturne. Il est le commandant du bord qui veille à la sécurité de tous. Et chacun, se sentant à l'autre bout du monde, infiniment fragile, se tourne en fin de compte vers lui, pour le remercier d'être là.

⚜ ⚜ ⚜

Par devant M. Barrois qui s'effaçait discrètement, madame Rougemont expliquait à Hélène que la glace au corossol était faite avec la pulpe d'un gros fruit vert. Il semblait à Hélène qu'elle mâchait une pâte de fleurs odorantes. Après que les boys eurent passé les aquamaniles où une feuille de citronnelle découpée et repliée suggérait la forme d'un insecte, Ternier se leva et l'on s'en fut à travers le hall et dans les vérandas, tandis que Tubinque avouait à Hélène qu'il avait trop mangé, qu'il aura encore mal aux reins demain, mais que ça ne valait pas l'ancien commissaire de police qui, après un repas comme ça, — dites ! — avait encore faim et, rentrant chez lui, avalait une salade de pommes de terre et huit œufs durs, avec les coquilles, et buvait trois canettes de bière coup sur coup, — hein ! — sans en crever.

Les groupes ne tardèrent pas à se reformer. Les hommes coupaient les bagues de cigares de Manille à bout noué et l'odeur des Three Castles que fumaient les femmes glissa, diluée par les « vire-vire » comme les appelait le docteur.

— Vous ne vous ennuyez pas trop ? demanda Ternier à Hélène, en lui apportant son café.

— M'ennuyer ? Je suis ravie. Dîner parfait, tout réussi.

— On dansera tout à l'heure.

— Aussi ?

— Aussi. Toutes les joies. Vous jouez ? Un bridge ?

— Non, j'aime mieux circuler.

Deux tables de bridge étaient déjà garnies.

Dans un angle du salon, un jeu de *ma-tsiang* s'organisait entre trois dames et un officier et l'on entendait, à travers le brouhaha, le frottement sur le bois et l'entre-choquement des cent quarante-quatre dominos que les joueurs mêlaient. Hélène tenta de suivre quelques parties de ce jeu importé de Chine depuis deux ou trois ans et qui faisait déjà fureur en Indochine et dans les colonies anglaises.

Une des joueuses lui expliqua sa « muraille », « les saisons » finement gravées et coloriées dans l'os, l'as bambou qu'un oiseau, les ailes ouvertes, traversait, toutes ces images aux significations si variées. Les dominos s'étalaient de plus en plus nombreux, multicolores et précieux comme un puzzle fait de pièces décoratives et délicates. Dans un langage choisi, conformément aux règles originales, on disait d'un domino à poser à tel endroit « qu'on fleurissait la colline ». Prendre tel autre, c'était « pêcher la lune au fond d'un puits ».

— Jeu difficile et assez long à apprendre, disait l'initiatrice, mais qui se joue facile-ment lorsqu'on le sait. Les combinaisons qu'il offre sont infinies.

⚜ ⚜ ⚜

Hélène passa. Madame Rougemont la rejoignit. Un groupe se désagrégea pour leur faire place : deux messieurs et le capitaine Thévenet. Le regard de l'officier toucha celui de madame Gassin. Après une imperceptible indécision dans son pas, elle s'arrêta net.

— Eh bien ! Capitaine, avez-vous réparé cette butte de tir ?

— Mais oui, madame, c'est fait.

— Et c'était vos tirailleurs qu'on entendait, hier matin, à l'aube ?

— Le vent portait. Il y a eu en effet exercice de tir.

— Je croyais à une attaque !

Madame Rougemont s'éventait, la figure trop indifférente. Un peu de sang teinta les joues d'Hélène.

— Vous dansez, capitaine ?

— Mon Dieu, madame, médiocrement.

— Nous contrôlerons tout à l'heure.

L'officier tortillait sa moustache, indécis. Hélène ne laissa pas à son silence et à sa gêne le temps d'être perceptibles. En souriant :

— Et j'imagine que vous m'inviterez ?

— Je vous remercie de cet honneur...

— Et vous, madame, dansez-vous, demanda Hélène à sa voisine en l'entraînant par le bras.

— Il fait bien chaud, madame. Et puis je ne suis plus à la mode. On ne danse que fox-trot et shimmy et j'en suis restée au boston.

Peu après, une jeune femme mince et à la figure souffrante prit le piano. Les boys dégagèrent le hall et une douzaine de couples glissèrent dans ce rythme si franc et heurté des danses actuelles.

— Ouvrons le bal ensemble, dit Ternier à Hélène en l'entraînant.

Le jeune caissier de la Banque l'invita ensuite et, le piano reprenant un fox-trot, le capitaine s'inclina devant madame Gassin. Elle fut dans ses bras, posément, droite, les yeux baissés. La plupart des regards les suivaient à travers les autres couples. De larges glaçures luisaient sur la robe lamée d'Hélène, pareilles à ces coulées qui flambent sur certains vases chinois. Des conversations de femmes se suspendirent. À un moment, les deux danseurs se trouvant un peu à l'écart, Hélène y maintint son cavalier et, toujours les yeux baissés, les lèvres presque immobiles à hauteur de son épaule, elle lui glissa rapidement :

— Ternier sait que je suis allée chez vous.

— Toute la ville...

— Que comptez-vous faire ?

— Soyez sûre que je ne parlerai jamais.

D'un geste nerveux, elle lui serra la main et, par un long glissement, ils se remêlèrent aux danseurs. Hélène souriait. Un peu de sueur perlait à son front. Elle lâcha un instant la main de l'officier pour reprendre une mèche rebelle de ses cheveux et l'enlacer aux autres. Son bras levé montra son duvet fauve.

Elle ne dansa plus qu'un one step et se sentit légèrement fatiguée car la chaleur, à laquelle elle n'était pas habituée, la surprenait. Elle partagea le reste de son temps en causeries avec les dames, recueillit les petits potins du poste et quelques informations contradictoires sur la vie aux colonies. La belle nuit coulait aux fenêtres. Ternier jouait au bridge. Et, de nouveau, les boys circulèrent, portant des verres à soda, des coupes et une marquise frappée dans un grand pichet de cristal embué de givre. Les bouteilles de whisky, de citron et de sherry, les limonades tintaient sur un plateau. Les ventilateurs chassaient les enveloppes en papier des chalumeaux. Lorsque le piano cessait, on entendait les joueurs discuter et le bruissement du *ma-tsiang*. Les conversations chuchotaient. Et aux pieds des piliers, dans leurs vases, parmi leurs gerbes, les lotus se fanaient.

X

Ils partirent pour Sisophon, l'après-midi du surlendemain. La Roland-Gassin contenait Hélène, le docteur et Ternier et la voiture de la Résidence, un secrétaire, le cuisinier et un boy. Les bagages avaient été expédiés le matin par un des camions de service qui font la navette entre Sangkè et Sisophon. À ce dernier poste où la route empierrée cessait, ils devaient laisser les automobiles pour monter à cheval et s'enfoncer vers le nord, sur la piste percée en forêt clairière, un premier tronçon de soixante-dix kilomètres. Au-delà, le tracé de la route future continuait, simple cheminement, obliquant sur le nord-est pour atteindre, environ vingt-cinq kilomètres plus loin, le seuil de la grande forêt de Chongkal. En raison de la présence d'Hélène, Ternier n'avait prévu que des étapes journalières de trente-cinq kilomètres qui les conduiraient en trois jours au point final du voyage.

Tous les trois ou quatre mois, Ternier allait ainsi visiter les travaux, stimuler l'activité des autorités indigènes et, chaque fois, il mettait pied à terre, plus profondément dans les chairs vives du pays. Parmi les nouveaux villages atteints, une partie de la population voyait alors pour la première fois un Européen, le *Louk Thom* : le grand monsieur, le maître de la province, celui dont vingt fois par jour le plus petit gardien de sala administrative jusqu'au Gouverneur prononcent le nom pour menacer ou promettre, stimuler ou conseiller.

⚜ ⚜ ⚜

La route chauffait à blanc depuis le matin. On la voyait devant soi, vibrer dans la réverbération entre ses deux accotements déclives couverts d'herbes, correctement traversés de rigoles tous les cent mètres. À droite, le télégraphe tendait ses fils où des libellules en nombre infini se posaient, l'abdomen dressé. Les poteaux, en bois imputrescible, la base noircie de coaltar, quittaient la route lorsque celle-ci formait une boucle. De distance en distance, des tas de pierre envahis par l'herbe étaient déjà préparés pour l'entretien et le rechargement. Et tout autour, jusqu'à l'horizon, la vaste plaine presque toute de rizières luisait comme une plaque de métal.

Où étaient les villages ? On ne savait. Dans ces bouquets d'arbres qui de-ci, de-là flottaient au lointain ? Sans doute. Ou bien, c'était parfois, sur des lagunes, deux ou trois cases de paillote montées sur leurs pilotis, mangées par le soleil, détachées du sol par l'ombre exiguë qui en tombait et où un porc se vautrait. Cette nudité solitaire où s'allongeait la route prenait un caractère âpre et étrange, car on concevait que quelque chose d'immense y vibrait et s'y préparait. Quoi ? Ne demandez pas à l'esprit humain de tout deviner. Laissez-le pressentir, redouter ou espérer.

Ici, le soleil travaille, fouille, cherche. Il couvre l'eau boueuse tel un mâle brûlant et gigantesque. Et déjà, partout, une buée d'un vert clair et fragile, délicat ; un vert de feuille qui se déploie, adoucit cette plaine. Il varie d'intensité dans les limites régulières d'un damier.

C'est le paddy qui lève, adorablement frêle, fluet et hésitant au cœur de cette fournaise. Il naît au talus de la route et, doublé par la mince couche d'eau qui le supporte, il flotte jusqu'à l'horizon, un horizon qui se déplace avec vous. À peine le paysan a-t-il remué cette terre de sa charrue primitive à l'époque propice des premiers orages : il a suffi. Cette terre a germé. Elle monte maintenant, se dégage des eaux tièdes — et verdit. Et tout est désert, silencieux, l'homme redevenu invisible.

Or, voici la route. Elle coupe en deux demi-cercles ces régions fécondes qui depuis des siècles germent ainsi, inlassablement. Voici la jeune route fine et dure, telle une lame posée dans le plateau d'une balance ; la route droite et impérative comme une belle idée. D'autres hommes vinrent la tendre afin d'équilibrer les forces de la nature et les leurs. Elle est l'ordre et la discipline, passe et contre elle tout s'agrège, vers elle tout converge. C'est vers elle, demain, que chaque tige de paddy inclinera sa tête lourde de riz et que chaque espoir humain, suspendu aussi à l'herbe comme le grain, se tournera.

Quelle belle route que cette route donnée par un pays à un autre, tracée par le plus fort pour le plus faible. Tu feras ta route, ordonne celui-là à celui-ci. Tu rêves et dégénères depuis dix siècles. On ne rêve plus à l'heure présente ; on forge. Aux chantiers, s'il te plaît, comme les autres, comme moi, dans mon pays. Crois-tu qu'elle me soit destinée, cette route ? Vous y passerez mille Cambodgiens pour n'y rencontrer qu'un Français.

Les tonnes de grès que vous avez rodées et sculptées jadis lorsque vous construisiez vos temples prouvent que vous savez travailler pour une idée. Eh bien ! La route va aussi loin que le temple — et plus droit. Regardez-la, nivelée, empierrée, étroitement surveillée, dépouillée de parure, maîtresse d'une nature jusqu'ici indomptée et où, depuis tant de siècles, les hommes de toutes races sont morts sans pouvoir lui passer ce trait qui la jugule enfin. Maintenant que le plus dur est fait et que vous avez peiné avec nous, prenez la bête en main.

Et les deux demi-cercles du pays sont déserts, semble-t-il, de chaque côté de la route. Rien, si ce n'est, dans l'irradiation du ciel et sur cette solitude trompeuse, dominant la terre où son œil scrute chaque motte de boue et les rides de l'eau, un aigle roux qui louvoie, tombe, suspend sa chute et remonte. Pourtant, à tout moment, le chauffeur ralentit et appelle. Comme des reptiles à écailles grises, les files de charrettes obliquent vers leur droite et les bouviers courent aux jougs pour rassurer les bœufs. Sous le roof, des femmes, somnolentes parmi des marchandises, se dressent afin de voir qui passe.

Il n'y a pas une heure que nous roulons sur cette route. Cependant, nous y dépassâmes ou rencontrâmes vingt camions, des automobiles aux vieilles carrosseries lépreuses et dévernies, des machines informes, rafistolées avec des planches, haletantes, déréglées, un nuage de vapeur et de gouttelettes d'eau bouillante fusant du radiateur, des torpédos déclassées roulant sur des bandages à vif, ceintes de paniers suspendus à leurs flancs et accumulés jusque sur le capot ; d'invraisemblables camions, écrasés par des piles de sacs ou retentissant d'écheveaux rouillés de fer rond pour le ciment armé, des tracteurs se mouvant à la vitesse d'un homme au pas, animés par la moitié de leurs cylindres ou bien les grands et confortables cars des services postaux et subventionnés, peints en marron.

Dans ces véhicules de tous les types, sortis la veille du garage ou rachetés en troisième main, au poids du métal, par dix, vingt entrepreneurs chinois de transports ; dans toutes ces voitures faites de bric et de broc, consolidées au fil de fer et au bambou, recarrossées et agrandies à l'aide de planches, assemblages ridicules de ferrailles dont le plus étonnant est de les voir avancer seuls, les indigènes s'entassent après les avoir attendus sur la route et pris d'assaut. Des bonzes s'incrustent entre un ballot de poissons secs et des caisses ; des Chinois s'enchevêtrent ; de mignonnes femmes annamites, un foulard de soie sur la tête, s'insinuent dans les failles des pyramides en levant leurs ombrelles et leurs baluchons ; les Cambodgiennes aux seins pesants, sous leurs vestes blanches et leurs écharpes, glapissent ; les gosses se mêlent aux paquets. Dans une vieille torpédo de quatre places, on compte trois Cambodgiens à côté du chauffeur qui mène, assis de côté, cinq individus accroupis le long des marchepieds ; derrière, ils sont huit. Et ainsi accrochés, ajustés, pénétrés, encaqués, coagulés, adhérents, ils rouleront sur deux cents kilomètres, à une vitesse de trente à l'heure sans compter les pannes ; ils resteront placides et hilares, chiquant leur bétel, partant à la recherche de leurs mains pour fumer, la face épanouie dans le vent de cette extraordinaire vitesse et avec l'idée vacillante qu'en cinq ou six heures ils parviendront au terme d'un voyage qu'ils mettaient, hier encore, cinq jours à effectuer. À leur tour, ces humbles et ces obscurs soulèvent la poussière !

⚜ ⚜ ⚜

Qu'est-ce donc qui les pousse ?

Ils se moquent du temps. Pourquoi, celui-ci, possesseur de deux bons bœufs et d'une charrette, vient-il sur cette infernale machine, recroquevillé dans une posture d'araignée qui a peur, au lieu de faire paisiblement son chemin, d'étape en étape, comme le faisaient ses pères ? Quoi presse cet homme de la brousse qui sait à peine calculer son âge ? Rien : et le voilà.

Lorsqu'il sera revenu, que dira-t-il à ses amis du village ? Il leur dira : il y a la route, il y a la voiture mécanique. Il ne conseillera pas à ceux qui, à leur tour, voudront partir : attelez vos bœufs, frères. Il leur dira : marchez droit vers le sud-ouest. Et lorsque vous serez sur la route, attendez. Car une heure ne sera pas écoulée, il sait qu'au loin, un nuage de poussière poindra et qu'un étrange bruit retentira.

Malgré les siècles d'art et de contemplation qui embuent encore les yeux de cet homme, il a fallu qu'une route blanche et droite passât près de sa liberté et de sa sagesse, de son dédain du temps et de sa pauvreté, pour qu'en quelques jours, sans discuter, sans songer à ses dieux ni à tout ce qui pourtant le sépare d'elle ; il a fallu qu'une route passât près de lui, pour qu'il s'y dirigeât ; une route nue, brûlante, où pourtant lui et tous ses frères de la région, réquisitionnés, ont cassé les cailloux.

Elle l'a ensorcelé. Il l'a vu accourir du sud et glisser vers le nord, divinité nouvelle. Il l'a approchée, a franchi son talus et son pied nu fut sur cette chair blanche qu'il frappa du talon. Et son talon qui laissait une empreinte dans toutes les terres foulées jusqu'alors, — son talon a rebondi. Puis l'homme avança. Oh ! que la marche lui parut légère le long de la ligne droite, rapide. Plus d'herbes à couper, plus d'arbres à contourner ni de taillis à percer, plus d'épines à travers ce sentier-là, plus de marécages où l'on s'enfonce jusqu'aux cuisses et d'où l'on ressort couvert de sangsues.

D'autres hommes s'y dirigèrent alors, de tous les points de l'horizon et prirent aussi possession de la route ; d'autres hommes qui jamais n'auraient imaginé de tendre ainsi dans les solitudes une bande de terre nue et dure. Et la région se trouva réunie en un long cordon d'espoirs et d'appétits. Ce qui était inconnu fut connu. Celui qui ne pouvait rien vendre côtoya vingt acheteurs ; celui qui n'avait pas de femme partit en chercher une. Or, elle est seule, cette route, à travers des milliers d'hectares de terre où les traditions de cet homme se suspendent aux palmiers. S'il la veut, qu'il la prenne. Il n'en a pas besoin ? Appuyé à la colonne centrale de sa case, qu'il l'efface au chant monotone de sa guitare.

⚜ ⚜ ⚜

— Vous ne pouvez vous faire une idée de l'intensité de la circulation entre Sangkè et Sisophon, dit Ternier. Chaque mois, c'est par dizaines que nous délivrons de nouveaux permis de transport en commun. Et remarquez qu'il ne s'agit là que d'un premier tronçon desservant à peine le quart de la région.

— Vous ne comptez pas les charrettes, dit le docteur. Avec leurs sales bêtes de bœufs qui s'écartent et se flanquent en travers et expédient les pauvres petites autos dans la rizière si l'on ne peut pas s'arrêter à temps.

— Docteur, vous êtes ingrat. Ne dites pas du mal des charrettes, vous en êtes un fervent.

— Dans la brousse, sur les pistes, oui, admirable ! D'abord je suis dedans. Sur la route, j'aime mieux l'auto.

— Et où voulez-vous qu'elles passent, les pauvres ? demanda Hélène.

— À côté, madame, à côté, répondit le docteur d'un air profond, car certain prince siamois que j'eus l'honneur d'accompagner m'ouvrit sur ce sujet des horizons imprévus. Une stupeur scandalisée se peignait sur sa figure lorsqu'il voyait la charrette d'un Cambodgien sur la route. Et chaque fois, comme le prince n'en pouvait croire ses yeux, il s'exclamait : vous leur donnez le droit de passer sur la route ! Je suis certain que cet homme aimable quitta le Cambodge convaincu qu'il venait d'être victime d'une farce et que nous avions disséminé des charrettes sur la route, pour la figuration.

— N'oubliez pas, en effet, dit Ternier à Hélène, que vous êtes ici en territoire qui appartenait avant 1907 aux Siamois et que, pour eux, les Cambodgiens ne sont que des esclaves.

— N'empêche, goguenarda le docteur, que dans une belle maison vous faites un escalier pour les maîtres et un escalier de service.

— La route de service existe en fait, car souvent, en région sablonneuse et lorsque les charrettes vont à vide, le Cambodgien préfère longer la route. Mais il est à tout moment obligé d'y monter pour passer sur les ponts. Tenez, continua Ternier après un silence, toute cette région-ci était inculte il y a trois ans. On n'y voyait qu'une forêt claire dévastée chaque année par les incendies.

De petites digues dentelées divisaient l'eau en casiers réguliers, vaste panneau décoratif enchâssé dans le réseau de plomb d'un vitrail où le peintre aurait oublié la ligne d'horizon et dans lequel on ne savait où ni comment finissaient les choses.

Soudain, devant les voyageurs, au loin, quelque chose se précisa au-dessus d'un nuage de poussière, un arc noir qui surmontait des masses mouvantes d'un violet mat. Le chauffeur débraya et, tandis que la voiture glissait en silence, Hélène perçut un son de hautbois qui, précédant l'apparition, semblait, tant il était faible et languissant, mourir au moment où l'oreille le recueillait.

— Madame, dit le docteur en se retournant, des éléphants.

Ils revenaient d'un long voyage. Leurs cornacs attentifs dissipaient leur fatigue en jouant sur le hautbois des airs mineurs. Et soudain, ils croisèrent la voiture sans que le moindre bruit de leurs pattes molles et précautionneuses décelât leur cheminement. Les uns allaient nus, les autres portaient la selle où le voyageur se couche sous un roof circulaire. L'homme qui jouait, emboîté au cou de l'éléphant chef de file, avait laissé la flûte pour prendre le croc et une longue cravache terminée par une boule de plomb afin de maîtriser la bête que l'automobile et les Européens inquiétaient.

Le défilé, jailli du soleil et touchant au ciel, se déroula. Le panneau décoratif, en mirage derrière ces silhouettes magistrales et leur mouvante architecture, devint de cristal. La troupe venait de passer un gué. Aussi, les têtes bossuées et les flancs étaient-ils d'un gris clair de poussière tandis que les jambes brillaient comme du basalte noir. En un instant, Hélène distingua des choses étonnantes et d'un autre âge : la cuisse nerveuse d'un cornac qu'éventait le grand battant déchiqueté d'une oreille doublée de rose et mouchetée de noir, une trompe étendue, des silhouettes d'hommes, l'écharpe autour de la tête et qui, vus d'en bas, immobiles mais balancés par leur monture, prenaient des allures de princes et un caractère augural. Et, sans doute, le convoi avait trouvé en cours de route le cadavre d'un éléphant disparu ou perdu l'un des siens, car on voyait, suspendu à une selle, un énorme fémur, noueux comme une souche et d'une blancheur délicate.

— De cet ossement, dit Ternier, un artisan sortira des montures de guitares finement sculptées.

La voiture repartit.

— Vous leur permettez la route, docteur ?

— Madame, oui. J'ai voué depuis longtemps aux éléphants une... Comment dirai-je ? Oui, c'est cela : une tendresse inquiète. Ce sont de braves gens. Lorsque j'étais au Darlac, j'ai beaucoup voyagé avec eux. Bien obligé, n'ayant pas d'autres moyens de transport. D'une fragilité extrême, savez-vous. Je voyais leur peau saigner sous la succion des taons. Aux haltes, on faisait du feu pour les protéger des moustiques tant ils en étaient incommodés. Mais quelle bonhomie à l'heure du bain, sous le massage des cornacs, et ces soins de marquis pour poser la patte en terrain douteux ; le volontaire arrêt, afin d'attendre qu'on ramasse le bagage tombé, ce dont personne ne s'était aperçu.

— Oh ! oh ! fit Hélène étonnée.

— Je vous l'assure, madame, des pensées constantes et coordonnées qui se suivent sous les bosses rocheuses du front, une sorte de philosophie permanente qui condescend volontiers aux petites choses de l'homme et daigne aider nos entreprises avec une obéissance qui devient aussitôt une protection.

Ternier ajouta :

— L'éléphant est un animal vénéré. Le cornac prononce certaines prières avant de fixer le tapis d'écorce qui isole le bât. Des airs de flûte spéciaux lui sont dédiés. Mais tout cela, c'est du vieux Cambodge qui disparaît. Une quarantaine à peine d'éléphants domestiques sont inscrits dans ma circonscription. Le Roi en a autant. Ajoutez-en une cinquantaine dans le reste du pays. Et c'est tout.

⚜ ⚜ ⚜

L'horizon s'anima et des touffes de palmiers se multiplièrent, se rapprochèrent : Sisophon, sa rivière, ses jonques, ses chaloupes. En bordure d'une place, dans un parc de manguiers et de cocotiers, la maison du Gouverneur.

Il avait paré la porte charretière de troncs de bananiers découpés et la porte paraissait en ivoire, sous un arceau de palmes liées. Ce Gouverneur était un petit homme chétif, à l'œil vif, vêtu à l'européenne et parlant très correctement le français. Les notables se rangèrent derrière lui afin de saluer le Résident. Tout n'était que frondaisons, arbres fruitiers sur lesquels mille palmiers éclataient. Quelques indigènes passaient dans les reflets d'un ciel opalin.

— Le Gouverneur vous a préparé une chambre chez lui, madame, dit Ternier, demandez-lui tout ce que vous désirerez. Moi, je suis à côté, dans cette maison qui n'est autre que le tribunal, mais où j'ai une chambre. Quant à vous, docteur, vous connaissez votre logis.

— Et devinez, madame, quel est mon logis ?

— Non, dites ?

— Mon logis, c'est l'in-fir-me-rie.

— Ici ?

— Ici-même. Une belle infirmerie, construite l'année dernière, trois chambres, lits en fer, douches — et des médicaments, je vous prie.

— Mais c'est merveilleux !

— Et un infirmier, breveté de l'école d'Hanoï ! C'est à cent mètres d'ici. Reposez-vous, venez voir et si vous voulez, je vous vaccinerai contre le choléra, la peste, la variole.

⚜ ⚜ ⚜

Le Gouverneur conduisit Hélène dans une grande chambre éclairée en chapelle ardente par deux lampes à acétylène, tous becs ouverts. Une carpette usée occupait le centre. De la cloison en bois jaillissaient, avec un mufle rose groseille et des yeux hagards, deux têtes de bœufs en plâtre peint, surmontées de cornes naturelles. Des photographies jaunies étaient encadrées et, sur un grand carton, une main patiente avait collé, les unes à côté des autres, les photographies d'actrices françaises qu'on trouve dans les paquets de cigarettes. Sur une table, Hélène vit une carafe, un verre, des cigarettes dans une coupe d'argent, un sucrier en verre bleu, une boîte de biscuits, un pot annamite rempli de fleurs. Un grand lit garni du linge de la Résidence occupait un angle de la chambre. Dans un autre, un phonographe.

Le boy apporta les sacs d'Hélène. La femme du Gouverneur, sa mère, des enfants s'encadrèrent dans une autre porte, saluèrent la voyageuse en s'agenouillant et lui offrirent des grenades. Un petit garçon tout nu, le ventre en avant et le bras tendu, vint en chancelant lui donner une fleur échevelée de gloriosa.

Cette chambre ouvrait ainsi aux quatre vents, mais après que tout fut mis en ordre et les présentations terminées, elle se vida comme par enchantement. Sur le plancher, le frôlement des pieds nus s'effaça. Et madame Gassin demeura seule, entre des fenêtres béant sur une verdure assombrie où des lucioles luisaient, dans un lieu si bienveillant et si naïvement sincère qu'elle s'assit, attendrie, reconnaissante à ces braves gens appliqués à bien faire, timides et cérémonieux, de l'avoir logée là, dans leurs habitudes, et d'avoir réuni tout ce qu'ils estimaient posséder de plus beau. Elle n'entendait plus que le chuchotement lointain du village et, tout près, le bruit que font les palmes en se froissant. Sortant de sa torpeur, elle passa dans une seconde pièce. Au centre, une grande jarre de grès avait été remplie d'eau, un bol d'argent, pour s'asperger, posé sur une chaise. Et sur l'eau limpide flottait une poignée de jasmins.

Alors cette femme qui portait en elle un secret brûlant s'allongea sur le lit, bras en croix.

— Que c'est bon ! murmura-t-elle.

Et immobile, sans sanglots, elle pleura. Ses larmes longeaient ses tempes et se perdaient dans ses cheveux. Et ses larmes étaient fraîches. Et à travers ses larmes, elle voyait, suspendu au plafond, une sorte de pendentif circulaire, fine armature de rotin, entièrement revêtue de fleurs tressées. Il tournait sur lui-même, charmant travail des femmes cambodgiennes qu'elles exécutent de leurs doigts menus et suspendent, dans les pagodes, les jours fastes.

XI

Madame Gassin s'éveilla lentement dans la perception croissante des bruits et de l'aube. Elle entrevit, d'abord, les fenêtres ouvertes sur une buée. D'innombrables coqs jetaient leurs cris. Un mortier à paddy s'était mis à battre. Puis elle perçut des gémissements doux et graves, inexplicables, qui s'approchaient, venus de différentes directions et cessaient près de la maison. Quelques voix d'hommes leur succédaient et tout retombait dans le silence : les charrettes se groupaient sur la place. Hélène s'habilla et descendit. Ternier parut en même temps qu'elle.

Ces charrettes, qui sillonnent le pays et qu'elle regardait toujours avec intérêt, allaient aujourd'hui chanter pour elle, véhicules élégants, organisés comme un corps vivant et dont la voix des essieux susurre, gémit et module au moindre mouvement des roues et qui, aussi longtemps que la route s'allonge, module, gémit et susurre, plus sonore en forêt, grave le matin, aiguë dans le soleil.

Elles se suivent à la file dans les mêmes ornières, alternant avec les bœufs subjugués, le conducteur entre ceux-ci, sur le timon. Et l'ensemble fait corps, rampe, glisse, plonge et tangue, s'insinue dans les pistes creuses, flotte dans les savanes, saute sur les souches ; chacune, être unique à trois têtes et on ne sait combien de jambes, les pattes en V des bœufs, les pieds pendants de l'homme et les rayons des roues lustrés par le fouettement des hautes herbes. Sur les ridelles courbées en berceau et dont les abouts portent un décor sculpté, le roof tressé arrondit un dos de pachyderme et lance en avant son toit en bec d'oiseau. Au passage des rivières, les bœufs nagent, le véhicule flotte. Un cadre formant traîneau fait glisser le tout au-dessus des ornières trop profondes. Tout est fixé par des rotins et des emboîtements sans le secours d'un fragment de fer. L'essieu lui-même est un cœur de bois dur. L'homme et la forêt s'assemblent pour se mouvoir.

En voici huit, ce matin, en file, seize roues : un chœur. Au départ, deux chanteuses nouvelles entameront leur chant, puis chaque charrette s'ébranlant, deux nouvelles chanteuses enfleront la chanson. Alors, la poussière se lèvera et tous les airs à l'unisson monteront avec la poussière. Et des heures et des heures, la file serpentine balaiera, comme une traîne de soie bruissant, la torpeur des solitudes, de village en village, de point d'eau en point d'eau, de l'aube à la nuit, du sud au nord.

⚜ ⚜ ⚜

Tandis qu'on chargeait les bagages, Ternier parlait khmer aux bouviers, martelant d'une voix bon enfant les mots de cette rude langue :

— Hé ! Les hommes ! Êtes-vous prêts ? D'où sors-tu, toi, ce casque qui tient du concombre, de la patate et du sein de vieille femme ?

Et chacun de rire en ouvrant une bouche noire.

— Ah ! les beaux bœufs que tu as là, toi ! On dirait que tu passas leur dos au safran et leurs pattes au vernis ! Rudes tireurs, francs du joug et l'œil si candide. Bonnes bêtes, toi et eux ! Et toi, grand garçon, à l'air niais, tu pars avec un moyeu fendu ! Hein ? Quoi ? Il y a six mois qu'il est comme ça ? Merci ! Je ne veux pas assister à son dernier jour. Et ta roue ! Mais elle est polygonale cette roue ! Tu n'as pas honte de te présenter avec une charrette pareille ? Va-t'en ! Ô Khmer ! Khmer ! Peuple de linottes ! Toi, monsieur le vieillard, avec ta tête poivre et sel, ça va ?

Le Gouverneur glissa un mot à l'oreille du Résident.

— Ta femme a accouché hier ? À ton âge ! Faut-il que tu aies de bons amis !

L'homme éclata de rire en claquant sa cuisse nue. Ternier se retourna vers Hélène.

— Voilà, chère amie, le Cambodge. Depuis huit jours, tout le monde est prévenu. Chacun fait de son mieux. Sur huit charrettes commandées, six sont utilisables. Et nous allons perdre une heure pour les remplacer.

Le Gouverneur hocha la tête en souriant :

— Les Khmers ne savent rien.

— Les Gouverneurs devraient savoir pour eux, interrompit Ternier d'une voix brutale. On ne convoque pas un homme qui vient d'être père. Et lorsqu'on réquisitionne une charrette, Gouverneur, on regarde ses roues. Tenez-le-vous pour dit.

Le Gouverneur s'inclina.

— Voyez-vous, madame, continua Ternier en s'éloignant avec Hélène, ces hommes sont d'une placidité extrême. En voilà qui nous accompagnent. Quoi faire ? Ils ne savent marcher. Ils étaient si bien chez eux et ils partent parce qu'on leur a dit de partir, parce que c'est comme ça. Ils mangeront n'importe quoi, n'importe où — ou pas du tout. Peut-être encore un de leurs bœufs, leur fortune, crèvera. Telle est la volonté de l'Occidental pour des raisons qui ne sont pas les leurs, à eux qui nous suivent à plusieurs siècles d'intervalle. On les paiera, c'est évident. Et il faut bien qu'ils se soumettent à certaines conditions d'ordre général. Mais ce qu'il y a de certain, c'est que leurs mandarins les mènent sans ménagement et aggravent le plus souvent la rigueur de leur servitude. Huit fois sur dix, l'indigène préfère avoir affaire au Résident qu'au Gouverneur. Voici le docteur.

— Comment ! Dans cette tenue ? s'exclama Hélène stupéfaite.

Le docteur paraissait en pyjama à rayures bleues, les pieds dans de vieux escarpins aux nœuds absents, un fusil en bandoulière. Et derrière son lorgnon, voilé par la buée du matin, il ouvrait avec peine des yeux gros de sommeil.

— Madame, acceptez mes hommages et mes excuses. Tel est en effet mon costume d'explorateur. Ce fusil, que j'emporte toujours, sert à chasser, le cas échéant. Je le donne à un Cambodgien et, de la sorte, je suis sûr de ne blesser personne et d'avoir du gibier, car moi, je sais mal m'en servir. Ensuite, vous, le Résident, allez à cheval. Moi, j'ai horreur de cet animal. Lorsqu'on est à cheval on est au soleil et j'ai encore plus horreur du soleil que du cheval. Aussi, vais-je en charrette. Gouverneur, où est ma charrette ?

— Ici, monsieur le docteur.

— Venez voir, madame. Là ! Qu'elle est belle ! Un roof tout neuf et finement tressé, passé à la résine. Que voulez-vous de mieux ?

— Mais on ne peut pas s'asseoir là-dedans !

— On s'y couche, madame, on s'y couche, et c'est ce qu'il y a d'admirable. Tâtez ce matelas de kapok, une merveille ! Et ce bon petit oreiller ! Vous m'envierez, vous m'envierez bassement... du haut de votre cheval.

Tout à coup, le docteur éclata :

— Seigneur du ciel ! Qu'est-ce qu'ils m'ont ficelé, là-haut, au sommet du roof, avec au moins dix mètres de rotin ? C'est ma sacoche !

Il se retourna vers le conducteur qui souriait sans comprendre, car le docteur continuait en français :

— Tu veux que je meure ! Sais-tu ce qu'il y a dans ma sacoche ? Mon bloc-notes et mon mouchoir, la quinine, l'antipyrine, ma montre, une loupe, le stylo, de la menue monnaie pour jeter aux petits enfants des villages, mon canif, mes cigarettes, de la ficelle — et Horace ! Il y a Horace ! Et j'en passe la moitié, mâchoire d'âne ! Et tu ficelles, tu ligotes tout ça !

L'homme restait impassible.

— Il s'en fout, sauf le respect que je vous dois, madame, ce Cambodgien s'en fout !

Le boy vint remettre les choses en état. Les deux nouvelles charrettes arrivèrent et l'on fut prêt. Le docteur s'installa comme un roi mérovingien.

Huit charrettes, seize roues : un chœur. Chaque charrette s'ébranla et, chaque fois, deux nouvelles chanteuses enflèrent la chanson. Alors, la poussière se leva et tous les airs à l'unisson montèrent avec la poussière.

⚜ ⚜ ⚜

Dès la fin de la matinée, ils quittèrent les rizières et, désormais, la piste serpenta en forêt claire. Hélène et Ternier allaient devant, guêtre à guêtre ; elle, fine comme un jeune garçon, lui, trop grand pour son cheval. Afin de ne pas fatiguer la cavalière, il était convenu qu'on ne galoperait qu'une dizaine de kilomètres avant d'arriver aux étapes. Deux ou trois Cambodgiens les précédaient d'un pas élastique et allongé, presque nus, car ils avaient relevé le *sampot* très haut sur leurs cuisses.

La vie végétale était si variée, si mouvante que leur nudité ne s'y superposait pas, mais s'y mêlait et y participait. Les jeux de la lumière, favorisés par le poli de l'épidémie, liaient à l'ambiance ces magnifiques marcheurs par les reflets dont ils étaient inondés, car il n'est pas de plus belle danse que la marche de l'homme nu.

Tout est prestigieux dans cette architecture mouvante : thorax et dos bombés en boucliers ; ces deux armes : les bras, et les jambes, propulseurs de la merveilleuse machine. Attaque, défense ou fuite, ces principes élémentaires de la vie humaine se trouvent synthétisés en l'homme nu qui dément ainsi toute la vaine philosophie issue de son cerveau. Mêlé à la nature dont il n'est, en définitive, qu'une simple tige, il n'a qu'à paraître et toutes les vérités primordiales, l'initial bonheur et les combats qui l'achètent ou en résultent, remplissent son ombre. La confiance, la témérité cuirassent la poitrine de cet homme que déchire l'infime ronce de la forêt. Quelle sincérité, quel loyalisme peuvent être plus affirmés que cette franchise de la nudité : l'arme bien visible brille au soleil. Pas de parures trompeuses, pas de protections lâches, pas d'hypocrites embûches : l'adversaire rencontre partout l'élémentaire et voit, au centre du torse, battre le cœur. La faiblesse de ce torse s'encadre de la force et de la défense des membres. L'attaque roule dans les muscles. Les pieds se posent sans bruit sur le sol, dans un écartement léger de ventouse et y aspirent une stabilité qui devient aussitôt de la ténacité. Une opportune prévoyance dort au creux des mains adroites. Autre chose, enfin, rayonne de cet ensemble que l'air soutient et favorise : la liberté.

Ternier, qui voyait Hélène observer ces hommes, dit :

— Ces Cambodgiens sont admirablement faits aux pistes et à la forêt. Ce sont les vrais hommes de la brousse, les « têtes noires », comme les appellent ceux des villes. Ils flairent les points cardinaux, regardent le ciel, tendent un doigt qui paraît aimanté et se mettent en marche. Leurs yeux distinguent la feuille entre les feuilles, reconnaissent la bête qui fuit et que vous n'apercevez même pas. Infailliblement où je ne vois goutte, ils montrent le rotin qui se torsade, la liane dont on peut faire une corde, le nid de mouches à miel, la trace de bêtes dont nous ne savons ni le nom, ni la forme, l'arbre au bois dur, à huile ou à résine, les feuilles des tubercules comestibles ou vénéneux. On les devine, en route, qui repèrent des points mysté-rieux ou observent, dans les taillis, des choses qui leur servent d'indications. Le coupe-coupe alerte et toujours en mouvement, ils entaillent les arbres de marques régulières lorsqu'ils ont peur de se perdre. À la forme des mottes de terre et à leur couleur, ils savent quand il a plu ; à la couleur des mares, leur profondeur et depuis combien de temps un convoi s'y désaltéra. Chaque forme d'arbre est fixée dans leur mémoire avec la saison à laquelle il fleurit, l'espèce d'oiseau qui se nourrit de ses fruits, les vertus médicinales de ses feuilles. Ils ne soulèvent pas deux pierres de la même façon, car l'une doit cacher un scorpion, l'autre non...

Une biche traversa la piste, à trente mètres, fit quelques bonds, s'arrêta, dressa la tête, regarda approcher le convoi et, secouant ses larges oreilles, repartit.

— Eh bien, docteur, cria Ternier, votre fusil !

— Ohé ! Ohé ! répondit la première charrette.

Un bras, brandissant l'arme, souleva le mouchoir mis en store à l'avant du roof. Ternier la confia à l'un des guides.

— Et les cartouches ?

— Les cartouches aussi ! protesta la charrette. Où diable sont les cartouches ! Boy ! Boy !

— Oui, m'sieur !

— Où çà mettre cartouches ?

— Y'en a pas.

— Comment, y'en a pas !

— Non, m'sieur ! M'sieur n'a pas donné.

❖ ❖ ❖

À tout moment, cette piste qui traversait la solitude de la forêt claire s'animait de groupes d'hommes. Ils surgissaient au loin, postés, immobiles et faisaient de grands saluts lorsque les voyageurs passaient. Vingt kilomètres à la ronde, la tournée du Résident avait été signalée et les villages épars envoyaient des émissaires, en cas de besoin. On voyait ici une ou deux charrettes dételées et des chevaux bridés de rotin. Ailleurs, le chef d'un groupe de cases était venu lui-même porter un poulet, des œufs, un régime de bananes ou des cocos : humble hommage traditionnel. Ternier prenait, serrait la main du notable et, lorsqu'il y avait des femmes et des enfants, donnait des pièces d'argent neuves. Des mains jointes le remerciaient, des fronts se baissaient. Presque partout les émissaires demandaient de la quinine. Alors le docteur, qui avait rempli de comprimés des bouteilles, les versait de sa charrette.

— Ils ruinent l'État, ces bougres-là ! Tiens, toi, encore deux ou trois, là, et maintenant décampe.

Dix fois, le même cérémonial patriarcal se renouvela, sans bruit, tranquillement. Une confiance curieuse couvrait les visages. Chacun faisait ses petits salamalecs en conscience, posément. Il était venu, pour voir, avait attendu et allait repartir. On atteignait déjà les hautes régions, au fond du pays, avec, pour toute arme, un fusil de chasse sans cartouches. Qui pensait à cela ? Et pourquoi y penser ? Le Résident inspecte la piste. L'ordre a passé de bouche en bouche. C'est bien, logique, légitime. Allons voir le Résident ! Il paraît qu'il y a une madame. Et la forêt était ensoleillée, et la piste en bon état, car, depuis que l'ordre avait passé, vite on avait bouché les trous, repris les tassements, coupé l'herbe afin que le Résident ne poussât pas de cris.

On attend, en se frottant les pieds, après avoir marché quatre heures. C'est lui ? Pas encore. Un cavalier viendra d'abord qui préviendra. On peut dormir. Le voilà ! Il est à cheval. C'est la madame ? Non, c'est un garçon. Je te dis que c'est la madame. Ne parle pas si fort. Attention ! Et le chef de village, devant le groupe, s'agenouille, ou, s'il veut faire le faraud, quitte son chapeau mou et se casse en deux comme un Français. Ah ! Mais ! Tout se brouille, bruit et poussière. Le Résident a parlé. Qu'est-ce qu'il a dit ? Le chant des charrettes s'éloigne. Tout est fini. Nous avons vu. Il nous a vus. Tel était bien l'ordre.

Chacun met ses quatre ou cinq grains de quinine avec son tabac dans une boîte en fer-blanc. Allons ! Et l'on retourne au village, l'un derrière l'autre, le chef en tête ou le plus âgé du groupe. La vie est belle, chaque conscience allégée. À travers les arbres, une voix nasille :

Œung œuy œung œuy...

L'éléphant balance sa trompe,

Il berce, il berce le palanquin,

et berce, et berce tes seins, femme !

qui frémissent, qui frémissent dans ta veste...

Forêt claire, forêt claire, toujours. La vue ne trouve aucun repos, pas une joie. Des arbres espacés, rabougris, noueux, à écorce grise, presque sans branches, à larges et longues feuilles épaisses, ondulées et dures, couvertes de poussière. Un tiers verdit, un tiers jaunit, un tiers tombe. Par endroit, des troncs blanchis, jetés en biais sur les autres par la foudre ; des coupoles de boue sèche bâties par les termites. Perçant partout le sol gercé, les jeunes arbres se terminent par un gros bourgeon duveteux ou gluant. Sans interruption, des feuilles mortes, sur une terre mi-sable, mi-argile, tantôt blanche, tantôt jaune. Tristesse âpre, dur soleil, ombres trop petites, trop légères et déchiquetées. Chaque année, un incendie brûle les jeunes pousses, tord les arbres déjà hauts, les dépouille et arrête leur élan. Peu d'oiseaux, mais des troupes de cerfs et de daims. Pas de grands fauves : ils seraient trop à découvert. Aucun cocotier, nulle frondaison. La marche interminable vers les régions riches du nord, les grandes forêts sonores à l'humidité perpétuelle, les villages tapis dans un coin de sol moins aride, où l'eau passe et où, tout à coup, la rizière miroite et l'arbre heureux s'élance.

Cependant, la piste hardie et souple sait où elle va et sa tête intelligente s'est avancée dans ce désert, car son but s'étend au-delà. Elle a rampé dans cette disgrâce, couchant les petits arbres qui la gênaient. Elle oblique pour éviter la construction d'un pont. On la voit comme un tentacule palper le paysage, fuir le sable, longer le marécage et contourner la roche. Parfois, elle hésite, se dédouble. Une erreur fut reconnue, un arbre tranché ferma la voie fausse et la piste repartit. Elle se creuse, se bombe, elle est terre. Elle garde encore le modelé des terrains qu'elle armera plus tard d'un axe autoritaire, lorsque, plus rigide, elle percera ce ressaut du sol qu'elle contourne aujourd'hui, lorsqu'elle sera pierre. Déjà, de loin en loin, voyez les blocs de grès que les casseurs de cailloux débiteront. Des charrettes, par centaines, en amèneront d'autres. Ces ponts ne sont que provisoires, faits de troncs à peine épannelés et qui, remis en terre, bourgeonnent parfois. Plus tard, une arche blanche, d'un saut de fer et de ciment franchira l'arroyo. Des fils métalliques longeront cette piste, plus élevés que les arbres rabougris de la forêt claire. De mille mètres en mille mètres, une borne marquera un pas humain. La piste roule déjà cet avenir dans sa chair friable et sur son corps nonchalant.

⚜ ⚜ ⚜

Or, le Résident et des ingénieurs ayant, sous le ventilateur et près d'une limonade glacée, tracé un trait rouge sur la carte fausse et incomplète de ces régions encore si mal connues, tout autre chose est de reporter le même trait, large de cinq mètres à travers le pays. Les habitants, à tour de rôle, vinrent de leur district respectif couper les arbres, tasser la terre. Mais quel est celui qui planta, de distance en distance, le jalon blanc et rouge et, de sa lunette d'arpenteur, dirigea ce jalon, vécut dans ces solitudes desséchées aussi longtemps que la piste l'exigea et y reviendra séjourner pour faire la route ? Quel est l'homme qui, muni d'un ordre, s'est déjà avancé, laissant derrière lui cette trace étonnante ?

On cherche dans les dossiers. De bureau en bureau, des signatures se sont ajoutées aux signatures. Le Résident mit en lumière les nécessités de la région qu'il avait parcourue à cheval, en observant, en interrogeant l'habitant. Il a pointé les villages, repéré les rivières et les carrières. Quel Résident ? Demain, Ternier sera mort et son nom effacé. Des ingénieurs ont étudié sur de mauvaises cartes. Depuis quand ? On ne sait pas. Il n'est pas question de noms. Lesquels de tous ceux-là verront la route ?

Celle-ci ou une autre, bien plate, bien nette, se développe sur une table, on la plie en huit et on écrit dessus « approuvé ».

⚜ ⚜ ⚜

Hélène vit soudain une paillote, la première depuis le matin, édifiée à même le sol, prolongée par un préau. Des piles d'outils brillaient au soleil. Au pied d'un arbre, un tonneau, monté sur roues, tendait des brancards où une mangouste s'épouillait. Du linge séchait étendu sur les buissons. Plus loin, à travers le ravin d'un arroyo desséché, un pont d'une quarantaine de mètres de long dressait ses chevalets. Des indigènes en posaient le platelage. Aux alentours du chantier et de la maison, les copeaux et les écorces couvraient le sol. Les coolies avaient installé leur campement à une centaine de mètres et des poules, cherchant l'ombre, erraient avec tristesse.

Une femme française, brune, un peu forte, vêtue d'un peignoir bleu déteint dont le volant pendait derrière, pieds nus dans des espadrilles et coiffée d'un casque sale, vint au-devant du Résident.

— Eh bien ! Madame Carlaguet, comment allez-vous ?

— Tout doucement, monsieur l'Résident.

Elle se tourna vers la maison.

— Eh ! Émile ! V'là monsieur l'Résident.

Émile parut en serrant la ceinture de son pantalon kaki. C'était un long gaillard roux à figure ravagée, l'œil bleu et doux. Nu-tête, en plein soleil, ses cheveux flambaient. Il s'approcha à grands pas en se balançant et tendit à Ternier une large main velue et gantée de taches de son. Ternier présenta :

— Monsieur Carlaguet, Surveillant des Travaux publics. C'est monsieur Carlaguet qui a fait cette piste.

— Vous pouvez le dire, monsieur l'Résident ! Ah ! non de d'la. C'est pas tant la piste ! On n'a pas d'eau. Depuis que nous sommes à ce foutu pont, faut aller la chercher à sept kilomètres.

— Pas encore de pluies ?

— Si, quelques orages, mais la terre est trop sèche, al boit tout. Vous rentrez pas ?

— Non ! Non ! Carlaguet, merci. Nous voulons arriver avant la nuit.

— Rentrez donc, quoi ! Une minute. C'est pas ça qui vous mettra en retard. Le temps de boire un coco. Tiens ! Docteur. Ça va toujours comme vous voulez ?

— Adieu, Carlaguet.

— Vous tombez bien, on n'a plus de quinine. C'est pas qu'on a la fièvre, mais vous savez, des fois, comme ci, comme ça.

Ils entrèrent dans le logis. Terre battue. Quelques effets pendus aux cloisons en bambou. Deux pauvres malles à couvercles bombés, dans un coin, sur des briques. Un lit sous une moustiquaire sale, relevée. Au chevet, la photographie d'une fillette et de deux garçonnets endimanchés était accrochée à une ficelle, dans un cadre en coquillages. Sur une table, aux quatre pieds dans des boîtes en fer blanc pleines d'eau, à cause des fourmis, des bouteilles de Picon, de Dubonnet et de vin du Cap Corse, entourées de gros verres à pied, la tache bleue d'une boîte de sucre. Enfin, Carlaguet, qui était chasseur, préparant des souvenirs lors de sa mise en retraite, avait suspendu des pattes d'échassiers, une peau de python, la tête d'un toucan, des ramures de cerfs ficelées en fagot et des défenses de sangliers.

— Ça n'est pas bien beau, le château, dit madame Carlaguet avec un humble petit sourire confus. Asseyez-vous, madame.

— Vous vous battrez pas, y'a que deux chaises. Boy ! Boy ! Où c'est qu'il est encore el chameau ! C'est pourtant pas les distractions qu'y a autour, ajouta l'homme.

Le boy vint.

— Coupe les cocos, bellure ! Et fous pas tes doigts d'dans !

— Et vous habitez aussi ici ? demanda Hélène, terrifiée, à madame Carlaguet.

— Faut bien, madame. Qu'est-ce que je ferais toute seule à Sangkè. Comme ça, Émile et moi, on est nous deux. Il s'embête moins et moi aussi.

— Pour un sale coin, c'est un sale coin. C'est la faute du pont, madame. Si c'est pas malheureux, faire un pont et y'a pas d'eau ! Pas moyen d'enfoncer les palées tellement que la terre était dure. Et dans deux mois, l'eau coulera comme une vache ! C'est vexant tout de même.

— Depuis combien de temps êtes-vous sur la route ? demanda le docteur.

— Sur celle-ci, docteur, nous v'là dans le onzième mois. Mais c'est pas partout comme ça. Et puis, quand il pleut, ça va mieux.

— Si, Carlaguet, dit Ternier d'une voix douce, c'est toujours à peu près comme ça. Si ce n'est pas une chose, ç'en est une autre. Pourquoi ne venez-vous pas de temps en temps à Sangkè ?

— Et quoi faire, monsieur le Résident ! Se transbahuter avec des malles, mettre un costume blanc, aller dépenser d'largent. Il en faut pour les gosses.

— Nous avons trois enfants en France, madame, dit la femme du surveillant. Ça coûte cher, à cette heure.

— Et puis, quoi ! On a l'habitude, pas vrai, la vieille ? Si seulement y'avait de l'eau.

— Vous vous réapprovisionnez facilement ?

— Y'a rien à dire là d'sus. Deux fois par semaine, la charrette vient de Sisophon. Mais, bon Dieu! Faire un pont, qu'on y est d'puis un mois, et pas avoir d'eau à mettre dans un dé à coudre, ça c'est raide !

— Et les travaux ?

— Ça va. J'ai presque plus de boulons par exemple. Faudra m'en envoyer. Et puis des touques vides. Tenez, vl'à un papier, j'ai tout mis dessus de ce qui m'fallait.

Le Résident prit le papier et demanda encore :

— Et les coolies ?

— Ça va. Y sont pas pressés, ces bougres de Cambodgiens. Tant qu'y faut remuer de la terre, ça va encore, pas besoin de trop gueuler. Mais pour le reste !

— Et vous, madame Carlaguet, vous ne vous ennuyez pas trop ?

— Ma foi, monsieur l'Résident, c'est pas la vie d'château. Mais enfin, on bricole, quoi ! Le temps passe tout de même. Si y'avait de l'eau, seulement, qu'on puisse se laver. Et le linge !

— Il est dégueulasse, le linge, précisa son mari.

— Si vous avez besoin de quelque chose, nous repasserons dans quatre ou cinq jours, pensez-y.

Le convoi repartit.

— Quels braves gens, dit Hélène.

— Ils sont beaucoup comme ceux-là, qu'on connaît mal. Pas toujours faciles à mener, mais lorsqu'on les a pris, on en fait ce qu'on veut. Des nomades, presque toujours dehors, campés. Leur vie est rude et excuse beaucoup de choses. Voilà ceux qui font réellement la route...

Après un silence, Ternier continua :

— ... de leurs mains, avec leurs mains. Ils logent dans les salas ou, s'il n'y en a pas, dans des abris comme celui-ci. Beaucoup, madame, quittent la route pour entrer à l'hôpital. Rarement leurs femmes les suivent, d'ailleurs la plupart de ces surveillants sont célibataires. Une *congaï* part avec eux : maigre distraction. Ils passent ainsi des mois de privation, dans l'isolement, ravitaillés à peu près, sur les terres remuées ou les empierrements qui réverbèrent le soleil. Ils vivent, un peu sur le pays, de poulets et de conserves, ne dépensant presque rien. Et puis, lorsqu'ils retournent au centre ou descendent à Phnom Penh, en permission, ils font une noce folle. Qui le leur reprocherait ? Seulement, ils gaspillent en huit jours leurs économies. Rien ne va, rien n'est possible en parole, avec eux ; en fait, ils viennent à bout de tout. Vous croyez avoir affaire à une tête forte, en trois mots vous retournez l'homme comme un gant. Eussiez-vous trouvé ce brave Carlaguet dans une villa somptueuse, au cœur d'un site enchanteur : il se serait plaint autant que dans cet enfer. S'il y avait eu de l'eau dans l'arroyo, Carlaguet aurait protesté contre l'eau, prétendu qu'on commençait le pont trop tard, et...

— Cette vache d'eau ! dit Hélène en riant.

— Cette vache d'eau qui l'eut alors gêné pour monter son pont. Et sous cette révolte hérissée et latente, des cœurs d'or, de braves gens qui frotteraient le pont au papier de verre eux-mêmes, s'il le fallait ; trimant et se privant de tout pour leurs enfants qu'ils font élever très correctement en France ; dévoués au service en niant tout principe d'autorité. Sans doute, il y a quelques agents douteux parmi eux, arsouilles ou fricoteurs qu'il faut avoir à l'œil. Mais dix Carlaguets rachètent la corporation. Ceux-ci ont en eux, obscurément, la trame des conquérants, l'intelligence active et ingénieuse, l'audace. Seulement, le sort les fit naître du côté où l'on obéit. S'ils obéissent, le subconscient gronde. Les ingénieurs sont des imbéciles : cette conviction allège leur tâche. Ils ont l'orgueil de leurs vertus manœuvrières, de leurs qualités pratiques et, le fait est que, souvent, ils connaissent admirablement leur métier. Quelques routes difficiles ont été étudiées par l'un d'eux, au jugé, en marchant dans la forêt ou sur le flanc d'une montagne et qui, trouvant ainsi les seuls passages possibles, fit un tracé remarquable.

⚜ ⚜ ⚜

Après deux nouvelles heures de cheminement à travers l'invariable paysage, les voyageurs parvinrent à l'étape. La sala apparut au centre d'un terrain bien battu, soigneusement désherbé. Une allée, bordée de jeunes cycas nouvellement plantés, conduisait à la vaste construction ouverte au centre et de plain-pied sous une croisée de toitures. À droite et à gauche, sur pilotis, des chambres formaient ailes, le tout en bambou, rotin, et recouvert de paillote épaisse : cloisons finement tressées, ligaturées aux colonnes, portes tournant sur des crapaudines en bois. Dans chaque chambre, une fourche d'arbre écorcée formait porte-manteau et une jarre avait été remplie d'eau pour la douche. Au centre, un cadre, tendu d'une claie et pourvu des quatre montants où l'on suspend la moustiquaire, constituait un lit très suffisant.

On apercevait à quelque cinq cents mètres le village dont la population accourait. Des coolies apportaient des bottes d'herbe pour les chevaux, et de l'eau dans des paniers calfatés à la résine.

Ternier expédia les salutations d'usage, tandis qu'on déchargeait les charrettes, reçut les poulets et les noix de coco, les œufs. Deux hommes, conduits par le chef de village, vinrent offrir un chevreuil pris au filet, le cou tranché, lié par les pattes à une traverse de bois. Le docteur distribua la quinine et fit faire la course aux enfants en leur jetant, en tous sens, des pièces de monnaie. Les femmes indigènes, qu'une Européenne, la première qu'elles voyaient, attirait, formèrent cercle autour d'Hélène et une vieille, le torse nu, tête rasée, les seins réduits à des peaux pendantes, un trou sous chaque pommette, poussiéreuse et pathétique, s'assit devant elle, lui sourit, lui prit la main avec précaution. Et elle tournait cette main de lait, fine et longue entre les siennes grises et nouées comme des sarments.

Lorsque Hélène entra dans sa chambre, elle vit le matelas pliant recouvert d'une fine natte, sa malle sur un chevalet, des serviettes accrochées, sa trousse posée sur une table et la grappe d'une orchidée à fleurs ailées suspendue à l'une des colonnes. Une fenêtre dont le volet tressé s'ouvrait en tabatière laissait pénétrer le soleil bas de l'après-midi. Un lézard à tête corail se sauva.

Les deux hommes occupaient l'autre aile et madame Gassin entendit le docteur, homme perpétuellement gai, chanter à tue-tête :

Madame à sa tour monte,

Mironton, mironton, mirontaine...

Il s'arrêta pour prévenir à travers les cloisons :

— Ne vous effrayez pas, madame ! Je chante lorsque je prends ma douche. C'est un phénomène pathognomonique dont je n'ai jamais su la cause. Et c'est toujours le même air !

Il cessa bientôt et l'on sut ainsi qu'il était douché.

⚜ ⚜ ⚜

Telle était l'étape. Le plus humble, le plus lointain, le plus misérable village possède une maison ouverte aux passants, souvent la plus belle et la plus propre, la sala, refaite à neuf lorsque le Résident est annoncé. Le site est choisi avec soin, sous de beaux arbres, près de l'eau : étang, puits ou cours d'eau. La fatigue, la chaleur de la route en augmentent le charme. Heureux les peuples qui travaillent traditionnellement à la douceur de la maison que le voyageur espère et vers laquelle il a marché tout le jour.

Soudain, il la voit, sa barrière, ses bambous. La terre piétinée marque la place des bœufs. La savane flamboyante dans les yeux, les cahots des véhicules ou le trot du cheval sur les reins ; dans l'âme, la tristesse de la forêt claire, puis, subitement, une pelouse d'herbe, la maison ouverte, l'eau endormie dans la jarre pour la douche délassante. Le chef du village a tendu sa plus belle natte sur le plancher. Ce calme ? Ce silence ? Les charrettes arrêtées ont cessé leur oraison. Des coqs, les « *kroukrou* » des tourterelles, des coups de hache dans le ciel, parmi les palmes, détachent les cocos qu'on vous destine en hommage, quelques voix...

À peine prend-on conscience de cet enveloppement que les charrettes dételées estompent leur groupe et, si l'on est en « semaine claire », la lune roule sur les arbres. Les conducteurs font le rond et, tour à tour, chaque bœuf fatigué se couche de côté sur ses pattes étroitement repliées — tel que surent si bien le sculpter les Khmers de l'époque héroïque, parce que Çiva le chevauche. Et c'est la nuit.

⚜ ⚜ ⚜

Lorsque madame Gassin sortit de sa chambre, une lampe à acétylène illuminait le centre de la sala et le tableau qui s'offrit à elle la combla de surprise. Sous une frange d'orchidées, la nappe avait été mise et les couverts d'aluminium brillaient comme de l'argent. Des coupes à champagne côtoyaient les gobelets. Le menu était écrit. Moutarde, pickles, cure-dents, aucun accessoire ne manquait. Les serviettes pointaient en bonnets d'évêque. Au-dessus de la table, suspendu à un entrait, un large panka tressé laissait pendre sa corde. Et les deux hommes en smoking blanc, une hélice de frangipanier à la boutonnière, se levèrent, cérémonieusement.

— Nous avons voulu, madame, vous faire une surprise, le docteur et moi. De même que vous avez su mettre dans vos bagages cette robe charmante, nous avons voulu ne pas rester en kaki.

— Ni en pyjama, madame, ajouta le docteur, surtout ce soir.

— Surtout ce soir. Car c'est aujourd'hui que vous faites connaissance avec la brousse, la vraie brousse, que vous allez y passer votre première nuit : dîner inaugural. J'espère que vous n'êtes pas fatiguée.

— Pas du tout, mais je suis stupéfaite.

— Tout ceci est très simple et cet appareil qui vous surprend ne nous a pas imposé un souci de trop, ni une caisse de plus. Ordre a été simplement donné au boy. J'y ai tenu pour d'autres raisons. Vous allez retourner en France et vous pourrez dire que vous avez pénétré dans les régions les plus reculées et les plus désertes du Cambodge. Vous saurez donc protester contre toutes les bêtises qui circulent sur la brousse indochinoise en général et cambodgienne en particulier. Sachez surtout que vous n'assistez à rien de spécial. Tout comme moi, un simple particulier trouve une *sala*, partout, gratuitement ouverte. Comme moi, il obtient les charrettes dont il a besoin et au même prix. Comme moi, il possède un boy et un cuisinier. Comme le docteur, il peut se promener en pyjama, avec ou sans fusil. À la faveur de tout particulier qui vient dans ma province, fonctionnaire ou non, je lance les mêmes instructions de bon accueil. Sans doute, il y a des randonnées pénibles et fastidieuses ; selon les saisons, des orages violents ; dans certains lieux, des moustiques ou des sangsues. C'est entendu ! Mais, tout de même, en France, dans les bois, il y pleut et il y neige, on peut être piqué par une abeille, incommodé par des punaises...

— En tout cas, interrompit le docteur, j'aime mieux cette sala qu'une auberge, même avec panonceaux du Touring. Voyez-moi cette nappe, ces orchidées ! Celles-ci poussent à foison sur le tronc des palmiers à sucre.

— Et cette nuit ! ajouta Ternier.

— Et toujours cette sensation de tranquillité parmi tous ces gens si dévoués.

— Vous dites bien, madame. Voyez-les préparer leur campement. Pensez-vous qu'ils vont dormir, ces charretiers, bien que depuis ce matin, assis en équilibre sur leur timon, ils aient poussé leur bête ?

— Je crois plutôt qu'ils sommeillaient en faisant cela, dit Maillard, si j'en juge par certains cahots...

— Leur race ne subit pas le temps comme nous. Les nuits sont trop belles et trop douces pour les perdre et ces gens-là les vivent — du moins jusqu'à ce qu'elles s'avancent trop et soient envahies par la buée.

Hélène voyait confusément le campement à la lueur de torches faites de copeaux et de résine. Un bœuf bougeait-il ? Aussitôt un sifflement humain le rassurait. Si les foyers, installés entre trois pierres, faiblissaient, une branche ajoutée les ravivait. Et, par intermittence, les hommes échangeaient une réflexion, se levaient, allaient boire, mangeaient un poisson sec tapé dans la cendre, fumaient, se déplaçaient dans le silence de leurs pieds nus, avec des allures de prêtres ou de confidents, ourlés de l'ocre des torches ou baignés du lait mystique que la glaciale éclaireuse, ronde et bombée comme une mamelle, versait sur les saillies de leurs muscles.

⚜ ⚜ ⚜

Les trois voyageurs rêvaient, attendant que le dîner fût prêt et tous trois, quelle que fût la différence de leurs âmes, communiaient. Chacun s'évadait dans la solennelle bienveillance de ces heures exotiques qui effacent toutes les autres ; de ces divinités crépusculaires qui, montées des arbres et de la terre, posent ensemble leurs mains sur le soleil. C'est en de tels lieux, sous les tropiques, loin du monde, qu'il faut les entendre parler.

Tu as quitté tes habitudes. Tu as dégagé ta tête du joug. Tu as laissé les conventions pour voir autre chose. Tu as compris ta pauvreté. Tu délias des bras qui te retenaient, afin de grandir. Libre, tu as voulu être libre ! Quel que soit ton talent, tu as compris qu'il tournait avec tous les autres talents de ta génération, dans la même atmosphère. La nature est morte entre tes villes ; ici, elle règne. L'homme de chez toi est inaccessible sous tous les masques qu'il emprunte ; ici, l'homme est nu, et, riche sous sa nudité, il s'oppose à toi, si souvent vide derrière tes artifices. Ici, l'âpreté et la violence du jour préparent la douceur et la fraîcheur nocturnes mieux que l'ombre de tes prisons. Tout est logique qui se soumet au rythme de la terre et de la lumière et tu n'aspires qu'à contrarier ce rythme. Du moins, ici, il te reprend et tu peux, en le retrouvant, évaluer ce que tu perds à t'en évader.

Regarde, là-bas, cette étoile que tu appelles « l'étoile du berger » et qui se nomme ici « l'étoile du village ». La vis-tu jamais plus brillante ? Ce qui vient de naître et te parvient, c'est le chant d'un orchestre, car, le village, les nuits de lune, joue et exhale les tendresses de son cœur. Combien de villages, chez toi, de dix maisons, même par les belles nuits d'été, chantent ainsi ? Combien ouvrent au voyageur une maison préparée et à lui destinée ? Prends garde que ta sagesse et ton savoir ne chancellent si tu les examines ici, dans cette ambiance et à ces heures ; si tu leur compares ce que celles-ci firent naître et mourir au cours des mêmes siècles qui t'ont vu grandir ? Car, es-tu bien sûr que d'ajouter toujours soit agrandir, plutôt que de couper, de retrancher, d'épurer ? Qui que tu sois et quel que soit ton dieu, tu n'es ici qu'un homme de Dieu, en ces heures — tu n'es pas l'homme d'un autre homme.

Hélène tourna la tête vers Ternier. Placide, il fumait sa courte pipe, solidement assis, les jambes croisées, les cheveux encore mouillés de sa douche, athlète moderne au repos — et pas celui au nez dévié par un coup de poing de vingt-cinq mille dollars or. L'homme bâtisseur et créateur, l'homme au poil déjà gris qui sait passer une journée à cheval ou dans une jonque et traverser un arroyo à la nage. L'athlète se reposant sur une piste aussi, tracée par son ordre, satisfait, orgueilleux, puisant dans l'heure immense sa bienveillance, sa fermeté et ses forces du lendemain. Il lutte avec tout un pays, sans arme, mieux qu'armé : convaincu. Il a posé des maisons les unes à côté des autres et cela a fait une ville et il se prépare à en construire une autre, plus loin, à l'extrémité de cette piste, le moment venu. Et il l'attend ce moment, il le désire, il le provoquera, juxtaposant notre vie civilisée à la magistrale liberté du pays, tentant l'audacieux métissage et une double transfusion de sang. Il met en pratique la leçon et ne veut point être seul à l'entendre, à s'avancer dans les domaines de la force et les cultures nouvelles. Il veut qu'on le suive. Mais, de race généreuse et rendu lui-même plus généreux par ces nuits, il désire qu'on avance plus vite que lui, plus sûrement, plus facilement — et il prépare la carrière.

Ternier regarda madame Gassin, mais elle ferma les yeux au même moment.

— Allons dîner, dit-il en se levant.

XII

Dans le milieu du lendemain, ils passèrent à Svay Chèk, l'avant-dernière agglomération qu'ils devaient rencontrer. Une large rivière somnolait sur un lit de sable. Tandis qu'on préparait le déjeuner et que Ternier traitait diverses affaires avec le Gouverneur, Hélène et le docteur parcoururent le village. Le long de l'emplacement de la future route, une dizaine de commerçants chinois avaient déjà installé leurs boutiques et, parmi elles, un restaurant situé à l'angle de la rive et du pont en bois, mi-parti sur le talus et mi-parti surplombant la rivière.

Venue du grand soleil, Hélène, pénétrant dans l'antre, ne distingua tout d'abord que l'eau jaune et lumineuse par les fentes du plancher. Puis, s'habituant à l'ombre du réduit patiné par la fumée de la cuisine et lustré par une authentique crasse chinoise, elle en fit l'inventaire avec son compagnon. Sur des rayons, des bouteilles de bière et de limonade jalonnaient un étalage de savons, de petites cuillers et de boîtes de conserves. Les bêtes rouges et noires de l'écriture chinoise montaient à l'assaut des paquets de thé et les rouleaux de baguettes propitiatoires, gainés de vermillon, voisinaient avec une pile de verres à boire pisseux, des jarretelles cousues sur cartons piquetés de chiures de mouches et quelques cruchons d'alcool de riz. Il y avait encore des tire-bouchons, des bâtons de craie, des soucoupes en porcelaine historiées de dessins bleus, des cigarettes, plusieurs boîtes de fruits de Californie. Un oiseau rare, dans un bocal, enthousiasma le docteur, car il était conservé comme un serpent sur l'étagère d'un musée. Le tout derrière des portes destinées à recevoir des vitres, mais dont il n'y avait encore que les châssis, fermés. Par terre, séparant la boutique du pont, un éventaire de champignons et de chaux à chiquer, d'oignons, de piments, de fruits et de gâteaux crûment coloriés bourdonnait sous un voile de mouches.

Le patron préparait les repas d'indigènes, voyageurs aussi, qui attendaient à croupetons sur des sièges en bambou. Sa silhouette se démenait entre son billot et ses marmites, vêtue d'un petit pagne à carreaux blancs et bleus, roulé autour des reins, si transparent à contre-jour que, lorsque l'homme écartait les jambes, on distinguait ses testicules qui tremblotaient. Il saigna un coq sur le parquet parmi des épluchures que soulevèrent des ailes agonisantes. Puis il découpa la volaille dont la carcasse plumée et vidée, suspendue à un crochet et à contre-jour, devint de corail.

Sur le bambou faîtier d'une autre boutique, un corbeau familier à l'aile cassée vacillait, poussé par un vent qui rebroussait ses plumes. L'un des gamins assemblés pour voir, du pont, les deux Européens, et qu'une fillette tenait à cheval sur la hanche, criait à la brûlure d'une plaie suppurante de la jambe où des mouches buvaient.

La femme du gargotier, son chignon mou sur la nuque, métis sino-cambodgienne, suivait Hélène d'une démarche somnambulique, les yeux mi-clos, la face triangulaire et figée dans une expression de sphinx triste. Lorsqu'elle se penchait en avant, deux longues mamelles pendaient sous la soie de sa veste. Un chat se sauva en s'allongeant et le Chinois essuya son billot et ses couperets d'un torchon grisâtre, pétri en boule, mouillé d'eau grasse et pareil à un paquet de tripes.

— L'antisepsie sera longue à pénétrer, dit le docteur d'un air résigné.

Lorsqu'ils sortirent, leurs regards furent attirés sur l'autre bord de la rivière et le toit d'une vaste maison par l'escalade d'une bougainvillée. Les fleurs, aussi nombreuses que les feuilles, faisaient une nappe de garance violette, glaciale et profondément triste malgré sa luxuriance et le soleil. Plus loin, plaqué sur le ciel blanc, un rideau d'aréquiers et de bambous formait fond.

❧ ❧ ❧

Mélange des races et des époques, humanité familiale ouvrant dans la rue et y vivant à moitié, intérieurs que le paysage pénètre, tout s'associe ici depuis des siècles. À côté du panonceau traditionnel chinois en papier vermillon moucheté d'or, la patente scellée aux armes de la République française, des Khmers mangeant une cuisine chinoise, des Annamites, des Siamois. Où ? Au fond du Cambodge. Que voit-on ? Un commerce sordide où échouent des marchandises européennes, une boutique à choléra, des hommes et des femmes de races différentes qui enfantent dans une végétation de jardin légendaires où la céleste lumière s'enlace aux palmes.

Ainsi, dans la brousse, loin du moindre logis, tandis que sous le soleil tout se pâme, le sable, l'herbe, l'arbre épanoui, que la cigale déchire son cuivre et que l'aigle tourne au zénith, tout à coup, passe la puanteur profonde et vibrante d'une charogne qui pourrit quelque part. Nature, civilisation et mort. Malgré la philosophie banale et ressassée du phénomène, poussant votre cheval au-delà de l'effluve et du fatal mélange, vous tournez la face vers la pointe des arbres et leur criez : voilà pourquoi vous êtes si hauts, si verts et plus beaux, vous autres, les impassibles !

⚜ ⚜ ⚜

Une heure après, la forêt claire reprit le convoi que la piste, toujours, portait vers le nord. Quelques mouvements de terrain parurent, légers, étageant les arbres. On traversa une zone de latérite. La piste fut rouge et les blocs d'une pierre spongieuse la rendirent raboteuse. Elle longea ensuite un pan de grande forêt où une troupe de daims s'enfonça. Le crissement des cigales parut plus sonore. Un étang luisait en contre-bas et Ternier montra à Hélène un chemin dans les hautes herbes qui reliait l'étang à la forêt et tracé par les fauves, la nuit. Des aigrettes immobiles ponctuaient l'eau de taches blanches. Puis les grands arbres s'espacèrent et la forêt claire reprit le paysage.

L'étape du soir, Thma Pouok, fut semblable à celle de la veille : grande sala, rideau de cocotiers, file de femmes revenant de puiser l'eau dans des paniers laqués recouverts de feuilles, orchestre nocturne et nuit constellée que traversèrent des bramements.

XIII

L e lendemain, au départ, le docteur, qui causait avec Hélène, remarqua ceci : lorsqu'elle aperçut son cheval qu'on lui amenait, une expression angoissée passa sur ses traits, puis elle marcha vers lui et fut en selle.

Ils déjeunèrent aux portes du grand temple de Bantéai Chhma, abandonné en forêt depuis des siècles et bouleversé par elle. Ils devaient le visiter le lendemain, en revenant, car l'extrémité de la piste n'était plus qu'à trois heures de là, avec la sala pour la nuit.

La grande forêt commença bientôt et ils y pénétrèrent. Les troncs d'arbres coupés longeaient les deux côtés de la piste. Celle-ci, molle, couverte de feuilles mortes, à peine touchée par les taches du soleil semblait se reposer, jouir de cette humidité et de la fraîcheur vers lesquelles elle s'étirait de si loin. Dix minutes de galop effacèrent le chant des charrettes. Comme les sabots des chevaux faisaient encore crisser les feuilles sèches, Ternier s'arrêta et, immobiles, Hélène et lui écoutèrent.

Les arbres, la plupart à tronc blanc, avaient poussé en hâte, droit, se disputant le ciel et des lianes les enchaînaient. On ne prend pas garde tout d'abord, au grand silence de la forêt, mais dès qu'on l'a « entendu », il s'impose, surprenant. On croit le percevoir par tous les sens. Il devient une impondérable citadelle murée autour de chaque chose et de chaque être : l'arbre immense ou la fourmi qui chemine. Ce n'est point la terre qui se tait, l'absence de l'oiseau, l'immobilité, non. C'est quelque chose de positif, ce silence. Il sature l'atmosphère et moule vos pas. Il paraît qu'on l'écarterait de la main et alors qu'on entendrait soudain la forêt s'exprimer dans son immense et logique murmure, comme si l'on sortait d'un caveau et entrait dans la foule.

Or, se trouver là, au milieu de cette vie incessante et formidable, au centre d'un orchestre qui jouerait le plus tumultueux des drames ; au cœur de ce monde où la naissance, la mort, la digestion de l'être et du végétal roulent des meules, serrent leurs mâchoires, happent comme des mains ; se savoir parmi la myriade de gestes par lesquels l'arbre s'élance, lutte avec l'arbre, tandis qu'à ses pieds, sur son tronc, de l'humus pâteux où il s'enracine à la pointe de ses bourgeons, l'insecte travaille de la pince, de la patte, de l'aile et de l'oviducte ; deviner qu'ici ou là s'enroule et se déroule la menace du reptile et veille peut-être l'attaque sournoise du fauve — et ne rien entendre ! Percevoir par l'intelligence un grondement, tandis que des cris de joie, de douleur et d'épouvante expirent et s'éteignent aux lèvres de chaque pore et de chaque bouche...

Quelle est cette forêt déserte ? L'oiseau est rare. Tout mouvement se cache ou se confond avec l'ambiance. Et le soleil ne montre nulle part cette joie de vivre dont il inonde les clairières, les rives et les plaines. Inquiétante immobilité. On se croit dans une cathédrale de paix et de béatitude et c'est un champ de bataille sur un charnier. La branche qui pend ne porte pas seulement des épines recourbées, mais aussi des fourmis rouges et guerrières. Le tronc mort ou vivant est rongé. En regardant de plus près une brindille ou une feuille sèche, on découvre deux insectes aux aguets, car l'un a la forme de la brindille, l'autre la rouille de la feuille sèche.

En ces climats sans saison, l'automne de la feuille en côtoie le printemps. Paré, en fleurs, en graines, l'arbre se dépouille. À toute époque, des branches mortes et des feuilles rouges tombent de frondaisons vert ardent. Et puis, il y a le combat de la liane et de l'arbre. On voit celui-ci, tordu par cette pieuvre, s'arcbouter, se gonfler aux endroits libres, doubler son tronc pour s'échapper, ressaisi, noué par des cordelettes vert tendre qui entrent dans son écorce d'où giclent des résines. Elles le suivent si elles ne peuvent le tuer, montent avec lui, aussi haut que lui, et retombent après, victorieuses, fragiles, parées de feuilles veinées de blanc, avec des poses molles et en spirales paisibles. Et cet arbre qui agonise ou lutte sous l'assaut de ces tenaces adversaires fait songer à une femme qui se lamente et tord ses cheveux.

Pas de soleil ou alors de ses taches salies par des lichens, la noirâtre pourriture du sol. Nulle part une échappée. Partout un invariable horizon qui n'a pas de sens parce que privé de ciel et dont le haut est aussi épais que le bas. Dans une clarté décomposée d'aquarium, c'est l'interminable et chaotique colonnade des arbres où s'enchevêtrent la liane et l'arbuste, des toiles d'araignée effilochent leurs haillons alourdis de déchets, la corderie des rotins et des branches mortes que rarement l'oiseau ne hante parce qu'il ne peut pas y voler.

Rien, dans cette serre hallucinante, n'indique le moment de la journée ni ne différencie l'aurore du crépuscule. Lorsque, entre les feuillages, on surprend le brillant du ciel morcelé par mille feuilles, on ne comprend pas qu'il puisse en tomber l'immuable jour où l'on baigne. Tout ruisselle d'une rosée qui ne s'évapore pas et mouille les jambes comme si l'on marchait dans un marais. Peu de fleurs et presque toujours blanches, aux pétales en papier de soie. Mais, de toutes parts, l'orchidée rayonne sur le sol ou laisse pendre de larges feuilles dentelées en barbes d'écrevisse et emboîtent aux troncs des arbres de monstrueux bénitiers. Durant de brèves époques, elles montrent leurs grappes fleuries aux tons éteints, des calices modelés en carène de galère, des sabots mouchetés de brun dans lesquels dort une eau pleine de larves.

⚜ ⚜ ⚜

Les chevaux repartirent. Et tout d'un coup, la piste cessa. Un arbre avait été laissé en travers. Un jalon blanc et rouge marquait l'axe de la dernière visée. La forêt opaque se dressait derrière. À droite, un sentier conduisait à la sala qu'on entrevoyait dans une éclaircie, à une trentaine de mètres. Ternier mit pied à terre et, pliée sur son cheval, les yeux excavés, pâle, Hélène dit :

— Voilà donc la fin de la piste !

— Un premier tronçon, le point où nous nous sommes arrêtés cette année, oui. L'année prochaine, on continuera.

— Ainsi, la route s'arrête ici, répéta Hélène d'une voix blanche, les yeux fixés sur le rideau d'arbres.

Elle se retourna péniblement. La piste ouvrait derrière elle un tunnel. Les Cambodgiens qui les accompagnaient s'étaient accroupis et attendaient. Les chevaux demeuraient immobiles, tête basse. Le crépuscule survint.

— Ici, dit Ternier en levant sa cravache vers la forêt où butait la piste, se termine un effort. Carlaguet est venu y planter cette fiche. Ce lieu n'a-t-il pas des significations profondes, madame, et je comprends, à votre trouble, que vous les saisissez. Nous voilà, en somme, à la fin de nos idées. Les vingt siècles de notre civilisation s'arrêtent, en pointe, ici, à ce jalon. Mais ils s'arc-boutent ! Au-delà, c'est l'inconnu, tout ce qu'on cherche et tout ce qu'on désire, donc ce qu'il faut acquérir. On ira ! La pensée hésite encore, mais voici venir, derrière nous, sur le chemin ouvert, tous les renforts de l'intelligence. Ils apportent l'action. Lorsqu'elle aura rejoint l'éclaireuse — celle-ci fera un bond de plus. Et nous pénétrerons dans de nouveaux territoires qui correspondent à notre ignorance actuelle.

— Être venu dans cette solitude..., dit Hélène qui ne semblait pas écouter. Et si l'on ne peut pas aller au-delà ?

— Qu'est-ce qui nous en empêcherait ?

— Et si l'inconnu n'était pas devant cette route, dans la forêt qui l'arrête... mais... à droite et à gauche de la route... Oui, dans le pays qu'elle a déjà traversé... Sans que vous...

— Oh ! mais qu'avez-vous, madame ?

Hélène vacillait sur sa selle. Le masque d'une grande souffrance couvrait sa face. Pliée en avant, elle appuya les mains sur son ventre. D'un bond, Ternier fut près d'elle et la reçut dans ses bras.

Il la tenait comme un enfant. Elle le remercia d'un sourire minable.

— Ce n'est rien... La fatigue, un peu de fatigue…

Il marchait à grandes foulées vers la sala. Des Cambodgiens s'étaient réunis là, avec des flûtes, un tamtam, et lorsqu'ils virent le Résident déboucher du sentier, le petit orchestre retentit. Il voulut le faire taire.

— Laissez, dit Hélène.

Il étendit la malade sur le lit de rotin et lui mit un mouchoir humide sur le front. Elle ne disait rien, immobile, les mains toujours croisées sur le ventre. La flûte chantait avec tendresse et le tamtam, frappé en sourdine et régulièrement, donnait à l'air aigrelet son appui bourdonnant. Les charrettes arrivèrent enfin et le docteur apparut. Ternier sortit.

— Eh bien ! Eh bien ! On n'est pas sage ?

— Non, docteur.

Il l'examina longuement sans dire un mot. Fièvre : 39,5, nez pincé, yeux creusés et soulignés de bistre, abdomen dur au toucher, douleur virulente dans la fosse iliaque droite, signe de Mac Burney, sensation d'empâtement sous les doigts.

— Vous ne sentiez rien en partant de Sangkè ?

— Non, docteur.

— Dites-moi bien tout, madame, je vous en supplie. Aucun point douloureux, à droite, avant de partir ?

— Non, docteur.

— C'est à cheval que vous avez éprouvé les premières douleurs ?

— Oui.

— Quand ?

— Ce matin.

— Et vous êtes restée en selle toute la journée ! Quelle imprudence ! Pourquoi n'avoir rien dit ?

— Parce que.

Eclairée par une lampe de chantier, madame Gassin demeurait les yeux clos, le visage barré. Le docteur jugea inutile de la tourmenter et la déshabilla doucement. Le moindre mouvement la faisait atrocement souffrir. Elle dit :

— Mon Dieu ! Que je vous cause d'ennuis... Mon pauvre ami, vous ne chanterez pas « Malbrough s'en va-t-en guerre », ce soir...

On fit son lit dans une autre chambre de la sala et le docteur l'y porta, enveloppée dans un peignoir de bain. Elle demanda son grand sac à main en cuir vert et le mit entre son oreiller et la cloison. L'interprète apporta la pharmacie de voyage.

— Il vous faut, madame, l'immobilité la plus absolue, sur le dos. Pour rien au monde, ne bougez. Ça ne sera rien.

— Je sais ce que j'ai, docteur.

— De la fatigue, un peu de courbature..., il tentait de la rassurer.

— Non, docteur : appendicite. Je n'ai pas peur.

— Vous avez donc déjà eu une crise ?

— Oui, à seize ans. On ne m'a pas opérée.

— Et l'on ne vous a pas interdit les fatigues, le cheval surtout ?

— Si, docteur.

— Eh bien ! Vous savez le traitement. Vous allez rester bien sage, là, sans bouger. La glace, impossible, nous allons faire le contraire : un cataplasme de riz très chaud. Ça ne sera encore rien cette fois et demain tout sera fini, hein !

— Oui, docteur, tout sera fini, peut-être.

Il alla retrouver Ternier.

— Mon cher, état très grave. Diagnostic facile : crise d'appendicite aiguë, rechute. Attendons demain. À parler franc, je redoute la péritonite. Elle souffre depuis ce matin ; demain, deux ; après-demain, trois jours. Si l'aggravation doit se produire, nous ne le saurons que demain au plus tôt. C'est qu'elle a un faciès qui m'inquiète et trop de température pour une appendicite simple. Comment a-t-elle pu tenir à cheval depuis ce matin ? Je me le demande. Elle n'a évidemment résisté que grâce à une volonté surhumaine, mais a aggravé la crise... Si elle ne l'a pas compliquée. Qu'est-ce qu'elle a donc dans la peau, cette petite bonne femme-là ?

— Est-elle transportable ?

— Non. Si elle ne fait que de l'appendicite, laissons refroidir dans la diète et l'immobilité absolues. Rien de mieux à faire ! S'il y a complication, le retour est inutile.

— Que voulez-vous dire ?

— Hé ! Ce que je dis. Car il n'y aurait alors que l'intervention chirurgicale immédiate. Or je n'ai qu'une pharmacie ridicule avec moi. Voyons, raisonnons. Aujourd'hui, jeudi. Si tout se passe bien, demain soir, nous pourrons nous mettre en route, civière bien suspendue, facile à faire. Marchant jour et nuit, arrivée à Sangkè deux jours après, donc dimanche dans l'après- midi. Là, opération ou non. Mais nous risquons le transport, la complication en route, l'intervention dès lors impossible, le manque d'eau. Mon cher, la solution n'est pas là.

— Dites ?

— Vous ne mettriez pas plus longtemps, vous, pour aller à Sangkè et revenir ?

— Certainement non. Changeant de cheval en route, je pourrai arriver demain vers midi et être de retour après-demain dans la soirée.

— Vous allez donc partir. Je vais vous donner la liste des instruments qu'il me faut et vous les rapporterez. Ainsi, nous gagnerons le transport et une journée et nous serons prêts à intervenir.

⚜ ⚜ ⚜

La nuit commença. Vers onze heures, Maillard vint voir Hélène. Elle ne dormait pas et regardait au-dessus d'elle. Sa température avait augmenté.

— Écoutez-moi, docteur, je vous affirme que j'ai toute ma lucidité. Si je meurs, vous m'enterrerez ici, ici dans cette forêt admirable, au bord de la route. Je ne veux pas être emportée. Jurez-moi...

— Cela, je vous le jure, madame, mais à votre tour, jurez-moi de conserver tout votre courage.

— J'en ai plus que vous ne supposez.

Après un moment de silence, elle demanda :

— Où est monsieur Ternier ?

— Il va revenir, obligé de...

— Oui. C'est bien cela. Et il va revenir bientôt, n'est-ce pas ?

— Mais oui, madame, ne parlez pas.

— Dans une heure, par exemple ?

Elle regardait le docteur et eut un sourire désespéré.

— Quel mauvais docteur vous faites. Vous ne savez même pas mentir. D'ailleurs on entend tout, vous savez, à travers les cloisons…

Elle s'interrompit dans une intense réflexion et reprit en fermant les yeux :

— Oui, on entend tout : un jour, deux jours, tant de kilomètres, on fera ceci, cela. Pas un mot de compassion. Et il est parti !...

Elle parlait d'une voix plaintive, monotone et releva les paupières, une lueur d'épouvante dans les yeux.

— Est-il sûr de me retrouver vivante ? Et il est parti sans même venir me revoir ! Les minutes sont trop précieuses pour qu'on en perde une seule à presser une main. On ne serait plus un homme d'action, n'est-ce pas, si l'on s'attendrissait ? Agir ! Agir ! Comme si l'on savait toujours où conduit l'action...

— Vous vous méprenez. Ternier a voulu, au contraire, vous éviter l'angoisse que l'explication de son départ urgent pouvait jeter en vous...

— Ne pouvait-il pas venir me revoir sans rien dire ? Non : il n'y a même pas pensé. Il est parti, voilà, c'est tout, c'est tout...

Le docteur allait répondre ; elle l'en empêcha d'un signe de main. Il ouvrit alors la pharmacie de voyage, flamba l'aiguille d'une seringue, brisa une ampoule.

— Qu'allez-vous me faire ?

— Un peu de morphine pour vous aider à vous assoupir et calmer ce cerveau tourmenté par la fièvre.

Après, il reboucla les courroies de la trousse et la poussa contre la cloison. D'entre ses paupières mi-fermées, glissant un étrange regard, Hélène avait suivi tous ses gestes.

XIV

Une aube triomphale lança bientôt dans la forêt les longues plaintes des singes-hurleurs. La buée délia ses écharpes et le soleil descendit de la cime des arbres à leur pied. Une lumière charmante emplit la clairière et baigna la sala. Des foyers, une fumée bleu pastel se dégagea. Les hommes s'éveillaient, étirant leur nudité de cuivre dans la volupté fraîche du matin. Tout n'était que promesse et jeunesse.

Ternier poussait sa monture renouvelée à Thma Pouok. Des paons et des coqs sauvages se levaient à son approche et sur la forêt claire, comme dans la haute forêt, le matin enchanteur jetait ses violettes. Paphnuce aussi courait jadis, parce que Thaïs mourait !

L'intense rosée des tropiques nacrait les feuilles. Quelle douceur et quelle nonchalance de tous côtés répandues et si indifférentes au galop de ce cheval ! On s'est tué un peu partout, ici, cette nuit. La panthère a éventré un cerf et un python étouffé un agouti. Le crapaud s'est repu de sauterelles. La sève a cessé de battre dans les branches et des fleurs tombèrent. Des nuées d'éphémères perdirent leurs ailes et la nuit elle-même est morte, avec tous ses astres.

Cours donc, conquérant, sur ta route. En ce moment, le docteur constate quarante degrés de fièvre sous l'aisselle moite de la malade, les vomissements surviennent et il ne doute plus que l'aggravation redoutée se produit. Pourquoi ? Parce que les gestes humains ont des conséquences imprévues. Ton orgueil d'homme t'a poussé sur cette piste du sud au nord pour conquérir et te voilà lancé du nord au sud afin de réparer. Eh ! Réparer quoi ? Moi qui raconte, qui sais le dessous des choses et la cause et la fin des événements au travers desquels tu te débats, moi qui sais ce que « cette sacrée petite bonne femme-là a dans la peau », je te dis qu'Hélène va mourir.

Elle est ce qui mourra aujourd'hui et qui doit peut-être logiquement disparaître. Elle est l'effort qu'a vaincu un autre effort — ce qui tombe d'une création. Qui sait même, si elle n'est pas aussi l'âme, la fleur secrète de cette région ouverte par ton soc ? Peux-tu certifier que ta piste n'écrase rien, ne détruit rien ? Non, cela, tu ne peux pas le certifier. Donc, avec ta conscience nette, tes scrupules, ton haut sentiment du devoir, tes plus nobles projets et ta clairvoyance, tu as tué bel et bien, de tes mains, cette femme. Non ? Si, car cette nuit elle mourra. Voilà le fait et si tu ne veux pas en accepter les causes que j'essaye de te faire pressentir, tu les apprendras bientôt, lorsque tu sauras à ton tour la fin des choses. Nous croyons nous mouvoir isolément, nous sommes tous des symboles. Souviens-toi d'une phrase que t'a dite un jour Hélène : une femme n'est pas toujours maîtresse d'elle-même. Et souvent, les événements que l'on croit isolés et sans rapports entre eux s'engendrent les uns les autres.

Ta route passe à travers une région et, comme une flèche, va la toucher au cœur. Le constructeur d'automobiles y lancera ses machines. Mais la région traversée le frappe aussi au cœur. La première Roland-Gassin qui roulera ici, vers le nord, s'avancera vers une tombe et ce sera sans doute un veuf qui tiendra le volant. À chacun de ces ponts, on a acquitté, on acquittera encore un droit de péage.

En ces lieux, un philosophe devenu dieu règne. Il ordonne à ses bonzes de regarder où ils posent le pied afin de ne pas écraser d'insectes ; de boire aux sources à travers une mousseline pour ne pas avaler d'animalcules. Illusions ! Vaines et puériles prescriptions ! Marche avec précaution, tu n'en écraseras pas moins le grillon que tu ne vois pas dans son trou. À travers ta mousseline, les animalcules plus petits que les mailles passeront. Et lorsque tu avances, si tu détournes ton pas afin d'éviter la fourmi, tu le poseras sur la chenille. Tu dis : je suis la civilisation nécessaire, dictée, désirée par les hommes. C'est possible. Je crois que tu as raison, mais cela signifie aussi que tu es, d'une façon ou d'une autre, le plus fort, comme tu l'as dit toi-même sur la montagne. Et quelle que soit la douceur avec laquelle tu poses ta large main sur le monde et les certitudes salvatrices que tu y déverses — tu tues. Rien à faire, je te l'accorde, mais sache-le.

⚜ ⚜ ⚜

Et la nuit revint. À la fin de la journée, la malade avait un peu plus de 40 degrés de fièvre. Toutefois, vers neuf heures, une légère rémission se déclara et Hélène parut s'assoupir. Le docteur, exténué, se retira dans sa chambre qu'une simple cloison séparait. Une voix effrayée le réveilla :

— M'sieur ! Madame partie !

— Comment partie ?

— Oui, m'sieur, lui plus là.

Le lit était vide, la trousse à pharmacie ouverte sur la table. Maillard, terrifié, prit une lampe et sortit, appela. Des Cambodgiens munis de torches fouillèrent les abords de la sala. Le docteur criait dans la nuit et ses appels couraient à travers les arbres avec les reflets des lumières. Une voix d'homme le héla vers l'ouest et il s'y dirigea, trébuchant sur les lianes. Aux pieds de l'indigène qui s'était immobilisé et levait sa torche tel un bronze antique, il vit Hélène, toute petite tache blanche, tombée sur le côté. Son peignoir ouvert montrait sa poitrine de fillette.

⚜ ⚜ ⚜

Lorsqu'il eut achevé la toilette du cadavre, le docteur mit de l'ordre dans la chambre. Il s'aperçut que le flacon de strychnine de sa trousse manquait et que le sac vert que madame Gassin avait demandé l'avant-veille et gardé, depuis, jalousement près d'elle n'était plus sur le lit. Après avoir cherché inutilement dans la pièce, il retourna dans la forêt à l'endroit où Hélène était tombée. Il trouva le sac ouvert, avec sa boîte à poudre, un mouchoir, des clés, des bijoux et de l'argent. Il vit à quelques pas une boîte d'allumettes, et, un peu plus loin, des cendres de papiers consumés avec des feuilles sèches, quelques brindilles à moitié calcinées et le flacon vide.

Des fourmis rouges exploraient la place où la chair de la morte avait touché l'humus. L'abdomen dressé, elles coulaient sous la lueur du fanal comme des gouttes de miel.

XV

Madame Gassin fut inhumée où elle l'avait désiré, dans la forêt, près de la piste. Dès son retour à Sangkè, Ternier télégraphia à Roland Gassin. Son télégramme revint avec la notation « destinataire inconnu ». Il fit faire une enquête rapide qui lui apprit que le constructeur d'automobiles n'était pas venu à Saigon et qu'il n'avait jamais été question de créer, dans cette ville, une succursale de la célèbre usine. Aux Messageries Maritimes, le nom de Gassin ne figurait pas sur les listes des passagers arrivés de France au cours des six derniers mois.

En interrogeant le gérant du bungalow et le receveur des postes, le Résident sut qu'Hélène n'avait reçu aucune lettre. Elle n'en avait envoyé qu'une seule, recommandée, à madame Annie Belgrand, sa sœur. L'inventaire des bagages de la morte, avant la mise sous scellés, ne donna aucun indice, aucun papier. Alors Ternier envoya deux câbles, l'un à Roland Gassin à son usine de Levallois-Perret, l'autre à madame Belgrand. Celle-ci télégraphia : « Suis désespérée. Envoyez-moi détails par lettre. ». Le mari ne répondit pas.

Toute cette obscurité obligea Ternier à pousser son enquête officieuse plus avant afin de tranquilliser sa conscience et de savoir, du moins, comment entreprendre les démarches officielles inhérentes à ses fonctions. Il convoqua le capitaine Thévenet et le pria, d'homme à homme, de lui dire ce qu'il savait sur la morte. Celui-ci ne la connaissait pas. Allons donc ! Elle était allée chez lui, une nuit. Le capitaine ne savait pas. Il y avait des témoins. Les témoins pouvaient avoir mal vu. Légion d'honneur, trois palmes, cinq blessures, quatre ans de guerre dans l'infanterie, trente-deux ans.

— Madame Gassin m'a avoué être allée chez vous.

— Madame Gassin a déclaré ce qui lui a plu.

— Mais songez que tout cela peut être extrêmement grave. Je me débats entre dix conjectures qui m'épouvantent. Je peux tout supposer. Que s'est-il passé ? Pourquoi madame Gassin m'a-t-elle dit avoir laissé son mari à Saigon alors qu'il n'y est jamais venu ? Pourquoi a-t-elle reconnu, devant moi, être allée chez vous, une nuit, cependant que vous le niez. Supposez une affaire grave, je serai obligé de dire ce que je sais, et vous voilà complice.

— Je serai complice.

— L'enquête la plus simple démontrera aisément si vous connaissiez madame Gassin ou non.

— Peut-être, mais je n'ai qu'une parole.

Ternier alla vers l'officier et lui posant la main sur l'épaule :

— Je comprends, je comprends bien. Et il n'y a qu'une seule personne qui puisse vous rendre cette parole. Je veux dire : il n'y avait.

Les deux hommes se regardèrent. L'officier ne répondit pas. Ternier lui serra la main, fortement.

⚜ ⚜ ⚜

Le soir même, il rédigea un rapport sans intérêt sur le décès de madame Gassin, voyageant seule. Il attestait qu'il l'avait connue à Paris. Toutes les formalités légales avaient été faites. La tombe se trouvait au point kilométrique 118 de la route coloniale n° 1 ; à deux cents mètres ouest de la sala dite « sala Prei Thom ». La défunte avait brûlé ses papiers. Ses bagages, sous scellés, demeuraient à la disposition de la famille informée par câble. En conscience, le Résident de France à Sangkè savait-il officiellement autre chose ? Non, en conscience, il ne savait rien de plus. Il signa. Le secrétaire, Tri, mit le cachet, enregistra et épingla à ce rapport celui du docteur. Une femme était morte et voilà tout.

⚜ ⚜ ⚜

Or, trois mois plus tard, une enveloppe bordée de noir parvint à Ternier. Il en tira deux lettres. L'une, en deuil, comme l'enveloppe, était de la sœur d'Hélène ; l'autre, pliée en quatre, tracée sur un papier azuré aux initiales bleu foncé. Ternier eut froid jusqu'aux os en reconnaissant le papier, les initiales et l'écriture. Voici ce que contenaient ces deux lettres :

Paris 26 juin 19...

« Monsieur,

« Vous pouvez imaginer la stupeur et le désespoir dans lesquels votre câblogramme m'annonçant la mort de ma pauvre Hélène m'a plongée et avec quelle angoisse j'attendais votre lettre. Elle m'est arrivée hier. Décidément, le sort ne m'aura pas épargnée. Il ne me restait plus sur terre que ma sœur à chérir. Et elle est morte loin de moi, après un long supplice. J'apprends par votre lettre toutes les suppositions que l'arrivée d'Hélène en Indochine soulève dans votre esprit et je réponds sans détour aux questions que vous me posez. Je vais sans doute vous faire du mal, ne m'en veuillez pas. En considérant où nous en sommes pour avoir gardé un inutile secret, je suis convaincue qu'il vaut mieux faire toute la lumière.

« Votre apparition jeta le trouble dans l'âme de ma sœur. C'était une nature fermée, volontaire et sensible. Votre tempérament, votre situation, votre métier la séduisirent. L'amour qu'elle conçut pour vous fut si rapide et si impérieux qu'il était trop tard lorsqu'elle voulut se reprendre. Vous êtes parti sur ces entrefaites. Votre absence activa cette passion. C'est alors qu'Hélène, désespérée, me la confia et que, depuis, je fus au courant de tout ce qui en résulta. Durant plusieurs mois, elle tenta, sans y parvenir, de se redonner à son mari. Il lui devint intolérable de rester près d'un homme qu'elle n'aimait plus. Elle le lui déclara et le divorce fut décidé. Hélène vint alors habiter avec moi et une vie nouvelle commença, bien triste, je vous l'assure.

« M. Gassin, injustement frappé, fut pris d'un désespoir profond. Il connaissait trop sa femme pour estimer désormais possible une vie que d'ailleurs lui-même ne pouvait plus accepter. Le divorce fut obtenu rapidement. Nous ne vîmes plus M. Gassin, car nous vivions isolées et lui, laissant toutes affaires entre les mains d'un fondé de pouvoir, partit en voyages interminables chercher l'oubli, refusant même que tout courrier le suive. Je ne sais où il est, ni même s'il connaît, à l'heure présente, la mort d'Hélène.

« Peu à peu, le désir d'aller vous retrouver grandit en Hélène. Elle dévora toute une littérature coloniale pour imaginer votre vie, vous suivre par la pensée. Et sans doute serait-elle partie dès sa liberté reconquise si la crainte que lui inspirait le jugement que vous porteriez sur elle ne l'en avait d'abord empêchée. Elle chercha cent moyens. Je lui conseillais d'attendre votre prochain congé. Elle ne put se faire à l'idée de rester deux ans encore sans vous revoir et dans l'incertitude. Finalement, elle imagina la fable dangereuse que vous avez connue.

« Elle ne pouvait pas vous dire qu'elle avait divorcé parce qu'elle vous aimait, ce qui eût signifié qu'elle venait s'offrir à vous. Néanmoins, et sans se départir de sa fierté, elle espérait, à la faveur de son subterfuge, une éventualité qui vous aurait ouvert les yeux. Avant tout, il fallait qu'elle vous revît et qu'elle tentât l'unique chance qu'elle croyait avoir de se faire aimer de vous, pour cela apparaître dans votre solitude, y partager vos enthousiasmes et se montrer, non pas dans une attitude empruntée, ce dont elle était incapable, mais telle qu'elle vous aimait. Elle avait, je le répète, par-dessus tout, peur que, sachant son divorce, vous supposassiez qu'elle venait à vous pour des raisons douteuses. Elle n'était pas de celles qui savent faire usage de leurs charmes et je vois que, malgré sa hardiesse, ma pauvre petite n'a pas su tenter sa chance aussi aisément que l'aurait fait une femme moins fière et moins scrupuleuse. Son séjour au Cambodge, si follement concerté, devait finir par un triomphe. Sinon, et pour ménager son retour, elle vous aurait dit que son mari la rappelait à Saigon, qu'il y avait contre-ordre. Elle vous eût alors quitté.

« Moi, que la vie a déjà brisée et que cette folie éclairait encore, j'estimais la situation sans issue, qu'Hélène la compliquait et qu'un miracle seul pouvait l'en dégager. Je le lui ai dit de toutes les façons. Elle me répondait invariablement : « Je veux le revoir, le reste m'est égal, tant pis ! Je n'ai rien à perdre. ». Voilà toute l'histoire, monsieur. Elle n'a plus rien à perdre, en effet, la pauvre chérie.

« Elle partit. Vous savez le reste. Elle ne m'envoya des escales que des mots hâtifs. Par une lettre de Saigon, elle me disait que tout allait à merveille, qu'elle partait pour le Cambodge le lendemain. Quelques jours après son arrivée à Sangkè, elle m'envoya la dernière lettre qu'elle devait m'écrire. Cette lettre ne parle que de vous. Je vous l'envoie. Elle vous expliquera mieux que moi (qui ne sais plus rien et ne peux rien juger) comment Hélène envisageait les choses. C'est parfois un bien grand malheur que la nature humaine soit si complexe et si simple et que la perspicacité de l'homme, pourtant si subtile, passe à côté de belles et profondes choses sans même les pressentir.

« Quant aux papiers qu'Hélène a brûlés, j'imagine qu'elle n'a pas voulu laisser derrière elle la révélation de sa fugue, mais vous faire ignorer jusqu'au-delà de sa tombe qu'elle vous aimait. Cette fierté, ou plutôt cette noblesse du cœur, eu égard à votre quiétude et à sa pudeur me manque peut-être, puisque ce secret qu'elle a scellé de son dernier souffle, je le divulgue maintenant. Je vous en ai dit les raisons. Je dois dissiper les doutes qui vous obsèdent, prévenir surtout l'enquête que la présence suspecte et les actes à première vue inexplicables d'une femme seule à la colonie pouvaient provoquer. Je sais aussi la noblesse de votre nature. Vous avez suivi votre route, monsieur. En tout ce triste roman, la fatalité demeure seule coupable.

« Je vous prie de témoigner au docteur Maillard toute ma reconnaissance. Si la chose est possible et ne vous paraît pas déplacée, exprimez à ce capitaine, dont parle Hélène, mon émotion et croyez, monsieur, que ma douleur grave dans ma mémoire un souvenir de vous qui ne périra pas.

« Annie Belgrand. »

⚜ ⚜ ⚜

Sangkè, mai 19...

« Ma chérie,

« Depuis sept jours, je suis près de lui, je le vois et il me parle et il me tue. Je comprends de plus en plus ma folie. Tout ce qu'il me dit me démontre l'impossibilité de mon rêve. Même par pitié, il ne tolérerait pas mon amour si je le lui découvrais parce que, ne me donnant rien en échange, il s'estimerait mortifié et, pour me guérir, il s'appliquerait à saccager mon cœur. Je suis le fruit tombé, comme il me l'a dit hier, celle qui s'offre. Il n'en veut pas de celle-là. Il m'a conquise et cette conquête ignorée de lui, non décidée ni poursuivie par lui ne masquerait pas ma donation. Il ne voudrait pas se prévaloir de cette donation qui m'amoindrirait dans son jugement. Oui ! Oui ! Tout cela, je ne l'invente pas, je l'ai entendu de sa bouche. Son orgueil égale son humilité.

« Peut-être devrais-je me faire conquérir, m'offrir prudemment, me laisser entrevoir. J'en suis incapable. J'ai trop peur qu'il ne décèle une telle manœuvre et dédaigne aussitôt une conquête si facile. Du moins ainsi, je l'ai un peu, je puis encore rester près de lui et ma passion, se dévorant elle-même, trouve quelque consolation à le contempler. Il est bon. Il me cajole comme une sœur, comme une petite fille, le misérable aveugle !

« Je suis une de ses provinces qu'il a pénétrée. Je vis dans cette unique pensée et cette comparaison m'obsède. Comme la province, j'étais paisible et heureuse, limitée dans mes habitudes, une vie choisie, et il s'est avancé en moi. Il m'a bouleversée par un monde d'idées et de passions nouvelles, assoiffée de richesses que je n'avais jamais entrevues. Comme les villages que sa route repousse et aspire, toutes mes pauvres pensées, mes projets et jusqu'à mes souvenirs sont méconnaissables. Et malgré tout ce qui souffre en moi, le dur et profond sillon qui m'écartèle, je me sens agrandie. Je suis vaincue, la plus faible, l'autorité du plus fort me tient dans les larmes et la peur, mais j'aime Pierre et si je paye des joies nouvelles par un désastre où je voudrais mourir, je ne changerais aucune des heures présentes contre celles de mon passé.

« Je sais, je sais, ma bonne chérie, tout ce que tu vas me répondre. Mais que veux-tu, je suis forcée d'être fière, aussi ! Je ne peux rien, rien tenter de plus et je suis une malheureuse. Tu me répéteras que je me forge des idées fausses sur la rigueur de sa conscience et qu'il est comme les autres. Je n'en crois rien. Si tu le voyais, ici, comme un maître ! Et puis, ce serait abîmer mon amour que d'en amoindrir l'objet. Moi aussi, je veux qu'il m'aime et me désire ! À son contact, à honorer en moi sa constante présence depuis que je l'aime, à me vouloir digne de lui, belle des vertus qu'il préfère, je me suis durci le cœur. Tant pis pour moi. Mais tant que je respirerai, je veux garder l'espoir qu'il m'aimera et me tenir prête, bien belle.

« Il faut que je te raconte un incident qui faillit me perdre et a tout compromis. À bord du paquebot, parmi les passagers dont je fis connaissance, se trouvait un capitaine Thévenet. Juge de mon affolement en le voyant tout à coup surgir, un soir, chez Pierre. Ce capitaine, que je croyais avoir définitivement quitté à Saigon, avait été affecté à Sangkè. Par une chance inouïe, il comprit à mon attitude que je désirais ne pas être reconnue. C'était un soir vers sept heures, je dînais chez Pierre et le lendemain, à l'aube, le capitaine devait aller avec lui je ne sais où. En sortant, j'étais folle d'angoisse et ne pensais qu'à une chose, prévenir le capitaine, inventer n'importe quelle histoire, mais lui demander son silence car il savait bien, lui, que j'avais voyagé seule, que Roland n'était pas à Saigon. Alors j'ai couru chez lui, dans la nuit. Avec une discrétion parfaite et sans même accepter d'explications, il m'a assuré, sur son honneur de soldat, qu'il garderait le silence. Quelle belle nature et que cette rencontre m'a fait de bien, dans ma détresse !

« Mais, hélas ! ma bonne chérie, je n'étais pas hors de danger. Ma visite nocturne s'est sue et, dans cette petite ville, je passe pour la maîtresse du capitaine. Pierre en fut informé aussitôt et, une heure après, il me poignardait. Comment pouvais-je nier la visite et comment lui en révéler le but ? Aussi, conçois mon épouvantable tourment. Certes ! Pierre est convaincu que je ne suis pas ce que la rumeur de la ville propage, mais il sait aussi que je suis allée de nuit chez un homme que j'avais vu quelques heures avant à la Résidence et ne paraissais pas connaître. Quelles idées doit-il se faire ? C'est d'ailleurs au cours de la discussion mortelle entre lui et moi sur ce sujet que je me suis rendu compte de mon infortune. J'ai constaté que ce que j'avais cru être une libération (mon divorce) ne pouvait être à ses yeux qu'une déchéance bien qu'il en soit la cause et que, dans ma folie, si je m'étais bien détachée de l'arbre, j'étais devenue le fruit tombé dont on ne veut pas, parce qu'il faut l'essuyer... La démarche par laquelle je me croyais sauvée assura ainsi ma perte d'autre manière et des paroles m'ont peut-être plus sûrement atteinte que des événements que j'avais conjurés.

« Je te demande bien pardon, ma chérie, de t'attrister en te racontant mes tourments. Cela me fait un peu de bien. Songe que je me surveille à tout instant, mesure mes paroles et redoute jusqu'à mes regards. Je voudrais me pelotonner en ses bras, sentir sa rude moustache sur mes lèvres, à jamais ! Et je dois jouer le rôle détaché d'une passante, d'une touriste ! Il y va de ma vie. Et il ne soupçonne rien. Il est en action comme une puissante machine. Il va, tout à sa tâche, dans la maîtrise de soi, l'égoïsme des forts, la lourdeur des esprits logiques. Il fait sa route ! Ses sens sont satisfaits : il a une femme indigène, belle et jeune que j'ai aperçue un matin, en sortant de la Résidence. Et j'en suis jalouse !

« Il faut que j'arrête. Ma santé est bonne, mais je me sens immensément lasse. Tout ce que je vois est admirable. Comment tout cela finira-t-il ? Allons ! À bientôt, Annie, je t'écrirai dans huit jours, par le prochain courrier. Toutes les tendresses de ta pauvre

« Hélène »

⚜ ⚜ ⚜

On sait comment tout cela a fini et pourquoi, par le courrier suivant, madame Gassin n'écrivit pas à sa sœur.

Vendredi, 2 mai 1924.

Phnom Penh.

FIN

Exotic Visions of French Indochina

1912 Exploration in Cambodia.
ISBN: 978-1-934431-90-0

A romance of colonial Cambodia
ISBN: 978-1-934431-94-8

First Study of Cambodian Dance.
www.CambodianDancers.com

Masterwork on Cambodian Dance
www.EarthInFlower.com

Exotic Visions of French Indochina

An American in 1920s Indochina.
www.HarryHervey.org

A sensual novel of East and West
www.HarryHervey.org

Fantastic folktales from ages past.
ISBN 978-1-934431-21-4

Paintings of 1920s Indochina.
ISBN: 978-1934431917

A Travel Journal of the Cambodian Mekong — 1929

Edited by Groslier biographer Kent Davis, foreword by Henri Copin, and literary translation by Pedro Rodríguez. This full color edition features 70 hand-tinted vintage illustrations, including Groslier's original photos; appendix articles by Paul Boudet, Dr. Paul Cravath and Solang Uk; and the complete original French text.

ISBN 978-1-934431-87-0

www.ingramcontent.com/pod-product-compliance
Lightning Source LLC
Chambersburg PA
CBHW080850190726
48292CB00010B/2943